DAWN OF SUBJECTION

Other Books by D.I. Telbat

The COIL Series: Christian Suspense

The COIL Legacy Series: Christian Suspense

COIL Legacy Collection: 3 Books in 1 Volume

The Resolution Series: America's Last Days

The STEADFAST Series: America's Last Days

STEADFAST Collection: 6 Novellas in 1 Volume

Last Dawn Series: America's Last Days

Leeward Set: Where Christians Dare

Never Lost Series: Trafficking Rescue Novels

Arabian Variable

Called To Gobi

God's Colonel

Soldier of Hope

Short Story Collections

DAWN OF SUBJECTION

America's Last Days

BOOK THREE OF THE LAST DAWN SERIES

D.I. TELBAT

IN SEASON PUBLICATIONS
USA

Printed in the United States of America

DAWN OF SUBJECTION: America's Last Days
/ D.I. Telbat -- 1st ed.
Categories: Futuristic Christian Fiction;
Christian Suspense

D.I. Telbat / In Season Publications
https://ditelbat.com
https://books2read.com/DITelbat

ISBN 978-1-7371777-8-4

Cover Design by Streetlight Graphics

This book is dedicated to
those Christians who endure through weariness,
serve while wounded, and share while hungry.
Their comforts are few, their possessions
are recycled, and their bodies are frail.
But they are precious in God's eyes as they trust
in a coming day when the Lord Jesus Christ
will show justice in judgment, bind up
the brokenhearted, and give flight to the faithful.

Acknowledgements

Publishing a series takes a special form of endurance from a whole team of editors, readers, and advisors. Friends and family have continued to faithfully offer direction as this COIL adventure continues to unfold (since 2004). Thanks to Dee for editing and working through another novel. Others, such as Jamie and Sharon, have shared in the work yet again, finding errors, and/or offering valuable feedback. My gratitude is extended to our group of valuable beta readers for their personal and helpful touch (I dare not name you for fear of leaving someone out, but you know who you are). May God bless each one of you for your faithful service to me and the Telbat Team.

Character Sketch

Alice Prine – one-armed black woman; leads & scouts for the group of Christian refugees; she is known for carrying a steel walking stick

Brian Steelman – Federation Enforcer whose violent past haunts him as he searches for the Serval, the man who showed him kindness long ago. Brian joins the COIL group to help Rex lead refugees from NYC to Colorado

Bruno – a bear-sized man who has dedicated the last decade to securing safe passage for Christians in the underground movement in New York and New Jersey

Chen Li – Nathan's wife who worked in Citizen Processing, using her position to help God's people endure the Federation's harsh treatment. She and Jenna become separated from the group of refugees as they escaped NYC, and now lean on God's direction for survival

Chloe Azmaveth – COIL's original public relations officer in her late sixties; now helps Rex lead the refugees from NYC to Colorado

Corban Dowler – founder of COIL; trained COIL's elite operatives to face dangers looming against God's people

Jenna Dowler – blind daughter of Corban Dowler, now nearly forty; became COIL's chief strategist who is often underestimated. As Radiant Shade, she ran the COIL mission, Operation Esther, to save the underground Christians in NYC. She & Chen Li become separated in their escape from the city

Kendrick Obrador – once the chancellor of the Federation; he has joined the Christian band for survival

Lena Travers – older sister to Owen Travers; a Federation Enforcer who terrorizes nonconformists in New York. Killing meant nothing to this vicious woman. She has a goal to claim the position of chancellor of NYC

Levi Caspertein – witty son of the infamous Titus Caspertein, known as the Serval. He and Nathan Isaacson leave the group to search for Chen Li and Jenna Dowler who have gotten separated from the main refugee group

Luigi Putelli – aged Italian, Corban Dowler's most loyal companion; has dedicated himself to protecting Jenna

Milo Rotham – a colonel in Philadelphia's Citizen Army; ambitious soldier who grew up on video games

Nathan Isaacson – also known as Eagle Eyes, is joined by Levi Caspertein to search for his own wife, Chen Li, and his blind friend, Jenna Dowler

Owen Travers – younger brother of Lena, the vicious Enforcer from NYC who terrified and killed nonconformists. He has joined the refugees to escape NYC

Rex Caspertein – giant son of Rudy Caspertein, cousin to Levi; leads the group of Christian refugees from NYC toward Colorado

Runner – bounty hunter who uses his black Labrador by the same name to help in his evil deeds; he has the job of finding and killing Jenna Dowler and Levi Caspertein

Scooter – one of the original COIL Special Forces team members. The Hispanic man is Nathan Isaacson's good friend, now helping to lead refugees to Colorado with Rex

Sean Harris – gruff sergeant who accompanies Nathan Isaacson from NYC; now helps lead refugees to Colorado

Shaker - Federation scout and trader whose life is defined by opportunism. His facade of gentleness draws strangers in, but he has evil intentions that are often discovered too late

Eastern United States Map

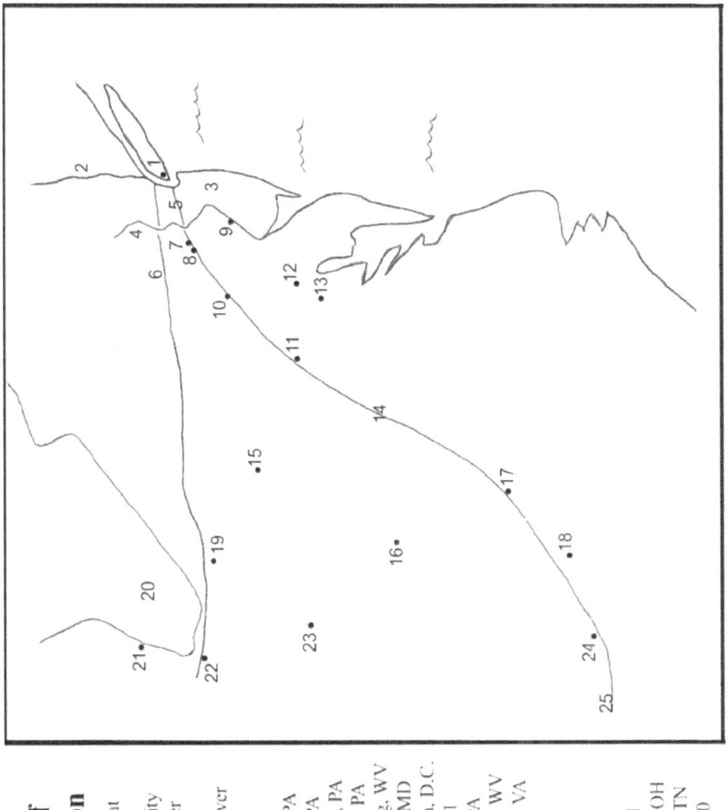

Dawn of Subjection

by D.I. Telbat

1. New York City
2. Hudson River
3. New Jersey
4. Delaware River
5. Interstate 78
6. Interstate 80
7. Bethlehem, PA
8. Allentown, PA
9. Philadelphia, PA
10. Harrisburg, PA
11. Martinsburg, WV
12. Baltimore, MD
13. Washington, D.C.
14. Interstate 81
15. Pittsburg, PA
16. Charleston, WV
17. Wytheville, VA
18. Erwin, TN
19. Akron, OH
20. Lake Erie
21. Detroit, MI
22. Toledo, OH
23. Columbus, OH
24. Knoxville, TN
25. Interstate 40

A Note from the Author

Dear Reader,

The next adventure for COIL, the Casperteins, and the Dowlers is before you! So much work goes into these novels, and I sometimes like to share with you a little of the research behind these projects, so you know what is real and what is fictional. Of course, the whole story is fictionally-based in the future, after a pandemic wipes out one-third of America's population, but a few local landmarks may interest you.

- Bethlehem, PA, is a real place, named by Moravian settlers. They found the Lehigh Valley beside the river to be a place of insignificance, much like the little town where our Savior was born. Later, the PA town became known for its industry, especially the steel factory. The old steel stacks are still standing today and are mentioned in the book where the space in front of the stacks is used for a market for traders.
- Allentown, PA, is another real town, and its Dorney Park is an amusement park visited by thousands every year. Dorney Park's several roller coasters and water park offer the backdrop for a pivotal moment in the novel. The names of the rides and brief descriptions are factual.
- The Martinsburg roundhouse in West Virginia is still standing today. As it appears in the book, it was once a turntable to shift locomotives onto other tracks. Since the building has a metal roof and its walls are sturdy, I imagined the structure would survive the fires and destruction of Pan-Day.

- The Loretto Mansion still stands in Wytheville to this day, across from the East End Cemetery, although it's one of Wytheville's many museums nowadays.
- The Erwin, Tennessee, fish hatchery and superintendent's mansion are still there today, nestled in the middle of the low mountain range. I imagined the hatchery would be an interesting food supply for the town in a post-apocalyptic scenario. It isn't far from where the legendary Davy Crockett was born.
- A decoction made from white oak bark (found across North America) can indeed be used as an antiseptic to clean wounds and rashes. Other antiseptics can be mixed from the juice of wild onion as well as garlic. The leaves of chickweed or the crushed leaves of wild spatterdock also work as disinfectants.
- When the Israelites left Egypt during the Exodus, it's understood by historians that they had worms from the bad Nile water piped into the region. This must've been why God had them drink wormwood, also known as tansy, to cure them of their worm infestation. Wormwood is high in alkaline and tastes bitter (Exodus 15:22-27), yet it would have cleansed the Israelites of their stay in Egypt, with much spiritual symbolism as well. Wild carrot leaves in North America is another remedy used to deal with intestinal parasites.

I hope you enjoy reading this book as much as I enjoyed writing it. Levi Caspertein, Jenna Dowler, Chloe Azmaveth, Nathan Isaacson, Brian Steelman, Chen Li, Luigi Putelli, Alice Prine, Scooter, Bruno, and Rex Caspertein are all looking forward to sharing their adventures with you!

May the Lord be honored by this novel,
David Telbat

Chapter One

Levi Caspertein tried to ignore the stench of death as he peered around the corner of a building at the New Federation soldiers a few blocks away. Dead bodies from the old regime were lined up on the street with the bodies of the soldiers of the new regime who had invaded the island of Manhattan. The battle had raged for a whole night, but in the end, Lena Travers had prevailed. Kendrick Obrador had run for his life, and a new era of subjection seemed inevitable.

Wiping sweat from his brow, Levi gauged the distance from his position west of the parking lot to the Bowery Hotel, the headquarters for the New Federation. He needed to cross three city blocks. Every step could attract the attention of someone who wanted to know who he was and what he was doing in a lieutenant's uniform.

Two days had passed since the battle for control of the East Coast, but cleanup was still in process. Three divisions from outside Manhattan had descended upon the city. The devastation appeared to extend two miles to the north. However, Levi hadn't been in New York in over twenty years, so he wasn't certain what infrastructure had been already crumbling, and what had been caused two days earlier. The reality was, the city was in chaos, and he hoped to use that to his advantage.

A crowd of soldiers in green uniforms walked down the street from the north. They were carrying an assortment of pilfered backpacks and rifles. Different patches on their shoulders identified them as hailing from a variety of military units. Perfect, Levi thought, and plucked off his lieutenant's silver bars. It was better to be a lowly private at this point, rather than a first lieutenant as Nathan Isaacson had been for several years.

Though Nathan was a large man by normal standards, his uniform barely fit across Levi's chest, and the pant legs were an inch above the top of his boots. But infiltrating the Bowery Hotel was their only shot at getting immediate intel on the status of Jenna Dowler and Chen Li. The women had been separated from the evacuating Christian refugees during the start of the battle and had been somehow left behind. The two COIL agents could be enduring torture that very moment!

Levi knelt and tied his boot laces as the party of twenty soldiers passed him.

"I'm sick and tired of cold meals, cold showers, and cold nights," one soldier said to another.

Glancing to his left and right, Levi hopped upright and fell in step at the back of the group.

"I bet that new chancellor lady isn't eating, sleeping, and showering in the cold," Levi grumbled, which barely drew a grunt from the previous complainer.

His group of soldiers walked past the crew organizing the dead, weaved through dozens of armored vehicles, then reached the Bowery. Levi hadn't had much time to learn the layout of the headquarters from Nathan, but he knew this was his stop, even if the soldiers were moving on to what he guessed were the barracks for the enlisted men.

The front doors of the Bowery were guarded by hard-faced men with assault rifles in their hands, so Levi waited to peel off from his group until he was out of sight of the guards. Around the east corner of the Bowery, Levi put his back to the wall and clipped his lieutenant's bars back onto his uniform. From his breast pocket, he drew out a folded, wrinkled piece of white paper. This was it—into the enemy's lair, armed only with a .22 pistol in a holster on his hip. The weapon was loaded with non-lethal gelatin tranquilizers, which wasn't much against five thousand rifles armed with lethal bullets.

"I'm in Your hands, Lord," Levi breathed, and stepped around the corner.

The guards stiffened as he approached. Levi steeled his face, narrowed his eyes, and corrected his posture. He was now their superior officer.

"I have intel on Chloe Azmaveth," Levi stated gruffly to a sergeant who wore a uniform with a bloody sleeve. No one seemed to have survived the battle unscathed. "The new chancellor needs to see it immediately."

The sergeant and the other guards took in his lieutenant's insignia. Then they seemed to notice his uniform, which barely fit. Finally, the sergeant frowned as he studied Levi's face. Levi knew a blond man his size and physique would normally be remembered. He'd shaved off his beard two days earlier, but he could still be identified as an enemy if he were questioned. They probably had strict orders about security so soon after the battle. The smell of gunpowder still lingered, and shrapnel still checkered the outside of the structure.

"I haven't seen you before." The sergeant reached for the paper. "Let me see what you have there, Lieutenant."

"Seriously?" Levi pulled back the paper. "You really want to get involved in this? Obrador and Azmaveth? You want to be the one hunting them down across the Plains Zone?"

The force of Levi's words checked the sergeant's curiosity. Levi himself didn't understand all the Federation politics, but Nathan had informed him just enough to spout the right names with the right attitude.

"You know where to go?" The sergeant moved aside and nodded to two of his men, who opened the nearest double doors to the hotel lobby. "Or do you need an escort?"

"I can handle a few flights of stairs!" Levi barked, and moved into the hotel.

Two plainclothes men and several women were cleaning up blood and debris from the floor and off the walls of the lobby. Apparently, the battle over the Bowery had reached even into its interior. Several soldiers stood against an old registration desk, watching the cleanup crew, so Levi paused only long enough to locate the stairwell that Nathan said was toward the back of the room, past the inoperable elevators.

He marched across the lobby and into the stairwell. Up one flight of stairs, he stopped on the landing and peered up the shaft. This was as far as Nathan had guided him. Now, Levi was on his own, moving into the unknown upheaval left in the wake of a bloody coup and an administration left in shambles.

With his right hand, he unclipped his holster so he could draw his sidearm with ease. The thought of Jenna Dowler in the hands of the new ruthless chancellor, Lena Travers, made Levi sick and angry. He'd looked into her eyes two days earlier and glimpsed her cold heart. And he'd heard enough from Nathan to know Lena would stop at nothing to glean intel from Jenna, who had been the Christian underground's voice of hope, even though she was a blind woman.

But Levi's concern wasn't about what intel Jenna had on the Christian underground. The Christians had been evacuated—over one hundred men, women, and children, including Levi's own wife—and were now fleeing west across New Jersey and Pennsylvania, in the protective hands of veteran COIL operatives. No, his concern was only to find Jenna and free her. Chen Li, Nathan's wife, had been with Jenna, so the challenge would be doubled—rescuing two women from the grip of a socialist regime. Levi had faced challenging tasks before. He was trusting God through this one as with others.

He steadily climbed the stairs, passed several descending officers, and reached the top floor.

There, he took a deep breath and checked his uniform. Although he was far from presentable for an inspection, his lieutenant's status had to count for something.

A long corridor spanned before him in which uniformed officials, suited civilians, and aids milled about, speaking in small groups. Levi walked casually toward them. Suddenly, he remembered his prop, and unfolded the bogus paper message he'd used to enter the hotel. With his head down, seemingly occupied with the paper, he weaved through the groups of officials. Nathan had been right so far. The diversity of three Army divisions who hadn't known one another, merging with the remnants of the previous administration's personnel—no one knew for sure who belonged.

Levi reached the just-as-crowded chancellor's suite, a windowed room with lavish furniture and a long dining table still cluttered from a forgotten feast. Cautiously, Levi edged into the room, hunching his back so his tall frame wasn't as conspicuous. Just because he'd shaved off his beard didn't mean he couldn't be recognized. After all, just two days earlier, he'd stood nose-to-nose with a military unit, forcing their retreat from the George Washington Bridge.

Sure enough, over the heads of several officials, at the side of the dining table, he spied Lena Travers. She wore a pressed Federation uniform, the green and white flag pronounced on both shoulders. She was a blond woman, her hair pulled back in a tight bun, which further accentuated her piercing eyes, small mouth, and thin lips. For years, she'd been a Federation Enforcer—arresting, questioning, and executing Christians. Levi remembered Nathan's warning about her hard line against anything and anyone that challenged her view of government. Almost singlehandedly, she'd beaten COIL out of the Bowery, forced Christians out of the city, and by violence decimated the previous administration. And more, she'd fired the shot that had killed Corban Dowler.

Suddenly, Levi recognized another figure, and he quickly turned away. Colonel Milo Rotham, a squinty-faced but ruthless military man from Philadelphia was there! Levi had tranquilized the man in his own city a week earlier, then questioned him for an hour while in captivity. *Lena and Rotham in the same room?* Both could ruin Levi's hope of finding Jenna and Chen Li.

With his back to the familiar faces in the room, Levi found himself standing at the edge of a group of three men and two women, each wearing a suit or uniform, and in deep discussion.

"She wants our support," said one woman with her hair down and a briefcase at her feet, "but she has no record of real leadership."

"She led the invasion," said a gentleman with a stained tie, "but never a country. We need a figurehead, a statesperson, not a loose cannon. She burned down the bridge, after all!"

Keeping his eyes down, Levi nodded thoughtfully, as if he were part of the conversation. Ironically, they were blaming Lena for tearing down the GW Bridge, but that had been a Caspertein stunt. As they continued to quietly discuss their apprehension over Lena's leadership, Levi stole glances toward one of the side rooms. If he could get alone with any of the people in power, he could question them about Jenna and Chen Li. He couldn't imagine that the blind woman and older Hong Kong operative had been able to evade capture, but if they had, Levi was searching for them in the wrong place. Every minute he stayed behind in Manhattan allowed his wife and the Christian refugees to move farther west without him and Nathan.

"What do you think, Lieutenant?"

Levi lifted his head to acknowledge an older man in an Army uniform. His shoulder insignia identified him as a Baltimore division officer. His eyebrows were gray but his mustache was dyed black with what appeared to be boot polish.

"Our choices have consequences." Levi frowned, not entirely sure of what they were discussing. Lena had forcibly taken charge, hadn't she? "As a military man, I'm fond of a firm and decisive hand. But I'm empathetic for the people who need a shepherd, someone benevolent and understanding. Maybe even someone who can be self-sacrificial. Does that sound like anyone we know?"

"Wise words from an Army lieutenant," said the Baltimore man. "It's settled, then. We vote for Morgan Branaugh, the people's choice, even if Lena Travers blows a gasket. The Federation would never run right with an Enforcer at its head. She got rid of the Christians and other troublemakers, so now we have no use for her."

"Send her to the Plains Zone to hunt noncompliants with the others." Another man with overgrown sideburns chuckled. "Of course, I don't think Colonel Rotham likes her too much, either. He's an able man. Young, but resolute."

"I like the choice of Morgan Branaugh," the other gray-haired woman said to Levi, touching his arm. She had long fingernails painted with toxic-smelling red polish. "We need more of you forward thinkers in the military, Officer."

Levi smiled, not sure who he had swayed, or for whom. He couldn't recall the name Morgan Branaugh from Nathan's briefing. Perhaps he was a newcomer. Whatever the case, the fireworks weren't finished in the Bowery. Lena's grab for power was apparently being challenged before it started. And there was a hunt for noncompliants in the Plains Zone?

Excusing himself, Levi moved to one of the unmarked side doors. He kept several groups of people between himself and Rotham and Lena, who were themselves each a part of different discussion groups. When he reached the door, he turned the handle and walked smoothly inside, as if he belonged there. Happily, he didn't find himself in a closet. Instead, as he closed the door behind him, two uniformed men with headsets looked up from the controls of a HAM radio. He'd entered the Bowery's radio room.

"Hey!" A middle-aged operator ripped off his headset. "You're not supposed to be in here!"

Reading the operator's face, Levi decided the man couldn't be reasoned with in the limited time he had. He didn't want the radio operator to cause a fuss that would draw attention from the room outside, and Levi couldn't return to the main suite very easily now. The other operator was in the middle of a broadcast, so Levi was facing only one demanding man.

Drawing his sidearm, Levi fired a silenced gel-tranq into the man's thigh, then shot the second operator in the shoulder before he knew what was happening. An instant later, both men were unconscious. Levi holstered his gun and dragged the men against the wall where no one would immediately see them if the door suddenly opened.

Levi had grown up with his father's radio, so he sat down and adjusted a couple knobs, then pressed the broadcast switch.

"This is the Bowery Hotel," he stated without donning the headset. "Attention all precincts and locales. The Bowery has been overrun by infiltrators. New York City has fallen into the hands of noncompliants posing as Federation loyalists. I am broadcasting from the Bowery this very minute. I repeat, we are overrun. Warn every state up and down the coast to stand in self-government. You have the authority to rule autonomously and govern yourselves. The Federation, I fear, is no more. This is the Bowery signing off for good. Be suspect of any further broadcasts from this location on this frequency. Once and for all, we're out."

Amused at his own misinformation, he turned off the transmit switch and ripped out both mic cords. His little bit of nonsense might further disrupt the oppression the Federation had been building against so many.

While he was considering where he could hide the mic cords, the door to the suite opened. Levi looked up and locked eyes with a uniformed man whose size filled the doorway. He had sergeant's stripes on his shoulder, and his nametag read Ibojka. Levi vaguely remembered tranquilizing him in Philadelphia, a man who'd been with Colonel Rotham's division.

"We have an announcement to send to the state capitals," Ibojka said, a clipboard in his hand. "They're almost ready for the vote that needs to be . . ."

The man's voice trailed off as he closed the door and noticed the two unconscious men on the floor. Since Levi didn't have his beard, he knew the soldier hadn't recognized him yet. Levi tossed the mic cords into the sergeant's face, then charged him.

He slugged the man hard in the stomach to take his wind. Ibojka dropped to one knee, and Levi quickly used the cords to bind the man's hands behind him. Then from behind, Levi drew his pistol and held it to Ibojka's head. A killer like Ibojka would never cooperate with a non-compliant. Again, misinformation seemed the best route.

"I don't want to hurt you, Sergeant, but I need answers and I need them fast. Someone came into this room before you and shut down the radio. Now, I just spoke out there in support of Morgan Branaugh. Where do your loyalties lie? Are you with Lena Travers?"

"Get your hands off me!"

"Keep your voice down!" Levi hissed into his ear. "If you're one of the loyalists, then you have nothing to fear from me. How do I know you're not the one who sabotaged the radio right in front of everyone?"

"This is ridiculous!" He shifted his head toward the unconscious operators. "Are they dead?"

"Well, it ain't siesta time, is it? Now talk? Your loyalties—now!"

"I'm not taking sides. I don't care who runs the Federation. Untie my hands! Who are you? All I'm doing is making sure we have a Federation still here when we get back."

"Where are you going?"

"It was already announced. Colonel Rotham is going after the noncompliants who escaped two days ago. We're fighting men. We're not babysitting politicians around here. We're leaving. You guys can duke it out here all you want. We're going after the Casperteins."

"Good." Levi cleared his throat. "Now, what about Radiant Shade?"

He used Jenna's code name, which he knew had been revealed days earlier.

"What about her?"

"Lena captured her. She was holding her, wasn't she? Has she talked?"

"Holding her? I've heard nothing about Jenna Dowler. I didn't know she was captured. I thought she was with that whole band who escaped over the bridge—before they burned it down."

"Thank you for cooperating, Sergeant." Levi relaxed his hold and moved in front of Ibojka. "But if you go after those Christians who ran away, you and I are going to keep meeting like this, and I'm going to have to keep tranquilizing you."

Ibojka's face changed from confusion to fury.

"You!" He cursed. "Caspertein!"

"It ain't easy getting bested by Christians every time we meet."

The man opened his mouth to speak or yell, so Levi shot him in the shoulder. The body count was piling up quickly in the radio room. Since he believed what the sergeant had said about Jenna not being in custody, Levi figured it was time to make his exit. Time was wasting. A blind woman and a middle-aged agent were out there all alone, somewhere on the island or the mainland, waiting to be found.

Levi opened the door a crack to see the room to the right. The doorway to the crowded corridor was in sight. By the time Ibojka and the two radio operators woke, he'd be on the bank of the Hudson, ready to meet up with Nathan to begin their search for the women.

"The ballots have been counted!" a man announced over the noise of the room. "Colonel Rotham, this is what you're here for."

Opening the door a little wider, Levi could see more of the room to the left. Everyone's gaze was fixed on Rotham, who took a can and shook what Levi guessed were ballots. Now was the perfect moment to escape, while nearly everyone was facing Rotham, except Rotham would be facing him. Hesitating further, Levi checked his sidearm. He'd fired three rounds of a nine-shot magazine. That meant he had six gel-tranqs left.

"I postponed leaving the capital to keep this transition peaceful," Rotham stated as the room became silent. "The New Federation will take effect at dawn. Sergeant Ibojka is in the radio room, gathering the votes from the governors of the other states, but even if those ten additional votes go the other direction, the winner is overwhelmingly obvious."

"Read the winner already, man!" someone cheered, drawing some anxious chuckles.

"Very well." Rotham lifted his chin on his small face. "By a landslide, even if the other states vote opposite, Mr. Morgan Branaugh is our new chancellor! Mr. Branaugh?"

"No!" shrieked someone in the front.

Levi rose onto his toes to see the shorter woman—Lena Travers—rush forward and rip the ballet canister from Rotham's fingers.

"This isn't right!" she yelled. "This is my office!"

"Lena!" Rotham thundered back. "We all agreed. The vote must stand!"

"I made this happen!" Lena panted and backed away from Rotham. "You all slept through Obrador's reign of weakness. I deserve this office. I earned it while you all avoided conflict. I demand reconsideration! This isn't fair!"

"Lena, you have to—"

Rotham was cut short as Lena drew her sidearm and aimed it at a quaint man with a white beard. Levi guessed he was the new chancellor, Morgan Branaugh.

"If you won't have me," she gasped, "then you won't have him, either!"

In a blur, faster than Levi had ever seen anyone draw a gun, Rotham raised his own sidearm and fired. Lena dropped from sight, and the window behind her fell in a cascade of broken glass. The guests screamed and backed away from the gaping window which looked down on Broadway many stories below.

"Stay calm!" Rotham holstered his weapon. "You and you, get her body out of here. Take her to the furnace. Ibojka? Where are you? Someone find Sergeant Ibojka. And get a sheet of plywood over this window. Watch out for the glass. Don't go anywhere, Mr. Branaugh. We'll swear you in and be finished with this as soon as we hear from the other states to make it official."

Levi saw his moment to escape the radio room in the midst of the ruckus. He slipped out the door and closed it behind him. In two steps, he was in the crowd, shuffling toward the exit. Although Colonel Rotham's voice was calm, the guests were far from settled.

"He executed her!" cried one woman in a plaid skirt. "It was so gruesome!"

"She deserved it," said a man with taped spectacles. "Didn't you see her? She was going to shoot Morgan."

"Nobody wanted her here," another said. "She's too unpredictable—a wild card. I'm glad she's dead and gone."

Levi kept his head down, but the press of bodies heading toward the corridor forced him to move with the flow of traffic.

"Make a path!" A soldier bumped Levi from behind. "Coming through."

Turning, Levi saw two men carrying the limp body of Lena Travers, her face bloodied from the bullet. He immediately saw her as his ticket out, and took one of her legs to carry her forward.

"Move aside," Levi instructed bystanders, then nodded at the soldier next to him. "I've got her, Private."

"Okay, sure." The soldier carrying the other leg abandoned it as Levi took control of her lower half, guiding forward the soldier who carried her upper body behind him.

They were in the corridor in seconds, moving rapidly toward the stairwell, when Levi felt Lena's legs twitch.

"Put her down!" Levi stopped in the corridor, halting the other soldier against the wall. "Put her down! She's still alive!"

The other soldier roughly set her on the carpeted floor. Guests walked past or milled about, apparently waiting for the window to be boarded up in the suite so the crowning ceremony could resume.

Quickly, Levi moved up Lena's body, examining her, but her only wound seemed to be on her face. Half of her jaw was missing. Then her eyes opened and locked onto his. She was struggling to breath past the blood and tissue mangled below her eyes.

The soldier swore and flinched away.

"She *is* alive!" He shook his head. "It doesn't matter. Colonel Rotham said to get rid of her."

Levi stared into her eyes. This was Lena Travers, the butcher of Christians, Nathan had said. Lena had been beat out by Branaugh who was probably more popular and maybe had more experience as a statesman.

"Turn your head to breathe," Levi said to Lena, and physically took the top of her head to shift it to the side. "Otherwise, you'll choke."

"Her whole mouth is gone." The soldier grimaced and studied her closer. "There's no way she'll live. Lieutenant? No offense, sir, but Colonel Rotham said—"

"I know." Levi held up a hand to the young man. He didn't have time to hang around. The three in the radio room could be found any minute, and then the Bowery would be on lockdown. "Let me take her. I'll put her in the ground when she dies. I've got her from here. You're dismissed, Private."

"I think . . . I should help you burn her. He said the furnace."

"You want to wait on her to die? That could take hours." Levi nudged the soldier aside and picked up Lena in his arms. "Or maybe you want to throw her into the furnace alive. Look at her. She's fighting to stay alive!"

Standing upright, Levi was surprised at how light the forceful woman was. Although Lena was indeed struggling to breathe, she didn't flail her limbs, which made it easier for Levi. He was able to hold her close, not caring that she was bleeding onto his borrowed uniform.

"The colonel was trusting me to burn her."

"It's okay." Levi nodded at the man. "You'll never see her again. Go on and get yourself cleaned up. I've got it from here."

Levi couldn't wait around any longer. Entering the stairwell, he descended as fast as he could with his extra burden. Lena needed medical help if she was going to live, and her straining wasn't helping the steady flow of blood from her missing jaw. It felt natural for him to pity her, even though he knew a little about what she'd done. He hadn't known the details of Corban's death, but he remembered now what Chloe had told him. Corban had wanted Lena to be given some sort of chance, if Levi ever came into the city. His mission to rescue Jenna and Chen

Li had been extended to saving the life of the woman who had hunted Jenna and murdered God's people for a decade.

When he reached the lobby downstairs, Levi paused and surveyed the loitering personnel. He'd never make it out unnoticed, and he couldn't imagine escaping the Bowery grounds with the wounded woman in his arms. Unless there was a miracle.

"Walk us out, Lord," Levi whispered, and stepped onto the floor. "It ain't easy . . ."

He walked straight ahead, and when he reached the doors, he used his foot to shove them open. The guards outside seemed like they wanted to say something. But they only stuttered and moved aside at the sight of Lena as he marched into the daylight. Every step he took, he expected a bullet in his back, or a call for him to stop. Stealing Lena's body was one thing, but his business in the radio room, tranquilizing Sergeant Ibojka, was likely to cause the Bowery to erupt in new orders for his arrest.

They reached Broadway and continued west. A block later, with his arms cramping, he stopped in the shadow of a building and lay Lena on the sidewalk. No one was around in that part of the city. He expected to find her dead, but then he saw her teary eyes. With her head tilted aside, she was breathing with difficulty, but she was still bleeding where her jaw was supposed to be.

"I don't know what else to do with you, lady, but to take you with me." He sighed and almost touched her face with his hand, but instead, he touched her shoulder. "You're in a bad way, and it's getting worse with the bleeding. I don't know what to do but to cauterize this . . . mess, and hope to save your life."

With surprising strength, she reached out a hand and grasped his uniform. He recognized pleading when he saw it. She lowered her hand to her neck and traced her thumb across her throat.

"You might feel like dying right now, but I'm not killing you. I know you're in pain, but you're in no condition to die, spiritually speaking. I guess I can help you that much."

He drew his sidearm, held the muzzle a few inches from her thigh, then squeezed the trigger. She flinched, then closed her eyes. He patted her head, studying her deformed face, wondering if she would ever wake up.

But while she was unconscious, he needed to cauterize her jaw. He picked her up again, shifted her head so she could breathe without choking, and ran west, toward the Hudson River.

✝

Colonel Milo Rotham adjusted the shotgun on a sling across his chest, then rested his hand on his sidearm. He stood in front of the Bowery Hotel and watched his men running to and fro, preparing the convoy to leave. The smell of diesel choked the lot, finally masking the stench of death from the two hundred dead, lined bodies, still waiting to be cremated or buried.

"Rotham, this is Ibojka," his radio crackled. "Come in, Colonel."

"This is Rotham." He held the radio in his left hand, keeping his right hand hovering over his pistol grip. "What is it, Sergeant?"

"We've searched the whole Hudson River bank. We see no sign of the Casperteins. The guy's a ghost. He either crossed the river already, or he's hiding in a million possible places in the city. Over."

"All right, Sergeant." Rotham sighed. Of course, it had been too much to hope for to capture Levi Caspertein before he'd left the city. "Bring the boys back. We're rolling out in ten. Out."

He clipped the radio onto his belt and walked down the line of ten vehicles where forty men scrambled with gear and supplies. Once Sergeant Ibojka returned with his ten men, the convoy would consist of an even fifty fighting men and women, the toughest soldiers the Federation could provide. Most of them were his own people from Philadelphia, and the rest had been chosen from the other Army divisions who'd participated in the coup.

"Get that fuel truck to the back of the line," Rotham ordered one of the engineers who was also a captain. "And make sure the turrets are manned every minute."

Rotham walked up to his armored command vehicle, a steel-plated commuter bus, and slapped the shielding on the side. He'd never ventured into the Plains Zone, but he couldn't imagine having a better equipped or fiercer unit about to face the unknown. His command vehicle even had a rusty snowplow mounted on the front, giving it the appearance of a death machine. Five Humvees, two SUVs, a fuel truck, and a Jeep for forward scouting completed the convoy.

Several hundred Citizen Army soldiers stood on the edge of the Bowery parking lot, watching forlornly as the ten vehicles made final preparations. Many of them had hoped to be chosen for the journey westward, but the final call had been up to Rotham. With Ibojka and other division commanders, only the finest marksmen, engineers, medics, and demolitions people had been selected.

"Colonel," someone called from behind him.

Rotham turned to look down at Chancellor Morgan Branaugh, and shook the politician's hand. Branaugh's five muscled bodyguards stood uncomfortably close to Rotham on both sides of him.

"Come to see us off, Chancellor?" Rotham gestured toward the vehicles. "We're about ready."

"You know I wouldn't be signing off on this little revenge mission if the Federation's interests weren't uppermost."

"Yes, I know." Rotham chose his words carefully, having heard a few stories of how brutal the little man had been in Baltimore. Despite his small stature, the new chancellor wasn't to be underestimated. Rumor had it the man had poisoned at least two others who'd stood in his way on his climb to the top. "We'll be scouting and mapping for Federation expansion."

"Good." Branaugh crossed his arms, seemingly unbothered that he was so short that he needed to look up at everyone. "But all said, unofficially, whoever this Caspertein family is, I want them wiped out, along with all the noncompliants."

"I'll take care of them."

"Please understand. I don't even want to see Obrador again. When you catch up to them, leave their bodies in the ditch, and continue with your orders, all the way to the Mississippi, if you can."

"The Casperteins will wish they'd never come to New York, Chancellor."

"It's curious, though, isn't it?" Branaugh took a few steps past his bodyguards to gaze at the command vehicle. "This Levi Caspertein person comes right into our territory, ruins our bridge, burns our cities, attacks our people in our own radio room—and he's not intimidated by any of this?"

"He's woken the beast, sir. Obrador was obsessed with the weak underground resistance. I'm going to show these Casperteins what defeat feels like."

"You're the right man for the job, Colonel. Make your Federation proud. Always caring, forever strong."

"Always caring, forever strong," Rotham repeated the national motto, and shook the leader's hand once more.

With his bodyguards, Branaugh returned to the safety of the Bowery.

As the scout Jeep drove onto Broadway and headed north, the other vehicles started their engines. Sergeant Ibojka marched up with his unit and dispersed amongst the vehicles.

"Branaugh was just out here, showing off his new command," Rotham said privately to Ibojka, knowing his right-hand soldier had the same feelings toward politicians. "I'm not sorry to be leaving this city already. No sign of Caspertein, huh?"

"We found a cold campfire and fresh blood over by the river, like he was wounded or something, but it could've been someone else." Ibojka cursed. "I'm ready to rip that guy's heart out. First, Philadelphia, then the GW Bridge, and now this morning? I'm still bruised from that tranquilizer."

"Believe me, I know." Rotham scowled at his own memory of being tranqed by the Caspertein weapons. "He risked his own life to come question us about Radiant Shade? What's a lame blind woman to him?"

"At least we know now that Jenna Dowler is still out there somewhere, and the noncompliants are on their way west." Ibojka tightened his belt. "Let's hope Obrador stays with the main party. He'll be easier to find that way."

"He will. He doesn't know how to survive in a place like the Plains Zone without a bunch of nurses caring for him. Just a week ago, he was eating caviar and drinking wine. But you and I were born for this. Let's load up."

Someone honked one of the vehicle horns, and a cheer rose from the Citizen Army bystanders. The reaction caused more horns to be honked.

Rotham ignored the ruckus and walked over to a slender young man clothed in earth tones, standing patiently against the Bowery wall. A thick-chested black Labrador retriever was panting at his side. The animal lowered her head as Rotham approached.

"Thanks for waiting." Rotham didn't trust the dog or the man enough to move closer to shake his hand. "We're pulling out. You know your targets?"

"Find this blind woman and use her to capture the blond westerner."

"Don't underestimate them." Rotham gave him a handheld radio.

"Don't underestimate us," the young man said, pocketing the radio, then he dropped his hand to the Lab's head. The dog barred her teeth in a silent snarl. "I guess we'll be leaving now, to do what we each do best."

"I guess we will."

Rotham didn't move as the bounty hunter walked away. The man couldn't have been older than twenty-five, but Ibojka had heard from Federation scouts who'd traveled in the Plains Zone that there was a young tracker known as the Runner who never lost his prey. A short crossbow hung from the bounty hunter's belt, and a tomahawk was fastened on his other hip. There was a small pack on his back, and for an instant, Rotham envied the youth. He was so free, liberated from the burdens of the Federation's Army politics, skilled enough to live off the land instead of relying on fuel, command vehicles, and dozens of men to make a kill.

Glancing down at his own weapons—the shotgun strap across his chest and the sidearm on his right hip—Rotham thought of his own start. He was in his thirties now, barely a teen when Pan-Day had struck America. Video games had been his military training, and his command in Philadelphia over the Citizen Army had hardened him while hunting and arresting thousands of noncompliants. But now, he was facing real threats. The Plains Zone was full of danger—packs of feral dogs, rogue towns occupied by militias, highways threatened by ambushes, landslides, and flash floods.

His heart beat faster at the thought of adventure and risk. He wasn't arresting and executing unarmed Christians anymore. Now his enemies were well-trained marksmen who knew the Plains Zone, and he felt certain they knew he was coming after them!

Andy Radner, known as the Runner, knelt next to the ashes of a recent fire on the east bank of the Hudson River. Not far to the north, the jagged remnants of the ruined GW Bridge hung, both sides seeming to reach for the other to close the ugly, smoldering gap. But Andy wasn't interested in the bridge. He'd already inspected it and heard the account of the man called Levi Caspertein who'd faced down Lena Travers and her whole army.

"Track 'em, girl," Andy said softly to his Labrador—also named Runner—who sniffed at the simple campsite in the corner of a ruined warehouse. He loved Runner, and it didn't bother him at all that they shared the same handle. "Where'd they go, girl?"

In seconds, Andy had read the sign available and deduced that two people had shared the fire sometime in the last few hours. He was a long ways from the mountains of Wyoming where he'd been raised by wilderness survivalists, but tracking and reading sign was the same anywhere.

There were bloody rags by a stack of iron to his right, and the smell of scorched skin mingled with sweat from an abandoned Army uniform next to the fire. After examining the uniform, he found blood on the outside of the shirt, not the inside. The scorched skin smell, he reasoned, must've been from a cauterized wound.

Runner whined for Andy's attention, and he knew she'd picked up the trail, but he was too fascinated with the unfolding story to move away from the ashes just yet. Levi Caspertein had worn the uniform to infiltrate the Bowery, but who'd been wounded that the person had bled on the outside of his uniform?

"What?" Andy said aloud, sniffing at the clothes himself. "No way . . ."

There was only one person who Andy had heard had been hurt earlier that morning. Lena Travers had been shot and killed by Rotham. She was dead. Besides, Lena and Levi were enemies, so it made no sense that it would be her. He decided whoever was wounded was someone else. Possibly a recovered friend, maybe even Jenna Dowler, for whom Levi was willing to risk his life rather than flee quickly from the Federation that was hunting him.

"Track 'em!" Andy commanded Runner, and charged after the dog.

Runner had been poised for several minutes, so she needed no further urging. She turned and bounded toward the river bank, her nose to the ground.

Andy jogged after her, his mind still puzzling over the actions of Levi Caspertein, a foe who both irritated and interested him. Ever since leaving his parents in Wyoming, Andy had employed his skills as a hunter by tracking down thieves, travelers, and runaway slaves. But this was the first time he felt he was tracking someone worthy of his skills. He had no doubt he would catch Jenna and Levi within days—and kill them—but he would enjoy the game in the meantime.

Runner led him to the river's edge where Andy found drag marks in the wet soil from something heavy. Not a boat necessarily, but probably something that could float. He peered across the river with his naked eye as his fingers dug into the breast pocket of his buckskin shirt for a short field glass. Through the monocular, he studied the opposite bank of the river a half-mile away. There were people fishing, and maybe even washing clothes. The water was murky and polluted, but it was as good as New Yorkers knew.

Then, Andy traced his scope to the left, trying to gauge the river's current and how far it would carry a floating object down river. If Levi was paddling, then he wouldn't be trusting merely the current to carry him away. Yes, Andy guessed. The man would've had a paddle or two to steer, and would have eventually reached the New Jersey shore.

With really only one way to track Levi from the river, Andy turned to search for the items he'd need. There wasn't time to go around through the Bronx to reach New Jersey. He wanted to cross the same way Levi had crossed so he could pick up his trail on the other side before sundown.

Suddenly, Andy paused and stared down the bank. A lone, gaunt man stood at the edge of the water. He was thirty yards away, but Andy's eyes were keen. The man was old, his frame a little slouched, but he'd moved up to the river without Andy's notice. Even Runner whined and looked to her master with uncertainty.

"It's okay, girl," Andy coaxed her, not caring if his voice was carried to the stranger. "He's just an old man. A nobody."

Andy reentered the structure where the fire had been built, searching for anything buoyant or hollow that could be fashioned into a flotation device. When he checked the river again, the old man was gone. He had no doubt the city of New York was filled with strange, lonely people, but there had been something about that particular man that triggered Andy's caution. Runner had sensed it as well. They'd been in the same place, looking in the same direction across the water . . . as if he and Runner weren't the only two on the trail of Jenna Dowler and Levi Caspertein.

Jenna Dowler couldn't remember ever being this frustrated with being blind. When her father, Corban Dowler, had been at her side, she'd been a fearless overcomer, compensating for her lack of sight by using her other senses. But now, her father was somewhere else and she was alone with Chen Li, who wasn't the elite agent she'd once been.

"It's almost daylight," Jenna said to her friend, trying to withhold the criticism in her voice. "We need to move. Walking will warm you up."

Beside her, under the cover of a thick tarp that smelled like oil and seagull droppings, Chen Li shifted her slender frame.

"How do you know it's almost daylight? I can still see the stars."

"The wind always changes before dawn along the coast. I can smell the scent. Come on. Let's go."

Jenna climbed to her feet and held out her hand to Chen Li, who was twenty years older. While crossing the Hudson River on three truck tires, they'd both gotten soaked. After changing into dry clothes from their small travel packs, Jenna was ready to march, but Chen Li couldn't shake her chill.

The older woman finally accepted her hand, and Jenna strained to help her to her feet.

"I think the river current carried us down the coastline of New Jersey." Jenna turned her head and clicked her tongue, discerning by echolocation that they were between two buildings. "Did you see how far we drifted?"

"We crossed in the night. I couldn't see land until we bumped into it." Chen Li rubbed her arms as Jenna held onto her. "Okay. Which way do we go?"

"Dad and the others probably met up with Bruno on the other side of the GW Bridge. That's north of us at least two or three miles. Lena's troops are probably swarming that whole area, which means we need to move away from them, but start heading west."

"We'll never reach Colorado like this, Jenna, just the two of us. We have no gear."

"Well, we never thought we'd get off Manhattan, either, right?" Jenna coaxed her with strained patience. "But God provided. We have to trust Him. Let's go."

When Jenna pulled her friend forward, Chen Li pulled back.

"No, we can't go that way. We're in a dead-end alley. We'll have to go around. And carefully. There's all kinds of scrap metal on the ground."

"Guide me," Jenna urged, "and let's cover some miles before we rest again."

Chen Li was still shivering, but Jenna was pleased that the woman finally started walking. Placing their booted feet carefully, and climbing over a few metal beams that had fallen from old buildings, they moved around the warehouse on the bank and away from the river.

"You're right," Chen Li said. "It's daylight. That was fast."

"Think of how we look to civilians." Jenna was used to strategizing with her father, so it was natural for her to keep her mind busy in this way. "Two women, one supporting the other, with backpacks on our backs. It'll look weird if you're seen leading me like this. People will notice and recognize me, and they'll turn us in for extra rations."

"Well, you can't rightly lead me, Jenna." Chen Li scoffed. "I don't see an alternative."

"Is the street clear ahead? I can walk beside you. As long as you keep talking, I'll know where you are, and you can steer me. It'll look more casual."

"Okay, what am I supposed to talk about?"

"Anything. Pray." Jenna forced herself to release Chen Li, then move a couple feet away from her. "Pray for Nathan and the others. They'll have started west ahead of us."

"God in heaven," Chen Li started, "we're lost and afraid, but we believe You haven't forgotten us. Send my husband for us. I know he's probably already on his way, but I don't know how it'll work out. Last night was pure fright, Lord . . ."

Jenna relaxed as she walked beside her praying friend. With Chen Li focused once again, Jenna was free to apply her mind to their dilemma. It was dangerous to be all alone like they were, but not necessarily gravely so, as long as they kept out of the hands of the Federation.

The screams and gunshots from the battle for the Bowery still rang in Jenna's memory. The years she'd spent intent on infiltrating the government had ended so abruptly, sending all the remaining COIL personnel running for their lives. Somehow, she and Chen Li had become separated from the others, and Nathan and Corban had had other concerns apparently, because no one had noticed in time that they were missing.

Or maybe they'd all been killed, Jenna thought in near-panic, almost coming to a stop next to Chen Li. It was too horrible to imagine, that the others might have died! But it was possible. She needed to steel herself for that reality. It would certainly explain why no one had found them yet.

But then her heart skipped a beat. Levi was still out there! He'd crossed the Plains Zone to save her. If Levi was still alive, he'd find her. She loved him more than if he were a brother, even though he was married to Lyla now. He must've still cared for her somehow, too, to have come so far for her. It was something to hope for since, as Chen Li had said, they'd never make it to Colorado alone and without supplies.

Sometime later, Chen Li called a stop to rest their feet.

"We're nearly at the outskirts of the industrial area closest to the river." Chen Li groaned. "Sit here. The grass is dead on this side of the street, but it's dry. Feel that sun? It feels so—"

"We need to find an interstate," Jenna said, not willing to rest. "Sorry to interrupt, but we can't stay on these streets. If we could travel on an interstate, we could avoid most civilians and move south or west more directly."

"Yeah, but so can the Federation." Chen Li yawned. "Besides, isn't that defeating our goal? The faster we move, the harder it'll be for Nathan to catch up to us."

"That's not all I'm worried about." Jenna faced the risen sun and tried to sense what lay behind them. "Lena promised to come after us. Even if the others were killed trying to cross the GW Bridge, she'll see you and I aren't among the dead. She'll be searching for us."

"What did you just say?" Chen Li climbed to her feet, and Jenna could feel her closeness, even her voice was uncomfortably near her ear. "What do you mean, if the others were killed? Nobody's died, Jenna. Nathan's coming for us. My husband wouldn't dare—"

"We have to prepare ourselves for the possibilities!" Jenna stepped away, angry at herself for the harsh tone of her voice. "I'm sorry for snapping, Chen Li. We can't wait around for what may not come. I don't want to think about it, either, but we need to get out of Federation territory. If we can get into Pennsylvania—"

"That's a hundred miles!" Chen Li's voice broke. "Jenna, I can't do that. Not like this. How could we?"

"We have to. If we are where I think we are, then it's only about fifty miles across New Jersey to Pennsylvania. We can do that in two days."

"Two days!"

Jenna reached out for Chen Li and found the older woman's shoulders. Using the sun as her compass, Jenna turned Chen Li to face northwest.

"Look in that direction. It must be near. What do you see?"

"A rusty crane. Trees. A few rundown houses. What do you think is out there?"

"Interstate 80 shouldn't be far to the north."

"But I thought we wanted to go south a little to avoid the Federation patrols."

"We may need to compromise our safety temporarily, if it means we can find a quick route west. Imagine if we could get on Interstate 80. We could follow it all the way to Meeker, Colorado, behind the others!"

"Yeah, but . . . with no supplies?"

"I'm working on that." Jenna chuckled. "One thing at a time, okay?"

Without warning, Chen Li threw her arms around Jenna and shook as she cried. Jenna stood and held her.

"You're so much braver than I am! I thought I could do this, but in my mind, when this happened, I thought I'd be with Nathan. He always makes everything all right. I never felt unsafe with him, not even all those years in Citizen Processing. Now look at me. I'm a mess, Jenna. I'm so sorry."

"It's okay. Look at it this way. We've both relied on different people so much, God may be forcing us to rely on Him like never before. He's doing this for us, to make us stronger in Him. See? This isn't all bad, right?"

"As long as we're not arrested. I never want to see Lena Travers ever again!"

"Look again to the north," Jenna directed. "Interstate 80. We find that, and we've won half the battle of getting across New Jersey."

"Okay. There's a cross-street up here." Chen Li guided her back onto the road. "We just have to keep moving, and I'm not thinking about the others being dead. We can't be thinking like that, Jenna. I don't want to. My mind doesn't work like that. You and your father always think about contingencies and what-ifs, but I don't, anymore. Not at my age. Just point me in one direction, like you've done before, and I'll get to it."

Jenna allowed Chen Li to ramble on. She knew the older woman was right. Corban had taught her to think strategically. Even in that moment, Jenna was thinking about who the Federation would send to track them down, return them to New York, and execute them publicly.

They'd killed thousands of Christians already. What was two more women?

Someone was behind them. Jenna couldn't shake the sensation. Maybe it was from God, or maybe it was just her imagination, but it made her weary legs walk faster. Even though she couldn't talk about the dread with Chen Li, or what was following them, Jenna hurried them on.

Being captured was indeed unthinkable, because Jenna knew Levi would try to rescue them, even if it meant his own death.

Chapter Two

Brian Steelman heard the first gunshots, and thought how they sounded remarkably like firecrackers. Then a grenade was thrown, and the explosion shook him into reality.

"Ambush!" Scooter yelled for the one hundred Christian refugees. The short Hispanic man with a crewcut waved his arm. "Everybody, down!"

The men, women, and children dove to the ground and covered their heads with their hands as rifles thundered, bullets whizzed, and an RPG screamed overhead.

Simultaneously, Brian and the others who carried COIL .308 battle rifles returned fire with gel-tranqs, pounding the tree line above the New Jersey freeway. Until the last two years, Brian had been a Federation Enforcer who had hunted unarmed Christians for the government. He'd traveled through the Plains Zone before, but this was only his second pitched gun battle.

He'd been near the middle of the caravan heading west when the gunfight had begun. They were only a day and a half out of New Jersey's eastern warehouse district, moving parallel to Interstate 80 on their flight toward the Rocky Mountains.

"Bruno! Brian!" Chloe Azmaveth shouted from her prone position. "Push them back! I'll get everyone to cover!"

Wide-eyed, Brian nodded once at the veteran operator, and charged toward the tree line. Bruno, an older black man nearly twice as thick in the chest as Brian, was on his left. To Brian's right, Lyla Caspertein knelt and fired her rifle methodically, no panic in her attitude. And Alice Prine, a one-armed black woman who'd been far out in front, was running back to the main body of refugees. She carried a rifle on her back, but in her grip was the steel walking staff she always carried.

"Come on, you Philistines!" Rex Caspertein roared as he charged the hill.

If Brian wasn't mistaken, the big cousin of Levi was laughing in the midst of the battle! Meanwhile, Sean Harris, the sergeant Nathan had recruited from the Bowery, stormed the hillside without any cover, firing every couple of steps.

Brian fired eight more rounds at the woods, then reloaded as he searched for an actual target in the trees. The others kept firing, driving a hard offensive, probably more than the ambushers had expected from a fragile, rag-wearing caravan of refugees. He glanced back and saw Chloe leading the retreat of the one hundred people into a ditch. Though ex-chancellor Kendrick Obrador and ex-Enforcer Owen Travers carried rifles, they were in full retreat without firing a shot. This didn't surprise Brian since he knew both men to be selfish Federation men. They were traveling with the Christian refugees only because the two men would be killed by Lena's forces if left behind.

A bullet zipped past Brian's head, snapping him back to attention. He needed cover, and fast! The closest cover at that point was to continue his charge to the trees ahead rather than retreat over exposed ground with the rest. Seeing how Rex was hollering challenges as if to the ancient Philistines, Brian followed suit and screamed with adrenalin as he raced toward the tree line.

But as soon as he entered the oaks and pines, he realized it was a complete forest, not merely a narrow stand of trees. With his shoulder against a thick pine, he scoped the shadows ahead. It was unnerving that the caravan of refugees had been attacked at all—inside

Federation territory! However, Brian decided he shouldn't have been surprised. Lack of food and water in the coastal cities had pushed people inland after Pan-Day. In rural areas like these untamed lands between cities, there were probably hundreds of rogue bands of survivalists, wild and cutthroat.

The forest was quiet now. He couldn't hear Rex's shouts any longer, and Bruno's gun had stopped barking. The attackers in the trees had either retreated or they'd been tranquilized. If they had been tranquilized, Brian doubted it had been by him since he'd fired blindly at the trees, seeing no actual target.

Then he saw them. Two men in tattered winter coats prowled toward him, their heads low and eyes wide, like wolves stalking a rabbit. Another enemy shifted from cover on Brian's right, but the man's face was turned toward the clearing. Moving only his eyes, Brian acknowledged two more men in the trees about twenty feet off the ground, standing in tree stands made of wood and metal framing. It was alarming to Brian that he'd entered the forest without them noticing, unless he'd been too close for the ambushers to spot since they'd been focused on the spoils of the large party below.

Swallowing down his fear, Brian searched around his position for better cover. He was severely outnumbered. Rex and Bruno were somewhere to his left, and Sean Harris was somewhere nearby, though Brian couldn't remember if he'd remained outside the tree line with Lyla Caspertein, or moved back to cover the refugees.

Sweat ran from Brian's hairline as he contemplated what he should do. Rex was a bit young and reckless, so Brian guessed the Westerner wouldn't wait patiently for long. Brian was still getting to know the frontiersman, and from what he could tell, the Caspertein man was a genuine man of faith and devotion, leading in such an outspoken manner that he drew even Scooter's approval. That was why Scooter hadn't offered to lead, he figured. In fact,

Brian reflected, he hadn't once seen any of the Christians fighting for leadership, not like he was used to in the Federation. There, people were always struggling with others for power. Here, since there was little personal ambition, if an idea was sound, they simply all moved in that direction.

Two gunshots blasted from an unseen position to Brian's left. He recognized them as battle rifle rounds. If Rex and Bruno were again on the offensive, then Brian wanted to keep up the pressure in his sector of the forest. Leaning around his tree cover, he aimed at one of the men in a tree stand and fired. The gel-tranq hit the man's chest, and he slumped unconscious against a harness around his shoulders.

At that instant, a gunman not ten feet away rose from the ground in front of Brian and threw off his camouflage. Brian leveled his rifle to fire as the other man shouldered his own weapon. Suddenly, a short burst of automatic gunfire whipped through the trees. At least two rounds pierced the stranger in front of Brian. Of course, Brian realized he'd been the target of those bullets, but the man from the ground had risen in front of his own people's muzzles, drawing their friendly fire.

"Hold your fire!" Brian shouted, and gritted his teeth as he fired rapidly at the two men who'd just gunned down their own man. He knew they didn't understand the rounds he was firing were harmless tranquilizers, so his demand to hold their fire as he continued to shoot would surely not make sense.

His flurry of gunfire tranquilized the other sniper in the tree and pushed the other two back and out of sight. Brian reloaded his rifle, then knelt over the man who'd been shot by his companions.

"Don't move," he said, and set his rifle aside. "I have friends who know medicine. We can help you."

Brian took off his backpack, then his own coat, which he draped over the man's lower half, hoping to keep him warm to guard against shock. In pain, the thirty-year-old with a sparse reddish beard squirmed under Brian's attention. He looked down at two bubbling wounds, one in the man's chest and the other in his abdomen.

"Someone help me!" Brian called. "Hold your fire! We've got a wounded man here!"

Desperate to stop the bleeding, Brian pressed his hands over the two wounds. The bleeding was bad, and Brian saw no way the man could live, but he had to try.

"Hold on, pal. Stay with me. Try to relax."

The irony wasn't lost on Brian. He was trying to save a man who was his enemy, just like others had saved him when he was their enemy. But the wounded man wasn't having it, and Brian's calls for help only drew other shooters. Two bullets smacked branches near his head, and as Brian ducked low and used his body to protect the wounded man, he noticed the hands of his patient.

Plink. The man tugged the pin from a grenade and stared wildly at Brian.

Whether the dying man was intent on ending his own suffering or trying to take Brian with him, Brian wasn't waiting to find out. He dove to the right, abandoning his coat, pack, and rifle. The force of the explosion lifted him off the ground and hurled him into a stand of saplings. Fire burned in his ribs as he settled onto the ground. He couldn't breathe. The ringing in his ears finally gave way to the automatic gunfire all around him. They were still trying to kill him!

He lifted his head high enough to check his surroundings. Five paces away, his pack and coat were shredded to pieces, and the wounded man was gone since he'd held the grenade over his own body. The battle rifle was nowhere in sight.

Brian held his ribs on his right side where blood was soaking through his ammo vest.

"He's over here!" a stranger voiced, followed by more gunfire.

Then a second and third rifle joined the attack, and the brush all around Brian seemed to dance from the assault of bullets.

Crawling forward, he forced his brow through the scratchy thicket, then he scrambled to his feet. A fallen log blocked his path, but he dove over it as moss and bark spit in his face from bullets slapping the wood. Brian rolled over, lunged upright, and ran.

Weaving past trees and hurdling over rocks, he gasped for air, trying to think past the pain in his side. He'd been wounded, but how badly?

Water gleamed ahead. It was a large pond with a wall of broken sticks and chiseled logs on one side. He waded into the cold water, then dove hastily into the depths of the pond. As if to send him on his way, a bullet clipped his shoulder, spinning him sideways as he submerged himself.

But he kept his wits enough to hold his breath as he sank below the surface. Opening his eyes, he saw blood from his wounds and scratches cloud the water, drifting around him like fog.

He swam deeper and toward the logjam he'd seen on one side of the pond. His lungs burned, but he still didn't surface. From six or seven feet under, he noticed a channel through the logs that arced up to the surface. It might just offer some cover behind or within the logjam. All he knew for certain was that he needed another breath of air.

The channel rose sharply, and Brian exploded upward for a breath. His head broke the surface inside a dimly-lit enclosure where he could see only a few slivers of sky through the sticks and logs.

Flopping onto a bed of twigs and weeds, he touched his side. When he held up his palm to the light coming through the jam, he saw dark blood, and he was scared.

Drawing his feet from out of the water, he listened for his enemies. While holding his side and panting, he peered through a small opening about head level. Two men with rifles moved into his field of vision, then they were gone, somewhere along the bank of the pond and the edge of the forest.

Under his palm, he could feel something sharp and foreign sticking out of his ribs. His fingers trembled over the ugly protrusion, afraid to find that it might be his bone. But it wasn't. It was metal shrapnel from the grenade that had lodged in one of his ribs. Snarling over the heightened pain he knew would come, he took hold of the shard of metal and tugged it straight out. It seemed to tear even more out of his side, and fresh blood flowed, but the thing was out of him.

He lay back on the bed of twigs and weeds, holding his side to keep pressure on the wound. For the moment, he was safe. There didn't seem to be any way out of the space he'd found except the way he'd come in, which would mean another dip in the icy water, but that didn't seem too necessary right then.

Weariness plagued him, and he knew it was a combination of the cold, the blood loss, and his adrenalin wearing off. He was with the Casperteins now, so they would take care of him. God had given him the Casperteins and all that COIL represented, so that was of some comfort.

And if he wasn't mistaken, this wasn't a logjam at all. It was a beaver dam. God was full of surprises! Now, whether or not he was the only occupant of the den . . . He decided with a smile that was something he could wait to discover after he rested a little more.

Rex Caspertein used an entrenching shovel to dig Brian Steelman's grave at the edge of the woods. The man's body had been so dismembered by a grenade that he and Sean Harris had to identify the ex-Enforcer by his gun, backpack, and coat on the scene.

"Did you know him well?" Rex asked Sean as they used their hands to pat the dirt.

"Not really," Sean said. His voice was gravelly, and his gray eyebrows stood at strange angles. "We'd talked a few times. He was someone I think Corban and Jenna Dowler brought in, along with Luigi and Scooter. I'm still learning names myself, of course."

Staring at the mound of dirt, Rex was saddened that he hadn't gotten to know better the newcomer to their group. In fact, he was so new that none of the refugees had even asked to attend his burial, once word reached them all. Of course, Brian had been an Enforcer for many years, and that grim truth didn't make him too popular.

"At least he was a believer," Rex said, surveying the forest nearby. He, Sean, and Scooter had rooted out the last of the ambushers, tranquilizing them back by a quiet pond. "That's all that matters in this kind of moment. I don't care if you're old enough to be my dad, Sean, I'll tell you to your face that if you die without a heart for your Creator and Savior, you'll perish forever in misery."

"You convinced Steelman of that stuff." Sean frowned. "Maybe there's some truth to it all."

"Rex?" Alice called from the middle of the meadow where she stood tall with her long staff in hand. "Chloe wants to get moving. We're exposed here, and the enemy will be waking up soon. You guys finished?'

Patting Sean on the shoulder, Rex walked down to Alice. When they reached her, Rex allowed Sean to go before them, down to the refugees who were still hunkered low in the ditch. Four adults had been wounded in the shootout, and one had been killed—shot in the back while running for cover.

"How are you doing?" Rex asked. "And don't tell me you're on top. Over the last few months, I thought I'd be getting to know Levi better, but he and Lyla were always batting their eyes at one another. Instead, you're the one I've gotten to know, Alice, and I know something's bugging you. Normally, you wouldn't have been misled by an ambush like that."

"Are you blaming me?" Her voice was cold, her dark eyes avoiding him as she gazed across the meadow.

"No, I'm just pointing out the truth to my closest friend, and wondering how we're going to get back to Colorado with all these people if we can't identify threats along the way."

"Fine. I'll tell you. We're supposed to be helping these people, but there's too many of them. They're loud, slow, and inept at caring for their most basic needs. We can't care for them and watch for ambushes at the same time."

"Okay, well . . ." Rex scratched his head. "Levi was the mouth and marbles of our little group. I don't know what to do about any of this."

"Well, I talked to Nathan Isaacson before he pulled out with Levi. He suggested we have two divisions, a fighting group, and an escort group. But no one's getting us organized."

"I think we've all just been focused on running for our lives, trying to get out of Federation territory." He noticed Chloe leading out with the refugees. The dead man had been buried above the ditch, and the wounded were being helped along by loved ones. "I'll talk to Scooter. He seems to know about military stuff. He was with COIL."

"You shouldn't do anything without Chloe. Levi said she's the best there is, remember? It was Chloe and Corban Dowler at the beginning of COIL."

"If she's the best there is, why are you telling me this and not her?"

"All mouth and no marbles." Alice scowled at him and walked away.

"Hey!" he called after her. "You can't use my own saying against me and just take off!"

He chuckled and sighed loudly as he moved in another direction, toward the rear of the refugee line, which trailed two hundred yards from where Alice took point again. Rex reached Chloe where she slowed to load gel-tranqs into a spare rifle magazine. Refugees filed past them.

"Sad about Steelman," Chloe said, "but not too sad since he was a believer, I heard Scooter say."

"That's what I told Sean, but that old coot is being stubborn. You'd think with all of us praying at breakfast and talking about God all the time, he'd be influenced."

"You never know." Chloe paused to use her binoculars to look far ahead, then continued walking. "He hasn't run off to be on his own, so maybe he's figuring it out. Sometimes the truth needs time to work through some barriers."

They walked in silence for a while, and Rex was painfully aware of how slowly they were moving. The refugees were well-equipped with gear, so their slow pace couldn't be blamed on lacking boots or other supplies. Rather, they were unhealthy and unaccustomed to marching. They were from the city, ignorant of the ways of disciplined travel.

"There'll be other Philistine attacks," Rex suddenly blurted.

"Philistine?"

"Bandits, raiders, whatever. I think we could prevent more deaths if we got organized."

"There's no organizing a hundred men, women, and children who've never been outside the city before."

"I'm talking about organizing us—you, me, Scooter, Lyla, and the others who're armed. Nathan had a plan. Maybe we should try it."

"Nathan's plan was to be with us by now, and he will be, as soon as he and Levi find Jenna and Chen Li."

Rex watched her out of the corner of his eye. She was somewhere in her sixties, but the way she carried herself, even wearily, she knew something about being stealthy. The refugees clomped along in their boots, trudging with light packs, their arms and shoulders hanging heavily. But

Chloe planted each foot with purpose, her boots laced tightly, and her heaping pack between her shoulders was centered but not jostling. And he vaguely remembered her firing her rifle at the ambushers much like Lyla had—no panic. Nothing like Obrador and Owen.

"I have some ideas that might be important for us," he pressed, "and we should all meet to discuss them."

"Ideas, huh?"

She frowned at him, making him feel younger than his thirty-two years. Since he was usually the largest person around, he'd gotten through his adult years without asking for much, using his size to push his points home. But that wouldn't work this time. Chloe and the COIL people wouldn't be won over by anything but sound reasoning. Or Caspertein wit, if he could muster it.

"I'm calling a halt before more of us get killed," Rex stated and double-timed his pace ahead of Chloe.

"Wait, Rex," she called. "We need to keep moving!"

Rex felt a surge of confidence as his determination to act rapidly evolved around his ideas. By the time he'd worked his way to the middle of the refugee column, his heart was set on facing down any opposition to his ideas. This was about saving lives. He knew Alice at least would have his back. Getting organized had been her suggestion!

In the middle of the column, he came upon Lyla Caspertein, her mane of black hair tied back, and her gray eyes full of humor as she walked between two shy teenage girls. They immediately hushed themselves when they noticed him, which made Rex wonder if they'd been talking about boys.

"The radio, Lyla?" he requested. "I need to holler at Alice."

Lyla didn't question him, but he was ready to stand his ground even with his cousin's wife if he had to. But Levi's wife had been across half the country with him, and even if Rex felt these COIL newcomers didn't take him seriously, he knew Lyla would.

He peeled off from the column to study the countryside as he fit the headset over his ear and clipped the box to his shoulder strap. They were between towns somewhere in western New Jersey since they hadn't yet crossed the Delaware River into Pennsylvania. Patches of thick forest stood between broad stretches of uncultivated farm fields and the occasional swamp.

"Alice, can you hear me?"

"I'm here," she responded from far ahead.

He noticed that she didn't stop walking. Tall and slender, the woman planted her steel staff, took three and a half steps, then planted it again.

"We're camping early today."

"It's not even noon."

"Lead us over to that stand of trees ahead to your left. We'll camp on the north side, in the shadows."

"You got it."

She changed direction, and like a snake's body following the head, the caravan traversed a small rise, then dipped toward the trees ahead. Rex walked far off to the side, parallel to the main group, and studied their whole procession from a distance, seeing his people as an enemy might see them. Their vulnerabilities were many, stretched out over two hundred yards, with only ten rifles, two of which weren't in the hands of dependable shooters.

"What's going on?" Bruno walked up to meet him as Rex rejoined the refugees. The large black man was six-six, the only one who came close to Rex's size and height. "Alice said you called an audible and we're stopping early."

"We're in danger," Rex said, pointing ahead. "Let's space out seven small campfires in a line along this tree line. No more large group bonfires like last night. We're letting the whole countryside know where we are. After everyone's settled into their tents and bedded down to rest, we'll gather so I can explain everything."

"Roger that." Bruno waved two fingers in a type of salute, and Rex was pleased there wasn't more asked of him right then. Levi had always made leadership seem so natural, but Rex had never had that privilege.

The refugees seemed exhausted already, so there were no complaints by any of them to stop early. Bruno and Scooter started two fires, then carried flaming sticks to start the other five. Several young men were dispatched by Sean to fetch more firewood. Meanwhile, Chloe gave Rex puzzled glances from where she was helping erect the tents.

"Alice?" Rex waved her over to him. "Once it's dark, we're going to set out again, traveling only at night from now on. Can you scout out a trail for us down to the interstate? And keep an eye out for Federation patrols. They know we came this way."

She jogged away, and Rex thanked the good Lord that he really did have dependable people with them. They only needed to adjust and find their strengths.

"Lord, help us," Rex mumbled, "but I need one of my strengths to be marbles for a change."

Ration packs and water bottles were shared around the fires, and sleeping bags were unrolled inside tents or under the blue sky. Rex walked among them, hearing their conversations about blisters and weary muscles, but he believed the Lord was with them. The ration packs on which they'd stocked up at Bruno's warehouse would soon be depleted, but he had no doubt that God would provide something else along the way.

Off to the side of the fourth fire where he could see everyone under his charge, Rex sat on the grassy ground and sipped from his canteen. He didn't have to wait long for the others to come. One at a time, all the right people came to him and sat down, gradually making a tight circle. First Lyla, then Sean, Scooter, Bruno, and Chloe. Even Nick Zoft, the chubby mayor from Hackensack grunted as he joined them. Rex had overheard the story of the man revealing that he was a Christian when it was dangerous to be one, so his faith was genuine even if he wasn't in prime physical condition. Sean was the only one of their number right then that Rex gauged wasn't a believer, but he was happy to see the man join their humble meeting. Of all those armed in the company, only Obrador and Owen were absent.

"Thanks for humoring me, everyone," Rex said softly to the six gathered around. "Bruno, you prayed for us yesterday morning when we left your warehouse. Would you do that again for us now?"

Bruno prayed a prayer with simple words that showed his gentle heart inside his bear-sized frame.

"I'm no Levi Caspertein," Rex began. "I've heard how some of you talk about my older cousin, and it swells me with pride to think that I've been at the side of the man you guys think is such a hero."

He elbowed Scooter and drew a few chuckles.

"But seriously, Alice made a suggestion I think is important, and I respect her as much as I would my own sister. We're running the risk of another attack if we keep traveling the way we're traveling—exposed, spread out, and not paying attention."

"Now that you mention her," Lyla said, "where is Alice?"

"She's scouting a trail to the interstate, which is how we'll be traveling from now on."

Chloe and Scooter both started to object at the same time, but Rex held up his hand until they were quiet again.

"I know we all agreed just yesterday not to travel by the interstate, because the Federation might use vehicles on the interstate to come after us. We'd be seen from far away, and it wouldn't take much for them to run us down and kill us."

"So, why use the interstate, Rex?" Lyla asked. "What's the trick?"

Rex smiled, appreciating the trust of his cousin's wife.

“The trick is, we begin to travel at night. No one will see us and we’ll see everyone.”

“Not necessarily, Rex,” Chloe voiced. “Not all the dangers ahead will be announcing themselves with lights.”

“The interstate is the route ahead,” Rex said. “We have a couple maps, so there’s no mystery of where our trail is if we stay on the interstate. Alice can continue to scout ahead if she knows we’re back here doing our job. And our job will be patrolling.”

“Patrolling?” Bruno leaned closer. “You think we have the manpower to put out our own patrols?”

“We’ve already lost two people in a day and a half of traveling. There should be two-person patrols on the left and right flanks, and a two-person rear guard to cover the refugees. We’ll have a warning in advance if we’re walking into an ambush. Before dawn every morning, we’ll move off the interstate and find cover to rest for the day.”

“I’m not sure I’ll be good at patrolling,” Nick Zoft said. He reached down and massaged one of his swollen calves. “I’m having a hard enough time keeping up with the pace we’re going.”

“It’s okay, Nick. We need a minimum of a couple armed people with the main body, and you would be a good candidate for a rear guard, too.”

“What about those two?” Sean thrust a thumb over his shoulder. “Why do they have rifles if they won’t use them? Seems a waste.”

Rex didn’t need Sean to say any names to know what two men he was talking about. Kendrick Obrador had a battle rifle only because he’d been given one back in Manhattan, and that was the case for Owen Travers as well. The ex-chancellor and his Enforcer had been traveling together the previous day and a half, talking in low tones between themselves.

“There are a couple dependable men who were with us at the warehouse,” Bruno offered. “They’re Christians, family men. We could see if they'll stand for the people if we give them those two rifles."

"Good." Rex nodded at the black man. "Can you reassign those rifles, Bruno? Does everyone agree? How does all this sound? I'm not trying to replace Levi or your Nathan Isaacson. I don't even know Nathan, though I shook his hand the night before he left. Otherwise, I'm relying on what I know about him. Can we operate like this? Is it a good plan?"

He remembered what Alice had said about needing Chloe's say-so, so he looked to her for approval. When he met her eyes, she lifted her head, as if she understood he needed her support specifically.

"I can't think of any downsides," she said, "as long as we all do our parts. We'll need to keep rotating our shifts, or we'll get too exhausted to be worthwhile. Otherwise, it sounds well-thought-out to me, Rex. Night travel on the interstate. It'll sure be easier than this terrain. Scooter?"

"Why do we need Nathan and Levi if Rex is going to do the job of two men like this?" Scooter joked, which drew a playful shove from Bruno. "I like it. I nominate my oversized friend here for the first patrol."

"And I second that nomination to my undersized friend," Bruno said just as quickly.

"Good." Rex gestured to two others. "Sean, Lyla—can you two spell them? You four work out some rotation that seems good to you."

"That leaves me and Nick for the rear guard?" Chloe asked. "Seems like a lot for two people every day."

"Bruno's going to find two more to rotate with you," Rex reminded. "After sundown every night, when we start walking, the rear guard will stay back, covering our trail. We don't have enough radios for everyone, so we'll need to rely on warning shots if anyone sees danger. Otherwise, we try to make as little noise as possible as we glide through this country."

"You haven't told us what you'll be doing," Lyla said.

"I'll be a rover, spelling Alice when she needs a break on point. She and I will use the radios for now, since one of us will remain with the main body as a rule."

After the meeting, they dispersed, but Rex remained cross-legged on the ground, quietly thanking the Lord for helping him speak.

"That went smooth," Lyla said as she offered her hand to help him up.

"I'm not sure how I would've reacted if someone wanted to argue." He accepted her hand and stood upright, towering over her. "You don't mind being on patrol? You'll get your share of walking in the dark."

"I don't mind. Just keep me at the top of the list for a new pair of boots if you find a stash."

"You got it." He gave her a half-hug. "The wounded are doing okay?"

"Their bandages are holding. I'm more concerned about their other conditions. I have enough spatterdock weed to use as an antiseptic on their surface wounds. The other issue is more sensitive, you know?"

Rex touched his beard in thought.

"Sensitive?" He lowered his head toward her. "Is that a female code word for something I need to know about—or not know about?"

"I thought you knew. All the people who were held in cages in New York have worms. Annette said a lot of people in the cities got them after Pan-Day, since there wasn't clean water to drink. All the Christians from New York have worms. They're dehydrated, malnourished, and they're not getting better without treatment."

"Is there treatment?" Rex cringed. "Worms? They can feel them inside?"

"No, they can't feel them, Rex!" She slapped his arm. "It's a parasite. You've heard of wormwood? That's what the Israelites drank after they came out of Egypt. Some historians understand that the Israelites had parasites from drinking the Nile's water, but God led them to drink wormwood to purge their systems."

"So, we find some wormwood?" Rex clutched his belly just thinking of their discomfort. "Is it around here?"

"We call it tansy in America. We'd be better off looking for another remedy—like wild carrot leaves. They're more abundant in this area."

"This is urgent. You need to find these carrots right away. No wonder these people are walking so slowly."

"Not the carrots, Rex. The leaves of the carrots. You make it into tea." She raised her eyebrows. "This is why it's sensitive. Get it? They all need to be purged. I thought you knew."

"You should know me better than that. I need things spelled out for me, or I'll just keep driving forward. Alice had to point out the flaw in our traveling, but once she did, I got it."

"So, you're saying you need a good woman at your side to keep you informed." She reached up and pinched his bearded cheek. "I knew there was a romantic under all that hair. There are a couple single ladies in the group who just might be a fit for you. Challenge accepted!"

Rex raised his hand and opened his mouth as she danced away. Finally, he found his tongue.

"Lyla, that is *not* what I was saying!"

But he didn't get to appreciate his Christian sister's teasing for long since Obrador and Owen approached him an instant later.

"That big oaf took our rifles!" Obrador shouted, drawing the attention of the resting refugees.

"Keep your voices down." Rex took Obrador by the shoulder. As a big man himself, Rex figured Obrador was used to throwing his physical weight around, intimidating people to get his way. But both Bruno and Rex were taller, wider, and more muscled than the ex-chancellor. And Owen was short and wiry, though with a hawk's eyes that made Rex wonder who had invited the vulture to the party. "You're both guests here. You shouldn't have to carry weapons when we're here to protect you. That's why we agreed to reassign your rifles to someone else."

"Who agreed?" Obrador snapped. "Who's the *we?* You're talking about you and that big oaf?"

"Bruno's not an oaf. You watch your mouth, Obrador. I'm talking about the leaders of this group, those with experience at hunting and fighting."

"Give us back our rifles!" Owen hissed. "We need to protect ourselves. We can't count on you guys. You already got some of us shot! We're not like the rest of these pathetic—"

"Now, you watch your mouth as well, pal!" Rex let go of Obrador to take hold of the smaller man's whole jaw, muffling his voice and cutting him off before he upset anyone. "You all ran into our protection on that bridge. I won't have you talking down about these people. Besides, the way I hear it, they wouldn't be as sick as they are if it weren't for you two. A little humility is in order when you compare yourselves to them. You're this big in my eyes, understand?"

Rex released Owen's face.

"We need our weapons!" Obrador pressed. "You can't leave us unarmed out here."

"This morning, you were both armed," Rex reminded. "I heard that neither of you fired a shot. You were too busy running and hiding. That's why we took the rifles back. If you want a weapon, you earn it. If you show yourselves approved, I'll give you back a rifle myself, but not before."

"You'll regret this!" Owen snarled, shaking his finger at Rex, then he turned away to walk into the woods.

Obrador was starting to move away as well, but he wasn't fast enough. Rex grabbed the older man's arm and held him fast.

"Why are you acting like this? I heard that Corban Dowler died for you."

The man raised his head, and Rex could see everything but brokenness in the man's face.

"I'm not saying I'm not grateful for that man's sacrifice for me. I just know better than other people what I need. Lena Travers is hunting for both Owen and me. You hear me? She's hunting *us*, not you. *Me and him!*"

"She's hunting all of us," Rex said. "I saw the blond woman you're talking about on the bridge. She was there to kill everyone in this group. We're all in the same boat."

"Don't you understand? She can get by without ever finding you idiots, but she won't be able to move on with the government unless I'm dead. You hear me? *Dead*. She has to kill me, or her government isn't legitimate."

"When was the last time you fired a rifle?"

"Just a few mornings ago, when we ran from Manhattan. And I fought in the Unification War after Pan-Day. I held the line with a rifle when you were in diapers, Rex Caspertein! Don't tell me I need to earn a weapon. I ruled this whole country with a weapon in one hand and a flag in the other!"

"And his sister pushed you out in one night." Rex narrowed his eyes at the man. "Whoever you were, I don't care. Right now, you're a pasty white guy wearing boots and a coat that Bruno gave you from his warehouse. You're welcome to those, but you have no right to a firearm. If you don't like that decision, you can push off across the countryside there. Just walk away. No one's keeping you here."

Obrador glared back at him.

"Maybe I will! You just wait and see."

Rex watched the brute stomp away, shove a refugee out of his path, then enter the trees where Owen had gone.

"That went bad fast," Bruno said as he approached. "I didn't hear it all, but I heard enough. You're not in the wrong, Rex."

"Thanks, but they both threatened me. Chloe knew them in New York, right? Are they a real risk?"

"We'll all keep an eye on them. Hopefully, they're all mouth and no marbles, like I've heard you say." Bruno waved two men closer. "I want to introduce you to Taylor Tharp and Hank Lowery. The rifles went to them."

"I see that." Rex shook both their hands, then tugged on Taylor Tharp's rifle sling, which was hanging over his shoulder. He was a short, stocky black man with a ready grin on his face. "Your families are okay with this? You're able to do this work?"

"I talked to Shailene," Taylor said. "She agrees that it's only right that I take a regular shift to pull my family's weight. Besides, my boy Trenton needs a good example from his pops. Like God's Word says, if you don't work, you don't eat."

"Well, I won't mistake you for being lazy," Rex said. "And Hank, is it?"

"Yes, sir." Hank was a balding white man in his forties. Rex remembered seeing him care for a wife and two children, one of them a teenage girl. "It's a blessing to be doing something. My family was in those cages for nine months, and since we weren't denying Christ to pass the Citizen's Entrance Exam, we were only headed to the gallows. Carrying a non-lethal weapon is the least I can do beside you heroes."

"Taylor was part of the Citizen Army before he was found out as a Christian," Bruno explained. "He was a worker under Sergeant Harris, both him and his wife. Hank, what did you do for a living?"

"I was a nutritionist in Midtown." The man glanced down at his rifle. "I hunted a little after Pan-Day. I'll do my best."

"I have no doubt." Rex shook their hands again. "Glad to have both of you."

Bruno dismissed the men, then stood next to Rex, a content smile on his face as they both admired the seven fires with people bedded down inside and outside the tents.

"Things are shaping up, wouldn't you say?" Bruno asked.

"I'm hopeful, but I'd rather be taking orders from my cousin."

"You're a Caspertein, son." Bruno nodded. "Leading is in your blood."

Nathan Isaacson walked slowly through a deserted town in north-central New Jersey. Sundown was approaching, but he'd already spoken with Levi about continuing through the night, as long as they could see well enough by the moon. They had to make up for lost time. Not only did Jenna and his wife Chen Li have a two-day head start, but caring for Lena Travers had slowed them down.

"I hear You, Lord," Nathan whispered to the wind, and clutched his battle rifle tighter. "Patience."

He stopped next to a fast-food restaurant and surveyed the town. They'd traveled through a dozen towns just like this one, tracking Jenna and Chen Li. Already, Nathan was learning that appearances could be deceiving. Some towns were truly abandoned, due to the Meridia Virus, food shortages, or forced relocation by the Federation.

Since Nathan had lived more than a decade inside Manhattan's strictly-controlled environment, he was still experiencing the culture shock of America's losses. Following Pan-Day, he and other COIL operatives had gotten busy on Operation Esther, infiltrating Obrador's administration. Nathan, like the others, hadn't witnessed the death and destruction outside the city. Sure, Obrador had facilitated his own chaos inside New York, but now Nathan was seeing how little the Federation had actually cared for its citizens on a broader scale. Socialism had failed, like it had everywhere else in man's history.

The skeleton of a horse blocked the sidewalk ahead, and Nathan stepped around it. Two cars that had crashed into one another years earlier had been left in the street, their bumpers still interlocked, as if in an eternal tug-of-war. The glass from most windows of the shops on the main street was missing, and leaves from trees were scattered everywhere. In one window, a dead body swung stiffly out over the sidewalk. As Nathan drew closer with his rifle poised in case it was a trap, he found the body to be only a mannequin.

A shrill whistle from far behind echoed up the street. It was Levi, but Nathan didn't turn back. Instead, he held up his fist—the signal to hold fast while he scouted around a little more. Their packs were light, but filled with valuables, not to mention their rifles and ammunition. A small band of thieves could attack them and walk away with their food, clothing, and weapons.

Then Nathan heard it—the cry of a baby! Before anyone could silence the baby, Nathan identified the location of the sound and ran straight toward it. He leaped over a tipped-over motorcycle and climbed through a bridal shop display window. His boots crunched across broken glass. Stepping over a dark computer screen as he reached the back room of the shop, he threw open the door.

A young man with a scraggly beard stood close to the door. He raised one hand while his other arm protectively covered his young family behind him. His wife, a Hispanic woman, was holding the baby in her arms, and a boy of about three knelt partially behind his mother.

Nathan immediately directed his rifle muzzle elsewhere, and offered his open left hand.

"It's okay, it's okay. You're not in danger from me. Is anyone else here? Come on, talk to me. I just don't want to be shot in the back as I walk through your town."

"Guns are illegal." The young father swallowed, his wide eyes falling on Nathan's weapon. "For most of us, anyway."

"The town's empty?"

"There's another family who lives across the street. They're unarmed, too. Sometimes, we trade with them. Are you . . . an Enforcer?"

"No, I'm just a . . . Christian soldier." Nathan shook his head at himself, realizing he needed to figure out how to interact with people on the fringes of survival so he would exhibit benevolence rather than prompt fear. "Did you see two women walk through your town in the last day or two? They're friends of mine."

"Two women?" He shook his head, and finally lowered his head. "No. We've seen no one since . . . maybe three weeks ago. A Federation truck turned around at the edge of town. We've left the street cluttered on purpose."

"I saw that. Smart." Nathan heard footsteps behind him and saw Levi prowling up to join him. "It's okay. Just an unarmed family hiding out."

Levi lowered his rifle.

"It ain't easy seeing you tear across the street like that. I thought we were being bushwhacked." Levi stuck his head through the doorway. "This is my kind of town—nice and quiet. I'll wait for you on the street."

Drawing an energy bar from his ammo vest, Levi tossed it to the startled father, then he left the way he'd come.

"Just curious," Nathan said to the father. "How do you guys survive out here? You don't get Federation rations, do you?"

"Chickens, goats, and a garden. We have our own. My wife does the gardening. We make do. I'm sorry, but we don't have anything to share right now."

"That's okay." Nathan smiled. "God provides, until we go to eternity, right?"

"Uh-huh."

"Goats and chickens?"

"Uh-huh."

"Okay. You take care now. You can let the baby cry, ma'am. We're gonna move on now. Stay safe."

Nathan walked out the way he'd come and emerged from the bridal shop onto the sidewalk. He found Levi there with Lena. She was squeezed into a baby stroller that had three large wheels. It was the kind that Nathan remembered jogging mothers once used in the suburbs. He drank from his own canteen as he watched Levi unwrap Lena's face then help her drink water from a straw from Levi's canteen. It was a messy affair—the missing lower half of Lena's face as well as her attempt to drink water.

"It's okay," Levi said as he held the canteen and she held the straw. "Take your time. We're not in a hurry."

Lena suddenly gagged and coughed, and Levi held her as she leaned over the side of the stroller to drool water and blood. Though Nathan wanted to help, he just stood there instead. Levi had taken the wounded woman as his own responsibility. Nathan was still shaken about Levi's news that Lena had opposed the vote in the Bowery, and then Colonel Rotham had shot her!

Recovering her breath, Lena cried in an open-throated way, since she couldn't close her mouth. Nathan looked away as Levi held the broken woman. She sounded like a crying kitten, and it was enough to bring tears to Nathan's own eyes. Levi's compassion had shut Nathan's mouth the last two days—every time he opened it to argue that they could move twice as fast without her. Eager to catch up to his wife, Nathan had even considered going ahead, leaving Levi to trail along with Lena. But that would be too dangerous for them all. Finding the stroller had taken them hours the day before, but it had been necessary since Lena couldn't yet walk. The pain from her missing lower jaw was simply too much to endure every jarring step.

"Let me see." Levi coaxed her. "Let me see. Lower your hands. It's okay."

Nathan leaned closer, seeing Lena's naked wound without the bandage on it. Lena's glare, as if Nathan's gaze was a violation of her privacy, made him straighten up and divert his eyes. He'd seen enough, anyway. Levi had had to cut away flesh and cauterize blood vessels that first night. Both men had remarked that they couldn't believe she had survived that long.

"There's no infection," Levi said. "It looks healthy. Just tissue that looks like your gums. The clean air is probably the best thing for you so I'm not going to bandage you up too much. Just a covering to keep the dust off. The bleeding is minimal. You got enough water for now? Okay. In a couple hours, we'll stop and fix something to eat. Nathan, can you grab some of that lace there? That'll make a good bandage after we boil it."

Nathan looked through some of the tattered wedding garments still in the window of the bridal shop and found a veil on the floor he thought would work. He tore off some of the length. Though it had yellowed over time, it was soft material. He handed the upper portion to Levi, who tucked it into Lena's coat. The irony of what the bridal lace meant for Lena wasn't lost on Nathan. Her hands were anything but clean, but it was hard to think badly of her past when she was like a crippled animal in the present. Lena was approaching fifty, but she was a child in Levi's hands.

"I'm pretty sure we're catching them slowly," Nathan said, hoping he could get a little of Levi's attention. "They must be zigzagging west and north, trying to throw off anyone following them."

"I've been thinking about that." Levi removed Lena's straw from his canteen and slid it into a pocket. "I think they're looking for something."

"I don't get it." Nathan gazed to the northwest, past the end of the town. "Chen Li has no clue of what it's like out here. She can't be looking for anything."

"That's why I think it's Jenna who's leading them. Someone with eyes doesn't zigzag like this. And north? It's dangerous, putting us back in the path of the Federation. They can't hope to catch up to Rex and the refugees, even though that would be best. Jenna probably knows the map of this area."

"I wouldn't doubt it." Nathan tightened his pack straps. "So she's looking for a highway west, the first one possible? Boy, I'm glad Chen Li has Jenna!"

"And I'm glad Jenna has Chen Li!"

They laughed, and Levi pushed the stroller into the street.

"Did your dad ever tell you how he and I first met?" Nathan asked.

"Gaza. Same place you met my mom the first time."

"You sure remind me of him, especially without that crazy beard you had."

"It ain't easy trying to grow a bird's nest on this chin. Just call me Patches."

Levi laughed, but Nathan wondered if mentioning the word chin at all would make Lena uncomfortable. Since she didn't have a chin, and she couldn't chew without a mandible, Levi had boiled a thick broth for her the night before. He'd encouraged her to eat, even when she choked and spilled. Nathan wondered if his own time undercover had hardened his heart. He envied Levi, his care for Lena, even his care for the family in the back of the bridal shop. Levi hadn't hesitated to share his own short supplies with the frightened father.

They hiked until dark, then lit a fire to fix Lena hot food and to boil the bridal veil to use it as a facial covering. During this meal break, Nathan stood away from the light of the fire, gazing westward. His wife was out there, definitely anxious, but he sensed now that God was teaching them both through their separation. Nathan was learning from Levi, and Chen Li was surely humbled while she relied on Jenna's sightless sense to guide them.

Behind Nathan, Levi stomped out the fire and came to him in the dark.

"She's good for now," Levi said quietly. "I filled up an empty bottle with broth for her next meal, so we don't need to stop and cook in the morning."

"Smart." Nathan motioned at the distance. "I think that's an overpass up there. Maybe an interstate. It's got to be what Jenna was looking for."

"I hope they didn't get on it. That's Interstate 78." Levi sounded like he growled. "That's going to take them southwest. We won't be following Rex and the others if she went that way."

"Maybe Chen Li will notice in time and break north."

"Yeah, right into the path of a Federation armored truck—which I'm sure is heading this way."

"You did sort of antagonize them." Nathan chuckled. "The bridge incident might've gotten under their skin."

"That might explain why we're being followed from behind as well."

"What? Us?" Nathan was tempted to turn around and level his rifle at whoever was out there. "How many? I can circle around and catch them by surprise. Or maybe it's just Luigi watching over us."

"Slow down, Nate." Levi touched his arm in the dark. "I don't think we need to do anything. Whoever it is came up on us in the dark a few minutes ago. They had a chance to attack us when I was busy feeding Lena. But they just stayed out there, watching us around the fire. There's only one or two, I think."

"Maybe they didn't attack since I was away from the fire, because they couldn't see where I was."

"Maybe. We'll set up a trap for them tomorrow night and find out their intentions. If they're still following us. Let's go."

Nathan wanted to talk about it some more, but Levi left him and returned to Lena. It was hard to rely on a man who'd been just a teen last time Nathan had seen him. But this was Titus' son. For twenty years, Titus had kept his son at his side, sharing his knowledge, raising him in the things of God, training him to use the skills that had made Titus a world-renowned operative. And now, Nathan was seeing the outcome of Titus' hard work—a man who was sensing predators in the dark better than even Nathan knew how!

Chapter Three

Colonel Milo Rotham stood on the roof of his armored command vehicle and gazed to the west. The sun was setting, and he cursed the wasted day on the open road. He heard movement behind him and turned to see Sergeant Ibojka climbing onto the roof to join him.

"The men are repairing the last couple of tires," Ibojka reported. "We should be able to pull out in twenty minutes."

"If I didn't know any better, Ibojka, I'd think the gods were conspiring against us. We're not fifty miles from New York City, and we've already come to a screeching halt."

"It was unavoidable." The big man held out his arms for balance as the bus rocked, the powerful jack underneath elevating the vehicle. "We couldn't have known some Federation resistance groups had put caltrops all over the road. It could've happened to anyone."

"Yes, but these things can't happen to me or you. We can't tolerate such inadequacy from our men, not this early in the mission. It's humiliating, like Caspertein tranquilizing you in our own radio room. We need to make an example of someone, like we did years ago in Philly. It could lift morale."

"Or destroy morale."

"It's too early in this operation to think weakly, Sergeant. That's what I liked about Lena Travers. She was decisive. Too bad I had to kill her, but I need that from you right now. We've wasted a day out here. The caltrops are to blame, but who's at fault? *Nine blown tires!*"

"Any of the drivers should've seen them. I can execute the driver of the scout Jeep."

"No, both men in the Jeep are too valuable. How about the second or third vehicle? Any drivers we don't care for?"

"You chose them all." Ibojka shrugged. "They're all good men. Shooters, all of them with kills over the years."

"Good men, but not good enough, or we wouldn't be stranded out here on the interstate!" Rotham closed his eyes to the sun's last rays. "Pick one of the drivers. Disarm him and hold him for me. I'll be down in a minute to remove him in front of everyone."

"Let me do it." Ibojka's voice lowered. "Let me make the example. Some of the men from other divisions don't know who I am yet."

Rotham opened his eyes and smiled at Ibojka.

"I like this side of you. It's the old Ibojka I once knew. Fine. You'll execute someone. Pick someone out, but none of our women. They're few enough as they are. I'll be down in a minute. I have something to say first, then you can finish it."

Ibojka left the roof of the bus, and Rotham watched the growing shadows across the landscape. They were still in Federation territory, but he hated to admit to himself that this was yet untamed land. He wouldn't want to wander alone over the hills or through the forests and ghost towns. Cities like Philadelphia and Manhattan were functioning civilly, but out here? They may as well have been in the Plains Zone already, fighting for their lives against rogue armies and feral dogs.

Levi Caspertein had haunted his dreams the previous night. Ibojka had reported that the mouthy traveler had cut off his beard but Rotham knew him only with hair on his face, so the tall blond noncompliant had been bearded in his nightmare. The dream had left him feeling helpless. In the haze of night, he'd been wounded and left by the roadside, and his soldiers had walked past without giving him aid. The line of troops had smirked with disdain as he'd bled to death, but they didn't stoop to help him and he couldn't do anything to stop them. Right before Rotham woke, Levi Caspertein had stood over his wounded body, shaking his head at Rotham.

Helpless? Rotham cursed the thought. He would show everyone he was far from helpless! He was the mighty Colonel Rotham. He would show Levi Caspertein!

As he climbed off the command vehicle, he remembered the bounty hunter he'd brought in from the Plains Zone. The man known as the Runner might have caught up to Levi already, or have executed Jenna Dowler. Rotham didn't care how it was done, as long as both went away so he could focus on catching up to Obrador and Chloe Azmaveth. Then he could give his attention to mapping the Plains Zone for the Federation.

Two mechanics on the ground were tightening lug nuts on the last tire while Ibojka had gathered the rest of the fifty men and women against the guard rail. A man in his thirties was on his knees, his hands bound behind his back. Ibojka already held a gun to the man's head after someone had stripped the condemned soldier of all valuables, including his knife and boots.

"We're a fighting unit!" Rotham shouted over the gathering, glaring at their hard faces one at a time. Both men and women scowled back at him, calloused, unforgiving, vicious, just as he'd trained them to be. "You are killers. We destroy what stands against the Federation, because nothing—*nothing!*—will be permitted to humble our proud nation. If it falls, we fall. And *we will not fall!*"

He licked his lips, finding his own words ridiculous. A couple years had passed since he'd moved from the loyalty he'd once felt for the socialist state. But the words gave them a purpose for which to strive together, and the Federation gave him his authority.

"If you're negligent in your duties, you will be disciplined. If you make this operation and this company seem the fool, you will be terminated. You stay alert! One mistake can quickly become a dozen errors. That's why we haven't moved an inch today, not since dawn. I won't tolerate negligence and laziness. We must all remain alert, each one of us, or we're all at risk. You are a reflection of this whole company. We will not fail. Sergeant?"

Rotham watched the faces in the crowd, looking for weakness as Ibojka pulled the trigger. The faces before him had the appearance of stone monuments, chiseled from Rotham's own thrusting words. It brought a smile to his face. They were ready to continue.

"Now, let's load up and finish this!"

No one whined or objected. They rushed to climb into their assigned vehicles.

Rotham finally looked down at the deceased soldier whose eyes stared blankly up at him. They were the eyes from his dream. They were his own eyes. Helpless eyes.

"You okay, Colonel?" Ibojka asked quietly. "You said to pick anyone. Did you know him?"

"It's nothing." Rotham shook off the haunting feeling. "Let's find those Casperteins!"

In the dark, Andy Radner used a leather harness to tie his dog Runner to a tree. He hadn't used a leash or collar on his hunting partner when they'd been in the city, but this was different. Not even Runner, as stealthy as she was, had the instincts necessary to sneak up on Levi Caspertein.

He'd been following the party of three since he'd crossed the Hudson and Runner had picked up their trail. He'd first thought he was tracking only Levi and his larger older friend with the slanted eyebrows. But now, he knew they still traveled with the woman in a stroller. If it was Jenna, then Andy could end his hunt here and now.

It made sense that Levi had put Jenna in a baby stroller. Since she was blind, Levi could travel faster with her in the wheeled cart. But the bloody bandages Andy had found at several sites made little sense, unless Jenna had been wounded.

"I'll be right back, girl." Andy held Runner against his cheek. "Shhh, now. You just rest. It'll be a long walk back to New York tomorrow."

He was a half-mile from where he'd seen Levi and his party stop at the edge of a small town and enter a house to sleep for the night. Andy preferred the open air, but some people liked the familiarity of a house, even if there was no electricity or running water.

Andy crossed a set of railroad tracks and paused to listen to the breeze. This was nothing like the Wyoming wilderness. The smells were all wrong. There were so many artificial odors on the wind—asphalt, oil, and the unnatural decay of the remnants of a spoiled civilization.

Reaching the neighborhood, Andy recognized the blue residence with the empty carport where Levi had inspected and entered. Even Andy, a product of the mountains, knew only to enter a house where there were no vehicles out front. If there were vehicles, it probably meant that whoever owned those vehicles were still inside, rotting, their bodies possibly still transmitters of the virus even years later. Residences without vehicles were often the empty ones and safer to enter. Andy had used several himself during occasional thunderstorms.

Finally, he stood in the driveway of the house and sniffed the air again. *Wood smoke*. Whatever this Levi's history, he was no fool. He'd picked a house with a chimney and fireplace, where the light of their flames would be hidden within. But Andy's nose was keen; he could still smell the fire.

This house had windows still intact, the shades drawn, so Andy circled the first floor twice before he found an oak tree with a stout limb that stretched close to an upper story balcony. The doors on the first floor were no doubt barricaded from inside. He'd left his pack and crossbow with Runner, so with only his skinning knife and tomahawk on his belt, he climbed the oak and leaped silently onto the balcony. Again, he paused to listen and to wait. He and Runner had approached Levi too closely the previous evening, and Andy had wondered if Levi knew he was being followed—and by whom. But there was nowhere to escape, no authorities to whom they could run. Levi was a fugitive, and Andy wanted only to kill him and the blind woman. His contract required no less. The sooner he fulfilled this contract, the sooner he could return to the Federation capital and write his own ticket to continue doing what he did best: hunting and killing.

The balcony door was unlocked. One window pane had been broken by wind or hail, so Andy stepped over the broken glass as he crept into what seemed to be the master bedroom. It was empty, as Andy had presumed, but he'd nevertheless drawn his tomahawk. It was a Kangee t-hawk, with a sharpened top edge for an extra cutting option. He could throw it or use it like a knife blade by gripping the handle around the neck. By its edge, he'd killed before, and if the situation was right that night, he'd use it to kill again.

The stairs leading down to the living room from the bedroom were a risk for noise, but Andy saw no other route by which to reach the area below and to the left, just out of sight. He could hear the dying fire crackle occasionally from an unseen area. As he descended the stairs, he placed his feet closest to the wall, avoiding squeaky boards, and skipped every other step to reach the bottom. *Perfect silence.* He was born for this kind of stealth! If the people back in River Camp, his childhood community, could see him now, they would faint in dread at the deadly predator he'd become! What a thrill. What expertise and dominion he'd achieved over a civilization that had forgotten the art of hunting in the wild!

Andy barely breathed. He planted his soft-soled boots, sewn by his own hand, before the open doorway to the living room, and stared inside. The fire was dwindling from an open hearth. Before it on the floor lay three bundled masses. The closest to the fire was the smallest of the three—Jenna, Andy guessed. If she was smaller and wounded, it made sense that she would be closest to the heat. Then, Levi and his dark-haired friend were spaced under sleeping bags beyond Jenna.

His feet barely whispered as he approached the woman closest to the fire. There, he crouched. His left hand reached out while his right hand held his tomahawk, cocked for a death strike, silent and decisive. The two men might rise up, but they would be groggy from their slumber, so he'd have the advantage. He hadn't gazed directly at the fire coals, therefore his eyes remained adjusted to the dimness of the room.

Gently, he drew back the edge of the woman's sleeping bag. Already, he could see by the low fire that her loose hair was brown. It was Jenna. He pulled back the covering more to expose her neck, and gazed down at her two open eyes, staring up at him. What was worse is what he found below her alert and daring eyes. Where her mouth should've been, it had been replaced by a void where crimson-stained white lace was loosely draped.

She lifted her head and raised up on one elbow to cringe away from him. It wasn't Jenna Dowler! In moving, the lace dropped from her face, and Andy looked upon a deformed creature from his nightmares. A light cry came from her throat, the back of which he could look into since she had no mouth.

The nearest sleeping bulk threw off his sleeping bag, and Andy wildly swung his blade at the brown-haired man's neck. Andy hadn't been prepared to fight like this, but now he was facing the man with angled eyebrows. Levi hadn't even joined the conflict yet!

The man raised his rifle at the last instant and blocked the tomahawk blade from decapitating him. Andy jerked his weapon free and lurched to the left toward the door. Having lost the sense of surprise, he needed to escape before Levi got the upper hand! As an assassin, Andy preferred secrecy and mystery. Now discovered, he didn't like the odds. If he survived the night, he could kill another day.

As suspected, the front door was blocked by furniture. He returned to the stairs and bounded up them three at a time, not caring about the noise he made. Though he expected to be shot in the back by the rumored tranquilizer ammunition, he arrived unscathed in the master bedroom. Running with full momentum, he leaped off the balcony and misjudged the distance to the oak branch. It was closer than expected.

Grunting as he plowed into the branch against his belly, Andy let go of his tomahawk and clawed for a hold of the tree, any hold, even a finger-hold! Instead, he clawed and kicked through the air as he dropped. He landed on his shoulders on the uncut grass. His breath didn't come right away, but he rolled over anyway and felt in the darkness for his tomahawk. When he found it, he lunged upright and ran down the driveway. It wasn't the most covert path, so again, he expected to be shot from behind, but he didn't know where else to go!

Yet, no one shot him. There was no barking of guns in the night. Crossing the railroad tracks minutes later, he stopped, panting and trying to calm his heart so he could hear the night sounds. He slid his tomahawk into his belt and leaned on his knees to gather his senses.

Levi's friend hadn't been as unprepared for an attack as Andy had hoped. Who slept with their rifle like that? And what kind of woman were they caring for? Now that he thought about it, the woman's hair hadn't been brown like he'd been told Jenna's was. Once he had seen more of it, it had been blond, just unwashed.

But that wasn't what chilled Andy's blood that very minute. He'd been warned that Levi was some sort of untamable force. He'd burned half of Philadelphia, single-handedly torn down the GW Bridge, and sabotaged the long-range radio in the Bowery—during the crowded election event. Why hadn't he moved against him in the living room?

Andy knew the answer before he arrived back to where he'd tied Runner, and his suspicions were confirmed when he did reach his whining canine. The contents of Andy's own pack were laid out on the open ground under the glow of the moon. He'd left his pack outside Runner's reach so she wouldn't mischievously tear it open. Actually, his pack wasn't even torn. It was emptied and folded nicely on the ground next to his meager supplies. Even the short-range, handheld radio that Colonel Rotham had given him was lying in plain sight.

Kneeling on the ground, Andy counted what he saw. Nothing was missing. Wait. He picked up his crossbow. The six short arrows he kept braced in the carbon fiber supports were gone. His crossbow was useless without the arrows. Since Andy relied on the crossbow for the silent hunting of critters for food, the theft of the arrows was a true blow to his ability to provide for himself. It meant he'd need to catch his food, or steal it. Or find birds' eggs, which he despised. Runner caught and ate her own kills, rarely sharing with him unless she had an abundance. The loss of an effective crossbow changed the way he would be able to track anyone.

He felt his cheeks grow hot from humiliation. Who was the real predator and tracker? Now he understood why Levi's form in front of the fire never moved. He hadn't even been there. While Andy had thought he'd silently snuff the lives of his prey, the real predator had prowled back and sorted through his pack. Runner hadn't barked or made a sound that Andy had heard, so the renowned

Levi Caspertein must've offered the mutt something to eat. While Runner had eaten, the invader had rifled through his belongings.

"Traitor," Andy accused, and she whined as if she understood the charge.

But Andy's anger reached much deeper than his irritation over a foiled attack. His enemy hadn't fought back, not really. Levi's friend had deflected the tomahawk, but hadn't shot him. Levi had taken the arrows, when he could've easily killed Runner. Even at that very minute, Levi could've been watching him as he violently shoved his few belongings back into his pack.

It was unnerving, Andy thought, to be treated like he wasn't worthy of a fight. He'd been disarmed without a conflict, as if he wasn't a threat at all. As if he were a child!

"I'm going to kill Jenna," he said aloud, not guarding the volume of his voice. "Taking my arrows won't stop that. I know now you've been trying to catch up to her. I'll show you who I really am!"

Andy waited for a response, but all he heard was more whining from Runner. But the dog did glance toward the woods and perk her ears. Levi was out there, Andy felt, but there was nothing he could do about it. Yes, it was time to move on to more innocent prey. Blind prey.

Chen Li was walking faster on the interstate, but she couldn't stop looking behind them. Although Jenna had encouraged her to walk beside her without touching an arm or hand to guide her along, Chen Li was now tugging on the blind woman's coat sleeve, trying to draw her ahead at a quicker pace.

"They're gaining on us!" Chen Li tried to guard her voice from sounding frantic, but this was the first time she'd ever crossed anyone outside the city. "One thing for sure—I'm not thinking about my sore feet right now!

"We have to figure out where we are," Jenna urged.

"I don't know. All I'm thinking about is those people behind us!"

"Describe the highway or freeway we're on."

"Um, there are four lanes. It has to be Interstate 80, right? Do you think we should get off and let these people pass us? What should we do? I have the tranq-pen. Should I use it?"

"How many are there?" Jenna asked much more calmly than Chen Li thought she should sound. "Describe them to me. Think clearly. Nothing's actually gone wrong, has it?"

"You're right." Chen Li took a deep breath and turned, studying the approaching party for several seconds. "There's a man leading a horse. It looks like a pack animal. He's in front, and there are several others behind him. They have lots of stuff with them, like they're traveling with baggage."

"So, they're going our way. Let's stop and wait for them."

"Are you serious?"

"You have a tranq-pen." Jenna stopped and cautiously moved to the right-most lane of the highway. Abandoned cars sprinkled the interstate, but Chen Li saw none nearby. "It'll be safer to travel in a group than alone. Our enemies aren't travelers with horses, Chen Li. Hopefully, these people will let us join them."

"Right." Chen Li waited next to Jenna and watched the travelers draw nearer. Finally, she raised her hand and waved. "Can you manage a couple more to keep you company?"

"That's good," Jenna encouraged her. "Let them know we're friendly."

Chen Li forced herself to smile, but she held the tranq-pen in her left hand while her right hand gripped her pack strap.

The man in front stopped nearly even with them, and his tired horse on a lead rope halted as well. The others in the group—three older men and one woman in her fifties—appeared exhausted, as if they'd been walking for hours, even though it was only ten in the morning.

"There's always room for more." The lead man spoke softly, but he wasn't looking at Chen Li when he spoke. He was looking at Jenna, sizing her up. He was balding and clean-shaven, which she thought was rare for people outside the cities where razors were probably harder to come by. "It's just the two of you? Well, join us, by all means. Trust me. You'll be better off with us. I'll keep you safe."

He opened his coat to show he was armed with a long-barreled revolver.

"I'm Chen Li and this is Jenna." Chen Li noticed how awkwardly Jenna tilted her head, not even pretending to look in the direction of the travelers as she angled her ears to hear everything. When she noticed Jenna was drawing quizzical looks, she cleared her throat. "Um, she's been having trouble with her eyes. She'll be okay."

"Do you want some glasses, miss?" The man moved back to his sorrel mare, which was burdened high with three packs. He opened one flap and produced a case with glasses. "Sunglasses. They might help your eyes. No charge. I trade in all kinds of things. Go ahead. Keep them."

Chen Li accepted the glasses for Jenna, and passed them to her. But in the back of Chen Li's mind, she thought nothing was free in America anymore. Jenna pushed the glasses onto her face.

"Thank you," Jenna said. "You're very kind. What's your name?"

"They call me Shaker. You see?" He drew a breath mint container from one of his breast pockets and rattled it. "Hear that? It's the best way to test the quality of things these days. You shake them."

"He's a trader," Chen Li informed Jenna. "It's nice to meet you, Mr. Shaker. We'll just tag along at the back, if that's okay."

Shaker started his horse forward, and the others in his company moved past the two women. Chen Li was nervous, but by the suspicious looks from the other four showed that she wasn't alone. Everyone was suspicious of everyone those days. Meanwhile, Jenna smiled politely and nodded as if she were a stewardess greeting new boarders.

The man at the rear of the band was towing a metal wheelbarrow. Chen Li pulled Jenna to step in line behind him. At the rear, she could guide Jenna with no one noticing, and they could still blend in with this rabble.

Chen Li was still adjusting to the idea of traveling with their new companions when she gazed ahead.

"There's a red and blue sign up there," she said quietly to Jenna. "This is the interstate!"

"We're a lot farther north than I thought," Jenna said.

"We're on Interstate 78," the man with the wheelbarrow said over his shoulder.

"Okay, then, we're farther south than I was hoping," Jenna corrected. "Interstate 78 angles south soon. Chen Li, we have to get off this freeway and go north. The others—"

"There's not an exit ramp for another mile." The wheelbarrow man towed his one-wheeled contraption with a harness over both shoulders, so his hand was free to point. "See?"

"It says one mile." Chen Li read the sign to Jenna, then muttered a prayer for the Lord's help. "Now we have to find another road? You're sure?"

"The 476 is at Allentown," Jenna recited. "We can go north when we reach Allentown."

"That's true," the wheelbarrow man said. "Gal knows her interstates. Looks like you'll be with us for a few days."

"How far away is Allentown?" Chen Li whispered to Jenna. "I'm not sure how long we want to be with these people. I don't trust—"

"I know." Jenna took her friend's arm as they walked. "But we can trust God. We have a long way to go. Let's be thankful for the people the Lord provides, whoever they are. It's not Lena Travers, right?"

"Yeah." Chen Li accepted Jenna's rebuke, but wondered if Jenna realized there were many other dangerous people in the world besides Lena. Jenna hadn't seen many of the evils before Pan-Day; she'd been merely a kid. But Chen Li had faced those evils, and she recognized wickedness in the face of Shaker. "I'll trust God, but I don't trust them."

"What's rolling?" Jenna asked. "I hear something rolling."

"It's a wheelbarrow. An older man is pulling it."

Before Chen Li could stop her, Jenna hurried ahead.

"Excuse me? Can I help you pull your wheelbarrow? It would help me walk."

"Really?" The man stopped, considering the offer, then took one harness strap off. "Put your pack on the back, and take this. I surely don't mind getting help, even if it is by a young gal."

Chen Li chuckled and shook her head. Just like that, Jenna was already making friends. She blindly stowed her backpack on the heap of bundled possessions already on the wheelbarrow, then took the strap offered.

"I don't believe in sharing the weight of a wheelbarrow with a man whose name I don't know." Jenna leaned into the harness. "That's your cue to tell me your name."

He said he went by the name of Lisbon, on account of his family being from Portugal, but he sounded to Chen Li like he was from America's Midwest. Nevertheless, his friendly way of talking with Jenna helped Chen Li to loosen up and walk beside him. That way, if anyone tried anything with Jenna, Chen Li could be the first to pounce with her tranq-pen, which she still held tightly.

After Lisbon shared how he'd been part of the iron workers union in St. Louis, he introduced the other two men and one woman who were following behind Shaker.

"His name is Dusty Thomas," Lisbon gestured to a man in his seventies. "He doesn't talk too much."

"I'm not a conversationalist," Dusty informed after turning to look at Jenna. He held up a large round wall clock which appeared to be stuck at noon, or midnight. "There isn't the time."

"There's no time to have a conversation?" Jenna asked, unable to see what the man carried. Chen Li hoped to describe him to Jenna as soon as she could. "How much time do you need to have a conversation, Dusty?"

"I don't know." The man scratched his head and hugged his clock closer. "I'm not a conversationalist."

"And this is Al Hayes and his daughter, Tyra," Lisbon continued. "He's good for conversation, if you like a lot of facts. His daughter's a good gal, just special."

Chen Li moved up next to the man's daughter to get a closer look at her. Although she was in her fifties, Tyra's hair was golden blond and wavy. She noticed Chen Li, then glanced down at a number of shoelace necklaces around her neck. A compass hung from one necklace, fingernail clippers hung from another, and a stainless steel cross hung from the last one.

"Do you want to use it?" Tyra asked Chen Li, holding out her compass. It wobbled inside its water bubble. "You can use it. It tells you where to go."

"No, that's okay." Chen Li smiled. "I like the cross you're wearing. Do you know what it means?"

"Do you want to use it?" The woman released the compass and fumbled for the cross, but she found the shoelaces tangled. "Oh, no. This is bad."

"It's okay," Chen Li assured, then noticed her father move closer. "I'm sorry. I didn't mean to upset her."

"She's not upset," Al Hayes said. He was heavy-set, and appeared to be wearing three layers of sweaters instead of a coat like most wore. "She just likes to share. Two-point-nine-four percent of sixty-year-olds have cognitive difficulty."

"Oh, I see." Chen Li nodded. "I think I understand."

"Like I said," Lisbon stated to Jenna, "she's special, but she's a good gal. She can cook and take care of herself."

Chen Li surveyed her travel companions differently than she had moments earlier. It was a band of misfits following Shaker—exactly where she and Jenna belonged.

"We're all special," Jenna said, "each in our own way. I believe that's just the way God made us. We're all unique. What do you think about that, Mr. Hayes?"

"Eighty percent of Americans claim to believe in one God."

"Interesting." Jenna was working hard on the harness next to Lisbon, evidenced by her breathing. "How about you, Dusty Thomas? The Good Lord made you. Do you ever talk to Him?"

"I'm not a conversationalist," the old man declared and sped up to walk beside the horse.

"Tyra here has a cross on her necklace," Chen Li said, intended for Jenna. "Maybe she'd like to share with us why she carries it?"

"I have fingernail clippers, too." Tyra pulled on the shoelace. "Do you want to use it, Jenna?"

"Not right now, Tyra. Maybe later. But it means a lot to me that you know my name already. A lot of people don't care to pay attention to names nowadays."

"I remember your name," Lisbon said. "A good gal who helps pull this stuff with me—I'll remember her. Shaker always says to make room for others."

"Thank you for that, Lisbon. Tell me about St. Louis. Why are you so far from home?"

Chen Li plodded beside her new travel companions, and indeed thanked the Lord for whom He had provided.

She didn't know how far away Nathan was, or if he had survived the battle over the Bowery, but God wasn't absent. How could He be when Jenna saw every opportunity to share Christ's compassion? He was in them and He was going before them, everywhere they went.

With a sigh of contentment, Chen Li slipped the tranq-pen into her pocket. She wouldn't be needing it after all.

Brian Steelman woke with a shiver and opened his eyes to a sliver of morning sunlight piercing the beaver dam. He stirred in the dimness, and several creatures of the forest and pond scampered away. A frog hopped into the water nearby and disappeared. Only a field mouse remained stubbornly braving Brian's wrath as it tugged at a thread on his pants where the knee was torn. When he swatted at it, the critter only backed away as far as the pair of beavers across the den.

The beavers seemed just as unalarmed at his presence as they had the day before when they'd risen together through the water channel and met him face to face. Since there were already these other creatures in the den, Brian guessed as long as he didn't fuss too much, they wouldn't bother him.

This wasn't the first time Brian had been wounded and left alone, he thought as he sat up straight and touched his two most serious wounds. The shrapnel wound on his ribs had sealed up, but moving his right arm at all caused fire to move up and down his whole right flank. To add to his movement troubles on that side, the bullet had grazed his right shoulder. Though it had scabbed over, he could feel an ugly groove in his flesh, and any movement caused the scab to crack and trickle blood inside his shirt.

"I can think of worse places," Brian said to the black-eyed beavers a few feet away. He'd never heard of beaver attacking people, but anything was possible after the Meridia Virus had seemed to infect everything. "I could still be in the sewers of New York City."

Although he would've liked to recuperate longer in the den, he had no supplies, and begging for soggy roots from a couple of beaver or eating insects wasn't going to fatten him up.

The day before, he'd done the math—he'd been left for dead. After he'd shed his coat, pack, and rifle next to the dying man, his friends would've thought he was the grenade victim.

It saddened him that he wasn't going to be with the refugees heading west. He'd seen it as an opportunity to lead the people after Levi had asked him to do so. There were good COIL agents among them, though not Corban, Luigi, Nathan, or Levi. The group had sort of drifted the first day and a half. He'd wanted to fill that leadership role, and learn to be guided by God to watch over His people. But it wasn't meant to be, and now he knew he'd lost too much time and distance to even catch up to them. Besides, he had no weapon, coat, sleeping bag, or food. All he had was a knife and a full vest of gel-tranq ammunition for a rifle probably lost in the explosion.

"Thanks for your hospitality," Brian said to the beavers, and tossed them a spent brass shell casing from his rifle. "If you're anything like otters, maybe you like shiny objects, too."

The beavers ignored the shell casing for a few seconds, then the darker male reached out one paw and clawed the casing up to his nose. After one sniff, he swept the brass under his furry body. Gift accepted.

Brian peeked through a number of openings in the woven stick and log dam, but he could see no humans moving around the pond. Nevertheless, they were probably still around. His COIL friends would've only tranquilized the enemy, not run them out of their woods. He'd need to be very careful leaving the forest.

He took a deep breath and pushed himself headfirst into the channel through the woodpile. The water was cold, but he knew his wounds and flesh needed a little washing. A moment later, he cautiously surfaced and looked around the pond. A doe lifted her dripping muzzle on the bank, and the alert startled a heron farther away. Smoothly, Brian stroked to the bank from where he'd splashed over a day earlier. As he climbed onto dry land, he held his shoulder wound where his thermal layer clung to the scab.

At the edge of the trees where the dawning sun could reach him, he stripped off his clothes and rung them out one by one. Thankfully, it was mid-spring and not winter, or he would've needed to start a fire. But he wasn't interested in sticking around to draw attention to a smoky fire, not with enemies certain to be nearby.

Finally ready for travel, he entered the trees where he'd exited them during the gun battle. It didn't take him long to find where he'd nearly died trying to save the ambusher's life. Instead of leaves and pine needles alone, he found a disturbed grave. He guessed Rex and the others had buried him, but the ambushers had later dug up the mound of earth to see who was there, since they'd come up missing one of their own.

Wary of gunmen who were lying in wait for travelers, Brian crouched and ran south. He found the creek that wound from the pond and used its bank as cover to reach the ditch where the refugees had sheltered. Briefly, he searched for anything they'd left behind, but found only another gravesite. Since there was no marker, he wondered who'd passed on. In the week since he'd begun to lead the refugees—first in the tunnel in Manhattan—he'd learned to care for people like he'd cared only for himself. Again, he was troubled that he couldn't continue that experience. All he could hope for now was that God would raise up a leader among the COIL personnel who would try harder to avoid such ambushes in the future.

While he'd been in the beaver dam, Brian had decided what direction he would take. He wanted to arrive in Meeker, Colorado, where the refugees were going—and he couldn't wait to see their faces when they learned he was still alive! But Interstate 80 wouldn't be his route. When he'd first run away from the Federation two years earlier, he'd taken Highway 78, then the 81 West through the South. It was a route he'd left on and returned on, so he knew most of its haunts and dangers already. But Interstate 80 was full of unknowns, and as an unarmed man alone now, he needed to travel a road that was familiar.

He headed off cross-country, still southward, and crossed Interstate 80 a mile later. After only a glance left and right at the empty lanes, he pushed on, knowing Interstate 78 was a day's hike farther.

As the sun rose higher, his clothes dried, though they smelled a little mildewed. He realized this was the first time as a Christ-follower he'd ever been alone with God. The thought exhilarated him, and he found himself talking, even shouting to God about everything on his mind. The more he shared his thoughts and concerns with God, the more he found peace in all that had happened thus far. It was just like he'd read in the Bible—*God was with him!* And it was just like Jenna Dowler had told him that first day in the print shop. She'd touched his face and told him of peace and love. Oh, to see her again and tell her he'd found what she'd told him about!

Halfway across a farm field near evening, he heard the crack of splintering wood, and he stopped to find its source. Beyond an irrigation canal, he spotted a humble homestead, far away from any highway or town. He walked up on an elderly man splitting firewood. A lever-action carbine was leaning against the outside of the house where a year's worth of wood was already stacked. The rifle was older than even the aged man. Brian picked it up and checked its load. The action was well-oiled and the weapon was loaded with snub-nosed lead shells—reloads.

When he looked up, he met the eyes of the old woodsman ten feet away, his axe in both hands. He had dark, curly hair, though graying, and a crooked nose along with crooked teeth.

"I'd be happy to split some of that wood for you," Brian said, "if I could trade you for a little food and a dry rug to sleep on. I haven't eaten for a few days."

Brian flipped the rifle around and offered it by the barrel to the owner. The man hesitantly chewed on his lip. It was likely that very few people had found this homestead, Brian figured, since it was so far from civilization, though still in the middle of northern New Jersey.

"Yeah, you look it." With one hand, the homeowner sunk his axe into a chunk of firewood. "By the look of that shoulder, you shouldn't be trading any chopping for food. My wife would make me sleep out here on the woodpile if she found out I made that kind of trade."

His tone was firm but his words were friendly, so Brian didn't feel concern when he took the rifle and cradled it loosely in one arm.

"We don't mingle much." He pointed at Brian's ammo vest. "Is that some kind of uniform? You belong to a military or something?"

"Not anymore. I'm just a traveler, heading west. This is my ammunition vest. See? I have a bunch of .308 cartridges, but my rifle was lost."

"A .308 shooter? Huh." The man studied him for a moment. "I guess you look too worn out to be ornery. I'm Wyman, and that'll be Mrs. Wyman inside. You got a name?"

The man held the door open for Brian as he answered, and they entered the two-room cabin together. Brian's knees nearly buckled as he smelled food.

"This is Brian, Mrs. Wyman." The man set his rifle on a rack above the stove. "He needs food and a rug, then he'll be moving on tomorrow morning."

"Yes, sir." Brian understood the hint. He offered his hand to a pointy-nosed woman with light gray hair. Her eyes were squinty, but kind. "It's a pleasure, Mrs. Wyman. I'm sorry. Do you shake hands?"

Brian withdrew his hand, remembering that rural places were still haunted by the Meridia Virus and recurring outbreaks.

"We're not superstitious!" The woman dismissed his concern by waving the air and firmly shook his hand. She smelled like fresh bread and garlic. "This is a surprise. No one's been here since . . ."

"It's been about nine months." Wyman sat at the table, which was half-cluttered with canned vegetables. "The Springfield's cow wandered up and I caught her. Then they came knocking, glad to see we hadn't killed and eaten her. We got a gallon of milk from them for free for that. Have a seat, Brian. You're going west, you say?"

Though Brian was famished, even to the point of being lightheaded, the promise of food helped him focus enough to visit with the couple. He summarized the power struggle of the Federation, and the flight west with persecuted Christians.

"We don't mingle much," Wyman said, "but we never criticized anyone for their own religion. You've got your own religion, and I've got mine."

"With respect, Mr. Wyman, wasn't that the error that Cain made? Cain—the son of Adam and Eve—thought that he could decide what kind of religion he would have. When God wasn't pleased with Cain, Cain became jealous of his brother, and later killed him in the field. I only know that myself since I've read that part of the Bible. I don't think God is pleased when we make up our own religion."

"What're you saying?" Wyman leaned across the table. "My religion don't count with God?"

"Mind your manners!" Mrs. Wyman said from the stove, her back to them.

"I'm saying from God's own Scriptures," Brian said, "we don't decide what pleases our Creator. He decides that. We should be pleasing to Him. I've learned that I go to His Scriptures to find out how to live for Him. That keeps Him in the driver's seat, not me."

"I think you've got more learning to do." Wyman sat back in his chair and thought a moment. "Or maybe you're right. I haven't read that part of the Bible since I was a kid."

"What's stopping you?" Mrs. Wyman started filling three plates at the stove. "If you read more and belly-ached less, we'd both be happier. Heaven knows we could both use a little more peace and happiness around here."

"We don't mingle much," the man repeated. "I weary her."

"Do you two have a Bible?" Brian overlooked the promise of food for a moment. "They were banned years ago in the cities on the coast."

"Nobody's banned anything in this house!" Wyman went into the bedroom and returned a moment later, wiping cobwebs off two books, one small and one large. "Lookit here. Two Bibles! Hah! Who's got religion now?"

"Look at these!" Brian's hand trembled over the leather covers as if they were made of gold. "A full Bible, and then a New Testament?"

"They're rare?" Wyman asked. "Worth something?"

"Only for your soul." Brian sniffed the binding, still not opening the cover. "Thousands have died along the coast for having one of these—or even just talking about what's inside these pages."

Mrs. Wyman set the three plates on the table with steamed vegetables and small chunks of meat.

"Hah! Ground squirrel!" Wyman laughed until he started coughing. "For fifty years, they ruined our fields. They breed faster than rabbits, I think. Now, they keep us fed. But you got to be sharp. Every new generation learns how not to be caught."

"Thank You, Lord," Brian said, with a Bible in one hand and a spoon in the other. "This is more than I expected when I only hoped to chop a little wood for you!"

"We don't need two Bibles, Rud," Mrs. Wyman said. "Give him the big one. You'll probably never read through it all, anyway."

"You don't know what I'll do!" Wyman grumbled as he stuffed his mouth.

"No, I couldn't." Brian blew on a steaming spoonful. "I've already read the Old Testament. You should keep the big one. That way, you'll have the whole thing. God's changed my life from these truths. I used to be a killer for the Federation. I hate to admit it, but I used to arrest people for having contraband like this."

"Take the smaller one, then." Wyman set the New Testament next to Brian's plate. "She's right. I don't need both."

"I'm sorry I don't have anything to trade. Wait." Brian drew out his knife. "How about a combat knife?"

Wyman's eyes widened at the double-edged blade.

"We don't need more knives, guns, or bullets around here!" Mrs. Wyman spat around a mouthful of food. "We should be passing stuff on, Rud, not collecting more. And none of our grandkids live anywhere near us."

Accepting his correction, Wyman shoveled more vegetables into his mouth. Brian reluctantly sheathed his knife, then slid the small Bible into a pocket of his ammo vest. He couldn't wait to get alone and explore its pages!

As exhausted as he was that night, he lay on a couple blankets on the floor in front of the stove for an hour. He stared at the ceiling, thinking about the Wymans and how providential that God had led him there. And though he had very little, he had what he needed most—a Bible. With the Lord showing Himself strongly at the beginning of his journey like this, Brian had little doubt about God's omnipresence as his travels unfolded in the days ahead.

In the morning, he woke rested at dawn, though aching from his wounds and travels. Outside by the woodpile, he read the Book of Philippians in his new Bible until Wyman found him there.

"I haven't had any .308 shells for this in a half-century." Wyman shifted another antique rifle in his hands, an older model than the one he'd had the day before. "My dad used it in the Korean War. Or maybe it was my uncle in Vietnam. Either way, it was passed down, and hasn't been fired since I've had it. You might want to give it a test-fire when you're down the road a ways, just to make sure it doesn't blow up on you."

"You're giving me this rifle?" Brian accepted the heavy bolt-action rifle with a wooden stock. "It's beautiful!"

"No, it's not, but you're not likely to find another long barrel for all those shells you've got, and you'll be needing a rifle where you're going."

Brian checked the chamber. The magazine held five shells, more than enough for what he needed. It was no COIL battle rifle, but it would have the same range and impact.

"I'm undeserving of this, Wyman," Brian said, his heart softened from time with God that morning, and from the kindness of strangers. "My thanks don't seem enough."

"Well, we don't mingle much, but you've been good company. You could've shot us when you first came here, and taken everything we own. But you didn't. If I woulda seen you first, I mighta put your skeleton where I throw those dead gopher bones."

"I'm glad you didn't." Brian shouldered the rifle on its sling, then rested his hand on the old man's shoulder. "I feel that God has done something between us in our meeting, Wyman."

"Yeah." Wyman cleared his throat, wiped at his crooked nose, and looked away. "Maybe you should say goodbye to Mrs. Wyman. She has a sack for you."

A few minutes later, Brian was on his way, a sack of food over one shoulder, and a loaded rifle over the other. From a distance across the field, he looked back, and both Wymans were outside. He waved and they waved back.

"Oh, Father," Brian prayed, "get Mr. Wyman into your Word."

Heading into some woods, he knew Interstate 78 was only a few miles away.

Rex Caspertein dove into a shallow ravine at the first sound of a vehicle on the interstate. A dead coyote he'd shot was over one shoulder, so it cushioned his head as he landed on stones at the bottom. Disoriented for a moment, he lifted his eyes to the rim of the ravine and listened to the sound of the engines growing louder.

It had to be the Federation coming to hunt down Obrador, Levi, Chloe, and Jenna. Since Rex was still adjusting to sleeping during daylight hours, he'd instead gone hunting. Now, he chastised himself for stepping into open ground within sight of the freeway.

Setting the coyote down, he climbed the ravine to the rim about ten feet high and peered in the direction of Interstate 80. He caught sight of ten vehicles, including a huge armored bus, as they cruised slowly away to the west. Their speed didn't slow and their course didn't change, so he sighed with relief. It seemed he hadn't been spotted, and thankfully, the refugees were bedded down in the shade of a line of spruce trees. After he'd warned everyone else to remain out of sight, he'd nearly been caught himself!

He allowed a few more seconds to pass, then he recovered his coyote at the bottom of the ravine. It was a dry creek bed, which he guessed ran into the trickling creek farther north. Following the ravine one hundred yards, he came to the creek, and only then did he climb onto the high ground to approach the seven low campfires the people had started that morning.

For two nights, they'd been using his new system for travel on the interstate, and for two days, they'd been hiding and sleeping a short distance from the freeway. Granted, they'd only covered about twelve miles each night, but they'd done so in the relative safety of darkness, with both flank and rear guards deployed.

Ever-vigilant Alice was awake, her staff in her hand, when Rex reached the slumbering camp.

"Did you see that?" Her eyes were wild with fright, but she kept her voice low so none of the people were disturbed. "This changes everything!"

Chloe lifted her head from where she lay in a blanket on the bare ground. Rex waved at her to join them. Sean sat against the largest spruce nearby on his watch shift. He started to rise, certain to be reading in their body language that something had happened, but Rex held up his hand, halting the man. Sean didn't protest, but tightened his grip on his rifle and peeked around the tree, more alert than before.

Rex led Alice and Chloe down to the trickling creek where they filled several containers.

"Ten vehicles just passed us," Rex told Chloe. "They had a tanker truck and two fuel trailers, plus a big ol' bus with plating on its sides. I've seen it before."

"Philadelphia," Alice stated gruffly. "It's got to be that Colonel Rotham again."

"I know about him," Chloe said, her face betraying her concern. "He's young and ambitious, and he was second only to New York when it came to the execution of Christians."

"So, now they're in front of us," Rex said. "We can keep moving with that information."

"I should scout farther ahead." Alice lowered her head. Rex had seen that look in her eyes before. She was a hunter, and she reveled in going out alone to spot the enemy before the enemy could spot her. "If we know where they camp every night, we won't accidentally run into them when we're traveling."

"But they'll double back," Chloe said. "I give them one or two days before they realize they've passed us, and then they'll scour this whole countryside."

"That's probably their plan," Rex agreed. "To get ahead of us, then set up a net."

"Ten vehicles." Alice gripped her staff tighter. "What do you think? Thirty soldiers?"

"Probably more," Chloe said. "When Tentmaker chased after the last exodus west, he took trucks packed full of personnel. You remember what you guys dealt with in Meeker last year? Rotham could have as many as sixty men. I'm actually surprised he's the one who Lena sent after us. I thought she was going to use him in her new administration. Something must have happened in New York after we left."

"Well, Rotham's searching for us," Rex said, "so he'll be moving around during the daytime. If we keep traveling at night and laying low during the days, we should be safe."

"Until we try to get through the net they're casting," Alice said. "They'll probably cover all the roads west within a hundred miles, since they know that'll be the easiest way for us to travel."

"We don't know that this is the only convoy Lena sent after us, either," Chloe said. "She could've sent this one on Interstate 80, and two or three others on parallel roads."

"I'll head out now."

"Keep your radio on," Rex said, but he knew Alice never turned it off, keeping the radio powered through a flexible solar panel fastened to her shoulder when marching. "I'll do the same."

"Are you going to carry that thing around all day?" Alice pointed at Rex. "Or is your neck cold?"

Rex suddenly realized that in the excitement, he hadn't left the coyote in camp. It was still draped over both shoulders.

"Maybe I've grown fond of the little fella." Rex chuckled.

Alice marched off, and Rex was left with Chloe, who he noticed was grinning at him.

"You miss Levi, don't you? I remember that's the way you and Levi joked with each other for two days straight at the warehouse."

"Hey, she started it," Rex said in defense. "She's already serious enough. If she didn't kid with me once in a while, I'd get worried. But yes, I'm worried about Levi. This far out, and he still hasn't caught up to us? He and Nathan could cover three times in a day what we're doing in one night."

"They're traveling with Jenna and Chen Li now. I hope so, anyway." Chloe winced. "Jenna's blind and Chen Li hasn't been physically active for twenty years."

"You're holding up fine, aren't you?"

"I climbed dozens of flights of stairs every day at the Bowery." Chloe slapped one of her thighs. "I'm approaching another decade in age, but the pace we're going—I can hold it together."

"Another decade? What, like thirty? Forty?"

"Exactly. Thirty or forty years older than you!" She chuckled. "But thanks for the compliment."

At the edge of camp, Rex butchered the coyote near the men's latrines, which had been designated to be dug at every campsite on the east end of camp. The women's latrines were always dug on the west side. The coyote wasn't large, but Rex cut small steaks and strips off the creature. They'd need to keep hunting every morning, he decided, to feed the one hundred mouths.

He disposed of the canine carcass, then leaned against one of the spruce trees as he spied Alice at a great distance hiking westward. She was walking about two hundred yards north of the interstate, which was wise in case more Federation vehicles drove up the lanes. With Alice so far ahead, someone else would need to take point during the night march, and that would spread them thin somewhere else. They had only so many rifles and able shooters.

Two figures walked into camp from the creek. Rex wouldn't have thought anything of it, except both people were in deep discussion, the tall one talking, and the other one nodding attentively. It was Obrador and Owen. While everyone else rested quietly, Rex guessed they were up to something suspicious.

"It's good you're keeping an eye on those two," said Nick Zoft as he hobbled up and sat down with a grunt at the base of Rex's tree. The chubby man set his rifle across his knees. "Taking their guns from them two days ago was a slap in their faces. To them, guns are power and control. I may be from Hackensack, but I've known those two for years. I went to Manhattan every couple months, accompanying shipments of vegetables to the capital. Obrador always hosted me at the Bowery during my visits."

"I noticed Chloe watching them, too." Rex focused on Nick. "How did you survive as a Christian all those years?"

"Honestly, I thought it was a miracle every time I took the Citizen's Entrance Exam and passed. I knew I'd failed each one. Now I know there were people like Radiant Shade and Chen Li in the Citizen Processing Department who were fixing my exam results, keeping me alive. The exam left no room for error. I was unmistakably a Christian according to my answers, but I just acted natural, and no one ever arrested me."

"Those COIL people saved a lot of lives."

"Yeah. I guess we're all COIL people now." Nick sighed contentedly. "It's a nice feeling, isn't it? To be part of something that belongs to the God of the Universe. I could die today, and my smile would be the same."

"You were still part of it," Rex said, "even when you were in hiding as a Christian."

"Yeah, but I never uh—what do you call it—fellowshipped. I just lived every day wondering if I'd die that day. I guess I got closer to the Lord, though. I fellowshipped with Him, so I didn't miss out on that. But I believe the Bible teaches us to be part of what other servants are doing. Now look at me. I feel like a bodyguard for these people. Our people."

"You're a shepherd," Rex agreed.

"No, you're the shepherd."

"I barely know what I'm doing, Nick. I wasn't blessed with the marbles in my skull to be a regular leader. Did you meet my cousin Levi at the warehouse before he left? I'm bigger than him, but he has the mouth and the marbles to go the distance."

"I think God has you exactly where you're supposed to be, shepherding these people. And part of that shepherding job is watching out for the wolves." Nick nodded at Obrador and Owen. "Those two."

Rex left Nick to speak to Sean, Scooter, and Bruno about the convoy situation. The threat had been elevated, so their caution needed to elevate as well. Meeker, Colorado, was a long way off. And there was still the worm situation . . .

Chapter Four

Levi used his hand to feel inside his pack, careful not to prick his hand on the six arrows he'd confiscated from the stalker behind them. The threats yelled in the night by the young man with the black Lab still rang in his ears. *Jenna was being hunted!*

"Nope, that's it." Levi withdrew his hand and zipped up his pack. "We're officially out of food."

"You don't sound too disappointed." Nathan shouldered his own pack. "In fact, you sound downright satisfied. We've only just crossed into Pennsylvania, and we're already out of food."

From the shoulder of Interstate 78, Levi gazed over the guardrail at the squatters' camp below.

"Look, I want to catch up to Jenna and Chen Li as much as you do, but we should stop here and see if they're feeling generous. It'll be faster than hunting. Besides, maybe they've seen our two ladies."

Nathan didn't say anything, but instead, peered up the freeway. Levi could see the worry on his face. Even though they'd found sign of Jenna and Chen Li now traveling in a small group, Nathan wanted to see his wife's condition for himself.

"That doesn't explain why you're not more worried than I am," Nathan said.

Levi leaned lightly on the handles of the baby stroller, making the front wheel pop up a couple inches. He didn't like discussing their plight in front of Lena, not when he wanted to set an example of unshakeable faith for the woman. She was already downcast as it was without witnessing their own worries. Although Levi would never say it, their slower pace was because of her, besides being a third, unplanned mouth to feed.

"Honestly, Nathan, we're not in any real trouble. Worst case scenario, we stop and forage or hunt for a day. Jenna and Chen Li seem fine, even if they are headed farther south than we'd like."

"If we catch them by Allentown, we can turn north together. I'm aware of that."

"Well, they're probably almost to Allentown already. And they have maps, too. I'm sure Jenna knows the route from New York to Colorado. She's the one who arranged the last exodus, remember? And there's another thing."

"What other thing?"

"Them." Levi smiled at the squatters. "All those months I spent heading east, I never came across people that God didn't design for us to meet. Aren't you curious?"

"Curious?" Nathan threw up his hands. "What are you talking about?"

"What might God have for us to do here?" Levi turned the stroller around to jog back to the off-ramp. "Come on, Eagle Eyes. It ain't easy going slow when you could be running ahead, but this is God's way."

When he reached the off-ramp, he looked back and saw Nathan dragging his feet. At the bottom of the ramp, on both sides of the access road, a collection of about thirty tents stood, half of them dome tents, and the other half wall tents. As Levi pushed the stroller up to the perimeter of the encampment, the residents glanced up at them, some even stepping away from smoky campfires for a better look at the newcomers.

"Phew!" Levi exclaimed to Lena. "They could do something about their sewage!"

"Aah," Lena responded, which Levi guessed was all she could ever say with the gaping throat and partial tongue, though she kept the lower part of her face covered with the bridal veil.

North of the access road and above the tents, Levi noticed there was only one shelter that could survive a strong wind. A leaning sign out front read, "Martin's Mufflers." Whatever car garage had once stood there had collapsed and been rebuilt with odds and ends of boards and sheets of metal wired together at the corners.

Levi slowed to a stop next to one tent in front of which a thirty-year-old woman held a wooden stick over a low fire. On the end of the stick was a gnarled piece of meat, blackened and smoking. Her other hand was wrapped in a heavy scarf.

"I hope you're not planning on eating that," Levi said, only half-joking. "I've heard eating charcoal makes you vomit, but it makes good soap."

"It's the healer's recipe." The woman's dome tent was unzipped, and Levi could see another person lying inside. One side of the tent material was also blackened from the smoke. "My hand will be healed soon."

"A healer told you he can heal your hand if you eat that thing?" Levi grimaced. "What is it? Burnt horse tongue?"

"No, it's a toad. He said I have to cook it until it falls off the stick, then it'll be ready. Eat half and use the other half to rub on my hand. No offense, but I'm supposed to be focusing my energies on this."

Levi knew more than a few natural remedies for ailments, but burnt toad was a new one. He pushed the stroller to the next tent where a man in jean cutoffs was repairing a pair of leggings.

"Is the healer healing you, too?" Levi asked.

"No, it's my son." The man pointed his threaded needle at a boy with crutches leaning against a mound of earth. "His foot got crushed."

"What's this healer told you to do to heal a crushed foot?"

"He hasn't told us yet. We're waiting for the stirring of the waters near the next new moon, then the first one into the water will get to see the healer. It's in the Bible."

"Let me guess," Levi said, "that woman who's eating charred frog over there was first in the stirred waters at the last new moon?"

"That's right. But it'll be my son's turn in a week. I'll get him there first. You'll see."

Shaking his head, Levi walked with the stroller to the end of the camp, then stopped at the road to wait for Nathan. His travel companion was walking through the row of tents above the road, occasionally speaking to the campers.

"Aah?" Lena shifted her head in the stroller.

Levi knelt next to her, surveying the camp from her angle.

"I know. It's ridiculous. I've seen this before. Someone is using a piece of something from the Bible to captivate others. It could be a hoax, or it could be real, but it's definitely not of God. The stirring of the waters in the Bible was about people in Jerusalem holding to a myth that an angel would heal the first person into the pool after it was stirred."

"Aah."

"Yeah, I know. It's silly. God is real, and His Son cares for the sick and injured, but this isn't how He works. When Jesus healed, He made sure people understood their freedom from sin, made possible by the only God who can make people right before Himself. But this? This is the opposite of liberty. Don't look at this, Lena, and think that the Bible is the problem."

"Aah."

"No, Bibles are a blessed responsibility. Shameful people misuse the Bible's truths, twisting them, and then you get a woman eating charred frog. Look at her vomiting over there. What'd I tell you? It ain't easy trying to keep your food down after you've eaten burned-up frog's legs."

"Aah!"

"Exactly my sentiments. I bet this healer guy is trading his treatments for all kinds of valuables from these people."

Nathan walked up, his face grim.

"Did you hear what's happening here?"

"Some healer misusing the Bible." Levi tapped a finger on his battle rifle. "Sort of makes you want to tranquilize someone, doesn't it?"

"He's living up there in that shack." Nathan pointed. "If that's what you call it. There's a pool of water right in the middle of those tents over there. It's mostly mud with some waste draining into it from the outhouse over there. If people are jumping into that to get healed, my guess is they're climbing out with more diseases than they started with."

"I want to meet this healer," Levi said.

"Aah!" Lena reached out of the stroller and roughly grasped his arm.

"What?" He didn't shake himself from her grasp since he'd been trying to involve her in all their conversations. "No, not for you! He'd have you rubbing dandelions on the inside of your eyelids or some such thing, telling you your jaw is going to grow back. No, I want to confront him. We need to set all these people free."

"This isn't just some scam, Levi," Nathan said. "This is spiritual. There's probably some demonic stuff going on here."

"Let's deal with it." Levi shrugged. "We know how to."

"What? Exorcism? *Seriously?*"

"Exorcism?" Levi chuckled. "No, I was thinking about praying, tranquilizing this healer, and then you can preach the gospel to these people."

"We don't have time for this, Levi." Nathan shook his head at the camp. "Remember the guy who threatened Jenna? We need to get going."

"Time. Good point." Levi waved his arm at the people standing around their tents. "These people are facing time eternal if we don't take the time. Lena? You want to wait down here or go up with us to the shack? I can't promise what'll happen."

"Gaah!"

"Okay, but you're gonna have to walk."

"This wasn't part of my COIL mission briefing," Nathan joked. "If these people knew what you're about to do to their healer, they'd riot. Lena and I would prefer not to be drowned in that pool of sewage water, Levi."

"Just back me up." Levi helped Lena stand upright, leaving the stroller on a patch of grass next to the road. "We have more than enough gel-tranqs to take care of this lot."

Lena held onto Levi's left arm as she delicately stepped up the grassy slope toward the shack. Levi didn't rush her. She'd been moving around only a little at their evening camps. Her wounds were no longer bleeding, but the nerves in her jaw, connected to her throat and neck, were extremely sensitive. Tripping and falling would be terribly painful.

Nathan walked ahead of them and arrived at the shack first. He spoke to two men outside the shack before Levi arrived with Lena.

"They say the healer doesn't like to be disturbed when he has company," Nathan said quietly to Levi. "When I asked what company, they said a woman from down there."

"Probably someone trying to gain the favor of the healer." Levi looked past Nathan at the two guards. "They're carrying sidearms, but they don't appear to be professionals, just poor men duped by a wicked clown. I don't intend to make this easy on them."

"You're a Caspertein." Nathan rolled his eyes. "When do you guys ever do things the easy way?"

"He's exaggerating," Levi said to Lena. "When I fell in love with my wife, it was easy."

"Why don't you hurry up," Nathan pressed, "so we can both catch up to our wives?"

"On the count of three, move to your right." Levi drew his silenced .22 pistol. With Nathan blocking, the two guards couldn't see the drawn weapon. ". . . One, two, three . . ."

As Nathan moved, Levi raised his sidearm. Two loud clicks later, both men clutched their legs where Levi had shot them, and they crumpled to the ground.

"I think this is the door." Nathan tipped his head at the plywood. "Ready?"

"Ready. Lena, stand on your own for a minute." Levi nodded.

Nathan threw open the door, and Levi barged through. The single-room shack was cluttered with a variety of camping gear—certainly spoils from his spiritual hustle—but Levi easily identified the elaborate bed with two figures in it. The woman was no older than twenty, and when she cried out in surprise at the strangers, Levi shot her in the side with a tranquilizer.

The man in the bed raised his hands and stood up on top of the wrinkled sheets, wearing only his shorts. Nathan bundled up the woman in a tattered quilt, and lay her on the floor, which appeared to be carpet rolled over the bare ground.

"Get your pants on," Levi ordered the dark-haired, olive-skinned forty-year-old. The man complied. "Now sit on the edge of the bed."

Moving to the shack's door, Nathan kept an eye on the squatters' camp below.

"What's your name?" Levi holstered his pistol inside his jacket.

"I am a healer."

Levi narrowed his eyes, recalling how his father years earlier had dealt with a fortune teller who'd extorted citizens of San Diego.

"Where are you from?"

"I am from nowhere and everywhere."

"You have enough property in here for a hundred people." Levi picked up a guitar with a white sticker on it that read "Sammie." He set the guitar down and lifted up a sheet to find a sewing machine, a cookware set, and boxes of canned food. "We'll be giving all of this property back to those people down the hill."

"No, it's mine!" The healer rose to his feet, but Levi easily shoved him back down on the bed.

"It may have been given to you, but it isn't yours. You misled these people. That's why you have all this stuff."

"I showed them the power of healing."

"No one's been healed. I just walked through camp."

"They all have the power within themselves. I've shown them how."

"You've misused the Bible to take advantage. That's why I'm giving you the opportunity to return their belongings voluntarily, or you can give it back by force."

"And you're a thief if you take what's mine."

"No, I'm a saint of the Most High God, saved by the blood of Jesus Christ, and indwelt by the Holy Spirit who gave me new life. I'm telling you that your scam is over."

"You can't suppress the true self within, Levi Caspertein!" The man flexed his muscles. "Yes, I know of you, and you know of me. You know this isn't a scam."

"What's he talking about?" Nathan shifted on his feet. "You know this guy?"

"No. He said he knows of me, and I know of him." Levi took a step back. "We've never met, at least not in the flesh. But I believe him. This is real, like you said. Satan and his demons are real. This isn't a scam. This is the actual thing. The earth is consumed by violence and selfishness. Why wouldn't we expect some heightened demonic activity?"

"You can't stop me," the healer said calmly. "Come to me, Lena Travers. It's you. I have what you've longed for. I can show you the way to true strength from your true self within. Come, child . . ."

Levi turned and noticed Lena was making no move toward the man. Instead, her eyes were full of shock, even fear, where she stood at the door.

"Don't be afraid," Levi said to her. "Jesus Christ of Nazareth disarmed the demons when He died and rose again, reconciling all things to Himself. God is love, and we don't need to fear the likes of this creature, even when they do impress us with little tidbits of information. Place your confidence in God Almighty, Lena, and your soul will be eternally secure."

"Tranquilize him already!" Nathan yelled. "And let's take care of the people!"

"Stupid Nathan Isaacson," the healer hissed, his face twisting into a snarl. "No toxin can shut my mouth. No chains can bind my power. You know that! You saw me in Germany, in the Pacific, and now I'm here for you. I am eternal!"

"You may have the advantage over the fallen realm," Levi said as he drew his pistol, "but we serve the King of kings, who is sovereign over the seen and the unseen. He'll bind you once and for all someday. Our job is just to stand for the truth of who Christ is in contrast to who you are."

"I am not bound to the rules you live by, Caspertein!" The healer scoffed. "I fill the void. I am the new age. I am the connection. I am the global unit of togetherness. I am within and without. I am—"

Levi shot him in the bare chest. The healer blinked once, then fell back onto the bed.

"It ain't easy being a demon inside a physical body." Levi sighed and glanced at Nathan. "There's no reasoning with that. Once they've subjected themselves to whatever spirit that was, only the gospel can deliver. When they reject that, the conversation's over."

"That went on longer than I was comfortable with." Nathan looked at Lena. "You okay? Levi's right. You don't have to be afraid of that spiritual stuff, not if your life is hidden with Christ in God. We can explain more to you later, but right now, this camp needs to be dissolved. Any ideas, Levi? This was your plan."

"Ideas and plans?" Levi chuckled. "Oh, my old friend—and I say that as my father would—you overestimate my abilities. The simplest seems best. Carry these two outside, give all this stuff back to the people, and burn the shack."

Picking up the healer, Levi carried him outside and laid him on the grass. Lena emerged, stepping carefully, with a tablet of paper from the healer's pilfered possessions. After Nathan laid the woman next to the healer, he returned to carry the possessions outside. Levi helped Lena sit on the grass beside the woman. He offered her a pencil from his own pocket.

"I use this to mark up my Bible when I study. Go ahead. You can use it to write. It's about time you communicated."

"Aah." She accepted it.

"You're welcome."

He set his pack beside Lena and helped Nathan empty the shack. It took only fifteen minutes to lay everything all over the upper part of the slope. With the shack empty, the walls and structure appeared much less sturdy. By lifting and pushing on various sections of the walls, the flimsy roof caved in, and the rest collapsed on itself.

"You want to speak to them?" Levi asked Nathan as they acknowledged the campers begin to gather below. "Set them free, brother."

"They might shoot the messenger." Nathan hooked his thumb over his rifle sling and smoothed down his mustache, which he was regrowing. "Protect Lena before me, if it gets sticky."

Levi stood closer to where Lena sat and where the healer lay.

"Come closer!" Nathan called to the people, waving his arms to welcome them. The sun was at their backs so they could look up at him without squinting. "I have an announcement to make. Everyone, come up here!"

Reading the defeat on the people's faces, Levi decided they wouldn't react violently. He cradled his rifle and sat down with Lena.

"This should be good," he said quietly to her. "I was just going to tell them the healer is closed for business, and they can all have their stuff back, but Nathan has something on his mind. I grew up hearing stories about him traveling the world and sharing the gospel. What's that?"

Lena held up the notepad where she'd written one line: "I've wanted to ask you why you're doing all this for me."

"That's your first question?" He nodded. "I think you know already. You and I are a symbol of something much larger that's happening."

"Aah?"

"You don't deserve my favor, do you? I mean, it's me, the one you threatened on the bridge that day. You wanted to kill me. It makes no sense that I now prefer you over my own life, or that Nathan would want me to protect you before himself. You agree that makes no logical sense?"

"Aah."

"This is all a picture of how you and I are seen in the eyes of God. We don't deserve His favor, but out of His love for us, He offers it to us. I love you, Lena, not based on what you've said or done, but based on your need to be loved. When Corban Dowler was dying, I understand he said he wanted you to know about God's grace. I learned that from the Bible, and that's why I'm doing all this for you."

"Aah?"

"My wife is somewhere out there, maybe far away and in danger. Jenna is somewhere up the interstate. But you're the one I'm sitting here with. I saw Colonel Rotham shoot you. I saw those men carry you out to throw you into some furnace. But their intentions are made weak by the power of God. There's no force on earth, not even death that can separate you from the love of God. You've been chasing power and control, Lena, but you've been missing out on love. And I'm not talking about physical love. Here we go. Nathan's about to start."

Levi put his arm over Lena's shoulders, and she melted against his side. She was a few years older than he, but he guessed his words had touched her heart, because she curled up against him like a child seeking her father's protection.

"We're fellow travelers in this world!" Nathan shouted, his voice strong for the crowd of about ninety. "Whatever your life path has been in the past, now we are here together. You have hoped in something miraculous to give your life meaning. I'm sad to say that most of you have even given away your belongings—and in some cases even compromised your morals—to this crook who is up here sleeping on the grass. He said he would heal you, but he's driven by his own appetites to control you. He's ruining you, destroying your lives even as he tells you that he's helping you.

"Even if this charlatan were able to heal you, our lives, my friends, consist of more than flesh and blood and bone. I'm here to tell you today that true hope lies in much more than health or wealth or temporary pleasures. My name is Nathan, and I care for you. Today, I'm here to give you back your belongings, and to remind you that you have an eternal soul that is more valuable than even the physical healing this liar was trying to sell you."

Gazing across the faces of the listeners, Levi prayed for open hearts. Their faces appeared eager for truth, but they hadn't learned how to discern truth from lies. Nathan's words would ring true to those who knew their need, Levi believed, and that included the broken woman under his own arm.

"Look what we found inside this liar's shack!" Nathan finally said, after he'd shared the complete gospel. He held up two black objects. "Bibles! Seven Bibles! For those of you who can read, these Bibles are for you. In these pages, you'll learn that God doesn't require you to compete for His care, or to jump into a muddy pool full of sewage! You did that in ignorance, but now you've been told the truth. Believe on the Lord Jesus, and be set free from sin's penalty. Turn from your wicked ways, and look to God's grace to teach you how to live for Him. Now, come and retrieve your belongings, my friends. Take only what's yours, then disperse what's left among yourselves. Who can read? A Bible for you . . . and you . . ."

"Look down there." Levi pointed for Lena. "That lady just took the stroller we left behind. I guess that means you're walking from now on."

Lena shuddered beside him.

"Don't worry. I'll carry you where the ground is uneven." He stood and helped her to her feet. "Okay, it's time to go."

"Thank you for that." Nathan shook Levi's hand. "That reminded me of the old days for a few minutes."

"Aah?" Lena asked as Levi steadied her.

"I used to extract persecuted Christians," Nathan said, "or anyone else who needed help in violent lands. It gave me a chance to speak to people about the truth. So, what'll we do about him?"

He gestured at the healer.

"You've told the people the truth." Levi helped Nathan into his pack. "It's up to them what they want to give their lives to now."

"Seems we're hunting for dinner tonight," Nathan said. "These people just grabbed up that canned food they'd given the guy. I guess I don't feel like asking them for a handout after all."

"Maybe that woman has some burnt frog to share," Levi suggested. "I can ask . . . for some leftovers for you."

Levi picked up Lena in his arms, and she hooked an arm around his neck.

"Careful, Levi." Nathan took the lead down the slope. "There's always that muddy pool someone could accidentally bump you into!"

Chen Li and Jenna accompanied Shaker and his travel companions off Interstate 78 at a small town called Bethlehem. Because the town shared a name with Israel's birthplace of Jesus, Jenna asked Chen Li to describe the layout as they walked up the highway and could see the town from a distance.

"I don't know what you're expecting," Chen Li said. "It's just another quiet town. I don't see any real signs of Pan-Day, except some abandoned cars in the ditch. The map we picked up shows more than I can see through the trees around the river ahead. It's called Lehigh River."

"But why do they call it Bethlehem?" Jenna begged from where she walked behind Shaker's horse. Lisbon and his wheelbarrow and Al Hayes with his daughter were on Jenna's heels. Dusty Thomas trailed farther back. "There must be a reason."

"Moravians settled here and named it Bethlehem," Al Hayes shared. "It wasn't much to look at, like the first Bethlehem, so that's how it got its name."

"Thank you, Al," Jenna praised. "As usual, that's interesting and helpful trivia."

Chen Li smiled and tucked away her map. Al Hayes had shared facts about every town the last two days, so she wasn't surprised he knew something about Bethlehem, Pennsylvania, too. The man was a regular almanac.

"Nowadays, it's known for a trading post," Lisbon said, pulling his wheelbarrow alone at the moment. "See the smoke stacks up there? That's where the market is. I've been here twice with Shaker."

"Does this work for us?" Jenna quietly asked Chen Li. "Can we get to Interstate 476 from here?"

"Yep. To our left must be Allentown. As long as the bridges are still there, we can head north and reach Interstate 80 in a couple days."

"You're leaving me?" Tyra Hayes asked. She fingered her compass on the shoestring necklace. "Do you want to use this?"

"No, thank you, sweetie." Chen Li noticed Shaker glance back from where he led their band, as if he'd heard their plans. "We have to meet up with some friends of ours."

"We shouldn't stay here long," Jenna said. "We're already behind. Fill up on water and keep going. Do we even have anything to trade?"

"Nothing we can spare."

Again, Chen Li noticed Shaker turn around and look at them. He hadn't been a conversationalist, like Dusty the last two nights at camp, and Chen Li hadn't liked the way he kept looking at Jenna. But she'd kept her perceptions to herself. At least he'd shared a little of his food with them, and Chen Li had been first to see to the horse's pack repairs, as well as cleaning of the cookware. She'd even fetched extra firewood for their cook fire so that they were an asset and not a burden upon the small group.

The closer they drew to the smoke stacks, Chen Li noticed more people along the streets.

"There's a Federation flag on a house," Chen Li informed Jenna. "It must be some sort of regional office. This town is definitely occupied."

"We're only about three day's walk from Philly," Jenna said. "Let's stay in our group until we have to split off. We probably won't be noticed, just two old women."

"Correction—I'm middle-aged. And you're still young."

"Well, I'll pretend to be anything you want," Jenna said, "if you get us up to Interstate 80. Can you imagine being with the others soon? I've never met Rex Caspertein, but I hear he's huge. It'll be nice to have someone else worry about us for a change."

Chen Li didn't know what day of the week it was, but she was surprised to see what looked like a weekend farmer's market in front of the smoke stacks that towered over the pavilion area. The industrial area had clearly been shut down for decades, but the open space in front of an old raised railroad trestle made for a perfect expanse for traders. Tents and stalls of every color and size littered the dusty concrete. Three hundred buyers, sellers, and children milled about, some with farm animals in tow.

"No one wander off," Shaker said, and handed his lead rope to Lisbon. "I'm only here to pick up some fabric."

"Mr. Shaker?" Chen Li stepped up to him. "Jenna and I are actually parting your company today. We're expected up north on the next interstate. It's been a pleasure traveling with you, and we thank you for helping us on our way."

She held out her hand. In fact, it hadn't been a pleasure traveling with Shaker since he seemed so suspicious, but it hadn't been a horrible experience. At least they'd been safe, and the others in the group had been the pleasant part. She would never forget the odd personalities she and Jenna had gotten to know on their trek the last couple days.

But Shaker didn't shake her hand. Instead, his gentle face dipped toward her.

"You may leave if you must," he said, "but Jenna is better off with me. We're going south, staying on the 81."

"No, we're not." Chen Li felt Jenna's hand touch her arm. She was listening. "We have friends who are—"

"You're just saying that." Shaker offered an empty smile, one that didn't reach his eyes. "It's okay to travel with us. We want you to. Jenna, I know you can't see at all. I've been watching you. I gave you those glasses, and I've shared my food and company. It wouldn't be right for you to abandon us now. It would be impolite. The two of you wouldn't get far without me, if you left."

Chen Li felt panic rising in her throat as she tried to remember in which pocket she'd placed the tranq-pen. To make matters worse, a pair of Federation soldiers in green, with rifles over their shoulders, were strolling through the bazaar. A sense of helplessness like she'd never known froze her mind and stole her nerve. Jenna couldn't help her, Nathan was nowhere around, and no one in the marketplace seemed aware of their situation. She wanted to protect Jenna, but here was an insistent man, weathered and strong from travel and hard living, telling them what would happen!

"You're forcing us to go where we don't want to go?" Chen Li again noticed the Federation officers not far away, now stopped at a livestock stall, checking the teeth of a pair of goats. "This isn't right, Mr. Shaker."

"Trust me." He finally took her hand in his. His hands were softer than she expected. "I won't let anything happen to you or Jenna as long as you're with me. We're going to Erwin, Tennessee. After that, you're free to leave."

"Both of us?" Chen Li asked, tugging her hand away from him. "Will Jenna be free to leave as well?"

"That'll be up to whoever becomes her husband." He addressed Lisbon. "Give me a few minutes to get these fabrics, then we'll return to the freeway."

Jenna clung to Chen Li, just like the night they'd fled the Bowery Hotel. Except now, Chen Li saw no way out, no avenue down which to flee.

"Lisbon, sir?" Jenna asked. "Will you stop us from leaving right now?"

"You're both good gals," the old Portuguese man said, "but Shaker's the boss here. I don't have a gun. It's against the law. But Shaker has a gun. Nobody does anything with his property he doesn't want done."

"That's right. He does have a gun!" Chen Li felt a shimmer of hope. "We can turn him in. No one but Citizen Army personnel are supposed to carry sidearms, right?"

"He is Citizen Army," Lisbon stated. "He works for himself, but he's a Federation scout. That's one good reason why I stick by his side. He can protect us. You listen to him. He makes good business deals. Why do you think I tow this wheelbarrow for him? I'll get rich off his sales."

"But he wants to sell Jenna!" Chen Li was so furious, she felt her own shaking more than Jenna's. Finally, she found which pocket contained the tranq-pen, and she drew it to use on Lisbon, but still hesitated. "Lisbon, you can't allow this. You're our friend!"

"Sure, you're a good gal, Chen Li." Lisbon leaned on one arm over his wheelbarrow. "Shaker'll make sure Jenna has a good husband."

"Chen Li, let's just leave," Jenna urged. "We can be far away by the time—"

"Hey, Mr. Hayes?" Chen Li interrupted Jenna, since her blind friend couldn't see that the two Federation soldiers had come over to see Shaker's horse, and she didn't want Jenna to say anything about their situation. Surely, news was widespread of the fugitives who had escaped from New York. "How far is it to Erwin from here?"

"Erwin, Tennessee, is five hundred miles from Allentown, Pennsylvania. Right now, we're in Bethlehem, Pennsylvania, which is two miles from the town of Allentown, Pennsylvania."

"Do you want to use my compass?" his daughter offered Chen Li.

"No, Tyra." Chen Li's knees felt weak. The Federation men walked away. "Erwin is five hundred miles in the wrong direction! There's Citizen Army officers all around, Jenna. What're we supposed to do?"

"If we can't get away safely," Jenna said, her voice calm, even if her trembling hands holding onto Chen Li's arm betrayed her fear, "then we trust God with where He's planted us to grow."

"Nathan won't stop looking for us," Chen Li said. "If he's alive, at least."

"Let's focus on what we have and know." Jenna reached out and found the wheelbarrow. "If we're being forced to walk a mile with Shaker, then let's voluntarily go the extra distance as Christ would want."

"You're thinking of ministering to him at a time like this?"

"We can't beat him physically," Jenna said, "but we are more than conquerors in the spiritual realm, because of Christ who saved us."

Chen Li wept on her friend's shoulder, the despair greater than her composure could stand. A few minutes later, she saw Shaker return, and she told Jenna. Instead of responding to Chen Li, Jenna moved toward Shaker.

"Mr. Shaker?" She found his back as he fastened bolts of fabric onto his weary horse. Her hands moved down to his arm. "We've decided to travel willingly with you. We hope to be such God-given blessings to you that your unkind intentions toward us are brought to the surface in your own heart, and you change from your ways before it's too late."

"Not only are you actually blind, Jenna . . ." He took her hand and squeezed it until Jenna cried out, ". . . but you are naive. I won't be fooled by your passive-aggressive tricks. Remain obedient as you have been since you joined us, or this will be the least of the pain you feel from me."

Slapping his hand, Chen Li drew Jenna away from him.

"We'll go with you," Chen Li stated firmly, "but know this—when my husband catches up, you'll be the one who's asking for mercy."

"Your threats amuse me." He took his horse's lead rope. "Is everyone ready? Lisbon, make sure no one gets left behind."

Shaker led them away from the steel stacks, and Chen Li hesitantly started after him, with Jenna on her arm. From a distance, Chen Li looked back at the market, but no one seemed to be aware they'd been kidnapped. Only a slender young man with a crossbow and a black Labrador retriever walked after them, going the same direction.

"We'll wait for the right time," Jenna quietly encouraged Chen Li, "and then we'll leave. You figure out when. I'll be ready. Until then, we are servants of Christ, even to our unreasonable master."

Chen Li didn't respond. She couldn't yet see their predicament as an opportunity for Christ. Their bad situation had just become worse, and in five hundred miles, it would become unthinkable. She couldn't focus on helping others while she was so focused on her own deliverance!

Andy Radner was feeling pretty good about himself for having gotten around Levi Caspertein and his friend, and catching up to Jenna Dowler! Sure, Levi was on his mind to kill, but he felt he understood the big blond man's game. Levi had taken his six crossbow arrows, but left him and his dog alive. Now, Andy was willing to return the favor—by allowing Levi to live long enough for him to see Jenna taken from him—by the edge of his tomahawk!

When Jenna left the crowded market in Bethlehem, it definitely worked in Andy's favor. He preferred the solitude of the mountains, but when that wasn't available, he preferred just plain solitude. Crowds were not to his liking, and Runner seemed to agree, since she'd growled at anyone who came too close to them in the narrow aisles of the smoke stack marketplace.

Finding Jenna had happened purely by accident, Andy reflected as he walked down the interstate after her. Without arrows for his crossbow, he hadn't been hunting regularly, which meant his food stores were getting low. He'd trolled through the market only long enough to find someone to steal from. After all, he was traveling light with nothing to trade. However, he'd convinced one salesman that he had a dozen rifles to trade, plus ammunition, behind a tent. When the buyer had followed him back, Andy had swiftly attacked, then stole enough food from the salesman's booth to get Andy down the trail a ways.

He'd still been adjusting to his heavier pack full of provisions when he'd spotted the tall, young woman wearing sunglasses standing next to a horse and an odd group of travelers. Before he could reach them, they'd pulled out of town. Close on their heels, he now kept peering around him as the interstate wound through Lehigh Valley on a southerly angle. This was too perfect! Jenna had made her escape from New York, and she was traveling steadily into the Plains Zone where she would be more vulnerable.

Andy loved this moment of the hunt when he knew his prey was within his grasp. He remembered his adoptive father teaching him to make quick, merciful kills when hunting animals in the forest. But Andy, when no one had been looking, had learned to appreciate the power he could harness by bringing the hunted to a point of hopeless fear. Only when he'd run away from his childhood River Camp did he come upon the prospect of hunting people. People were an even bigger thrill than animals!

The fact that Levi was close behind didn't worry Andy. He'd made the mistake of underestimating the stealth of the Caspertein man, but that wouldn't happen again. Jenna was blind and isolated, except for the small band of travelers she was in. Now with ease, he could get even closer to her, and at the instant that he would need to kill her to provoke Levi, she'd already be in his grasp.

It was almost *too* perfect, Andy thought, as he checked his surroundings again. Soon, the interstate would be cutting through rural patches of forest, but right then, the comfortable community of Allentown's suburbs lay all around. He could see covered bridges, maple and oak trees, old mills, and farms. Only one lonely man walked far behind him. Probably a local, Andy thought, noticing the traveler carried only a rucksack and an old rifle. *A rifle?* Yes, he realized. These were the borderlands of the Federation. The Citizen Army didn't pressure the people about Federation laws as much on the outskirts of its reach. Travelers with firearms would be more frequent, but Andy wasn't alarmed. He'd never been in the South, but he was an expert at survival, a master at hunting, and practiced at killing. Nothing could surprise him or catch him off-guard.

Runner darted off the freeway by leaping over the metal guardrail, and into a patch of forest on the southeast side. She was the only companion Andy wanted, but to complete the contract he'd made with the Federation, he'd need to tolerate a few more people. Without much strain, he quickened his pace to overtake Jenna's band ahead.

Around the next bend in the freeway, Andy came upon them suddenly as they had stopped at a creek to water the horse and fill up their own containers. The interstate was flooded since the culvert beneath had been clogged, so there was no way forward except to wade down the asphalt.

"You're going my way," Andy called to the man with the horse. "Can I join you for a stretch? My dog is a good tracker. Maybe we can help bring in some game whenever we stop to camp."

The leader, a cautious-eyed yet soft-faced man, seemed to study him, and Andy recognized a profiteer when he saw one. He was a man with an eye for advantage.

"Keep your goods separate," the man said in acceptance, "or I'll make them mine."

After that, Andy received all the introductions from a man named Lisbon, where he stood next to his wheelbarrow. He pointed out Dusty Thomas, who wasn't a conversationalist, then Al and Tyra Hayes. Al offered Andy a factoid about Pennsylvania's Native American culture, and Tyra offered him fingernail clippers from her necklace. Then Lisbon directed Andy to the band's latest additions, Jenna and Chen Li.

This was Andy's first up-close look at the two women he'd been tracking for days, but he didn't allow his eyes to linger. As a man who read sign for his livelihood, he knew not to leave a trace for others to read, not even on his own face. But it took only a glimpse to see the weariness on Chen Li's aging face, her bloodshot eyes, her sagging shoulders. Jenna greeted him with friendliness, and as Andy shook her lovely hand, he hoped she couldn't feel the electricity pass up his arm. She was pretty, and he almost hated to put her down, but a contract was a contract. Yet, that didn't mean he couldn't appreciate her until he needed to take her life in front of Levi.

"What brings you to this lonely road?" Jenna asked. "Did you say your name is Runner?"

"Yes, same as my dog's." He stooped to refill his own canteen from where the stream flowed from the forest. "I'm from Canada. My parents live down south, so I'm going to see if they're still alive. Actually, I have several relatives I want to try to locate. How about you guys?"

"We're going to a gallery in Erwin," Lisbon said. "They'll trade anything in Erwin."

They didn't delay long at the stream. In minutes, they'd waded through the flooded portion of the interstate and were moving again.

Andy noticed the single traveler behind them had gained much ground. He was close enough now that he was able to make sure it wasn't Levi with a long-barreled rifle.

At the back of the band of travelers, Andy studied Jenna until he realized suddenly that Chen Li, Jenna's older friend, was watching him watch the blind woman. Quickly, he smiled at the Asian woman, knowing he'd been caught admiring her, and looked away. Actually, he'd been watching the way Jenna moved, wondering how much of a struggle she'd present when it was time. Obviously, Chen Li would need to be disposed of first.

They lodged that night on the far side of Allentown in an empty house in a lost community off the interstate. Andy intentionally focused on what normal people would expect him to do, and did that. When he'd been alone before joining this group, he did as he pleased and when he pleased, and Runner did the same. But now, he wanted to blend in, and although he hadn't been too social the last few years, he thought he could read the others and copy them in doing what was acceptable.

He gathered firewood from outside, and found a bedroom with a window where the other men with him could lay their bedrolls. Jenna, Chen Li, and Tyra laid their few possessions in another room, but they all gathered in the den of the house to sit around a fire. Andy thought the time was right to share his stolen food, so he passed it around—a loaf of bread, a container of honey, and cheese. The salted pork and other food he kept hidden in his pack.

After they'd eaten, there was very little talking except by Al Hayes. Andy wandered outside to see where the lone traveler had gone for the night. And, of course, there was the anticipation of Levi and his big friend showing up, but they were burdened with tending the deformed creature in the baby stroller. He still remembered her face—or what was left of her face—staring up at him in the diminished glow of the fireplace. Whatever had happened to her, Andy didn't expect her to live long. Surely, someone missing their mandible couldn't even eat food, he pondered.

Andy saw a flicker of light in the night, and he crept away from the house to spy out the nearby glimmer. Through one glass window of a small shack, he peeked in at the man who'd been behind them. He seemed to be in his forties, his lips moving as he read a little book by the light of the fire. His beard was trimmed and his clothes were neat, except for a few rips. He seemed to be a nobody, so Andy didn't consider the passing traveler to be a threat. Someone traveling alone would certainly pull ahead of Shaker's slower group in the morning.

Content that there was no nearby danger, Andy was returning to their shelter when Chen Li darted up to him and grabbed both his arms.

"Please, listen to me!" she whispered, her voice strained as she led him to the side of the house. "We have only a couple minutes. You must help us—me and Jenna!"

"What's wrong?" Andy's heart pounded. What a thrill! The prey was asking for the predator's help! "Tell me."

"That man, Shaker, is making us go with him. We've been kidnapped! He's taking Jenna to Tennessee to sell her. He may be doing that with Tyra as well. Will you help us get away? Shaker carries a pistol in his belt. Have you seen it?"

"Yes, I've seen it." Andy noticed Runner pad quietly past them as she hunted for her dinner. Runner didn't seem too threatening toward the women in the group, of which Andy disapproved. "What do you want me to do to him? I thought you wanted to travel this way."

"No, we're trying to go northwest, not southwest. Jenna and I just want to get away. We have friends traveling up on Interstate 80, and the longer we spend down here, the farther they are getting from us. Will you,

I don't know—make sure he doesn't come after us? Jenna can't travel too fast. Maybe you could tie up Shaker. See this? It's a tranquilizer you could use on him."

"You want me to stay behind after you escape?" Andy considered how he could turn this idea into a benefit. He couldn't let them get away. And if Shaker was indeed holding the women captive, then he was doing exactly what Andy wanted to him to do—until Andy grew weary of the trader. "Where is your tranquilizer?"

"See?" She thrust it into his hand, but didn't release it to him. "It's just like a pen. You click the top, and a short needle comes out the pointy end. It'll tranquilize him for an hour, no more."

"This pen can do all that?" He grasped one end of the pen and ripped it violently out of her hand. With his other hand, he shoved her away, making her stumble backwards. "Thanks. This might come in handy. Now, inside!"

"But, you—"

He grabbed the older woman's jacket collar and threw her against the side of the house.

"I said, get inside! And don't let me hear you talking any more about running away from Shaker. Just act normal, like you're going along with his demands. That'll be easier on everyone."

Inside the house, Andy waited until they reached the den, then he pushed Chen Li hard from behind, sending her sprawling into the bedroom the ladies had claimed.

"What's wrong?" Shaker looked up from the fire where he was stirring a pot of food.

"She asked me to help them run away in the night." Andy went into the other room and gathered his pack and bedroll. "I'll be sleeping outside with my dog, just in case they try to leave or someone else comes around. I can't hear anything inside these walls."

"You're turning into more than just useful, traveling with us," Shaker said, and spooned food onto a plate held by Dusty. "The food's hot."

"I'll eat something outside."

Andy stood in front of the house for a few minutes, thinking of the latest development. Now he wasn't alone in keeping Jenna exactly where he wanted her.

"Come to me, Levi," he said into the night, though not wanting the hunt to end.

Runner whined for attention at his side, and he patted her head. With her by his side, no one would escape his notice. Levi might've been on his way down the interstate, but Andy knew he had time to play with until Jenna and Chen Li met their end. They were confused and afraid, more now than they'd been about being Shaker's captives. For sure, he would kill them, and he couldn't envision anything getting in his way from that reality. He had only to decide when to do it. Since Levi had toyed with him, it seemed only right that he toy with Levi!

Chapter Five

Brian Steelman woke the next morning feeling strengthened, even after reading by the firelight late into the night. Since he was already on the outer boundary of the Federation, he wasn't keeping his Bible or his rifle a secret any longer. He'd also determined to travel during daylight hours, though he knew he was a wanted man by Lena Travers.

He'd been a Christ-follower for only two months, having been born again in the tunnels underneath New York City. With the resistance, he'd been able to read the Bible freely, but hadn't finished reading the whole Book. Now with a New Testament all his own, thanks to the Wymans, Brian was exploring truths he'd never known. Having read the Book of Romans the night before, he was praying about understanding terms like justified, condemnation, and adoption. He knew the words, but he sought a fuller understanding as to what God wanted them to mean. Luigi Putelli had told him that God was faithful in answering prayer, so he prayed.

As Brian walked west from the suburbs of Allentown that morning, he noticed the group of travelers he'd nearly overtaken the evening before. Since they were pulling a wheelbarrow and leading a burdened horse, Brian wasn't surprised that he was overtaking them again a couple hours after dawn.

They appeared to be merely humble travelers until he drew close enough for one young man's black Lab to growl threateningly at him. The wary-eyed man with a crossbow and a tomahawk glared at him.

"Easy there, doggie." Brian moved into the next lane of the freeway to give the band a wider berth. "You don't want to eat me. I'm all bone and gristle."

His self-deprecating joke didn't ease their suspicious glances, and the dog's owner in the rear didn't chastise his canine, either. The gentle-faced leader who held the lead rope of the plodding horse watched Brian without reacting, but Brian had been an Enforcer and a detective for too long to miss other signs of strife that warned him to reconsider joining this humble-looking lot.

The young man with the dog and crossbow wasn't masking the warning in his glare. But it was the body language of the other three men and three women that heightened Brian's curiosity. From the next lane over, he watched the troupe move on ahead. One man directly following the horse, carried a round wall clock. He appeared ignorant of Brian's presence, staring off at the forest on the right side. Next came a heavy-set man who wore several sweaters, his arm hooked around a spacy-looking woman as he hustled her forward while watching Brian.

A lean man pulling one side of a wheelbarrow was next, his eyes repeatedly glancing at Brian. Yet, it was the woman pulling the other side of the wheelbarrow who almost made Brian call out her name. It was Jenna Dowler, the blind daughter of the old printer, Corban Dowler! He immediately recalled how those who'd escaped Manhattan had said Jenna and Chen Li had gotten separated after leaving the Bowery. Nathan and Levi had gone back for them. Yet—here they were!

Though he knew Jenna's eyes were sightless, she was nevertheless turned toward him, her eyes behind dust-crusted sunglasses. She must've heard and recognized his voice! Chen Li was walking directly behind the wheelbarrow, a woman Brian had seen only occasionally over the years. He wouldn't have noticed her except he was aware that she'd been with Jenna so he knew to look for her. After Chen Li noticed he was looking at her, he wasn't surprised that she kept her chin tucked into her coat, but she didn't seem to recognize him. Unlike his days with the Federation, he now wore a trimmed beard, and two years had passed since he'd been an Enforcer who'd frequented the Citizen Processing Department.

Suddenly, one of them stopped in the road as the others continued.

"You should move on ahead of us," the crossbow man said, standing in front of Brian. He was probably in his twenties with a light complexion. But his blue eyes were hard. "One word from me, and Runner will tear you apart before you can shoulder your rifle. You were looking at our women. I saw it in your eyes. Don't even think about it."

"Your women?" Brian's eyes narrowed, righteous anger rising in his soul. Jenna and Chen Li were *not* his women! "You talk like a man, but you don't look older than twelve."

"Try me." The young man set his hand on the head of the tomahawk in his belt. "I swing this like a man. You go your way, and we'll go ours. Unless you want problems with the Federation."

The man drew out a handheld radio and held it up to his mouth, as if he were about to talk on it. But Brian knew in that hilly part of Southern Pennsylvania, with forest sprinkled across the landscape, the signal wouldn't reach more than a mile or two.

"The Federation?" Brian grinned, realizing he was about to risk his life for Jenna and Chen Li. He reached into his ammo vest pocket where he still carried his Enforcer papers and laminated card. "I'm on patrol as an Enforcer."

"Let me see those!" The man yanked them from Brian's fingers and compared his face with the photograph. "Brian Steelman? It says you're from New York City. You work out of the Bowery?"

Brian noticed that Jenna and the others were steadily pulling ahead while he was talking to the daring young man with more authority than he'd probably earned. He didn't look like a Federation officer, but Brian recognized an inventory sticker on the side of the radio. It was definitely from the Bowery.

"That's right. I've been undercover for a few months, tracking down infiltrators. I'm to report to Lena Travers herself."

"Lena's dead." The man handed Brian's papers back to him. "You've been out of touch, Steelman. You should go back to the coast and find out your new orders under the new administration."

"Lena's dead?" Brian felt his bluff collapsing. "I knew there was a battle and some changes. She died that night?"

"No, a few days later, from what I understand." The young man's tone softened, and his dog seemed to sense the change and stopped growling. "Colonel Rotham shot her, I heard, when she opposed the vote for the next chancellor."

"So, Rotham is chancellor? I remember Milo."

"No, he's chasing down Obrador and some insurrectionists farther north."

"I should still investigate my leads out this way," Brian said. "Even if Lena is gone, my concern for the Federation hasn't changed. Our interests in these regions are just as important now as they ever were."

"Well, I don't want you with us," the man said. "I'm doing something, laying a trap for someone who's nearby. You'll be in my way."

"Laying a trap with those people?" Brian smirked. "Come on. They look like they've been wandering for days without food. You should use me as a backup."

"Backup? All you have is that old rifle? Does it even fire?"

"It's part of my cover. Yeah, it fires. I can't be carrying around Federation issued weaponry out here. This is the

Plains Zone. Tell me your name, and we can figure out our play as we catch up to the others."

"I work alone. I said I don't want you around!"

"Now you're making me suspicious." Brian turned his head to peer at the man from another angle. "I've been a Federation Enforcer for more than ten years. What exactly are you, and why would a true citizen turn down help from another loyal friend way out here?"

Brian noticed his words were having an impact. The man shifted on his feet, his plans clearly destabilized. Whoever this guy was, Brian knew he didn't have much Federation experience, no matter where Rotham had found him.

"Fine, but listen closely. They call me the Runner, same as my dog. And I'm in charge. You just keep yourself under cover around those people. If anything goes bad, you back me up."

Nodding, Brian shook the Runner's hand. Together, they turned and continued after the others.

"So, what's our play?"

"Two female fugitives in this band are bait for two fugitives behind us."

"Behind us?" Brian checked the freeway to the east, but it was empty except for the glare of the risen sun. He knew who the two behind them had to be. What providence! "Are they dangerous?"

"Not to us, but to the Federation, yes. Colonel Rotham, who's following Chancellor Branaugh's orders, wants all four dead. No one else matters, even though this crazy trader with the horse wants to take these women down to Tennessee to trade them for supplies."

"Trade them? You mean, he's a flesh trader?"

"It's more common in the Plains Zone than you realize."

"Of course." Brian recalled his own two years in the Plains Zone, witnessing the horrors of a collapsed society trying to survive at the expense of the lives around them. "I've heard about it."

"Just stick to your cover and leave the rest to me."

"Part of my cover is being a friendly nobody on the road. I should try to visit with everyone at least a little. It's only normal, Runner."

"Fine. Just don't mess anything up. I'm warning you, Steelman!"

Rex Caspertein felt his frown deepen as the steady rain fell even harder. Several hands struggled to erect a few tarps between trees as he watched and listened to his people cry for dry clothes, clean water, and warmth. He felt their misery in the rain, his own hair matted and his beard like a sponge. After hiking all night, there was nothing but more rain alongside a wide river.

"The wood is soaked!" Sean Harris grumbled, his wiry eyebrows not protecting his eyes as water streamed down his face. "How're we supposed to start a fire in this?"

To make matters more uncomfortable, the people had been undergoing their worm treatment, thanks to Lyla's plant remedy. Their cleansing was necessary but challenging.

Before Rex could answer Sean, lightning struck nearby and thunder rolled across the gray landscape of Central Pennsylvania. The engorged Susquehanna River threatened her banks a stone's throw away, but Rex had chosen the site anyway. The people needed to bathe and wash more than they needed to concern themselves with the river flooding at that minute. But washing wasn't as much of a priority for them when they simply wanted out of the cold rain.

"The last of our beans got wet," Bruno said, the only one of their number who could look him eye to eye because of his size. "They're spoiled, all of them. I haven't checked the powdered milk, but it wasn't covered very well, either."

"We're short on everything," Rex said. "Thanks, Bruno."

"The joys of leadership, huh?" Bruno clapped Rex on the shoulder. "We'll get these tarps and tents up, then get fires started. This'll pass."

Next, Lyla approached him.

"We need the latrines dug now, Rex, if we're going to camp here for a couple of days. The women—"

"It's too wet to dig, Lyla." Rex waved at the woods behind them. "Just tell them to find a log and go wherever. We have other things to worry about right now."

He watched her take a deep breath, but she held back whatever she wanted to say, and walked away. Only then did he wish she would've said something, because he felt he hadn't helped her. She was right, of course, in trying to encourage a little dignity among the women who'd been mistreated within the Federation's cages. When he looked after Lyla again, she was walking alone into the woods, her rifle and a shovel in her hands. That was Lyla, he thought to himself, solving problems on her own. If he had more people like her, maybe the fires would already be lit and fewer people would be standing around complaining—including himself.

Finally, he had to dismiss the others from the confusion and take down two tarps to erect them higher and at an angle, so the rain could run off the back instead of the side or front. The people who couldn't fit inside the tents huddled together under the tarps. If Rex was reading them right, they were grumbling about him, casting him sideways glances, as if he were to blame for the weather and their miseries.

"I saw the rain clouds coming," he admitted to Chloe as she stood with him in the rain, her slicker hood over her head. Except for the few COIL men, she was the only one who seemed to be at perfect ease under the strenuous circumstances. "We should've stopped sooner to find cover."

"We were on open ground, Rex," Chloe said, not looking up at his tall frame since she would've turned her face into the rain. "There was nowhere else to find shelter. A little water won't hurt us. The guys will have fires going in no time."

Sure enough, Scooter drew everyone's attention as he created a competition between himself and Bruno to see who could get a roaring fire lit first. Scooter kept calling Bruno his little friend, trying to disrupt the large man's attempts to ignite the wet tinder. Some leaned out their tent doors to catch the comedy.

"Our food's gone," Rex said quietly to Chloe as they watched the competition.

"I know."

"A group this size—I don't know how to keep them all fed except by stopping more often so we can hunt and forage."

"There's no way around it, Rex. Armies have always struggled to cover distances while remaining supplied. Why would it be any different with us?"

"Levi and I came through here just a few weeks ago. We'd shoot a deer maybe every week. Lyla collected greens, and Alice scouted for campsites. I don't remember ever taking a day off to hunt and forage. We hunted as we hiked."

"You can't do that with a hundred people to look after. There's nothing wrong with walking for two days, then resting for one to hunt. The Lord knows my old bones could use the slower pace."

Rex listened to the rain and watched Scooter's fire flicker to life. The people cheered. Bruno drew more laughter as he rushed over to Scooter's fire and stole a burning log, and dragged it to his own waning flame. In the process, people scrambled and slipped out of the way, enjoying the banter and entertainment of the two COIL men.

Movement near the river drew Rex's eyes.

"What should I do about those two?" he asked Chloe about Kendrick Obrador and Owen Travers, who strolled through the rain, their shoulders touching as they talked. "You know them. What're your latest thoughts?"

"Give them an ultimatum. If they won't work, they don't eat. Everyone else here, even a couple of elderly, were gathering a few sticks and helping out. What do they do? Eat our food. Drink our water."

"I'll pull them aside when the rain is gone."

"They don't fit in here," Chloe said. "I hate to say it, but even Brian Steelman was welcomed by the people. And look at Sean, right in the middle of them all. Brian and Sean both hurt these people, but they were accepted because they showed a little compassion and care."

"Sean's been asking Bible questions, too."

"He's close to coming to Christ, and he takes a shine to you." Chloe elbowed him. "Scooter calls him Little Rex. You might get the honor of seeing him saved."

"Why do you think Obrador and Owen haven't changed like everyone else has?"

"They were shamed," Chloe said, "but not humbled, so there hasn't been any repentance for their pasts."

"It's hard to believe that man birthed the Federation." Rex sighed. "It doesn't matter now, though. He's not the chancellor any longer, and he needs to pull his own weight."

"Or go out on his own," Chloe stated. "Give him that ultimatum. His behavior has gone on long enough. I can't tell if he's encouraging Owen or if Owen's encouraging Obrador to separate themselves, but it'll begin to jeopardize the others before long, causing division and fear. Maybe even insurrection."

"Yeah?" Rex stiffened. "Yeah, you're right. I'm sure glad you have some marbles in your skull, Chloe. I wouldn't have foreseen all that, except for the nuisance they've become."

Alice plodded up then, her cap drenched, and her heavy staff dragging after her weary march through the night.

"Rotham has begun to close the net toward us," she informed as she leaned on her staff. "His command vehicle is parked at Lock Haven, and he's using the other vehicles to comb the area eastward, from Bellefonte to Wellsboro."

"How concerned should we be?" Rex asked.

"As long as we stay away from all the roads during the days, they might just sweep right past us. They'll be here in two or three days."

"We're a mile off the freeway." Chloe surveyed what terrain they could see through the rain. "Once this weather clears, we'll set up smaller fires. In the trees, no one'll notice. I hope."

"Everything's happening all at once." Rex nodded at Alice. "Get some rest. I'm going to take Taylor Tharp and his boy Trenton with me down to Lewisburg. We brought the town some meat when we came through here a few weeks ago. Maybe they can return the favor."

"Just watch out for that patrol," Alice said. "Rotham is probably knocking on the doors of the locals and applying pressure, too. Word will get around that we're in the area if you're seen too much."

"She's right," Chloe added, "and people have radios. Anyone looking to gain the favor of the mighty Federation could turn us in."

"We'll stay out of sight," Rex said, "but I don't see another option. We need help or we'll starve. I've got to trust God that He'll watch our backs since we can't do it ourselves."

"Just don't forget to deal with Obrador and Owen," Chloe said.

"I don't know what you guys have talked about," Alice said, "but I second that. Those two are beginning to creep me out, always whispering off on their own."

An hour later, Rex headed off with Taylor Tharp and pre-teen Trenton on a search for food. The town of Lewisburg was only a couple miles away, but it meant crossing the interstate in daylight. Short, muscled Taylor had been with the Citizen Army, so Rex wanted to take the young father and get to know him outside of camp. And some of Rex's own best memories of childhood were those which involved his father Rudy, so twelve-year-old Trenton seemed like a good addition. The boy was wide-eyed and energetic, and hadn't shown any sign of weariness or whining along the trip.

As they neared the interstate, Rex allowed Taylor to crawl closer as Rex stayed back with the boy.

"Your father has good instincts," Rex said to Trenton as they waited together behind short bushes. "See the way he listens before he moves? And the way he pauses to look around? Your dad's a hunter."

"He hasn't gotten any deer."

"Maybe not yet, but he will. And you will, too. It's good to be useful for the people you take care of."

"I don't really take care of anyone."

"Sure, you do. You're with me and your dad right now. Our Christian friends are counting on us to find something to eat out here, something besides grass or insects."

"I'm just glad we're outside the city." The boy looked up as the rain stopped and the sky brightened. "We were always hungry in those cages."

"That was an adventure God didn't choose to give to me, but you should hold that time in the cages close to your heart, young man."

"Why? I want to forget about it."

"You were in the cages because you wouldn't deny Jesus Christ as your Savior, right?"

"Yeah. Dad said that no matter what, never turn your back on God."

"See? That's nothing to forget about. God isn't forgetting about the time you suffered for His name. You stood for God, so I'll bet you have a better eye to notice how God stands for you. Here we go. Your dad is waving us to join him. The freeway must be clear. Stay low."

The boy hustled forward in a crouch, and Rex jogged after him. When they reached Taylor's position, the man looked both ways, then darted across the lanes now empty of traffic. Trenton crawled up to the freeway, then ran across to his dad. Rex trusted his ears as well as his eyes, making sure no vehicles were approaching as he also crossed the road.

But they weren't out of danger yet. They ran together, three abreast, across a grassy field of spring grass already thigh high on Rex. They leaped high as the wet blades soaked their pants even more, and safety came in the form of a shallow gully they hadn't seen ahead. They tumbled and rolled to the bottom of the gully and lay there panting and laughing, their nerves needing release from many days of tension.

After Rex and Taylor checked their rifles, Rex led the way down the gully, then hooked to the right a quarter-mile later. They arrived at a walled community, erected sometime after Pan-Day, with one gate on the east side. Two gunmen on a gate platform held assault rifles over the wall, but they returned Rex's wave in greeting.

"It's me, Rex Caspertein." Rex smiled up at the men he didn't remember personally. "My cousin and I brought you a couple deer quarters a few weeks ago. We knew you'd had a hard winter and could use the meat."

"Yeah, I recognize you," said one man with a sleeveless jean jacket. "But we're not opening the gate. We got a visit from some soldiers. They warned us that we'd better not help you."

"I was afraid of that." Rex gritted his teeth. "Colonel Rotham beat us here, huh?"

"They drove right up to our west gate. Their attack vehicles could plow right through our walls if they'd wanted to. We're just family people here, mister. We have women and children to think about. I'm afraid you're on your own."

"We have women and children, too," Taylor said. "That's got to mean something, right?"

"Yeah, but we don't want any trouble with the Federation. We've known they would come someday, and now that they're aware of us, we're aware of our vulnerabilities. We can't shelter you here."

"Oh, we're not looking for shelter." Rex wished Levi were there. He was far better at lifting the mood in tense situations. "We've been on the road for days and we're short on food. Even a little would help."

"We were hurting a month ago when you Casperteins helped us. We're doing no better now. But it's not up to me. The elders agreed we can't risk a confrontation with that Colonel Rotham by opening the gate to you. I'm sorry."

"You're letting wicked military men tell you who to be hospitable to?" Taylor asked. "You should be ashamed of yourselves. We're God-fearing men, women, and children. These Casperteins fed you, but you won't return that kindness? What kind of community is Lewisburg, anyway?"

"Taylor, it's okay." Rex set his hand on the shorter man's shoulder. "We've been blacklisted, so we'll just need to move on."

"How about a milk goat?" young Trenton called. "Give us a milk goat and we'll call it even. You don't even have to let us into the city."

Rex looked from the boy to the sentry on the wall. To his surprise, the two gunmen above exchanged whispers.

"Give me a minute," the guard finally responded.

"How'd you know they had goats?" Rex asked.

"Goat droppings." Trenton pointed at the ground. "Our neighbor in Queens had goats, remember, Dad?"

"I remember." Taylor walked away from the wall a few yards. "It looks like they have a whole herd, too, by the way all this vegetation is chewed back from the wall. Good eye, Trenton!"

Minutes later, the gate opened a couple feet, and a woman in patched overalls led two milk goats outside and handed their braided lead ropes to Taylor.

"I heard you're traveling," the woman said, and swiped at loose hair to pin it behind her ear. "Goats aren't really traveling animals, but they're good for milking, even if they look skinny."

"It's more than we expected a few minutes ago," Rex said, then lifted his head to the sentries. "Thank you! You just may have saved some lives today."

"We don't want it said that Lewisburg was cruel to travelers who were good to us."

"Lewisburg will be a blessing on our lips!" Rex vowed. "Every time we milk these gals, we'll remember where they came from. God bless you, Lewisburg!"

The woman backed into the gate, and it closed.

"It's not a bag of oatmeal or crushed wheat," Taylor said, handing his son one lead rope, "but I'd say this is a mission accomplished, eh, Rex?"

"Everyone will be impressed!" Rex led the way back to the gully. "I'm impressed! We have an impressive God. Now, maybe He'll impress us some more and help us get safely across that freeway again."

The goats were older and mild-mannered, so Taylor and his son had little difficulty leading them back the way they'd come. At the interstate, Rex took point and checked the lanes for movement from the edge of the guard rail. As far as he could see in both directions, the freeway was quiet. He was about to wave Taylor and Trenton closer when Rex noticed movement far to the west.

Quickly, he drew his binoculars from his coat and held them to his eyes. Two men were walking away from them, one short, one tall and heavy. He couldn't see who they were, but he felt certain they weren't any of his people. None of the Christian refugees would be out on the road. It had to be some locals, though Rex would've warned them of the Federation's presence if they were nearer.

Rex waved Taylor and Trenton up to the guard rail, and helped them lift their sixty-pound goats onto the pavement. In a few seconds, they were across and into the bushes on the north side.

"We'll still need meat," Taylor said to Rex. "A couple of milk goats for a hundred people?"

"I hear you. At least we're not returning empty-handed."

Rex was pleased with their short side-journey, and relieved to be back safely in camp with his people. In minutes, they'd chosen names for the two goats—Ruth and Naomi—and Rex finally sat beside one fire where he could take off his boots. After walking and scouting all night, then running down to Lewisburg, he was exhausted. Alice was bedded down in the trees, and others were yawning with glassy eyes around the fire. As Rex lay on his back and crossed his arms, he sensed from God that he still had much to do to care for the people, but this was time to sleep. Someone needed to find more food for the people, but he couldn't continue physically unless he rested.

As he drifted to sleep, he remembered that only Scooter and Hank Lowery were on patrol duty right then. With the Federation closing in, more safety measures would need to be employed.

He woke suddenly to a woman's scream. After tugging on his boots, he grabbed his rifle while others around his low fire were still rubbing sleep from their eyes. It was mid-afternoon, and he ran into the woods from where he'd heard the shriek. Alice joined him from another angle. When he noticed Bruno and Sean coming as well, he stopped them.

"Go back! Stay with the camp."

It's all he could yell as he leveled his rifle at someone running straight at him through the trees. Alice moved to the left and took up a defensive posture with her steel staff.

A moment later, Rex recognized Emma Lowery, Hank's teenage daughter, with another young lady. The two bumped into saplings and tripped over roots in their haste and distress. He heard their gasps and sobs, and then saw the tears on their cheeks.

Now that he'd identified the girls, he shifted his gaze to the forest behind them. They were only forty yards outside of camp, but the trees were close together and the foliage grew thicker the deeper Rex looked.

Emma reached Rex, and he grabbed her arm, shaking her to her senses. Her eyes were wild with fright.

"What is it?" he asked sharply, but not loudly. "What's out there?"

"It's Lyla!" the girl sobbed. *"She's dead!"*

Rex didn't believe it.

"Get back to camp. Go!"

As soon as they were a safe distance behind him, he prowled up to Alice's side, where she stood stoically, staring to the west.

"What were they doing out here?" Alice asked. "The women's latrine is in the other direction."

"Something about Lyla." Rex met her eyes and saw the fury there. "I know. Whatever it is, we'll deal with it. Go left. I'll go right. Slowly, now."

Rex set off, arcing wider than the path the girls had taken through the trees. Being raised in the Colorado mountains, he knew how to track and how not to cover up sign. As he prowled carefully forward, he tried to recall the last time he'd seen Lyla. It had been that early morning in the rain, after they'd marched all night, and she'd come to him about a problem he couldn't recall now. But he remembered she'd walked off in this direction. Surely, she'd been in camp since then. Someone would've noticed her missing, wouldn't they?

He found her behind a fallen log. From a few yards away, he could see by the way she lay that she was dead. He crouched and studied the scene. There was blood, and her rifle and belongings were missing. So this hadn't been an accidental fall while climbing over a wet log.

The site was trampled. A small excavation of earth lay at Lyla's feet, as if she'd been digging. Of course—the latrine she'd asked for! A man-sized boot had crushed a cluster of wild mushrooms in the shadow of the log, and closer to the body, fern branches had been broken by another body. Two people, Rex guessed.

He held back his grief, even as it rose. When Alice appeared on the other side of the wood, he raised his hand to stop her there.

"Rex," she called, her face like ebony stone, her lips trembling, "this is murder."

After a moment, he moved closer, noticing that whoever had stripped the body of gear had even taken her shoelaces, but left her boots.

"It was a couple of men," Rex said, waving Alice nearer, pointing out his findings. "The grass is trampled here and here, where two different men knelt and picked off her rifle, shoelaces, and canteen. I think she had a shovel, too. Her boots are in good shape, but they didn't take them, so they probably have larger feet."

"We're not that far from camp." Alice peered westward. "We would've heard her scream. Or maybe in the rain—"

"There was no scream." Rex turned his head away, vomit rising in his throat. "She wouldn't have screamed because she knew her attackers. When we were coming back from the Lewisburg outpost, I saw two men walking on the interstate. I was thinking they were locals, but . . . now, I'm not sure."

"Who was it?"

"You know." Rex wiped his hand over his face and down his beard. "You already know. What have I done? How am I ever going to look Levi in the face again? His own wife was—"

"This wasn't your fault!" Alice jammed her staff into the wet earth. "Don't make this worse by blaming yourself. Listen to me! It was Obrador and Owen? Then we go get them! I can catch them, even if they have a few hours head start. Which way were they going when you saw them?"

"No." Rex reached out and closed Lyla's eyes so they didn't stare blankly at the sky. "I'm not sending you after them. They're armed now. We took their rifles from them a few days ago, and now they took one back. They're killers and we're not."

"Yeah, but we're hunters," Alice said, her voice sounding like a growl. "They're from the city. They have to pay, Rex! It's the only justice there is out here. If you don't want me to go alone, then let me take Scooter or Bruno."

"And leave these people with two less defenders if we're attacked?" Rex shook his head. He began to weep. "I want them to pay, too, but we can't, Alice. Let's think this through. We save lives, not take them. We came all this way to deliver people. Levi would say that's unconditional. You remember what he's told us. He's been merciful to his own enemies before, even when it went against everything in his body. I have to think that he'd want us to stay the course now, even if this is . . ."

Rex couldn't finish, and Alice doubled over in quiet sobs. It was too horrible. He didn't want to move Lyla. He wanted to bring Levi to the glade and receive his older cousin's permission to move his wife, to bury her, and to leave her behind.

After some time, he wiped his nose and dried his eyes. Lyla was light in his burly arms, even though she'd not been a tiny woman. Alice walked stiffly in front of him as he carried her back to camp. Halfway there, he met Chloe and Bruno, who held their rifles, prepared to fire. The two girls who'd discovered the body had spread the news, and Rex couldn't speak or meet their eyes.

The people wailed and crowded around a central fire where Rex laid her. The people smelled like mildew from the rain, and they were already weary from long nights and restless days. They hadn't needed such sorrow on top of their grief. Lyla had been a mother figure to all the refugees, and a sister to all the Christians. Rex couldn't imagine losing a more loved person from their number.

Taylor and Hank's wives prepared the body. Bruno and Sean dug a grave below an old pine. Even though they laid her to rest out of sight of the camp, Rex didn't think the people would want to stay there for long now, even though they needed to rest, wash, and dry out.

Bruno presided over the funeral, and though he did his best to celebrate the life of Lyla and her graduation to glory, the sense of dread, the gruesome crime, and the miles ahead of them seemed to chill everyone from any type of rejoicing. By faith, Rex knew he would see Lyla again, but that didn't help his feelings in the moment.

At sundown, the leadership gathered with Rex near the river. Out of all the people who had fled from New York and were still alive, only Obrador and Owen were missing from their ranks.

"I know you're disappointed in me," Rex said. "I've let you down. I'd understand if you—"

"Stop it, Rex," Chloe interrupted. "It was Jenna's decision to try to save Obrador and Owen. At the warehouse, Levi didn't raise any objections to them coming with us, knowing they were dangerous. You never met Corban Dowler, but he supported trying to help those two men, too."

"We show mercy," Scooter said, his head low, "and sometimes we get burned."

"God is still just," Bruno reminded. "Lyla's suffering is over. The Lord will have His way with Obrador and Owen, unless they repent."

"I know how you're feeling," Nick Zoft said, and Rex lifted his head to acknowledge the chubby man. "I'm not a fit soldier or marksman like you all, but I was mayor of Hackensack for years. Some people were lost in my city, and I couldn't control it. I felt responsible. But the reality is different. These things are in God's hands, beyond our control. Lyla helped everyone from the cages get over their gut-worms. Now, we stay on schedule. Nothing changes. We've lost Lyla, but we've also lost two dark souls who didn't want what we all hold to—the hope of the resurrection."

"Well said, Mayor." Scooter nudged the man's arm. "Nothing changes."

"No, I'm sorry." Sean Harris' voice was harsh. "I don't have the faith like you guys do. Maybe I'm the only one here who doesn't. So, this is crazy! That's what I think. Look at the firepower we have in this circle right here. In two days, I could catch up to Obrador. I served him for years, so I know how selfish he is. And Owen Travers is the worst kind of person alive. You don't know me too well yet, but I can't sit here for two days while those jackals walk away with blood on their hands. I'm going after them. Who else is going with me? We could be back before the people here are ready to move on."

Rex was already feeling his confidence renewed from Nick Zoft and Scooter's words, although his grief was no less. He couldn't yet imagine explaining the situation to Levi, but somehow he would have to face his cousin.

"If you few aren't too tired of me leading," Rex said, "then I'll continue to have the final say on things that affect all of us. But I won't pretend to know everything, or tell you what to do with your own lives. Sean, you were a friend of Nathan's?"

"I was his sergeant for years. I think he'd want me to go after these two jackals."

"Well, you know Nathan better than I do," Rex continued, "but I can tell you this: God's way of operating is usually the opposite of how things are done in the world. The firepower you see in this circle isn't just for show. My dad raised me on the true stories of these people risking their lives to save others. Many times, with God's grace, they stood outnumbered against enemies who had bigger guns."

"So, let's go get 'em!" Sean pressed.

"It's not our way." Rex sniffed. "What those two did is . . . unspeakable. But the people you see right here, we've come to know the love God has for us, and we're not going to play God over Obrador and Owen by taking their lives. Oh, they're in a heap of trouble with their Maker, but we need to remain inclined toward forgiving them, not killing them."

"Forgive? Seriously?" Sean surveyed their faces. "Lyla didn't deserve this."

"Maybe Levi is better at explaining these things." Rex took a deep breath. "I'm not going to stop you, Sean, if you want to go after them. But I'll ask that you not take a battle rifle with you, if you do go. We need it here, and arming you for an act of revenge would be the same as joining you."

"Well, I don't have another firearm." Sean's fingers touched the stock of the battle rifle. "I'm not going anywhere in this country without being armed."

"Sean?" Chloe said. "Nathan and Levi aren't here. We've lost Steelman and now Lyla. I'd like you to stay with us, build us up, help us hunt a little, and heal. Leave Obrador and Owen in God's hands."

"But I'm not . . ." Sean winced. "Okay. I guess if I know those two, they'll find themselves in their own trouble soon enough, wherever they go."

Rex sighed, thanking God for calm from everyone. He still hadn't told anyone in which direction he'd seen the two murderers walking. That would be his secret—that they'd been heading west ahead of them. If Rex wanted anything from the killers, he wanted only the rifle they'd stolen from Lyla. It wasn't comforting that he'd lost a battle rifle to them, because it could be used for evil purposes in the hands of wicked men.

Lena Travers woke as the sky brightened and the sun shined on the upper reaches of the elm trees over their small camp. She glanced at the other two bedrolls around the fire. Nathan's bed was empty, but Levi was there, sleeping, his face turned toward her. Although her first impression of the Westerner on the bridge had been that he was a troublemaker towards the Federation, she'd found him to be immensely gentle. Without any doubt in her heart, she knew he had saved her life.

She wasn't surprised that he was still sleeping since she and Nathan had eaten boiled roots and gone to bed while Levi had been out hunting late into the evening. Well after midnight, he'd returned and she'd woken as he'd stoked the fire and butchered a small deer. As her eyes had returned to slumber, she remembered him glancing up at her, winking, then continuing to work into the night.

Levi seemed to have dedicated himself to her well-being, Lena thought, and she didn't know what to do with his care but to receive it. She knew he had a wife out there somewhere, because he spoke of her with affection. And Jenna Dowler was far ahead, the sign showing that she was traveling with a small band. But Lena realized even Jenna didn't take priority before herself.

Lena remembered her last words to Levi when they'd faced off on the GW Bridge—she'd sworn that she'd hunt him down. And he'd stated with amusement that he didn't care. The thought of her threat still rang in her ears, and she touched what was left of her face. She was a horror to look upon, she knew, so she kept the bridal lace over her lower face, except when it was just her and Levi. He didn't seem to mind her true appearance. After all, he'd treated her wounds with the boiled-down extract of white oak bark as an antiseptic to stave off infection as her now-deformed mouth had healed. It was far from healed, with pink skin covering where her mandible should've been, but at least the wounds were closed and no longer oozing.

In her limited capacity, Lena had begun to care for herself, although she appreciated Levi's attention. He was a handsome man, especially when he was shaved, and she didn't mind that he was a proper gentleman in caring for her, without actually being intimate with her. She couldn't remember being this close to anyone, not even her brother, Owen, or trusting anyone as she trusted Levi. And he was supposed to be her enemy!

Without disturbing him, she picked up the camp water pot and walked through the elms to a brook with tall grass along its banks. They were on the western edge of Allentown, and a number of other travelers were camped nearby since the town was located at a crossroads of a number of different highways. It would've been a mystery that so many people had gathered in the same sparse forest, except that a two-hundred-foot-high roller coaster rose high above the tree line, beckoning all who passed that way to see what it was. Dorney Park, an amusement and water park, had become both a local community hub and trading post.

After filling the pot, Lena returned to camp. All of her movements were slow and intentional. Tripping and falling, or bumping the nerves in her jaw, or re-opening her wounds was such a risk. Even as she'd begun to walk on her own since the stroller had been taken, Levi had kept his left hand tightly gripping the back of her coat. Twice the day before, she'd stumbled, but he'd caught and lifted her off her feet and into the air, by only his one arm, until she could right herself safely and pain-free. He was her protector, and in that moment, as she settled the water pot into the warm coals of the fire, she looked again upon his face as she might have looked upon a lover she'd known for twenty years.

Snorting softly to herself, Lena admitted that she was incapable of love, and she was incapable of being loved. She'd been Lena Travers, the most brutal Enforcer of the Federation, and now she was a pitiful creature who caused strangers to grimace. *Love?* She'd have to grow a heart first, she told herself, and growing a heart was about as likely as her growing another mandible to fix the missing part of her face.

She lifted her head at the sound of a woman's laughter coming from where the roller coaster frames were. A local man from the market had explained the evening before that there'd been seven roller coasters in Dorney Park, not to mention other rides for adults and children. It was strange to Lena, but she wanted to see them all with Levi, even though none of the rides actually worked anymore. While in Manhattan, she'd been devoted to rebuilding and controlling, but that life was lost to her. Now, she wanted to appreciate the simple things of a life that was once happy—if not her own life, then others' lives of a day when laughter and play had covered the grounds of a place called Dorney Park.

Lena walked away from camp toward the laughter. Since Nathan wasn't back from his own foraging, they wouldn't be leaving right away, so she wouldn't hold them up if Levi woke. He'd know she'd wandered to the brook or to the sound of voices within the park.

It was still early morning, so she walked among the trading post booths as sellers set their wares on tables and shelves. Nearby, the amusement ride called White Water Landing was tended to by locals, its reservoir of water from its days as a ride now transformed into life-sustaining drinking water for a whole community, fed by the nearby brook.

On a table, a merchant set out pocketknives and other trinkets of value for survivors of the area. At another booth, a woman unloaded a suitcase of cookware while her husband complained about the shave he'd gotten from a barber the day before.

Then Lena approached a booth where a merchant was setting out camping gear. Tents and boots, and even a couple compound hunting bows, were up for barter. It was a treasure trove for her party, Lena thought, since they were traveling and camping their way along the interstate. But unlike Manhattan, there were no ration incentive cards to trade or barter, and Lena had no gear of her own with which to pay.

In an instant of justification, Lena knew she was going to steal something. She turned to the side and acted as if she were studying a display of fishing poles, which were valuable in their own right. But really, she was watching the merchant of the camping gear. As he came and went from the front of his booth, there were short periods of time when his back was turned. In the back, there was a shanty where Lena saw other people moving about. Maybe they were the merchant's family living in the back. Nevertheless, there were two dome tents bundled tightly in canvas at the front of his booth, right on the table!

The merchant set a small cook stove on plywood on the ground, then returned to the back. With her head low, Lena approached the display. She placed her hand on one tent, saw a tear in the canvas, and chose the other. It was cradled in her left arm an instant later, when she noticed a cache of unlabeled canned food on a lower shelf. Not caring what kind of food it was, she grabbed two with her right hand and hustled away. As she walked, she tucked the cans into her coat. *A tent!* Sure, Levi and Nathan didn't mind sleeping under the stars, or under the scratchy, stained tarp against their faces, but she was a city girl. When they couldn't find a house to shelter in, she wanted a tent!

Another tall roller coaster named Thunderhawk loomed above her, and only then did she realize she needed to change directions to return to camp. But she determined to avoid the camping gear merchant by all means! It wouldn't be difficult, she decided, since the population of Allentown was beginning to fill the marketplace. Even a line of barbeques were set up, with various vendors competing for drifters' attention. Horse, dog, and pig seemed to be on the menu, but Lena preferred the deer meat she'd seen Levi bring back in the dark.

As she rounded the White Water Landing reservoir, three men hustled toward her on a crosswalk. The camping gear merchant was among them! The man in front pointed at her. He wasn't tall, but his sturdy frame, broad shoulders, and stern face identified him as some sort of authority in the park.

Turning in the opposite direction, Lena was met by a walkway overgrown with tall weeds. She stopped at the dead end, a chill coursing through her body at the thought of falling while climbing through the bramble of vines and bushes, all to escape her potential accusers.

"Excuse me, miss?"

Lena didn't turn toward them right away. Her eyes were wide as she imagined what would happen. She'd left her pencil and tablet back at camp, so she couldn't even communicate! And although she'd maimed and murdered hundreds in the past, she couldn't fight her way out of this. If she were struck or scraped violently on her injured face, her wounds would reopen, and no one but Levi would know how to help her—and she'd left him back at camp!

With humiliation in her heart, she turned toward the three men.

"That tent . . ." The stern one pointed at her arm, ". . . belongs to this man."

"And the cans of food."

The merchant threw down the tent bundle and clawed at her coat. One of Lena's hands hovered over her lower face, protecting herself, and the other hand batted away his heavy groping. Since her coat zipper was stubborn, he swung at her head, buffeting her on the ear, which sent waves of pain from her jaw into her skull. Paralyzed, she dropped to the walkway. Cursing and spitting, the man finally tore her zipper by force, and reclaimed his food.

"There was more, Mitchell," the merchant said. "I know she took more! Where'd you hide the rest, lady?"

"I didn't see her take more than just the two," the one named Mitchell addressed the third man, who wore a suit from another era. "What do you think?"

"We have a law." The man frowned. "It doesn't discriminate between citizens and visitors. Or the diseased, in her case."

"Yeah!" The merchant collected his tent, his voice sounding whiny and high. "Don't catch whatever she has!"

Weakly, and still recovering from being struck, Lena reached for her bridal lace. With horror, she realized it had been torn off in the scuffle. It lay on the ground next to her head. She rolled over to grab it when Mitchell jerked her to her feet. She fell against him, her knees weak from the pain.

"Do I have to restrain you?" he asked, holding up the metal bracelets as he gripped one of her arms.

She shook her head, almost deliriously. Levi often gripped her arm, but not with such force. The man named Mitchell walked her toward the tall tower where the blue letters of Dorney Park were painted on the frame over a ride called the Dominator. Three tattered flags hung limply on poles high overhead.

"Most of the country don't have laws," Mitchell said, "but we do here in Dorney Park. Even where there are no laws, people know not to steal from one another. You put me in a bad situation. Miss, I wouldn't mind letting you off with a warning, but that's the mayor of Dorney Park, and I'm the sheriff. I wish I wouldn't have seen you steal that stuff at all, but that idiot Adkins had the other merchants rising up in arms before we went looking for you. You've got to pay."

"Aah!" Lena made a weak attempt to pull away.

"Now, don't fight me! We have to do this. It'll be worse if you fight it. I've seen the whip cut much deeper than it needed to when people fought it."

As they continued through the park toward the Dominator tower, the crowd gathered, and the whiny merchant named Adkins boasted in the recovery of most of his belongings from a crazed wild woman with no face.

Finally, they arrived at the base of the tower's steel structure where the sheriff walked Lena up to the vertical beams and drew his handcuffs. Lena didn't fight him as he took off her coat with the torn zipper, then removed her button-up plaid shirt, leaving her in only a thin thermal top, which Levi had given her. The sheriff fastened one steel bracelet around her right wrist, looped it over a horizontal steel brace above her head, then fastened the other side to her other wrist. Her back was to the crowd and her front was facing the tower's superstructure. Small blessings, she thought, since the crowd couldn't sneer at her face. But the sheriff had said . . . *a whip?*

"This'll teach her to steal from our hard-working citizens!" the merchant spat.

"Get back, Adkins!" Sheriff Mitchell ordered. "Get back behind the line with the others."

"Get the whip and the charter," the mayor said in his perfect suit. "Let's make this official. I don't like it any more than you do, but let's set a good example while half the town is here."

Lena turned her head and looked past her arm as the sheriff entered a paint-chipped administration building, and emerged with a book and a whip. At the sight of the whip, a whimper escaped her exposed throat. It wasn't long, but it was thick, and the leather wasn't smooth. She would die now, she thought. It would kill her. The pain alone would drive her insane.

"Quiet now!" the mayor ordered the crowd. He took the book from the sheriff and held it high for everyone to see. "Let us be civil about this! We are Dorney Park. Whether you're visiting or you live here, the law must be followed."

Hanging from the cuffs for an instant, Lena tested the strength of the steel. The edges dug into her wrists. Of course, there was no give. Panic threatened her mind. She remembered saying similar words countless times about the Federation's laws. But her words had always preceded executions, never whippings.

"Today, Sheriff Mitchell himself caught this thief stealing a tent and canned food from a local vendor. I was there when the items were recovered from inside her coat. This is the woman! There is no doubt she's guilty. For simple stealing, the first offense, the charter requires ten lashes. She may be a vagabond or a citizen of Dorney Park, but justice is blind. The law stands. Sheriff?"

Mitchell approached Lena's side and hung the whip on a beam next to her. Instead, he drew a folding knife and clicked it open.

"I'm sorry, but I have to cut the back of your shirt off. It'll be worse with it on. Pieces of the shirt will end up inside the cuts and they'll get infected. It's safer on a bare back. Trust me."

She felt his blade on the back of her neck inside her collar.

"Hold on there!" a loud voice shouted.

The sheriff paused, then withdrew his knife. Everyone, including Lena, turned to see Levi on the roof of the administration building, his battle rifle aimed at the sheriff.

"You'd better explain yourself real quick!" Levi's voice was harsh and threatening. "It ain't easy holding back right now. You have one of my people chained to that tower, which means you have ten seconds before I start shooting!"

"She was caught stealing." The sheriff raised his hands, folded his knife, and pocketed it. "There's nothing foul happening here, stranger. I saw her myself take a tent and two cans of food. I wish she hadn't, but Allentown has laws. We're still civilized here."

Lena felt warmth instead of panic climb up her spine. Her protector was there. Levi would never let them hurt her. She watched him study the crowd, most of whom Lena couldn't see behind her. But Nathan didn't seem to be with him.

"If this is true," Levi said, "then the offense will be paid for in proportion to the crime. I'm a man who obeys local authorities. But if it's not true, this will be no easy day for any of us."

With seemingly little effort, Levi leaped off the roof and landed poised, his rifle still aimed at the sheriff. He walked up to the man and lowered his gun. The mayor stepped forward, but Levi held out his hand without looking at the suit.

"Not you! I'm talking to the man with the whip. You have authority?"

"I'm the sheriff."

Lena strained to see Levi's face. Now she was afraid of disappointing him. After all he'd done for her, she'd done this to him by putting him in this predicament! All for a tent and food? *This?* She hated herself in that instant, for doing this to herself, and to Levi, in front of so many.

"Did I hear right?" Levi asked. "Ten lashes?"

"That's correct."

"You saw her face?"

"Yes. I'm sorry. Seems like she's had some difficulties and pain already."

"Ten lashes could kill her. She has barely any skin covering her wounds, and her nerves are nearly exposed on the surface."

"Maybe . . . she could work off her punishment." Mitchell shrugged. "Like restitution?"

"That's reasonable. We're traveling west." Lena heard sorrow in Levi's voice. He was hurt. She hadn't known him long, but she knew how his voice lowered when he was weary or saddened, like at the end of the day when he spoke of catching up to his wife's party—the very refugees Lena had tried to kill. "But we can't wait here even a day. Whoever's been wronged, let me pay the price, even double, with deer meat. I shot a small buck last night. I'm a law-abiding citizen."

The man in the suit stepped up to them. Lena tried to stand up straighter so her wrists weren't cut by the cuffs, but her arms were getting heavy. She wanted to cry, but not in front of all these people. What a fool she'd been!

"Sheriff," the mayor said just loud enough for Lena to hear. "What will people think if strangers can just buy their way out of the consequences? The law, Sheriff! This is your job!"

"No! This woman cannot be whipped!" Levi's words were enunciated to make a point. "I will not allow it. Let me see this law."

The mayor opened the book and held it for Levi to read.

"There are no loopholes, sir," the mayor said. "I wrote this myself. Your lady friend should've thought of the consequences before she stole from the town's sellers. If you just shot a deer, then she had no need to steal, which makes her crime even worse!"

Levi read the book a moment, tracing the words with his finger.

"Okay. I've seen enough." He pushed past the mayor and approached Lena, stopping close to her side. Only then did she see he'd recovered her veil. With one hand, he gently wrapped her lower face as with a scarf. "Did you do this? You stole a tent and some food?"

"Aah," she said, tears filling her eyes as she nodded. How she wanted to explain! But she couldn't. And there wasn't anything to explain. She'd been impulsive, thinking she'd get away with it.

"Their law is pretty cut and dry. It ain't easy trying to make sense of why you'd do this, Lena. Were you trying to leave? With a tent and food?"

She shook her head, her cheeks burning with shame and frustration.

"We're in some trouble over this, I hope you know." He set his hand on her shoulder, then lowered his head.

She saw his mouth moving silently as he stood like that for a few moments. Finally, he straightened and stepped back to the mayor and sheriff.

"I'm to blame," he said resolutely. "She wouldn't have felt she needed to steal if I were a better provider. The crime requires ten lashes. We all seem to be men of justice here. Your book doesn't explicitly state that the thief has to be the one whipped. It just says that the judgement must be ten lashes."

"Well, who else would suffer for a crime?" the sheriff asked. "What are you saying?"

"You know . . ." The mayor studied his book. "He's right, actually. I wonder if we should amend this for clarity. No one's ever noticed that before."

"I'll take the lashes," Levi said. "That way, she's not further harmed by your system, and the law is satisfied. Most of this is for the crowd, anyway, right?"

"How dare you accuse us of crowd-pleasing!" the mayor huffed and slammed his book closed.

"I'm not whipping you!" The sheriff looked at the mayor. "I'm not whipping him. And he's right. She's in no shape to be whipped. That kind of punishment could mean her death. We don't kill people for stealing in this town."

"You're the sheriff!" The mayor jabbed his finger into Mitchell's chest. "Maybe he's right. Maybe this is for the crowd. If the law isn't followed here, this book and city charter are a joke. We have to uphold the law, Mitchell. You must! Even when it's ugly, Sheriff."

"Unlock her arms," Levi said. "I'll take her place. It's okay, pal. Just do it."

Lena gasped with relief as the sheriff unlocked her wrists, but her shame wasn't lessened when she looked up at Levi's face. His gaze wasn't meeting hers.

"Levi?" Nathan pushed his way through the crowd and up to the steel tower. His rifle was held ready to fire. "Wanna tell me what's going on here?"

"As my dad would say, we got ourselves in a pickle." Levi nodded at Mitchell. "But the sheriff is a man of justice and he's going to square it. Right, Sheriff?"

"I'm not whipping an innocent man!" The sheriff shook his head.

"Don't think of it as whipping an innocent man. You're satisfying the requirements of the law. That way, everyone's happy."

"I'm not happy!" Nathan pressed up to Levi. "Is this some sort of joke?"

"Hold Lena back. And pray for me." Levi set his pack at Nathan's feet, then took off his coat and shirt. He placed the rest of his belongings at Lena's feet as she clung to Nathan. "We'll leave right afterwards, so be ready."

"Aah!" Lena reached for Levi, but he turned away.

Shirtless, Levi walked in an arc, surveying the people. Lena guessed he could see their hunger for blood better than anyone since he was the tallest in the park. Then, he walked up to the steel frame, spread his arms above him to grip the structure, and widened his stance.

The sheriff approached with the handcuffs.

"You won't need those, Sheriff," Levi said. "This is voluntary, remember?"

"Levi?" Nathan called, his voice shaky. "I don't like this! Tell me to stop it and I will!"

Lena's fingers dug into Nathan's coat, hating every second she witnessed Levi's cursed heroism, but she was too shocked to look away. This wasn't fair to Levi. But she knew it was fair, somehow, to satisfy the law and the people.

"Ten, Sheriff," the mayor voiced sternly. "We're all watching."

Mitchell stood a few feet behind and to the side of Levi. He flipped the whip and it uncoiled along the pavement in front of the park ride called the Dominator. Lena watched Levi's back muscles tighten as he inhaled, then he exhaled, relaxed, and held it.

The sheriff's arm swung, and Lena jerked against Nathan at the mere sound of the whip. Then it struck flesh, and that sound was even worse.

"One!" the mayor called out, relishing the moment.

The crowd mumbled, and Lena gazed at them, the gratification on their faces, especially the merchant named Adkins. He wasn't looking at her, but at Levi's agony.

The whip slashed again.

"Two!"

Already, the strip of raised skin from the first lash reddened, and the second lash ripped open the tender skin where it crossed with the first stripe. Levi arched his back, then relaxed in time for the third and fourth lashes.

"Aah!" Lena cried out, meaning to say to Levi she was sorry, but she could never express her sorrow now or ever again, not in a way that would remove the stripes and scars he would have permanently on his back.

"Quiet. It won't help him now." Nathan hushed her, then prayed softly. "Lord, please help him."

The last two lashes appeared to hurt the sheriff as much as they broke Levi. After ten lashes, Levi lost his grip on the steel tower, and he fell to one knee. His back was bleeding, his skin split open to reveal the healthy muscle beneath. Lena had been to a hundred executions, but never a lashing like this. She didn't know if she should go to him or not.

Levi rose shakily to his feet and turned slowly. The crowd was silent. Fury, sweat, and tears were on his face, but his eyes were downcast. His first couple of steps toward Nathan appeared to take all of his concentration. He held out his hand.

"Shirt," he said haltingly.

Lena bent down, picked up his shirt, and handed it to him. He took it, pushed his arms through, then tugged it over his head. The movement made him gasp.

From there, he bent and picked up his coat, and looped his rifle sling over his shoulder. He held his pack in his arms.

"We're leaving this place." Levi walked up to the sheriff, who still stood with the whip in his hand, his head bowed. "It wasn't your fault. It's finished now. We leave it in God's hands."

As Levi started away, the sheriff dropped the whip and fell to his knees. Nathan pulled Lena forward, following Levi as the silent crowd parted for them.

Lena wailed, walking next to Nathan. The noise from her throat didn't sound human even to her own ears. She wanted to die, but she couldn't now. Levi had just bought her life from the law of Allentown's charter.

She owed him everything. Even though she was guilty as sin, she had witnessed the whole thing as he had redeemed her life with his own! In that moment, as they returned to the interstate in pursuit of Jenna Dowler and Chen Li, Lena vowed never to disappoint Levi ever again. She couldn't. He was her savior.

Chapter Six

The pack horse nuzzled Shaker's back as he stood at the head of Queen Street in Martinsburg, West Virginia, eyeing the town and inhabitants.

"Welcome to Martinsburg!" A man in a straw hat waved as he passed by.

Shaker could hear his fellow travelers draw up behind him. They were noisily chomping on apples they'd picked from the orchard where they'd left the interstate. The group had been making good time, moving into the South where Shaker had run regular scouting trips for the Federation and trading excursions for himself. But now, here was Martinsburg.

"What's wrong, Shaker?" asked the new man named Brian. "You know this area, right?"

Hesitating with his answer, Shaker didn't trust this new man. He was the only one besides himself who carried a firearm, though the rifle looked to be a hundred years old.

"I've been through Martinsburg a dozen times," Shaker said. "It's always been empty, though. Now, there's all these people."

Lisbon pulled his wheelbarrow until he was even with Shaker. The old iron worker was Shaker's only friend, he thought, though he still preferred his horse over any fellow traveler. As near as Shaker could tell, Lisbon didn't care that he'd kidnapped more female companions to sell in Erwin—particularly Jenna. Lisbon only cared about Lisbon.

"I don't want to stay here," Lisbon said quietly to Shaker. "You?"

Shaker glanced at his horse, piled high with merchandise to sell, then turned and studied with a critical eye the rest of his band. Fools, all of them, but not to be underestimated. They were fools because they had no idea what was in his heart. He led them every day, and every day they traipsed ignorantly behind him. And every mile they walked, it was a mile closer to the place he would sell them, kill them, or leave them empty-handed after he stripped them of everything they owned.

All except Lisbon, who would return north with him, and Jenna, who he'd leave alive to sell. He hadn't really made up his mind about Tyra Hayes. She was on the downhill side of fifty, and if any merchants heard her talk, they'd realize she'd be as useless as the ridiculous trinkets on shoestrings hanging around her neck.

His eyes went to Dusty Thomas, the man who still carried the broken wall clock after a hundred miles. The man in his seventies lowered his eyes under Shaker's gaze.

"I'm not a conversationalist," Dusty said.

"That's okay, Dusty," Shaker said. "We don't need to have a conversation. I'm just looking us over, wondering how all these people see us. Maybe they're friendly, maybe they're not, but we're done-in for the day."

The man who'd introduced himself and his dog as Runner walked up from a side street. The young man with the empty crossbow and sharpened tomahawk was always scouting around. Twice, he'd seen Runner throw his tomahawk at squirrels, and his Labrador had fetched them, the critters cut in two by the little weapon.

Runner patted Shaker's horse casually, but Shaker had learned to read the tracker. Everything Runner did, he did with purpose, wariness, and intent.

"They're waiting to kill us," Runner said loud enough for only their band to hear. "About two blocks up, there's forty people with handheld weapons, waiting behind a barricade. The street ahead is red with the blood of other travelers they've already killed before us."

"Why didn't they kill you?" Shaker asked.

"I was behind them, so they didn't see me. Then I climbed onto the courthouse to look around. They're waiting all right."

Brian shifted his rifle, as if to take it off his shoulder.

"Act natural!" Shaker ordered them all. He cared for none of them, but they were vital to his journey. Even Dusty's foolishness with his clock helped him. They'd joined him for safety—and he'd let them join him to make himself appear as a simple trader. They used each other, but he'd have the final say about their lives. "We were turning here anyway. Stay close. Night is coming."

Leading his party to the left, Shaker headed down a dust-covered street away from Queen Street.

"You're acting a little too casual for someone who knows these people want to kill us," Brian said.

Shaker didn't respond. He loved it when people misread him, thinking he was calm, gentle, and harmless. Hidden under his coat was his fully automatic handgun, which had taken the lives of countless pilgrims, all of them thinking he was an insignificant merchant too weak to defend himself or his goods.

Minutes later, they reached the train station and its warehouses. One giant building beside the tracks was round, two-tiered, and iron-framed. He and Lisbon had camped inside its wide space several times before, and he was glad to see that the windows and doors were still intact, regardless of all the new inhabitants in town. Since they couldn't continue in the darkness, and they were too weary to travel, there was no safer place than the station.

As Lisbon led the others inside, Shaker waited by the tall train door. Moments later, using chains and counterweights, Lisbon and Brian opened the train door, just high enough for Shaker to lead his horse inside. The men let the train door slam shut, and Shaker led his mare to the center of the large room where old black railing still stood from the days when roundhouse engineers transferred train cars and locomotives to other tracks. Leaving his horse there hitched to the railing, he joined Runner at one of the tall windows that faced west.

"It's a defendable structure," Runner said, nodding. "Windows all around. No one can sneak up. And you can't burn the place down since the roof is metal. But Runner and I aren't staying in here. We'll be outside. I'll see you on the interstate tomorrow."

Shaker didn't stop the young man from leaving. That was one of his tactics for keeping people close. He controlled those around him with minimal effort, letting them think they had free reign, but really, he merely waited until their guard was down. The tomahawk and crossbow Runner carried would each fetch him a small bag of beans for himself or oats for his horse.

He turned from the window and unloaded his horse, setting the three packs on the plank floor. Nearby and against the wall, Chen Li and Jenna set their bedrolls and packs next to Tyra Hayes and her father, who was accurately sharing useless trivia about the Shenandoah Valley and how Martinsburg had established the state's first post office. Sometimes the crazy man had something valuable to say, but most of the time, Shaker simply ignored him.

Lisbon showed Brian where there was a stash of firewood below the track platform, and the two hauled up several armfuls for the night. Shaker set out beans and rice and dehydrated vegetables for dinner, and the others crowded around as the fire crackled to life.

Chen Li cooked, as she'd taken to doing, and Shaker leaned back on one of the horse packs to watch his band. Jenna was talking with Tyra about her God again, and Dusty was listening, though if anyone noticed, he'd declare he wasn't a conversationalist.

The windows revealed the glow of the moon. After they ate, they wiggled their stocking feet at the fire and checked their boots for another day of walking. Shaker used nylon thread to sew a new sole onto a spare pair of boots. He worked slowly by the light of the fire, but it was Jenna and Brian he was really studying.

Brian had been with them for three days, and not once had the newcomer conversed with anyone but Runner, as if the rifleman was intentionally avoiding the others. It wasn't natural, especially for a man who'd chosen to join them rather than travel alone. He had eyes like a fox—careful, studious. Shaker wasn't fooled by the man's old rifle. He wore an ammunition jacket with customized factory-loaded cartridges, and he probably knew how to use them.

As Shaker fell asleep that night, his back to the fire, his mind was dwelling on Jenna—blind and beautiful. Even after he'd threatened her and Chen Li, she hadn't spoken a harsh word to him. Yes, she'd make some Southerner a fine wife someday. If he found the right buyer, he might even manage another horse out of the transaction!

Brian Steelman lay against the wall, far from the dwindling fire near the middle of the Martinsburg roundhouse where Shaker, Lisbon, Dusty, and Al Hayes had gathered. Jenna, Chen Li, and Tyra had opted to bed down away from the fire against the outer wall, and Brian saw this as an invitation to approach Jenna and Chen Li when the time was right.

He'd steered clear of both women for three days because he didn't want them to react awkwardly or excitedly in front of Shaker or Runner. And Lisbon, who seemed so innocent pulling his wheelbarrow, was anything but innocent. Brian had witnessed the Portuguese man briefing Shaker about the others, keeping the leader informed. There was much more to Shaker than he tried to display, Brian realized, just as Runner had warned him.

For a few minutes, Brian watched the tall windows of the roundhouse. Shaker didn't seem too concerned about the townspeople attacking, but Brian was sleeping with his rifle in hand.

Suddenly, Brian sensed shadows moving beyond the glass, maybe people spying on the new visitors in town. Runner had said they carried hand weapons, so Shaker was probably counting on the people outside not attacking since Brian openly carried a rifle.

Soundlessly, he sat up in the dark. The fire in the middle of the room had died out and no longer lit up the building interior. Only barely glowing coals remained. He guessed he could stealthily reach the women in his stocking feet. Unless he stepped on a squeaky board—he hadn't thought of that! Shaker's back had been toward him before the fire had died out. But Shaker wasn't his only concern. Lisbon was every bit a rat.

He rose to his feet, crouching low. Just then, a body unexpectedly collided with him! In an instant, he knew it was either Jenna or Chen Li. Although he hadn't been certain if Chen Li had recognized him, he knew that Jenna had recognized his voice that first day.

The collision of the woman's body against his own both tripped her and knocked him backwards. In an effort to make no sound, he pulled the woman into a tight embrace and rolled onto his back on his bedroll.

For several breathless seconds, he and his burden remained still, holding one another, praying their soft noises hadn't alarmed anyone. Whoever this was, she'd had the same idea as he had—to finally talk. In previous camps on the road, they hadn't felt safe from wary eyes. Runner was so unpredictable!

No one around the dark campfire seemed to stir. Brian eased his hold on the woman to let her up, but instead, he felt her hands on his face, reading him as only a blind person would do. She'd done the same in her father's print shop in Manhattan when Jenna had touched his face and spoken of hope and peace.

"It's really you!" she whispered so lightly, the sound was barely a breath in his ear. "Did my father send you? Is Luigi here, too? As soon as I heard your voice, I knew we weren't alone!"

Brian felt her arms against him, needing his reassurance. No doubt, in her blindness, with only Chen Li to rely on, Jenna had been forced to accept whatever situation unfolded. But no longer.

"We can't talk long," he breathed back, her hair in his face. He hadn't been close to many women, but right then, no other woman mattered. Only Jenna's safety and care were his concern. "There are things I need to tell you. I know you can receive what I must say. You're Radiant Shade, after all."

"What is it? My father?"

"I'm sorry, Jenna, but he died that night in New York, in Nathan's arms. Chloe told me at the warehouse. Lena shot him."

"Lena?"

"But she was killed a couple days later, Runner told me. He's here to use you to ambush and kill Levi and Nathan, who're behind us just a day or two."

He felt her pause, breathing against his face, taking in everything.

"Where's Luigi?" she asked. "Did he get away?"

"The day after the battle over the Bowery, he disappeared from Bruno's warehouse. Nathan and Levi left the same morning to find you and Chen Li."

"Who sent you?"

"It must've been God." He chuckled silently. "After a gun battle in New Jersey, I was wounded and left for dead. I came south to find this route west since I'd used it two years ago. Finding you was by accident. Like I said—it must've been God."

"Yes, it's no accident."

Jenna lay in silence for a few moments. Brian never wanted to move again, not with her in his arms!

"Does Chen Li know about me?" he asked.

"I haven't told her. During the day, I can never tell when we're truly alone."

"You need to know that Shaker wants to sell you for a profit in Tennessee, maybe the others, too."

"Yes, I know."

"Human trafficking is a big market in the Plains Zone."

"What's your plan?" she asked.

"I was sort of waiting for Levi and Nathan to catch up, then keep you safe while they all fight it out."

"It's too risky. You need to control the offensive. Brian, you need to act before that. Shaker and Runner—"

"And Lisbon."

"Yes. Chen Li had a tranq-pen, but Runner took it from her. How are you armed?"

"An old bolt-action, and a vest full of gel-tranqs."

"Gel-tranqs?" she drew back, then eased closer again. "Then what are you waiting for?"

"Runner's too sneaky. Colonel Rotham sent him for you and Levi."

"Of course. The Federation still wants Radiant Shade."

"It's personal."

"Then we deal with Shaker and Lisbon when Runner's not around," she said. "Give me a gel-tranq. With enough force, they work the same as a tranq-pen. Okay. When Runner isn't around tomorrow, you say, 'I wonder what today's date is.' That's our signal. I'll get close to Lisbon, then, and tranq him. And you tranq Shaker."

"You're sure? Lisbon's a big guy."

"And I'm a grown woman. I'll take care of it. Then we'll disarm both men and leave them with their gear and no horse."

"Then there's Runner and his dog."

"We'll deal with them when we have to. We need Levi and Nathan with us. No one'll try anything with you three together."

"Okay. Um, it's not much of a plan."

"The Lord handles the details when we trust Him with our whole heart."

"Where've you been my whole life?"

He said it without thinking. Immediately, he regretted revealing his affections, even vaguely, but as her silence continued without her pulling away, he hoped he hadn't made her as uncomfortable as he'd feared.

"I can't believe my dad's gone." She sighed. "I was hoping he'd be around the next corner, standing with Luigi, rescuing us from Shaker's plans."

"Sorry. You'll have to settle for me."

"Oh, I'm not disappointed. I'd heard you'd come to your senses since we last talked in the print shop."

"You remember."

"Of course. My father said you later found the peace of God while in the tunnels with Luigi and Scooter."

"Yes, as you said, I came to my senses. Even a stubborn man can be taught humility."

"You're going to live in glory with our Lord. Nothing else matters."

"This moment with you feels like it matters."

"I'm grateful you're here, Brian, because you're someone safe. But I can't imagine anything else right now."

"Right. I understand." He hoped his sudden feelings of defeat weren't conveyed through his whisper, or through his arms around her.

"Don't be angry."

"I'm not."

"Since I was a child, I was trained to care for others. I don't know what to think of someone who . . . you know."

"Who loves you?"

"You don't even know me, Brian. You can't love me."

"I know all about you. The last three days, being with you but ignoring you, has been torture."

"Please, Brian, not now. We can talk more later, when we're on the road together, safe. Remember the signal tomorrow."

"Got it."

He expected her to leave, but she remained, despite the danger of them being found out as co-conspirators.

"I'm sorry I'm treating you as an asset," she said. "It's the only thing I know."

Then, she was up and out of his arms, moving unseen and unheard through the dark room. Brian stared after her, feeling foolish, blaming God a little for giving him a new heart of compassion as well as . . . a mouth that stumbled in love.

Love? Did he really love her? Of course, she was right. They didn't even know one another. And worse, she knew all about him, his past. She had to. She was Radiant Shade. He had executed Christians who'd been in her network. How could she ever love someone who'd killed her friends?

He lay back on his bedroll. His affections wouldn't be returned. It was something he hadn't imagined before his heart had been shared, but now he saw that it was the only way. The sooner he could part ways from the people who knew about him as an Enforcer, the better. So, he was only an asset to the woman who'd been in his arms. A boy with a crush—that's all it was. And to even think that God intended him to be loved by someone like her . . .

Colonel Milo Rotham hid behind his command vehicle as machine gunfire peppered the armor. He cursed as a rocket-propelled grenade hissed across the field and struck one of the five Humvees in his company. The heavy vehicle flipped through the air as if a giant had flicked it like a toy. It landed on its roof, crushing one soldier who'd been hiding behind it for cover. The man didn't even have time to scream. He was already dead.

Braving the shooters across the field, Rotham stepped from his cover and fired his sidearm at the rocket launchers. Two men were hustling to reload their tube. Rotham knew they were out of range of his pistol, but he just wanted to slow down their process some.

His other soldiers sprayed bullets at the attackers. Rotham ignored everything else for a moment and focused on crossing the ditch beside the road. When he came up the other side, he emptied his handgun at the rocket launchers, then holstered it. He couldn't lose any more vehicles to this bunch!

Close enough now, he drew the shotgun off his back. It contained five shells, and he started blasting. By the time he reached the last two shells, he was nearly upon them, so he cut them down. With a snarl, he kicked at the RPG tube, but it had been damaged by his own assault, so he couldn't claim it for his own.

When he looked around, he found with satisfaction that a dozen of his boldest soldiers had advanced toward the enemy with him. He'd merely been trying to take out the rocket launcher, but his push had been their inspiration. The enemy was now fleeing across the field two hundred yards away!

Standing in the battlefield, he reloaded his sidearm and shotgun, then picked over the two dead bodies for anything of value.

"I don't think those were the Casperteins," Sergeant Ibojka said as he skirted a hedge and approached the colonel.

Rotham knew the hundred-plus refugees from New York weren't all named Caspertein, but they'd labeled the group as such, and the label gave his soldiers a target.

"I agree." Rotham waved his people back toward the interstate. "The Casperteins wouldn't use lethal force, either. It's against their religion."

He meant it as mockery, but it came out sounding like respect in his ears.

"Who knows who these people were?" Ibojka cursed as he tried to jump the ditch, but his bulk was too great and the ground too soft. He slipped up to his knees in sludge at the bottom of the ditch. "If they would've talked to us before they started shooting, we could've told them we weren't after anyone but the Casperteins."

"They won't listen." Rotham gave his hand to his sergeant and pulled him to dry land. "This is the Plains Zone. We've read reports from scouts. Every time these towns see a convoy like ours, they think we're after their resources."

"I doubt anyone's seen a convoy like ours." Ibojka stomped his muddy boots, then gazed at their vehicles. "All that firepower, and all they did was tip over a Humvee."

"A Humvee we couldn't spare, Ibojka." Rotham clapped another soldier on the back as he passed. "The longer we're out here, the harder it'll be to come away with success from these little skirmishes with the locals. But we can't return in defeat to the Federation. We just can't!"

"Look!" Ibojka pointed south as two of their scout vehicles returned to the Lock Haven position in Central Pennsylvania. "They're coming in as if something has happened!"

Rotham glanced at their two dead and several wounded from the brief battle, then moved with Ibojka to greet the two arriving vehicles. They surely needed some good news. Combing the countryside for the Casperteins had been fruitless for four days. Their supplies wouldn't last much longer.

The two vehicles lurched onto the interstate and screeched to a halt in front of Rotham. The men piled out, dragging a prisoner with them. At the most, Rotham guessed his men had captured someone who had intel for him, maybe about a weapons cache, a fuel depot, or the Casperteins' whereabouts. He didn't expect to recognize the prisoner.

They threw the captive at Rotham's feet. It was a man with shaggy hair and a torn coat. His right leg had been shot through the thigh. The prisoner shifted to his side, clutching his unbandaged wound while panting and whimpering.

Rotham crouched and looked into the man's face.

"Owen Travers. Well, this is fitting." Rotham chuckled. "The same man who killed your sister is about to kill you."

He watched Owen's eyes as he seemed to set aside his pain, and fear gripped him more fiercely. Like a rabbit at the mercy of a fox, the ex-Enforcer shrunk back against the pavement.

"Do you think we should tell him?" Ibojka joked loudly in front of Owen. "He didn't need to run away from New York at all. His sister didn't last two days. All he had to do was wait out the wildcat."

"Lena's dead?" Owen's chin lifted a little, but his face still reflected the pain from his leg. "We're not enemies, Rotham. I remember you from Philly. I only ran because of Lena. I'm lucky you found me."

"Found you?" Rotham cursed and looked at his scouts for a report.

"We found him east of Bellefonte," the soldier briefed. "He and another male were crossing a field, moving south. The other was a big guy, balding. They returned fire with this weapon, but the other fellow got away."

Rotham took a compact battle rifle from another soldier who offered it. He recognized the weapon as one the Casperteins had used to invade and burn Philadelphia up to his doorstep. It was a .308 rifle, and none of his men had ammunition for it, but he knew it was a powerful weapon in the right hands.

"Where are they?" Rotham asked, hanging the rifle over his shoulder.

"Who?" Owen grimaced. "My leg. Patch me up, Colonel, and I'll tell you anything you want to know."

"I never liked you, Travers," Rotham said. "You don't get treatment for free. You've got to earn it. Where are they?"

"Who?"

"Who do you think?" Ibojka kicked the foot of the man's wounded leg. "You think we're on a field trip out here? The Casperteins! Talk, now!"

"The Casperteins?" Owen cried in pain. 'Obrador and I left them back at Lewisburg. They were camping about a mile north of the interstate. I swear it. We haven't seen them for almost three days."

"What do you mean you left them?" Rotham cocked his head. "You would've been safer out here by staying with them. Why would you leave them?"

"We just did, okay? My leg. Come on, Rotham . . ."

"You left them because you did something to them, didn't you? You coward!"

Anger rose in Rotham's chest, then he felt it rising to his neck. When it reached his eyes, he turned away and disguised wiping at tears in his eyes by touching his forehead, as if he were sweating in the spring sunshine.

"What're you thinking?" Ibojka joined his side. "Obrador's out there alone?"

"I'm thinking you and I have wasted our skills hunting the Federation's garbage for ten years. Now we finally come face to face with a worthy adversary, and Owen and Obrador are in the middle of it, complicating things."

"I don't . . . understand, Colonel. Catching Owen is a potential lead on the Casperteins."

"The Casperteins wouldn't just give Owen one of their guns. He did something. Get it out of him. I want every detail. Then leave his body in the ditch that you fell into."

"With pleasure."

Entering his command vehicle, Rotham decided to change his socks. In an old book he'd read as a youth, he remembered that infantry soldiers needed to protect their feet above all else. In the back of the bus, where his private bunk was situated, he untied his boots and slipped off his socks. It was then that he noticed his hands were shaking, and he admitted that this mission was causing a wreck of his emotions. One minute, he was in a gunfight, and the next, he was tearing up from anger over his enemy being taken advantage of!

In a fit of rage, he threw one of his boots against the back wall. It crashed into a box of rifle cartridges, knocking them onto the floor.

A scream from outside made him pause. Ibojka was torturing Owen for information. Field interrogations could be particularly gruesome, but Rotham saw no way around it. They needed information and fast. Besides, Owen had always been a viper. He'd done something against the Casperteins. Why else would he and Obrador be all alone out there with one of the battle rifles?

Rotham eyed the compact rifle on his bunk. He wouldn't hesitate to kill any Caspertein he found, but not because they were Christians or weak. More than anyone else, Rotham knew the Casperteins to be a sturdy foe. That Levi Caspertein—now there was a warrior! It was hard not to envy the man, a skilled survivalist and hero of his people. And Owen had gotten in the way!

He hefted the battle rifle, imagining himself trekking across the Plains Zone, surviving on his wits and non-lethal ammunition as Levi had done for perhaps years. What stories the man must have!

There was a knock on his door. He opened it to find Ibojka, a knife in his fist.

"Well?" Rotham asked.

"You were right. Travers killed Levi Caspertein's wife and took the rifle, him and Obrador."

"Caspertein's wife? He just murdered her?"

"Sounds like it. But Levi's not with the main group. He and Nathan Isaacson, a Federation lieutenant, are out searching for Chen Li and Radiant Shade, like we suspected, somewhere in the southeast."

"So, we're not even chasing who we want to chase." Rotham shook his head. "We're still cleaning up Lena's mess—Owen and Obrador."

"It's a soldier's job, Colonel. We clean up messes."

"Soldiers." Rotham tossed the battle rifle onto his bunk as Ibojka stepped farther into the bus. "Radiant Shade is a blind woman I sent that bounty hunter after, and we're out here torturing a coward for information about a bunch of women and children."

"It's not much different than the rest of our career the last few years." Ibojka was quiet for a moment, then continued. "Well, Obrador is still out there. We at least have to get him."

"Owen really killed Levi's wife?"

"Some woman named Lyla."

"Lyla." Rotham sighed. "What else? Are we near the Casperteins?"

"He says they travel at night up the freeway. During the day, they camp out of sight behind some cover."

"No wonder we never see them. They're sleeping during the day."

"They're led by a big guy named Rex Caspertein."

"Big, is right. Remember him from Philly?"

"And Chloe's with them."

"Chloe, Nathan Isaacson, Radiant Shade . . . These are names I grew up hearing about, Ibojka. Now we're hunting them like dogs."

"We're bringing closure to the old administration for the New Federation."

"It's closure for us all." Rotham glanced up. "Any word on the radio from Runner?"

"Nothing's been relayed. You have much faith in a bounty hunter who isn't Citizen Army?"

"I looked into that kid's eyes. He's a killer. He'll find Radiant Shade and finish on his end what we sent him to do. The question is, will we finish what we were sent to do out here?"

"How do you want to find the Casperteins now?" Ibojka wiped his knife on his pant leg and sheathed it. "They walk in the dark and hide in the light."

"They haven't gotten past us, and now we know they stay close to the interstate." Rotham raised a finger to point at his trusted man. "But we'll go on foot now. The Casperteins may not kill us, but they'll take out our trucks without blinking, using their acid rounds. And I won't be caught out here without our trucks!"

"Foot patrols it is."

"And one more thing."

"Yeah?"

"Spread the word—dignity."

"Dignity?" Ibojka frowned. "For the enemy? I've got to ask, why now?"

"I have my reasons. Owen is gone?"

"He's in the ditch."

"When we kill the Casperteins, they deserve better than the ditch. Understand? We give them better than Owen gave Lyla Caspertein."

"Yes, sir. I'll pass the word."

"But if we find Obrador—I mean *when* we do—we put him down like Owen."

"You're not alone, Colonel. I mean, the way you have mixed feelings about these people. We're the baddest military unit this country has seen in twenty years, and we can't find a bunch of Christian civilians? They're surviving while we're fighting for our lives. It's hard not to admire them a little bit."

"For years, I didn't. But I guess I'm beginning to. Or maybe I'm just already missing the hunt that I know is about to end. We'll get them now. We know their tactics. I want to lead one of the hunting parties on foot myself tonight. The trucks can follow. Bury our dead and tell everyone we have another battle to fight. Just one more."

Alice Prine allowed her tears to flow as she crept through the darkness. In such low visibility with only starlight to illuminate the countryside, she relied on her ears more than her eyes to sense for danger ahead.

This was the second night that Rex had instructed her to lead them through the fields and forests of Pennsylvania, instead of on the interstate, since the Federation was almost certain to be combing the area eastward. Thus, walking was slower over the terrain. But slower was better than dead, Alice thought.

Her grief continued to distract her that night. Even though Lyla Caspertein had been laid to rest three evenings previous, Alice couldn't let her go. She'd been Lyla's closest friend, besides Levi, who wasn't present. He could even be dead, too, she realized, and that burdened her heart more. The world would be a worse place without the Casperteins. However, it might've been to Levi's benefit if he were dead, so he wouldn't have to hear the sad news about his wife. It was all too terrible to think about.

The one person Alice felt she could now most relate to was Rex, and Rex was busy trying to lead a people he hadn't planned on leading. What a shock for the young man, she thought, since he'd merely joined Levi for an adventure, yet had needed to replace his cousin as the shepherd of the Lord's people.

Alice ascended a small rise next to the interstate and stopped to listen to the night. She was surveying the landscape when she heard men's voices ahead.

Withdrawing from the rise, she shifted her staff to hold in the stump of her left arm and took her radio in her right hand. On the transmit button, she clicked the squelch button twice, then twice more, querying Rex.

Rex responded with the same response.

Then, she clicked it two more times, and stopped. It was the code for "negative." She imagined Rex drawing up all the people about a half-mile behind her to wait for the all-clear.

Without waiting to find out who or how many were ahead of her, Alice cut to the north. It could only be the Federation hunters out there led by someone she'd come across in Philadelphia named Colonel Rotham. He was closing the net on the refugees, certainly searching for Chloe, Obrador, and Jenna, but it was up to Alice to misdirect the hunters.

She planted one booted foot on top of the interstate guard rail and leaped onto the pavement. A moment later, she was across the lanes and into the foliage on the north side. There, she ran recklessly, darting left and right as she sensed stumps or bushes that might impede her flight.

Minutes later, she halted and listened wide-eyed. No longer did she weep tears of grief. Now, she was living her calling, to endanger herself for her people, Levi's people, God's people. If she died for them, it would be a worthy death. And since Levi had led her to Christ, and she had been growing in the truth of the power of His resurrection, she was unafraid of dying.

Raising her battle rifle, she aimed at the sky, and fired a short burst. After a few seconds, she fired again. The noise was deafening, roaring across the rolling hills of Pennsylvania.

A moment passed, and she saw headlamps and flashlights bobbing in the near distance. They were running toward her, hopefully all the soldiers that Rotham had with him.

Alice aimed at one cluster of flashlights and fired another short burst of gel-tranqs. But that was all the time she could spare. They'd be on her in sixty seconds if she didn't flee, using the darkness and their haste against them.

"It's working," Alice said into her radio. "Go for it, Rex, but quietly."

Then, she sprinted straight east. The flashlights were gaining on her, and she could hear their voices. Looking back, she saw the headlights of a couple vehicles cruising up the interstate, joining in the pursuit. It seemed they were buying the diversion so far—thinking someone in their number had stumbled upon the whole party of refugees.

In Alice's heart, she felt the dread of capture. The previous year, General Brogdon had captured and tortured her for information about Levi. But God's hand had prevailed, and Levi had rescued her without a shot being fired. She knew that Christians wouldn't always enjoy such victory in the world, but they could enjoy victory eternally when free from this world, and to this transcendent truth, Alice held to as tightly as she gripped her steel staff.

Splashing across a creek, she scrambled up a ravine and tripped into a thicket. After scratching her cheek on a sharp branch, narrowly missing her eye, she slowed her pace and looked back. Smiling, she saw the flashlights widespread, searching and disorganized. And they were all on the north side of the interstate now.

Before Rotham realized he'd been duped, she hoped Rex could hustle the people through the search pattern west, and across the land to the south. Otherwise, a large band of men, women, and children couldn't possibly evade an elite force like Rotham fielded.

For added security, Alice fired at a couple near flashlights, then ran off, zigzagging north now, drawing them away from the interstate and their vehicles. Soon, they'd give up, she hoped, or she'd be found on the landscape, visible in the daylight. Yet for now, she had the cover of darkness.

She wished Levi were there with her, enjoying the chase. And Lyla. Oh, she missed her Christian sister.

Chapter Seven

Off Interstate 81, southwest of Martinsburg, Andy "The Runner" Radner waited for Shaker and his party to catch up to him. Runner, his Labrador, continued to run circles around an acorn tree, unraveling the trail of a possum or squirrel, but Andy's eyes were on the treetops of the forest of Berkeley County, West Virginia. Sure, he'd never been this far from Wyoming, nor seen some of the wildlife and vegetation, but animals and humans behaved the same everywhere. He relied on birds that took flight to indicate when people were near. Deer were spooked when disturbed, or so he'd thought.

The night before, he'd chosen not to spend it with his companions inside the roundhouse. Instead, he'd investigated his back trail, confirming his suspicions that he was being tracked. And not by Levi Caspertein, it seemed.

Even as the Martinsburg population had prowled in the night, seeking a way into the roundhouse that wouldn't get them shot, Andy had scouted the town and nearby forest for evidence that he was being tailed. Of course, he knew Levi Caspertein, the deformed woman, and his large brown-haired friend were coming along after Jenna, but there was someone closer, Andy sensed, and he'd spent too many years hunting mountain lion and bear and deer in Wyoming not to depend on those instincts now. Someone was out there, but it was someone the wildlife didn't react to as often as Andy expected. It was as if whoever was out there was part of the forest, and the wildlife regarded him as part of nature as he moved through it. It was someone who *belonged.*

Even as Shaker and the others approached him on the freeway, birds took flight and squirrels chattered their agitation. However, the previous night, before the moon had set, Andy had glimpsed the form of a gaunt man, with no pack or weapon on him, moving across an open expanse outside Martinsburg. Three seconds later, he was gone. Silent, like a ghost. He was terrified that someone with such stealth seemed to be keeping pace with him, day after night.

Andy wondered if it could be the same man he'd seen on the bank of the Hudson so many days earlier, tracking Jenna. It seemed unlikely, since he'd been an old man, but who else could be out there? And who were they helping? Jenna Dowler couldn't possibly have more resources than he knew about. Levi was wily, but he was burdened by the deformed woman, and the last Andy had seen from a distance, she wasn't walking very quickly, though she was now out of the baby stroller.

"Anything to report?" Shaker waved friendlily at him as he drew even.

Glaring, Andy knew the trader only seemed calm and gentle, yet he was so much the predator. Once the man had served his purpose, guiding Jenna as bait for Levi to catch up, Andy would have to cross the trader once and for all. Jenna wasn't going up for sale in Erwin. The Federation wanted her gone.

"Nothing's happening," Andy reported. "The road's clear ahead, but keep your eyes open."

Dusty Thomas trudged behind Shaker and his horse, clutching his clock. Al Hayes and his crazy daughter Tyra were visiting with Chen Li and Jenna, and Lisbon and Brian brought up the rear. Andy nodded at Brian, seeing him as an ally only as far as the cautious man would keep Jenna from running, and help him put Shaker down when it was time. The old rifle Brian carried was probably less effective than other assault rifles available, but Andy wasn't going to argue with a man about his weapon preferences. After all, he had only a tomahawk in his arsenal since Levi had earlier taken the arrows from his crossbow.

"But I'll get 'em back," he mumbled, which caused Runner to lift her head and perk her ears. "Don't mind me, girl. Go track 'em!"

Runner put her nose to the forest floor and trotted off more vigorously on the hunt for Virginia's varmints.

As Shaker's group passed southwestward and out of sight, Andy withdrew into the shadows of the forest trees about forty yards. He didn't mind scouting on foot for enemies, but after a night on the move, he needed the rest. Waiting in ambush to see who was indeed closely trailing seemed to be time well-spent, so he sat down against a leafy tree, facing the interstate. Killing Levi wouldn't be this easy, he guessed, since it was daylight, but he wouldn't mind seeing the man again from a distance, measuring him, toying with him. Someone as crafty as Levi would probably even know what he was doing, but Andy didn't care. He'd kill him when it could be done safely, as someone with his skills was inclined to do, risking little.

After checking the morning shadows to measure the passing of time, he allowed his eyes to close. Birds chirped nearby, and he trusted Runner to reestablish contact with him every few minutes as she was prone to do, so he didn't expect to sleep long. After all, he wanted to catch up to Shaker by nightfall.

However, sometime later, he woke and blinked wearily, realizing he was no longer alone. His first moment of recognition was that the shadows had shifted and the sunlight was directly overhead now. That meant Runner hadn't checked on him or nuzzled him in a couple of hours!

And thirdly, the gaunt old man from the Hudson River stood against a tree, facing him, not ten feet away. Andy studied the man for weapons, but saw nothing, not even a backpack to carry his gear. He wore jeans and a flannel shirt. His skin was dark, his face Hispanic, but Andy had been only five when Pan-Day had struck, so he'd never learned the origins of different people groups. The man's boots were in good shape, the leather weathered and flexible, which attested to his silent stalking.

Andy turned his head, searching for Runner—or maybe her corpse—before he focused again on the dark eyes of the man in front of him. In ten years, Andy couldn't remember ever sleeping so soundly, or maybe this man was simply such a woodsman that he'd approached without himself or Runner detecting him. Not even the birds or squirrels had sensed anything amiss.

"My dog?"

The man didn't speak or move. He didn't even blink. Andy tried to show a casual front as he looked around a little more, even adjusting his arm to feel his tomahawk on his belt. Ever since he was a child, he'd used the tomahawk to kill game, chop wood, and build shelters. As easily as lifting his arm, he could draw the weapon, and as naturally as exhaling, he could hurl it at this stranger.

The minutes passed, and Andy began to worry. Why the wait? As a youth, he'd learned that patience was the hunter's first virtue. He could discipline himself to be patient, but his adoptive father had warned him that patience didn't seem to be one of his natural attributes. Eventually, that impatience had led him to leave River Camp, his family's settlement. Impatience and ambition. His father couldn't hold him back from exploring the world around him, finally! And it turned out Andy had deadly skills certain cold-blooded people sought to employ.

Except lately, his skills didn't seem to be adequate. How could an old man sneak up on him like this?

When Andy shifted his leg, he saw the gaunt stranger tense his right arm. His thumb was hooked inside his belt. As a hunter, Andy relied on the details to tell him the whole story, so his eyes didn't miss what appeared to be shards of glass on the man's belt buckle. This was the prowler's weapon? His belt loops appeared slack, loose enough to draw the belt perhaps more quickly than Andy could throw his tomahawk.

"How long are we going to—?"

"Quiet," the stranger hushed.

With clenched teeth, Andy bristled. He'd never appreciated his elders telling him what to do in River Camp, and he certainly didn't like it out here in this forsaken land.

Then he noticed movement beyond the trees on the interstate. Not until the party was in full sight did Andy recognize Levi in the rear, the deformed woman in the middle, and Levi's friend leading the party. The deformed woman's gait had improved. They were making good time, sure to catch Shaker by the following evening since they were just a half-day behind.

Andy glanced at the stranger in front of him. The man didn't turn his head to look at the three travelers, as if he'd been waiting for them all along. Suddenly, Andy narrowed his eyes, understanding more. This old man was a hunter, too! Maybe Colonel Rotham had hired more than one bounty hunter to kill Levi and Jenna. This man was his competition!

"We can work together," Andy said quietly.

Levi and the two others walked out of sight, oblivious to their observers.

"I work alone," the stranger said.

"So do I, normally," Andy said, wondering if he could distract the man enough through conversation to attack him. "Seeing we're after the same prize, we'd be safer to move together. We can finish the job and part ways. We both win."

"Who loses?" The man's eyes widened, his amusement read by Andy as interest.

"Jenna and Levi, of course. I don't care about the others."

"So, the Federation sent you to kill them?" The man scoffed. "I wasn't sure, but now I understand. Your mission is over, boy. Go home."

Andy's chin trembled. *Boy?* Who *was* this over-confident—?

"Aren't you after them? You're hunting them the same as I am."

"You track to harm. I track to protect. We're not the same. Your journey ends here. If you continue, you'll meet only disappointment."

"I go where I want. No one tells me where to go or what to do."

"I once thought that, too. Then I met Corban Dowler."

"Dowler? A relative of Jenna's?"

"Yes. Her father, whom I was sworn to kill, as you've sworn to kill Jenna."

"I'll do it, too. I've never failed."

"Nor had I before Corban Dowler. Through him, I learned that my determination was inconsequential against the protective hand of the Lord God Almighty."

"What?" Andy gasped. "Don't tell me you're a Christian! I was raised with that stuff."

"Jenna is under God's watchful eye—until He wants to take her home."

"She's in Shaker's grip now. He's going to sell her to the highest bidder in Tennessee."

"We're a long way from Tennessee."

"And you're here to protect Levi as well?"

"Protect Levi? Levi Caspertein?" The stranger grinned, his teeth stained but straight. "You should know by now that no Caspertein needs any help protecting themselves, especially from someone like you."

"Levi's protected by God as well, you're telling me?"

"You're learning."

"Who's protecting you? If I have to kill you to get to Jenna, I will. I've killed many already."

"Not nearly as many as I have," the gaunt man said, "although it's the mark of a foolish and shameful man to say such a thing."

"I am where I am today because I'm not ashamed to kill."

"And where are you today? You're seated on the ground as your targets walk past you on the pavement. An ancient and weary skeleton of a man has shut your mouth and made you useless. That's where you are today, and you had best turn from this evil before God wearies of you altogether."

Andy felt the punch of the man's rebuke. He was better at killing, not talking. Where was Runner?"

"You're one of *them*, so you won't kill me."

"For once, you're right about something."

"I'm getting up now." Andy set his right hand on the ground. "You won't do anything to me?"

"I didn't say that." The stranger didn't move. "But I won't kill you."

Watching the man, especially the hand over the belt, Andy slowly climbed to his feet, his back still against the tree.

"I'm leaving now." Andy lowered his head, ready to draw his tomahawk, charge, and kill. "You won't stop me."

"How can you leave without that?"

The man didn't point with his hand, but with his gaze. Andy tilted his head up and saw, about twenty feet up the tree, his tomahawk stuck solidly into the bark. He reached for his belt, but there was nothing there. Sure enough, while he'd slept, Andy's weapon had been confiscated and tossed so high, it would take time and energy to climb and recover it.

"It doesn't matter. I'll still—"

Andy stopped talking—because there was no one there to talk to. The gaunt man had disappeared while his back was turned. Ignoring his tomahawk for a moment, Andy jogged toward the interstate, then studied the tree line to the left and right, listening, sensing. But there was no sound and no sight of the man. He'd vanished!

Returning to the tree, Andy studied how he might rig a simple harness around the tree to climb it, but his nerves were on edge. Days earlier, Levi had bested him in the night—without any warning. And now this old man had bested him in the daylight. After several years on his own, Andy had thought he was the top predator, that his stealth and craftiness went unrivaled. Now, in the span of two weeks, two different men, both much older than he, had made him look like a fool. An old man taking his tomahawk while he'd been sleeping was by far the most irritating of all!

While still considering a route up the tree, Runner padded up, dragging the back haunch of a dead deer. Andy had never struck his dog before, but he felt like it then.

"Traitor," he scolded her for only the second time in her young life, knowing the gaunt man must've baited her away from her master.

But Runner had also brought him a gift. The deer leg still had plenty of meat on it. From scouting around and now needing to retrieve his tomahawk, Andy figured he'd lost a half-day of travel. As he took the deer remnants from Runner to carve off some meat for himself to boil, he contemplated abandoning Jenna Dowler altogether. And Levi. Too many people knew about his activities now. He'd lost his advantage. Shaker could have Jenna, if he was dumb enough to try to fight Levi and the gaunt man for her. Not to mention the brown-haired companion traveling with Levi.

"We've always gotten our trophy," Andy said to Runner, who began to gnaw on the bone he'd returned to her. "So, we can't give up now. We have a reputation to uphold."

With that thought, Andy set his mind to thinking on how he might kill Levi and Jenna without being a part of her traveling party at all. Since he knew where they were going, he didn't even need to track them. He had only to get ahead of them and lay some sort of trap.

Swinging Runner's rarely-used leash around the tree, he fit it around his waist and started to climb. Before he was halfway up to his tomahawk, he heard a rifle shot drift over the tree tops. Even Runner below lifted her head from her meal of deer.

Andy tried to discern from which direction the gunshot had originated, but it was impossible with the trees all around. But that wasn't what crept up against his heart, trying to steal his breath. The gaunt man had said that God protected Levi and Jenna. What if that was true? Growing up in River Camp, Andy had heard the stories from the Bible about God's faithfulness to a people long dead and gone. He'd also heard stories about his father who had faced countless enemies sworn to kill him, yet he was still alive. If God wanted someone alive, they were immortal.

"I don't believe it!" Andy swore and cursed the last few shuffles up to his tomahawk. In a fit of fury, he tore the tomahawk out of the bark.

He wouldn't be intimidated. He wouldn't stop the hunt. He would kill his targets, whether God was involved or not!

That day, Brian Steelman waited until the afternoon before he readied himself to tranquilize Shaker as he and Jenna had planned the night before. For hours, he'd been hoping to catch sight of Runner coming or going, so he knew where the young hunter was, but not even his dog had been spotted. Whether Runner was within earshot or not, Brian guessed that Jenna was growing restless about him making his move.

At the back of the party of travelers, Brian took his rifle from his shoulder and chambered a gel-tranq. No one in the group looked back at him. He was still embarrassed about the night before with Jenna. She hadn't returned his affections, and that was beginning to make him wonder if he belonged at her side at all. Certainly, he needed to keep her safe from Shaker, but what about long term?

He thought of Rex Caspertein and Chloe Azmaveth somewhere far to the north as they headed straight west. They all had their sights set on Meeker, Colorado, but now Brian wasn't sure he would join them. Of course, he knew he would be welcomed as a fellow Christian, but as someone interested in courting Jenna, he'd already received a chill from her. As soon as he could do so privately, he wanted to search the New Testament he carried to see what God had to say about marriage and relationships. And prayer would help bring the mind of Christ into his dilemma, he decided. What was he supposed to do with the body of Christ now?

"I wonder what today's date is," he said loud enough for the whole group to hear him. He watched Jenna carefully for a reaction, but she made none. She was a pro. "What day of the week do you guys think it is?"

"Do you want to use my compass?" Tyra Hayes asked, turning to him.

Immediately, her father began to explain how the exact date could be figured out from the consistent movements of the stars.

"It feels like a Thursday," Chen Li offered to the group, which sparked everyone to make an observation about which day they felt it was.

Everyone but Shaker got engaged in the discussion. Even Dusty Thomas spoke quietly about it feeling like a Saturday, until he realized he was speaking aloud, and suddenly declared himself a non-conversationalist.

"Lisbon, let me pull with you for a while," Jenna said, her hand outstretched, reaching for the man.

With his harness over his shoulders, and without stopping, Lisbon guided her to walk in front of the wheelbarrow, and passed his second harness strap toward her. In some panic, Brian realized Jenna was already holding a gel-tranq cartridge, ready to spring her trap! Brian picked up his pace for a better angle on Shaker's back. He didn't want to risk hitting anyone else while trying to tranquilize Shaker. After all, with only the bolt-action rifle, he would have time for only one shot.

Jenna took the harness strap from Lisbon and looped it over her shoulder. Then, feeling with her empty hand, she latched onto Lisbon's arm. With more force than Brian thought necessary, she swung her other arm in a downward arc.

"Ow!" Lisbon cried out as he was jabbed with the gel-tranq.

Brian was still passing by the wheelbarrow when Lisbon crumpled to the pavement. Jenna stumbled awkwardly away from him, dragging the wheelbarrow with her. But Lisbon's strap tugged in the other direction, and the wheelbarrow tipped over.

As Shaker glanced back to see what the commotion was about, Brian swung his rifle to his shoulder and sidestepped once. He was shooting past Chen Li. As long as she didn't step into his view . . .

Shaker's gaze seemed to find Lisbon's fallen form, then an instant later, his eyes widened at the rifle aimed directly at him. Brian fired the shot. Chen Li screamed as the deafening muzzle blasted so near her head. Tyra covered her ears and shrunk to the pavement. Her father knelt protectively over her.

"I'm not a conversationalist!" Dusty stated, one hand holding his broken clock, the other raised in surrender.

Brian ejected the empty shell and chambered another round. But no one reacted as he swept the muzzle over the travelers. Even Shaker's horse idled lazily, then nuzzled her unconscious master.

Chen Li was the first to react. She hustled to Jenna and stood between her and Brian.

"Whatever you want, Brian, just take it!" Chen Li said, her tone sharp, but her voice breaking. "We won't stop you. We can all just go our separate ways!"

Frowning in amusement at Chen Li, Brian reached Shaker and shifted the man's body so he lay more comfortably.

"It's okay, everyone." Jenna loosed herself from the wheelbarrow harness. "Chen Li, is Lisbon okay? I hit him pretty hard."

"But—" Chen Li looked from Brian to Jenna and back again.

"Hey, don't look at me," Brian said to Chen Li, and pointed at their blind companion. "Lisbon was her doing."

"Jenna?" Chen Li asked. "What's happening?"

"Take a deep breath, Chen Li," Jenna said. "This is Brian Steelman. Remember him? Before the Bowery battle, he was with Scooter and Luigi. Dad brought him in. You probably never met him, but he's a Christian now."

"Mr. Dowler didn't bring me in." Brian chuckled. "It was more like he abducted me. But it was all for the best."

"Oh, thank the Lord!" Chen Li bent over, her hands on her knees. "Oh, I think I'm going to be sick. I wasn't sure how to get away from Shaker. Please tell me that my husband sent you!"

Brian offered his hand to Al Hayes.

"It's okay, sir. I just tranquilized Shaker. He's a bad man, and Lisbon is his helper." Brian checked Lisbon himself as he explained to Chen Li that Runner had told him Levi and Nathan weren't far behind. Walking to the horse, Brian studied the three packs the animal carried. "But we're not safe here. Runner no doubt heard my gunshot. We need to move along, and hope Levi and Nathan can still catch up to us."

“Why don’t we just wait for them?” Chen Li shielded her eyes against the sun and stared up the empty freeway. “We’ll be safer with those two.”

“I’ll tell you why.” Brian tugged on a slipknot and dumped all three packs from the horse to the pavement. “Because these two will be awake in an hour, and Runner is out there. We can’t count on Levi and Nathan. They might be delayed. Get everything you own and put it on the horse. Empty-handed, we can travel twice as fast. It’s already afternoon, so let’s get a move on.”

Jenna took her backpack from the wheelbarrow to Brian. As he accepted her pack, his hand lingered over her own. He looked into her sightless face, trying to read her thoughts about him, even around the sunglasses she wore. But to him, her face seemed expressionless.

“So, we’re taking his horse?” Jenna asked.

“Do you disapprove?”

“No, not since I know he either stole it or bought it by others’ misery.”

Brian tied her backpack onto the horse and turned to find Chen Li lifting up her backpack.

“I didn’t even recognize you earlier,” she said. “Jenna did?”

“The first day I joined you guys.” He looked past Chen Li at Jenna, who was rousing Dusty, Al, and Tyra to leave with them. “But she sees me only as an asset.”

“And you want it to be more?” Chen Li frowned. “We’re running for our lives, and you’re thinking of romance?”

“Don’t worry. I was rejected.” He tied her pack onto the horse. “That’s it? This horse will begin to wonder what we have her for if we don’t put a little more on her.”

“Jenna isn’t used to what you’re offering,” Chen Li said softer to him. “Give her time. You rescued her. That’s got to count for something.”

“Yeah. You’d think so.” He moved from the horse. “Come on, Al. You and Tyra can put your stuff—”

"No!" Al covered his head with his hands. "Don't touch us. Stay away. I'll fight you if I have to!"

"Oh, Al, I'm not—"

"Please, take his stuff and leave us alone!" Al hid his face against his daughter's shoulder where they both huddled on the pavement.

"Al?" Jenna held out her hand, but didn't approach any closer. "It's me, Tyra, are you there? Listen to me, please. We're not going to hurt you. This is Brian Steelman. He's here to—"

"No!" Tyra ripped her necklaces over her head and threw them at Jenna's feet. "Just take 'em! Take 'em . . ."

"Shaker is evil," Chen Li stated, standing nearest Jenna. "Please. Dusty? We're trying to save you from Shaker and Lisbon's plans."

"So says you." Dusty clutched his clock closer to his chest. "They're dead now, but I'm not a conversationalist."

Brian gazed numbly at the people who refused to be helped. Jenna was the kindest person he'd ever known, but the Hayes's and Dusty Thomas weren't interested. As Jenna and Chen Li continued to plead with the three, Brian took two jugs of water from Shaker's packs and fastened them on either side of the horse, but left room for someone to ride bareback. Finally, he studied the freeway behind them, wishing Levi and Nathan were in sight to help him deal with Runner and his dog.

"We need to go." Brian guided Jenna by her arm to the horse. "Even if you don't ride her, we'll travel faster if you and Chen Li hang onto the horse. Chen Li?"

"But, Tyra—!"

"You can't help them if they refuse to be helped. We need to go! Come on! We haven't been through all this to sit in one place and get ourselves into worse trouble. Shaker will be awake in no time."

"I'm not a conversationalist!" Dusty shouted at Brian.

Pausing, Brian looked sternly at the man.

"That excuse will carry you only so far, Dusty. You're responsible for yourself now. Chen Li, now!"

Though Chen Li tried to grasp Tyra's hand, the younger woman shook her off.

"Chen Li?" Jenna called from the horse, her voice soft as she wiped her face of tears. "Let's go. Brian's right."

Brian led the distraught woman as if she were blind as well, guiding Chen Li to the horse and putting her hand on the animal's mane. But Brian sensed she was just in shock from those who refused to be helped.

In parting, Brian drew Shaker's sidearm, a .45 caliber, and threw it into the woods. He took the lead rope and clicked his tongue. The mare plodded forward, her back nearly empty of weight. Since leaving the Wymans, Brian had only a small sack and his rifle, so he continued to carry his few possessions himself.

From a short distance, he turned and walked backward for a spell, watching the people and the heap of belongings in the middle of the interstate lanes. No one had stirred. Runner would find Shaker soon, and Shaker would be forced to continue with little gear. Without his horse, he'd need to carry what he could, which wouldn't be much.

"Now we worry about Runner?" Jenna asked him, as if reading his thoughts.

"No worries." He faced forward, trying to sound positive. "Runner has only a tomahawk for a weapon. I don't think he's used to tracking people who know he's coming. He'll put it all together pretty soon and realize he's been had. Since he told me his whole plan, being hired by the Federation and all, he'll be wary of us."

"But won't that make him more dangerous?" Jenna moved closer to where he led the horse from the front. "He'll be acting unpredictably now, not visibly."

"It's possible." Brian smiled. "But remember, I was an Enforcer longer than he's been alive, so I might be a good asset to have around."

"That's not funny!" Jenna scowled. "That was just mean, Brian. You're more than an asset to me. I mean, to us."

"That's not what you said last night."

"What'd she say last night?" Chen Li asked from the other side of the mare.

"I am not talking about this!" Jenna stated, then tripped over her own feet on the pavement. If not for Brian catching her, she would've scuffed her hands and maybe her face on the hard surface. "I'm fine!"

She shrugged Brian's hand away while the horse didn't miss a stride.

"It's a long way to Colorado if we're not talking," Brian chuckled, enjoying the perfect woman's discomfort. "Maybe you'll tell Chen Li how she's just an asset as well."

"Not funny, Brian . . ." Jenna said, as if she were warning him.

"I've got a better one," Chen Li offered. "How about you tell us, Brian, how Jenna is not just an asset to you. What is she to you?"

"Oh, thanks!" Jenna scolded her friend. "You're getting in on this, too? On *his* side?"

Brian laughed until he was breathless, but didn't push her any more. His point had been made. And when he checked her face a moment later, she was trying not to smile—unsuccessfully.

It was then that he knew he meant more to her than just an asset, no matter what she said.

Levi was sore in places besides his whipped back. After carrying his heavy pack in his arms, his muscles ached in ways he couldn't imagine possible. Thankfully, Nathan had volunteered to prep and build campfires the last few nights, so Levi didn't have to move around more than necessary.

Lena's demeanor had changed drastically since Levi had been punished for her crime in Allentown. Levi had thought she'd been sorrowful in the days following their escape from Manhattan. Now, she wept openly, her throat making loud sucking sounds as she moaned and wet her bridal lace with her tears. Maybe ten times a day for the last four days, she'd handed him the same note from her notepad, which read, "Please let me carry your pack."

But every time, Levi turned down her offer. His muscle aches were minimal compared to the pain she would feel if she fell on her face while burdened with his sixty-pound pack.

That night, to the far southeast of Martinsburg, they made camp next to the willows of a pond fed by a stream. Nathan collected firewood and scouted around the forest as Levi surrendered to Lena's urgings to remove his jacket and shirt. As the fire crackled in front of him, he closed his eyes to Lena's touch. She applied the same decoction of white oak bark as an antiseptic for his back that he'd applied to her face when it had been healing.

As she worked on his back, she cooed and cried, but Levi was silent, wishing it were his wife caring for him. He'd nursed Lena like a father would a toddler, and now she was nursing him. But he didn't think of her in any way except as a wounded child. His own wounds would heal, but hers wouldn't, and he pitied her more than anyone he'd ever known. By praying for her spiritual breakthrough, it seemed God was heaping misery after misery upon her hardened soul.

For four days, she had cried for him, and offered many times to carry his pack, but not once had she written him a note that said she was sorry.

She finished smearing the antiseptic on his back, then helped him pull his shirt over his head to cover his wounds.

"It's ready," Nathan announced as he tapped a spoon on the edge of a tin camping bowl over the fire. "Soup a la Squirrel is served."

Levi stared at the flames as Lena offered his and her camp plates for the thick broth with squirrel meat. Earlier that day, Levi had used his .22 pistol to shoot three different squirrels in the span of a mile, using lethal brass bullets to save the gel-tranqs.

"I still think you could've made head shots," Nathan teased, filling his own plate last. "There wasn't much meat left on those frightened creatures after you were done blasting at them."

"Would you rather I use the rifle tomorrow?" Levi slurped his soup. "Yeah, that'll do. A .308 shell will solve our squirrel meat dilemma."

"Oh, please, no!" Nathan laughed. "You'll have me boiling down scraps of fur if you go after them with the rifle. I'm thinking you could maybe hunt for something besides a cute and cuddly critter."

"Anything larger than a squirrel?" Levi asked.

"Yes, anything."

"Skunk it is!" Levi saluted his companion over the fire. "It ain't easy eatin' skunk meat to stay alive."

Lena suddenly choked on her food, and if Levi wouldn't have taken her plate from her, she would've spilt it in the fire while she convulsed. But he said nothing as she recovered her breath, then handed her the plate again, which she accepted humbly, her head bowed.

More slowly now, she lifted the spoon to her makeshift mouth hidden under her veil where she could trickle the broth down her throat. There was a constant danger of inhaling the food into her lungs.

"I think we're gaining on the girls," Nathan said, referring to Jenna and his wife. "By this time tomorrow, we could be traveling with whatever group they're in."

"That'll be something." Levi finished off his plate and washed it clean with a swirl of water from his canteen. "I haven't seen Jenna since before Pan-Day, though we talked some through relays on the HAM over the years. We might've been something if I hadn't fallen for Lyla."

"Lyla fits you," Nathan said as he cleaned his plate. "She's tough and motherly to compliment you being soft and ornery."

"Oh, my brother!" Levi lifted his head and laughed. "You more than make up for my missing cousin! Your tongue is a little quicker, though, which I look forward to teasing Rex about."

"Don't make me the target of your freakishly large cousin."

Levi folded his hands and watched the fire, praying in his heart for God's watchcare over Rex and the others. Nathan's demeanor had improved the closer they drew to Chen Li, but he guessed none of them would be themselves until they were all reunited in Colorado.

Lena used his canteen to wash her own plate clean, then dried it with her sleeve. Levi smiled at her, but resisted the urge to put his arm around her. Though he wanted to keep encouraging her, he wasn't trying to give her a false sense of any romantic connection. He deeply missed his wife, and Lena's closeness or helplessness didn't change that affection.

"We're halfway through Virginia, huh?" Nathan unfolded an old highway map. "You familiar with anything ahead of us?"

"Well, we came east on Interstate 80." Levi shrugged. "I know the flavor of what we'll be seeing, and it's nothing pretty. Dad was raised in Arkansas. That's the direction we're going, but everything's changed since then. Hmm, I think . . ."

Levi narrowed his eyes at a place in the distant darkness where he'd glimpsed an orange flash. It was gone now, but he knew what it was: the reflection off metal from their own fire. Maybe a button or a rifle. Someone was out there.

"Yeah? You okay?" Nathan leaned closer. "You were about to say—"

"Keep talking and laughing with Lena," Levi said, and dropped his hand to his rifle. "It ain't easy being bushwhacked while eating squirrel stew."

He leaped to his feet and darted left, straight into the trees about twenty feet. As soon as he reached a tree large enough to hide behind its fire-shadow, he put his shoulder to the trunk while holding his rifle close to his chest. Nathan's voice droned on, mixed with light yet nervous chuckling, but Levi listened past the campfire noises. Someone was moving around out there, and he didn't like being watched.

A body scraped past a bush or leafy branch somewhere to his right. Levi went to one knee and one hand, then shuffle-crawled farther away from the fire. Whoever was out there was moving around too loudly to be an experienced hunter. If he could get beyond their perimeter in time, he guessed he'd be able to see them against the backdrop of the fire.

Another twenty feet later, he stopped and listened. Slowly, he eased his rifle into shooting position. There, just to the east a little, were two silhouettes. Their heads were together, speaking too softly for Levi to hear, but definitely more than one. Yet, were there more than two?

Without looking directly at the fire through the bushes, he studied the forest everywhere else. All else was quiet.

This didn't seem to be the man with the dog who'd threatened to harm Jenna. That man had been some sort of loner, and since Levi had disarmed him of arrows, he hadn't been too concerned about him as a threat. That man was still out there, Levi believed, but this was someone else. Maybe locals or other travelers had seen their fire and wanted their water, food, or weapons.

Their silhouettes shifted apart. Levi didn't want to lose them in the darkness, so he squeezed off a half-dozen gel-tranq rounds, raking from left to right to cover the two prowlers. They dropped from sight and the forest was silent. Not even night creatures chirped or squeaked. In case there were others yet undetected, Levi held his position and didn't rush forward. Even Nathan was quiet. Instead, the COIL operative had risen and was standing protectively over Lena, who huddled under him like a chick under a winged falcon.

Levi relaxed his posture, but didn't relax his vigilance. Cautiously, he walked slowly around their campsite counterclockwise, about thirty feet outside the illuminated camp, searching for more predators. Finally, he arrived back at the two he'd tranquilized.

"I'm coming in," he announced and walked into camp to join Nathan. "Two night stalkers. I don't hear anyone else out there, but I just alerted everyone for miles around."

"You may have saved our lives." Nathan helped Lena back to her seat next to the fire. "I didn't hear anyone while we were talking. Thank God you did!"

"It ain't easy being distracted by my wit."

"This guy . . ." Nathan scoffed and shook his head for Lena's sake. "He probably just tranquilized a couple raccoons that were hoping to lick our plates clean."

Together, Levi and Nathan dragged two medium-sized men up to the edge of the light. Levi returned to the trees to look for weapons, since he saw none on their bodies. He used a torch from the fire to light his search, but returned empty-handed.

"What could they hope to accomplish with no weapons?" Nathan asked as he finished binding each man's wrists with their own belts.

"I'm not sure, but I have a hunch." Levi ripped open the shirt of the nearest man, then turned him left and right in the fire's glow. "Remember that gunshot we heard late afternoon before we stopped? Does that mark look familiar to you? It's a little older than the welt I just gave him."

"A bruise on his back?" Nathan sighed. "I'm the best at this game, but I'm not keeping up with you, Levi. I know the report of a COIL battle rifle, and what we heard earlier today wasn't that."

"But you'd agree this is a gel-tranq bruise?" Levi let go of the man. "Two men without weapons out here must've been disarmed of their weapons by someone we know. Chen Li must have a COIL rifle after all, and we misheard the rifle report."

Lena frantically scribbled a message on her notepad and thrust it at Levi.

"She says she recognizes the balding one," Levi read. "He's a trader the Federation uses as a scout into this region. Name's Shaker."

"My wife would've had her reasons." Nathan rubbed his jaw, almost hiding his grin. "I'm sort of beaming with pride right now."

"It could've been Jenna, so don't get too excited," Levi joked. "If Corban trained her, anything's possible."

"After your display tonight," Nathan said, including a mock bow, "I won't argue with you. The fact remains, we have two crooks, probably disarmed by my wife and her sharp-shooting blind friend."

"This skinny guy probably has a bruise as well."

"I'll take your word for it." Nathan rested his hands on his hips. "You think they got handsy with our girls? I'm tempted to give them a few more bruises."

"Let's play this cool." Levi knelt and unbound their wrists. "They don't know we're with the ladies ahead. We might get some intel out of them."

"This isn't time for games, Levi. We've taken long enough to catch up to Chen Li and Jenna. They had to deal with these two on their own? Now I'm feeling even more anxious."

"Truly, I share your concern, Mr. Isaacson, but we have an opportunity here that we can't miss. I'm not trying to be preachy, but I grew up with Dad taking his time with rough characters like this in San Diego. I think this is one of those moments."

"Okay, Mr. Caspertein." Nathan roughly propped one prowler against a log opposite the fire from Lena. "You don't make it easy to argue with you, but I'm still holding my rifle on my lap when they wake up."

Levi set the other man next to his friend, their feet aimed at the fire. Then he sat down in his place next to Lena.

"You good?" he asked her.

"Not comfortable with this," she wrote. "Shaker might recognize me, report me alive."

"With me, I think you'll learn that discomfort can be a good tool." Levi smiled. "You can find out a lot about people, where they stand, if you don't mind being uncomfortable."

"That explains a lot about your back right now," Nathan said. "Sorry, Lena, but your guardian angel is a glutton for punishment."

Lena wrote on her pad and passed it to Levi.

"If you're wondering where I stand, I never said I'm thankful for Allentown."

He took the pencil and wrote back to her: "That's all I wanted to hear. Think nothing more about it."

Now that he thought about his back, he could feel the wetness of blood cooling under his shirt in the night air. All the moving around the last hour had obviously opened a couple of his back wounds. He knew it would all be worthwhile if Lena really grasped what Christ had done for her, not what *he* had done for her.

A few minutes later, the men stirred, the balding one taking in his surroundings first. The slender, older man seemed to check his friend's reaction, so Levi guessed the younger man was the alpha of the two.

"The way I see it," Levi said to Nathan, ignoring the two newcomers, "any one of us could die at any time. Yep. We've got to be ready for eternity. God isn't messing around about our eternal destination. He says so in His Word, doesn't He?"

Nathan's eyes twitched, and Levi could see the old field agent catching on.

"What do you think is really out there?" Nathan asked. "I mean, we should know, shouldn't we? What do you think we should expect in the afterlife?"

"A place of punishment, the Bible says, and a place in the presence and glory of God. From what I've read, our eternal destination is determined between the two by one simple reality."

"And what reality is that?"

"Which kingdom we belong to." Levi spoke with his hands, acknowledging in his peripheral vision that the two men were eyeing the camp with confusion, but he hoped they were also listening. "Are we servants of the prince of darkness? Or are we servants of the Lord Almighty, the just and loving King of kings and Lord of lords? It's about citizenship."

"But I'm only human," Nathan argued. "How can I be anything but a citizen of earth?"

"We're born into this fallen world that's under the sway of the evil one. We know we're condemned because we love only to please ourselves."

"So, I'm condemned? There's no hope?"

"Individually," Levi continued, realizing Lena was listening more intently than their two guests, "we each need to make a conscious decision of faith. We need to turn from our misplaced trust in ourselves, placing our confidence in God's provision to redeem us from our own living death and separation from God."

"What provision?" Nathan threw up his hands and raised his voice. "What could God possibly provide for me? Am I lost and dead in my sins? I've spent my life lusting and craving evil. I've killed and stolen, threatened and extorted. What hope is there for a sinner like me before a just God?"

"If you've become aware of your sinfulness and your need for salvation from defeat," Levi said, "then you qualify for God's grace. That's why His Son Jesus died on the cross. There is no other provision for forgiveness, no other cleansing of guilt available. God loves you, a foolish man, but only you can choose to believe to be saved. Do you believe? If you do believe, God will send His Spirit to dwell inside you. His life inside you changes the kingdom you belong to."

"I need it," Nathan stated, "and I do believe. I wonder what these guys believe."

Levi adjusted his focus to the two men. Suddenly, Lena thrust her notepad into his hands. She'd written, "What about me?"

"It's for you as much as it is for me." He looked into her eyes as they peered over her veil. "I didn't know you before, Lena, but God knows every evil thing you've done. How you've hurt others, how you advanced yourself. You've plotted, tortured, and killed. If you're like all the rest of humanity, your secret sins and thoughts are more horrible than your known ones. But God knows. He made you. He gave you life. You don't deserve His eternal life, Lena, but God is offering it to you, anyway. That's what His Holy Word says. You yourself know how close you've come to dying and going into eternal suffering and separation from God. I wouldn't wait another day in this scary world, if I were you, to trust in His love."

"What is this?" The balding man seemed calm, but Levi judged his eyes and saw uncertainty there. "Who are you?"

"We were just out camping, enjoying a little starlight and squirrel stew, when you two walked in from the dark." Levi received another note from Lena. It read, "How can I be so sure of what I believe?"

"No, this isn't right," the skinny man decided, and started to rise.

"Sit down and hush!" Levi snapped his fingers, which made the man drop back to his seat, then Levi turned back to Lena. "Once you realize you need forgiveness, and God offers to forgive you, all you have to do is match the problem with the solution. When your jaw was bleeding, we didn't throw a dead animal on the wounds. You treat the injury with what works, and nothing else. The Bible tells us, and I'm telling you—God offers peace between you and Him. Nothing else but accepting that by faith will do it."

"What if I try to forgive myself?" Nathan asked. "That was pretty popular before Pan-Day."

"Self-forgiveness is still me trying to fix myself, or to release myself from the shame and guilt I'm under. But God's forgiveness, found only in the sacrifice of Jesus, put an end to my burden of guilt, if I actually believe it."

"What about the past?" Lena wrote.

"Once you enter into His forgiveness, Lena, God won't be looking at your past. You should trust Him, let Him lead you into your future. That, my friend, will change you on the inside. You'll become a new person."

"How could I ever change?" Lena wrote.

"That's not for you to worry about." Levi reached out and took her hand. "It's for you to believe that God promises to change you. Your life for His Son's life. Rest in that promise, and in no time, you'll notice the old you is indeed dead, even though this flesh and old thoughts still linger. Are you really ready now?"

"Aah." She said.

"God will allow your faith to be tested. Are you ready for that?"

After a pause, she nodded slowly.

"Then trust God for His forgiveness. Let your past and your present fall into His ability to cleanse and—"

Lena dove into his chest, her arms wrapping around him. Levi held her as she sobbed in her throaty way. He let his gaze drift from their two guests to Nathan. Nathan nodded once, seeming to give his approval, which Levi thought was significant since he knew Lena best—how she'd killed, harassed, and afflicted Federation citizens and noncompliants.

"What are your names?" Levi asked the two men, even as he held Lena.

The balding one spoke first.

"They call me Shaker. I'm just a trader for the Federation. I travel this freeway year after year, but I've never been treated this way. I insist that I be freed to leave and return to my own camp through the trees over there."

"No one's stopping you, pal," Nathan said. "You came to our camp, remember?"

"And you?" Levi pressed, looking at the thin man. "What's your name?"

"Lisbon. My family's Portuguese." He glanced at Shaker, as if seeking permission to speak. "Can I leave, too?"

"You may leave," Levi said, helping Lena sit up on her own, where she wiped her eyes on her sleeve, "as long as you understand the danger."

"What danger?" Shaker asked. "Are you threatening us?"

"Threatening? No, I'm warning you." Levi pointed at Lisbon. "You, sir, should be warned that if you continue in your evil ways without trusting in Jesus, you will go to hell when you die. And you, Shaker, as you leave, are warned the same. Hell is a real place. Lena here is an example of the repentance you need to follow. Turn from your unbelief, or suffer in darkness for eternity. If you understand these things from God, you may go."

Both men climbed to their feet, picked up their belts, then bumped into one another as they backed away, seeming to worry that they'd be shot or mistreated. A moment later, they were in the darkness and could be heard moving south.

"Chen Li and Jenna could still be with them." Nathan rose to his feet and stretched his leg. "Any problem with me following them to their camp?"

"Handle it." Levi set more wood on the dwindling flames. "Fire a shot if you need a hand, and I'll send Lena while I rest my feet."

"At least I'll have back up that isn't afraid of shooting only squirrels."

Nathan grinned proudly at his joke as Levi's laughter followed him out of camp.

Lena passed Levi her tablet.

"I've burned Bibles," she wrote.

"Yeah, I understand." Levi unlaced his boots. "The Bible isn't a magical book that you'd be cursed for abusing, Lena. The Bible contains the truth about God and man, and God's eternal purpose to show Himself worthy of glory. Now that you know that, I don't think you'll be burning any more Bibles, right? Besides, God has always been able to preserve His Word no matter mankind's most determined efforts. Look at this." He drew his Bible from his coat and held it out to her. "It's a little sweat and tear-stained, but you can begin to read it."

Hesitantly, Lena reached for the Bible. When she did finally grasp it, she held it gingerly at first, then clutched it to her chest. She wept fresh tears, this time not reaching for Levi, and Levi hoped he became less and less her emotional stability as she leaned more on Christ. He'd seen the same transition when Alice had trusted in God for her eternal salvation. Ideally, he would've connected Lena with a mature Christian woman like his wife or Chloe, as Alice had had his mother, Annette. But Lena would have Jenna and Chen Li, hopefully soon.

Sometime after Lena had opened the Bible to read from the book of Matthew, Nathan walked into camp.

"They're about a half-mile that way." Nathan sat next to the fire. "You were right. I walked right into their camp and asked them about Chen Li and Jenna. Shaker's got a huge pile of trade goods, but no way to transport them, they said, since our girls disarmed them and took their horse."

"It ain't easy being shanghaied by a blind woman."

"I'd argue with you that Jenna had a little help from my wife, but it seems someone else named Brian Steelman joined them a few days ago. He turned on Shaker, but Jenna handled that Lisbon guy. Remember Steelman? Big guy about my size at the warehouse?"

Levi noticed Lena lift her head at the mention of the ex-Enforcer.

"I remember him." Levi said. "What's he doing with our ladies?"

"Beats me, but I'm glad he's there. He and Jenna had a connection a couple months ago. Scooter or Luigi led Steelman to Christ in the tunnels. More than that, all I know about him is that he was the only Enforcer in the early years of the Federation who killed more Christians than Lena—not to bring up old memories. Sorry, Lena."

Lena passed Levi her pad.

"She says Steelman hates her." Levi gave the notepad back to her. "That's the old Steelman and the old Lena. If Steelman's with us, and you're with us—you have nothing to fear."

She didn't seem convinced as she closed the Bible and stared again at the fire. Levi knew she was just beginning her journey with the Lord, and she had much to learn about God, herself, and other Christians.

"Long walk tomorrow," Nathan said, and unrolled his sleeping bag. "Remember, something larger than a squirrel for tomorrow's stew."

"We agreed on skunk, didn't we?" Levi lay on top of his bedroll next to the fire. The farther south they went and the further they moved toward summer, the warmer the nights became.

But Lena remained seated before the fire, feeding it sticks late into the night. Levi prayed and believed God would comfort the now-mute woman in her thoughts, her past, and her future.

Chapter Eight

Colonel Milo Rotham watched one of his engineers trying to plug a bullet hole in one of the fuel tanks, which had leaked several hundred gallons of fuel onto the ground after a firefight. A sniper from far away had punctured the tank using an armor-piercing round. It seemed everywhere they went, local militias were gunning for them. They had no respect for the might and authority of the Federation, and it left Rotham wondering more and more if they even belonged out there.

"Bad timing," he grumbled as he went to the mobile HAM radio station and donned a headset. "This is Colonel Rotham."

"Hello, Colonel. This is Lieutenant Grady. Chancellor Branaugh has commissioned me to be your comm-guy here at the Bowery. Are you reading me?"

"Five-by-five, Grady, but now's not a good time. We have a little patching up to do after our tenth attack by locals on the road."

"Your tech said you're making little progress because of those attacks. The chancellor will want a full report from me, sir, so please give it to me straight. We have news for you as well."

Rotham glared at his technician, who was listening in on his own headset. The man shriveled under Rotham's stare.

"Here's my report. The Casperteins are proving evasive. Owen Travers and Obrador broke off from the group, and we executed Travers in the field, but Obrador's still in the wind. Three nights ago, we attempted to sweep the area for the Caspertein criminals, but we were . . .

outmaneuvered and lost a day chasing a phantom trail. We're back on track, but to set up another regional sweep, we'll need to be resupplied."

"Well, you'll have to make acquisitions from the locals, Colonel. That was one of the chancellor's orders for me to tell you. Branaugh wants you back here, but not before you tie up the Federation's loose ends. And he said we can't spare any more trucks if you ask for them. He guessed you might be running into problems."

"Acquisitions from the locals?" Rotham felt his confidence wane as he acknowledged three more dead and five wounded from the last skirmish. Sergeant Ibojka stood over the dead as they were laid beside the command vehicle. "As long as you understand that'll require an acquisition by force, and that'll spread ill-will where the Federation hopes to expand someday."

"It'll be worse to have those criminals escape justice. Every day, Branaugh realizes more how Chloe Azmaveth and the Dowlers conspired against the government, making this rebuilding process more difficult. If you can't catch all the escaped prisoners, he wants at least Obrador and Azmaveth finished off. It would look good, I should add, if you return with that Caspertein dog mounted on your hood. I still can't believe that guy took down our bridge to Jersey!"

Rotham swore and felt like cutting off the connection altogether. He realized now the difficulty of taking on the Casperteins with their methods and armaments, but he couldn't explain that to politicians far away in the comfort of the Bowery.

"So, what's your news, Grady? And make it quick. We're in the middle of things here."

"We made contact with Europe! Or, I should say, they made contact with us. The virus affected them as well, spread all the way to China! The deaths were in the millions like it was here, but all the survivors are pulling together, including us. Branaugh is even setting up trade again, and a global effort is being arranged to find a vaccine that will eradicate the virus once and for all. The world is recovering, uniting under the banner of science, success, and solidarity. And Branaugh wants you to spread the news out there that we're a resilient people, able to achieve anything we set our minds to if we come together. All other government heads should lay down their arms in an effort to rebuild infrastructure and relationships. We're a new race of humans, Colonel, and Europe is saying that humanity is proving that we're evolving from what we were before the virus."

"That's great, Lieutenant. I'm sorry to be missing out on the progress."

"Some said that God had sent the virus to cause the world to look at our mortality. That's laughable now. All we're learning is to love ourselves more, and that makes us bigger than any god. Rotham, you've got to spread this news!"

"Yes, I hear you." Rotham looked down at his boots, which were blood-splattered from one of the wounded he'd tried to save. The comm guy's words sounded blasphemous against God, but Rotham knew no one really believed in such superstitions anymore. Except for the Caspertein crowd. "We're a new race with new hopes and dreams. I heard it all from Obrador years ago. That's what he said about the survivors in New York while we were starving to death."

"What's that, Colonel? I didn't catch your last."

"All right, I'll be home as soon as I can. I'll share your message, but I'm leaving a trail of blood, Grady. You tell that to the chancellor. I can't do this without force, but I'll get the criminals."

After the call, Rotham met with Ibojka and two captains in the command vehicle. Outside, the screams of the wounded cut through Rotham's soul as field medics did their best to patch up his people under the circumstances. They were out of morphine and antibiotics, and running low on bandages.

"Half our force is either wounded or dead." Rotham crossed his arms as he stood against the windows of the bus. "We're going to finish this operation if I have to kill Azmaveth and Obrador with my own hands, kneeling in the blood of our own people! The sooner we get this done, the sooner we can lick our wounds and head home."

"The wounded are sucking up our resources too fast to continue," Ibojka said. "I suggest we leave them behind and pick them up when we return."

"They'd be killed by the locals." Rotham considered his homecoming in the wake of so much loss and defeat. "Pack the worst wounded into one Humvee and send them back to New York. That'll stem the flow of our provisions to useless soldiers."

"I have a plan for going forward," one captain offered. He had a wound from a bullet on his neck, but he was still capable of serving.

"Let's hear it. It better not be a waste of our time."

Rotham realized his own efforts to catch the Casperteins had resulted in wasted time and life, but his demands from his men would keep them sharp. He moved up to the large strategy table where several maps of North America were unrolled.

"We need to lay another sweep," the captain said, pointing to the maps, "but not before we get resupplied. I propose we strike a town here in Ohio, just this side of Akron."

"That's two hundred miles away." Rotham nodded. "I see. Get way out in front of the Casperteins, take time to learn the routes, then close the net again."

"But provisions first, sir," the captain said. "With overwhelming force, we obliterate a town. Leave no witnesses to speak badly about the Federation, and take all the supplies we need. Some communities even have a little fuel left. We can scout ahead for one that looks promising."

"What do the rest of you think?" Rotham asked the others.

His rare offer for input left even Ibojka stuttering.

"It's not bad," the other captain stated, 'assuming the Caspertein's stick to Interstate 80."

"It's one decisive blow in two phases," Ibojka said approvingly. "Resupply, then use that ground to stage a fresh offensive. We know all their tricks now. We won't miss them again."

Rotham took a deep breath and studied the maps. As far as he knew, not a single one of Caspertein's people had been killed or captured. The exception was Owen, of course, but only because Owen had left the Caspertein's company.

"Let's get on the road. Captains, organize the troops. Send off one Humvee with the wounded. Ibojka, I want you in the scout Jeep. Find us a resupply town to reap from in Ohio. We've stalled long enough here in Pennsylvania. I want some progress by sundown."

Twenty minutes later, Rotham had changed his boots and socks, and had climbed into the lead vehicle. His Humvee was leading the procession west, though Ibojka was far ahead in the scout Jeep. From the passenger seat of the Humvee, Rotham studied the landscape as they moved through farm communities and towns. The Caspertein's were out there somewhere, but it was impossible to know where. All he could do now was get ahead of them and set up an invincible net that captured the whole lot of them.

Abandoned towns and burned-out homesteads flew by his window. Two of his soldiers in the back seat commented on the desolation that had already swept across the land. Armies and bandits had come and gone. It was little wonder that the survivors were aggressive against the Federation and determined to keep what little they had.

Hours later, the convoy stopped to refuel. They were nearly in Ohio, staying on the interstate except where it was destroyed at an overpass or at a collapsed bridge. There were other roads, and in no time, Rotham was glad to see his men were willing to charge forward. Since they'd lost a number of battles and fruitlessly chased the Casperteins for days, everyone was spoiling for a fight in which they could prove themselves.

That night, after they'd set up camp on the south side of the freeway where there was an adequate source of wood nearby, Ibojka returned in the scout Jeep. He had news, and Rotham didn't ask him to debrief privately. The troops silenced themselves in the middle of the camp, surrounded by the defensive circle of their vehicles.

"I found the perfect fort," Ibojka reported. "They set up a wall around themselves, but there's a hill nearby that'll give us higher ground for our artillery. If they refuse to supply us, we can threaten to destroy them. Or we can just destroy them and take what we want."

"Fuel?" Rotham asked.

"Definitely. They have at least a couple generators running on fuel. I saw the exhaust manifold and several barrels in two different locations. I drew a map."

"How many people?"

"About eighty, but it looks like only about thirty who are fighters."

"Fighting age out here is a lot broader." Rotham calculated the odds. "We'd be outmanned, even if we have more firepower."

"But they won't know that, and we'd have the high ground."

"Maybe they have a nearby ally?"

"No one within twenty miles," Ibojka said. "To make sure, we drove all around. A lot of locals are around, but nobody shot at us. We studied everything. That's what took us all afternoon. This fort is less than an hour away. The interstate is clear, and they're within sight of the freeway on this side of Akron."

"An hour away." Rotham looked down at the ground. "I don't want to rush things, and we're low on food, fuel, and first aid. Let's take a couple nights to rest and prepare. Twenty-four hours from dawn tomorrow, we're knocking at that fort's door. Any objections? Good. We'll hit them with everything we have, like our lives depend on it, because they do. We're too far from home for all of us to return, unless we take from everyone who has what we need. Let's get ready!"

Later, inside the command vehicle, Ibojka revealed his map of the Ohio fort, which they were calling Corn as a joke because of the surrounding cornfields. The other officers in the company leaned over the table.

"We could surround them first," Ibojka said. "Using our radios, we can organize our assault, relying on a couple spotters on high ground. This is the hill, here, about four hundred yards away. Meanwhile, Colonel, you can knock on their front gate, here, and demand their surrender."

"Whether they let us in or we force our way in, we leave no survivors." Rotham said. "It'll complicate things if we leave anyone alive, and we can't afford to help anyone who lives, anyway."

"It'll be close fighting inside Corn," Ibojka said. "And it's likely we'll ruin supplies while wiping out the citizens, so let's be careful."

"Then we'll make them surrender, and we'll erase them," Rotham said, his voice lower, feeling in his heart the coldness of his words. "No mercy. No trace. If we're lucky, we can even use Corn as a platform for our final assault on the Caspertelns, or lay in wait from there."

Since they were in such a remote part of Ohio, Rotham posted only two sentries on the perimeter that night. Before he lay in his own bunk inside the armored bus, he moved among his soldiers where they slept under the canopies erected between vehicles. These were his men and a few women, truly the best the Federation had produced. Maybe Europe was right; maybe they had evolved from what humanity once was. Hardship had brought them beyond weakness. Only those with the strength to endure and continue had prevailed. Men like himself. They weren't complainers or shortcut-takers.

He leaned against one SUV and crossed his arms. The moon was setting. Everything was still and peaceful. In a couple days, they'd take a town's supplies, and maybe have a little fun at the locals' expense. The men needed to blow off some steam. And then they'd complete their mission. It was hard not to be proud of himself at that moment. Hope swelled in his chest. He didn't care about a commendation from the chancellor, only succeeding for his personal glory.

How far he'd come! He smiled at the stars, feeling like he'd reached their very heights. Nothing could stop him now. What glory he'd already achieved, all from being a gamer in the basement of his parents' house! A whole generation had come of age since he'd learned to lead. No one under twenty even understood what it meant to be a gamer. All they saw once in a while were the heaps of computer screens and tech that rusted uselessly outside every town and community. That was all his past.

Rotham was lost in his thoughts of grandeur when there was suddenly a gunshot somewhere in the night. His first thought was that one of his men was outside the perimeter using the latrine, and they'd accidentally fired a shot. It had happened before.

But then another gunshot split the night, and he knew they were under attack. *Again!*

"Incoming!" he shouted an instant before an RPG exploded against the side of one Humvee, flipping it onto its side. The two tent ropes snapped since they were attached to the vehicle's bumpers, causing the soldiers below to be shrouded under collapsing canvas as they tugged on their boots.

As Rotham threw the canvas off the soldiers, two more RPGs flashed searing white heat into the perimeter. Another Humvee flipped over, and the scout Jeep disappeared behind a wall of smoke. With two vehicles missing in their perimeter, the enemy poured in. Now exposed, Rotham's people were taking incoming fire from at least two directions.

Eager to reach the safety of his armored command vehicle, Rotham crouched and ran across the expanse. There was no fighting such an ambush. There was only survival. Others in his command had the same idea, apparently, because he collided with them on the way to the bus. They were cut down by enemy fire as they ran. Screams from the wounded and dying sounded differently this time, Rotham thought in a split-second. Then he knew why. It was fear. In other battles, they'd screamed in courage. Even in other conflicts during daylight hours, the wounded had screamed in pain. But this was pure fear. They couldn't fight an enemy they couldn't identify or find cover from.

"Colonel!" Ibojka shouted for him from the doorway of the bus. The large sergeant, his companion in the ranks of the Citizen Army for over a decade, stretched out his hand to receive the commander, but then the arm disappeared.

Rotham dove to the ground as his friend and trusted officer was cut down and he fell from the bus. Several of his soldiers returned fire, but they were disposed of immediately. In fact, the enemy was storming inside the perimeter, already claiming some of their vehicles!

There was no reaching the bus doorway to his right, not for its safety and not for its armory. Instead, Rotham climbed underneath the bus, scurrying frantically on his elbows, and hid while gazing out at the fires where flaming bodies and wreckage spotted the ground.

Rolling over, he emerged on his knees on the far side of the bus. In the semi-darkness, he plowed into a man with a rifle who grappled with him. Rotham finally flipped his opponent to the ground, then before he could be shot, he darted into the darkness away from the vehicles.

He ran until he fell into a barbed wire fence. It cut him and tore his clothes before he managed to climb through it. Then, he ran again, zigzagging his way across an empty field, hoping his maneuvering was throwing off any pursuers.

Suddenly, he stopped in the field and looked back. He could hear no one following nor was anyone shooting at him. The gunfire back at camp had stopped, but the sound of cheers reached his ears—a victory chant of some sort. But they weren't his men's voices he heard. This wasn't his victory.

Moving a few steps, he wondered if anyone else had fled like he had. Certainly others had survived! But he recalled how even mighty Ibojka had fallen a few feet away from him. Once the enemy had entered their perimeter, the only escape would've been to crawl under the vehicles, and Rotham couldn't remember anyone else scrambling as he had for safety.

The screams of his people echoed in his skull. Their fear became his fear. No, he thought, he was trained better than to panic! But this new reality was undeniable. He was alone in Ohio, hundreds of miles from the Philadelphia he had ruled for so long. This was the Plains Zone. So much for the thoughts that he would be more ruthless and stronger than anyone in the lawless territory.

Just moments earlier, he'd been glorying in his greatness. It seemed so foreign to him now, that he'd imagined his own invincibility. Was it possible that he'd been so deluded, so mistaken—that he wasn't actually a conqueror?

Indeed, he thought as tears wet his cheeks, he'd done nothing but lose since setting off from the Bowery. Now, he was alone. With only his sidearm to—

His holster was empty. He felt his clothing, wondering if he'd maybe thrust the weapon into his belt, but his handgun was gone. Perhaps he'd dropped it under the bus or while climbing through the fence. So, this was worse than he'd first thought. Unarmed and alone, without supplies. Only vaguely did he recall the way the map had portrayed the highways and towns on the east side of Ohio. How was he supposed to navigate across four hundred miles back to Philadelphia, the Federation's most westward metropolis?

But then Rotham clenched his teeth. He couldn't go back. Not now. Not like this. Whoever had attacked his convoy this time had stolen his past and destroyed his future. Returning to the chancellor as a defeated commander could be an executable offense. Branaugh wasn't as temperamental as Obrador, but the new administration was trying to show strength, not weakness. And now Europe was seeking to partner and unite with America? For certain, Rotham couldn't return. Perhaps for the rest of his life, he would be alienated from the land he'd known since childhood. He would become a wanderer, never able to find a home on account of who he'd been. Unwanted back home and despised in the land of his wandering, he would be a man without a people. No family, no friends, no one to trust, and no one to trust him.

Rotham backed farther into the field. Besides the gunshots and explosions ringing in his ears, his own thoughts of killing an entire town was also fresh upon his conscience. How could he fall so far so quickly? What he'd intended to do to others, others had done to him. He tried to reject the idea that a God out there somewhere was responding to his arrogance by humbling him so low, ruining his career, and threatening his life in a matter of minutes.

As soon as he noticed he'd begun walking westward, away from Philadelphia, he stopped and peered to the east. Maybe he wasn't alone. Maybe he didn't need to fight and fend and fail until he died. The Casperteins were out there. One of their campsites had even shown signs of them having a goat or two. That was certainly more than he had going for himself!

But he remained still, not moving toward his sworn enemies, the Casperteins. It was unthinkable to sink to their level. They were a superstitious lot, believing the blood of their God would wash away their guilt. Some of those he'd arrested in Philadelphia had called their own wives their sisters. They were a plague in the Federation—a system of government that demanded complete and singular loyalty.

And yet, here he was with nothing, and there they were, about a hundred miles east, with everything.

There was of course the question as to whether or not they would accept him, but then he remembered who they'd already accepted. They'd allowed Obrador and Owen to accompany them. And they'd allowed the infamous Brian Steelman to join their ranks. They were an accepting people—naive, but kind.

He wondered what it would be like to look Levi Caspertein in the face and tell him he'd killed Owen Travers, the man who'd murdered Lyla. And he'd killed Lena Travers for them, too! Surely, that had to count for something.

Christianity wasn't to Rotham's liking, but he saw no way around it. He had to join the only people he knew in the Plains Zone. It would cost him his pride, but at this point, he didn't have much to lose.

Now walking east, he hoped to meet them before he traveled too far. Without even a sidearm, food would be scarce until he met them. And what about changing his socks? The ones he wore would probably rot off before he found a new pair to swap out.

The sound of a motor in the field caused Rotham to turn and see what the attackers were doing with his remaining vehicles. To his shock, the scout Jeep, which had only one remaining headlight, crashed through the barbed-wire fence, and bounced into the field. Its headlight flashed over him. *They were coming after him!* Someone must've seen him escape. Of course—the one he'd wrestled with behind the bus!

He turned and ran, lifting his knees high, trying to avoid falling over the uneven ground. At one point, the headlight shone far ahead, and Rotham glimpsed the rolling terrain of fields. It was never-ending. There was nowhere to hide.

The Jeep slowed on his heels rather than running him down. Winded, Rotham slowed to a stop in the headlight and placed his hands behind his head, just as he'd ordered hundreds of others to do for him.

"Throw down your weapon!" a firm voice shouted. "Do it, or we'll open fire!"

Rotham turned toward them, squinting into the headlight and opening his arms wide.

"I lost it. You can search me. I have nothing."

"Who are you?" Three men walked toward him from behind the headlight. The two on the sides twisted his arms behind his back and cuffed him. The one in the middle touched Rotham's shirt. "Colonel? So, you're the one we've been looking for. You were the leader of those invaders."

"We weren't invaders." Rotham looked into the man's hard face, wrinkled under a black beret. "We were capturing escaped prisoners."

"You're Appalachian Federation. That means you're invaders. I'm guessing you're with the other guy who killed two of our townspeople. Said he was with you, and if we didn't let him go, you'd rain bullets down on us. You must be the invaders he was talking about. He led us straight to you."

"I'm . . . not missing any men. You have the wrong party, sir. I assure you, all of my men were accounted for. Until tonight."

"Well, he refused to give us his name, but he knew all about you guys—enough to put us on high alert and put you down before you caused a problem. We here in Ohio know how to deal with invaders, let me tell you.

"I'm not an invader!"

"Say what you want." The man stepped closer, blocking out more of the light. He was clean-shaven and broad-shouldered with a jutting, sharp jawline. "These criminals you're after—where are they?"

"If I knew, I would've arrested them and returned to New York!"

"Worlawn!" called someone from the Jeep. "The riders from the border just called in a large group moving this way on foot. And they're armed."

"Throw him in the back," the commander named Worlawn ordered. "I'm getting to the bottom of who's who. No invaders will be tolerated in Ohio, let me tell you!"

Rotham was lifted by two sturdy men and tossed into the back of the Jeep. His head fell against a fuel can, then someone climbed into the back and sat on him where he lay. Miserable and in pain, he closed his eyes and wished for a painless execution.

Rex Caspertein measured the night hour by the turning of the stars around Polaris, the North Star. Dawn was approaching, and he'd already received a radio call from Alice not far ahead that she'd found a good campsite. And she'd seen horseback riders in the distance, but they hadn't approached her.

Even though the refugees hadn't been able to safely use the interstate to travel west, they'd found adjacent roads and even the occasional farm field to move across.

Nevertheless, the threat of the Federation's presence loomed even as they crossed Ohio's eastern border.

"Baah!" bleated the milk goat over his shoulders.

"Baah!" the second goat in their company responded, carried by Hank Lowery.

Whether Rex was carrying the goat named Ruth, or the one named Naomi, he wasn't sure. All that mattered was the welfare of the little animals along the journey, since their precious milk helped sustain them all. To keep the nannies from losing too much weight, they grazed during the day and were carried at night during travel. However, with all the people picking grass and feeding the goats while they were being transported—they may as well have been grazing all night, too!

The sixty pounds wasn't overly much for Rex's shoulders, but Hank's frame was a hundred pounds lighter. Yet the father of two and husband to Cobie walked without complaint.

"I see you," Alice voiced in his radio earpiece. "Come about to your right a little."

Changing his heading, Rex led the party of one hundred up to a single campfire Alice had already lit. Ruth and Naomi seemed thrilled to dig their hooves into solid ground, and once they were set down, instantly went to nibbling the sweet grass.

"Water's over there." Alice pointed in the growing light. "The freeway's about a quarter-mile in that direction, so we're way out of sight as long as we stay north of this spot."

"Any neighbors?" Rex patted the people on their shoulders as they arrived, letting them know they were acknowledged for their endurance through yet another night. "What about those horsemen you saw?"

"There's a farm in that direction, but no sign of any other activity around. Those horsemen were watching me, but they crossed over the horizon like I was nothing."

"Did they see us?"

"It's hard to say. I was way out front so I don't think so."

"Good." Rex slid his pack to the ground. "I'll make sure there's a watch on duty, then we can crash out."

"Sounds good to me." Alice said and walked off.

Rex didn't need to supervise the camp setup anymore. Everyone knew their duties—firewood, fire, water, food prep, tents, and after all that was in place, sleep.

By the time he confirmed that Taylor Tharp and Scooter had the first watch, Bruno and Nick Zoft strolled in from the west as the company's rear guard.

"All's quiet out there," Bruno said as he unrolled his bedroll across the fire from where Rex lay reading his Bible in the growing light. "I figure we're about a third of the way to Colorado, wouldn't you say?"

"That might be a little generous," Rex said. "More like a fifth. Everything's squished together out here in the East. The West goes on and on. You'll see."

"Well, Pennsylvania was a good hurdle." Bruno groaned as he lay back, the man's joints cracking. "My old bones needed it to be a third completed already. You sure? We're only a fifth into our exodus?"

"It's eighteen hundred miles from New York City to Meeker, Colorado. We haven't even done four hundred yet."

"What do I have to do to get you to carry me tomorrow instead of Naomi?"

"Naomi?" Rex joked back. "I thought I was carrying Ruth. In that case, it's between you two. I don't mind, but I expect your udders to be just as productive as hers by the end of the night."

"There are people trying to sleep around here, you hyenas," Sean Harris joined in, though he was still setting up his tent. "We walk all night, and you two want to talk all day. The least you could do is help me stand this thing upright."

"Kids and their tents." Rex scoffed, even though he was much younger than the sergeant. "You'd think they'd want to sleep under the stars."

"Oh, I love the stars," Sean said. "It's the rain I'm thinking of. You two will be begging me to unzip the door once it starts raining."

Rex lowered his Bible as Bruno and Sean exchanged banter. He studied the two goats as they stood alert, not grazing, their heads lifted, and their ears wiggling. They were just silly goats, but they were animals with keen senses, so Rex climbed to his stocking feet and studied what he could see of the terrain in every direction.

He snapped his fingers, drawing all those nearest him to immediate silence. The signal spread down to the six other campfires.

Suddenly, two sharp whistles cut through the morning chill, giving Rex a different chill. It was Scooter, the veteran COIL operative on their western flank. The man waved one arm and signaled beyond the tree line toward the freeway at something only Scooter could see.

But Rex had learned to rely on the experts around him. He didn't need to see to respond.

"Chloe, Bruno, to the north four hundred yards!" he ordered. "Alice, join Scooter. Sean, join Taylor. Hank, shoulder your weapon and wait for my word. Everyone else, stay down!"

His shooters scattered to the three angles to cover the whole camp from a distance. Still in his stocking feet, Rex pulled on his ammo vest and chambered a round in his battle rifle. Then, he faced the roar of motors as they drove around the trees and into sight. *The Federation!* Three Humvees and the armored bus pulled along the length of the refugees' fires. There was nowhere for the Christians to go. They'd been caught.

Rex snarled at the bullet-riddled exterior of the command vehicle. He imagined Colonel Rotham was inside, snarling back at him for leading them on such a wild and dangerous chase.

"Mouth and marbles, Lord," Rex prayed under his breath. "I need 'em both right now."

He didn't look left or right or behind him, to give away the positions of his shooters, but he hoped they lay prone and out of sight. They were the people's only chance. Maybe some of them could still escape. Rex would've preferred to be a good distance away himself, with his rifle against his cheek like he usually was when Levi had taken the lead and all the risks. But now, he was leading this caravan, and if that meant he would die first, so be it.

However, as the soldiers disembarked from the vehicles—nearly thirty of them—he saw no Federation uniforms except one on the tall, slender Colonel Rotham, whose hands were bound behind him! Now that Rex looked closer, the vehicles did seem more damaged than seemed reasonable for a convoy of elite killers.

A stern-looking man with a chiseled jaw stood near Rotham. His men, all wearing earth tones like Rex's people, carried assault rifles and grim faces, but their rifles weren't aimed directly at any of the Christians.

The two goats bleated and scampered out of the way of the commander as he briskly advanced. Rex stepped away from his fire, and in his stocking feet, looked down at the stranger.

"You've entered Ohio," the man informed, "so it's my responsibility to warn you that I'm responsible for these towns. I'm Deputy Worlawn, supported by our state to protect our citizens from invaders."

"Invaders?" Rex swung his rifle out of his way to hang it on the shoulder sling. He gestured to the goats nearby. "Ol' Ruth and Naomi are about the only invaders you'll find around here, Deputy. We're just traveling light, heading to Colorado where my family homesteads."

"This man . . ." Worlawn pointed with this thumb at Rotham, "says you're criminals."

"According to Federation law, these folks are criminals for having Bibles and talking about Jesus. I'm no Federation citizen, but if reading a Bible makes somebody a criminal, I'm the biggest criminal there is. I read the Bible as much as I can."

"The Bible?" Worlawn studied the people from the East. "You're all families? I see some children. Permission to look around?"

"Permission granted." Rex raised his right arm and shouted to the shooters, "Stand down! They're friendlies."

Worlawn hesitated as he glanced around.

"Who are you yelling at?" The deputy gazed out at the fields. "You have armed people besides yourself?"

"Just a few old veterans to escort these folks to safety."

With more caution, Worlawn walked past the first fire and surveyed the camp as far as the fourth fire, then he returned.

"You're not some cult group, are you?" Worlawn asked. "I've had to deal with some cults since Pan-Day."

"Nah, we're just simple Christians, sir."

"Not that simple. That's some rifle you've got there, son."

"It's the NL-X2 battle rifle," Rex said, emptying the chamber, then passing the weapon over to the deputy. "This is a standard .308, except we shoot tranquilizer ammunition."

"Tranqs?" Worlawn unclipped the magazine and studied a cartridge. "Fascinating. Can I keep one?"

"The rifle or the cartridge?" Rex smiled. "Of course, Deputy. Keep it as a memento."

The deputy passed the rifle back to Rex, but kept one cartridge and pocketed it.

"So, you know our prisoner?" Worlawn asked.

"I know of him. My cousin tranquilized him a few weeks ago. He's been chasing us ever since."

"That's not all they've been doing. Our neighbors in Pennsylvania radioed us and said they've killed their fair share of locals along the way, taking supplies and threatening some towns. We were ready for them when they reached Ohio. Caught them gearing up for another attack, it looked like. Even found a map inside that revealed their plans to hit a place near Akron."

"Well, you got their trucks now. They won't be doing too much harm, and that'll make our journey a whole lot safer."

"We serve everyone in Ohio, even guests. You have a name?"

"Rex Caspertein." Rex offered his hand. "You shake?"

"I will today." Worlawn gripped Rex's hand. "This Colonel Rotham didn't actually do anything in Ohio other than got found out before they killed our citizens. I've also got the Federation's old chancellor named Obrador inside the bus. He killed two homesteaders, so we'll be executing him once we get back to Columbus. Says he was with you, that you'd vouch for him. The guy said the same about Rotham, but Rotham isn't siding with him. I just need to give the judge the whole story. He's our prisoner either way, but can you tell me if Obrador was with you or not?"

"Sorry to say Obrador's time with us didn't change him, but yes, he was with us for some time." Rex sighed. "He killed my cousin's wife, then took her rifle and ran off with another ex-Federation man."

"We found Obrador alone." Worlawn signaled one of his men. "But as for that rifle you lost, this might look familiar."

Another deputy approached with a COIL battle rifle. Rex immediately recognized it as the one Lyla had carried.

"That's ours all right." Rex looked past the deputies at Rotham. "I might have some questions for your prisoner about why he had it."

"Ask away. We've disarmed him and killed all his men. Actually, we weren't sure what to do with him."

Together, they walked to the side of the bus where Rex scrutinized the colonel who didn't seem too intimidating in his torn and soiled uniform.

"I'm not too sharp," Rex said to Rotham, "so I need you to spell things out to me real carefully. This rifle? How did you get it?"

Rotham glanced at Worlawn and the other deputies who were pressing in on him.

"I caught Enforcer Owen Travers with it. Under torture, he admitted to killing Levi's wife for the rifle. Is Levi here? Do you remember me from Philadelphia?"

"You tortured a man?" Worlawn asked. "And the Federation's supposed to be some advanced society?"

"So, you talked to Obrador?" Rex asked Rotham.

"Yeah. He's inside." Rotham lowered his head. "Please, Mr. Caspertein, explain to this man that I'm only out here to arrest the criminals with you. I'm not doing anything nefarious to the locals."

"Rotham, we know you've been in skirmishes all across Pennsylvania!" Worlawn accused. "That's why we're here. I'm finding out the truth from you, Rex. I don't favor the Federation one way or another, until it touches the lives of the people I'm paid to protect. Obrador's going back to Columbus. Do I execute Rotham here for crimes against humanity as well?"

"It might mean more," Rex said, "if you leave him with us to deal with since we're the ones he's been persecuting and hunting for years."

"Then, he's all yours. Deputy?" Worlawn called on the nearest man. "Remove those cuffs. Mr. Caspertein seems like a capable man if Rotham wants to put up a fight."

"I've squished bugs with my bare hands that were bigger than this runt." Rex smiled, enjoying watching Rotham squirm. "If we had anything to spare, Deputy, we'd offer your men something to eat or drink."

"Never mind that. We all have families and gardens, so we're taken care of. Safe travels to you and yours across our fine state, Rex Caspertein. We're based out of Columbus if you need anything else."

Rex shook the man's hand and took hold of Rotham's collar with his left hand.

"Will do. Glad to meet friendly folks along the way. It's rare nowadays."

"Load 'em up, men!" Worlawn ordered, and the vehicles started up.

"What're you going to do with me?" Rotham asked.

"What do you think I should do with you?" Rex waved as the Ohio militia pulled out and drove away in the Federation vehicles. "I'll hear you out."

"Would you let me go?"

"Where would you go?"

"Well . . ." Rotham gazed into the distance, then looked up at Rex. "After my company was killed off, I was thinking of trying to find you guys. There's no future for me back with the Federation. Where's Levi? I feel I should tell him about his wife."

"You'll do nothing of the kind. I have one rule for you in camp. You never—and I mean never—leave my side. You visit the latrine when I visit the latrine. You walk where I walk and go where I go. Understand? I'm not having a repeat of another snake in the grass killing any of my people."

"I suppose I deserve that." Rotham didn't nudge Naomi away as she nibbled on his trouser leg. "But I'm not Owen Travers or Obrador."

"You're cut from the same cloth." Rex leaned over him. "Just don't make me whip you like a wayward teenager, because I will. You may be my elder, but I'll still put you over my knee and give you the belt like my father did to me. What's my one rule for you?"

"Go where you go."

Rex waved the shooters back to camp.

"Even if I'm sleeping, you stay at my side. If I hear you so much as step where I don't step, I'll flatten you.

Consider yourself my closest companion, Rotham. Now, I need some sleep."

"But I don't have anything to sleep on."

"God's good green earth ain't good enough for you?" Rex sat down on his bedroll. "Here's a tarp. Wrap yourself in that. And no complaining. I can only imagine what cushiony living you've enjoyed while these people have been starving and cold."

Chloe walked in from the field.

"What's he doing here?" she asked. "We adopting another stray, Rex?"

Rotham dropped the tarp, and seemed to take account of his appearance.

"Uh, Chloe Azmaveth," he stuttered. "It's been a long time."

"Rotham here will be carrying Ruth on tomorrow's march." Rex winked and lay on his bed. "The colonel's command was wiped out by the local militia. He's gonna be my best friend for the foreseeable future, never leaving my side."

Bruno resumed his place by the fire.

"Carrying Ruth?" Chloe smiled, as if she already knew what Rex was up to. "Seems fair. Welcome to your new porter status, Colonel."

She walked away, and Rotham unfolded the tarp beside Rex.

"Who's Ruth?" Rotham asked. "And why do I have to carry her?"

"Because she'll get too skinny if you don't. Now sleep. We move out at sundown."

Lena was walking abreast of Nathan and Levi, one on either side of her. She couldn't resist touching her face. It was finally healing! Well, as much as a face could heal where the jaw was missing. Because she was so distracted by her lack of pain where tougher flesh had grown, she'd nearly missed the faded sign that said they'd reached Wytheville, Virginia.

"Indoors tonight?" Nathan offered as they came upon Exit 73.

"I'd almost forgot what that was like," Levi said.

The trio took the exit and found themselves on Main Street in the midst of restaurants and motels. The motels appeared to be occupied and the restaurants smelled like their kitchens were still in use. Lena had a limited sense of smell since part of her tongue was missing, but she heard Nathan comment on the smells of grilled meat. He and Levi cradled their rifles a little tighter where there were signs of people, but they kept moving past the remnants of civilization.

Forcing her hand away from her face, Lena focused on the town they were beginning to enter. Two men were smoking pipes from a balcony on the fourth floor of a motel, watching the trio pass below them. Levi smiled and waved, which was friendliness Lena was still adjusting to. But both men gestured back, and Lena felt the lift of a smile, at least with what was left of her facial muscles. Was it a smile? She couldn't resist touching her eyes, wondering if she could still express a smile merely by revealing her eyes above the bridal lace.

"Your nerves are receding." Levi glanced at her. "You're feeling less pain and new sensations, right? Your nerves have receded from the surface layer of skin where your jaw once was. They're adapting to your new physiology as a defensive measure. God installed that. It's not evolution. It's not even healing, really. Your brain is adjusting to the new normal where your nerves are too damaged or severed."

"Aah." She nodded, happy he understood.

God installed that, she repeated in her mind. He was her God now. God had installed a lot of things in her, especially recently. The mind-numbing nerve pain was gone and she now was able to walk over uneven ground without agony or fear. Maybe it would've all happened naturally over time, but Lena couldn't separate her new facial sensations from her new spiritual sensations.

Spiritual? She scoffed at herself. Levi was rubbing off on her. No, she was way past merely being influenced by the handsome blond man who'd nursed her back from the edge of death. He'd convinced her that God was real, and that she needed to get right with Him. She'd never believed in miracles, but she couldn't deny the miracle that had happened inside her. Every few minutes, ever since confessing her faith in the Savior Jesus at the campfire, she'd searched for the anxiety and guilt she'd lived with for years. Life was different without them. Levi had led her to this new life, though she didn't entirely understand how that new life had happened. It was a spiritual death, he kept talking about, and then a rebirth.

Past the empty motels and restaurants, though still in sight of the interstate, they began to check the cross-streets to see if one led to any residences.

"Too exposed," Levi said at one street.

"Trouble down there," Nathan warned at another where there appeared to be a gang of youths with clubs strolling two blocks away.

They passed more cafes, then came to the top of the downtown block and stopped. Real estate offices stood adjacent them, but the rest of the downtown area had been vandalized, looted, or burned to the point of becoming a ghost town.

Levi led them to the right, suggesting they consider camping outside in the East End Cemetery, of which the lawn was overgrown but the atmosphere seemed peaceful.

"What about that?" Nathan pointed across the street. "'Loretto Mansion' it says. Some sort of museum?"

Lena walked up the driveway to a three-story white mansion with six columns in front. It was partially obscured from the road by trees, and vines had claimed its columns and outer walls, but it was standing, which was rare in the ravaged town.

"Hold it." Levi pointed his rifle at the roof where they could see faint puffs of gray smoke coming from the chimney. "Too good to be true. It's already occupied."

Nathan scouted around the side of the huge house.

"There's a horse tied over here, Levi."

Lena followed Nathan up to the mare. The animal's head lifted from grazing only when Lena touched her neck. A long tether connected her to the mansion's corner column so she could range about forty feet.

"It ain't easy stumbling across the very people we've been trying to find." Levi slapped his thigh. "You think it's them?"

Nathan grinned and hopped onto the porch. His footsteps were noisy, and Lena wanted to warn him to be more careful. It didn't seem prudent to make noise until they knew for sure who it was. But at the heart of her hesitancy to admit it was Jenna and Chen Li was a fear that Levi would forget her. She now knew the distance he'd come to rescue Jenna, his childhood friend. Of course, he'd had his hand in toppling the Federation over the blind woman! How could Radiant Shade not distract him away from her?

The latch to the front door seemed to be broken as Nathan pushed it open. Lena hid behind the column where the horse was tied.

"Chen Li!" Nathan called as he walked inside the darkened interior. "Brian? Jenna? You guys here?"

Levi waited next to Lena outside in the dusky evening. She wondered if this were the last time she'd have him all to herself. Of course, she knew he was married and she didn't expect him to remain exclusive in any way, but she felt their connection was much deeper than what he must've had with anyone else. After all, he had literally cradled her in his arms for days and miles, during the beginning of their flight from New York. Not only was he that strong physically, but his heart was that big.

"Jenna's going to be so happy to see you," Levi said brightly. "Not to *see* you, but to know you're . . . you know."

Lena frowned, now feeling foolish for any kind of jealous regard toward Jenna. The woman was blind. And she was a Christian. No, they were all Christians now. That's what Levi meant! Of course—Radiant Shade had been the champion for the Christian cause throughout the Federation, but especially in Lena's jurisdiction.

Then she began to doubt herself. Jenna might think her conversion wasn't real. She might think Lena was up to something, trying to get intel on the Christian underground, or even to exact revenge on Jenna for disrupting her attempt to remove Obrador and reign from the Bowery.

They heard a woman's squeal, then laughter—Chen Li. Nathan's own roaring laughter came next, followed by another man's boisterous voice—Brian Steelman. It was too much. Lena backed away from the porch, but found her hand enveloped in Levi's, and he held it tight.

"It's okay," he said softly, his eyes sad, as if he knew yet again exactly the emotional battle she was having inside. "We all have a history. Everyone has a past. No one's blaming you for having a past. Haven't I shown you that I've got your back?"

Lena's eyes welled with tears and she shook her head in frustration at herself. Of course, he'd been whipped for her, and that was before she'd even come to trust God for her forgiveness. Yes, she decided. That's what she needed to do now, was to trust in her forgiveness, which she'd received once and for all. That's what it meant to be a Christian and to possess eternal life. God lived inside her now. She couldn't feel Him, but she was already learning how He was changing her from the inside out and flipping her world upside down.

She was forgiven, and other Christians must've had an agreement. She guessed that they always held their own forgiveness before their own eyes so they didn't condemn others who'd also been forgiven from their own ugly pasts.

A slender, dark-haired man loomed in the front door, his smile broad, and his arms opened wide. Brian Steelman!

"Levi Caspertein!" Brian embraced Levi and they clapped each other on the back. "I heard you were behind us a ways. We had our troubles, so we couldn't slow down. Glad you eventually caught up to us!"

"Oh, we met Shaker and Lisbon a couple nights back." Levi pointed his finger at Brian's chest. "Last time we talked, didn't I ask you to lead the others west through Pennsylvania?"

Lena hadn't known the two men were so close. They treated one another like family! Had she not understood who Brian really was? Or was this the Christian brotherhood Levi had begun to tell her existed among believers?

"Would you believe I got shot a few miles out, and had to hide in a beaver's dam for two nights? By then, Chloe and Rex had moved on. I figured I'd find my old route west by coming down this way. Then I overtook Shaker and Runner. I guess you know the rest."

"Runner? Who's that?"

"Oh, you haven't met him?" Brian ducked his head a little, as if he suspected the man might be nearby. "Colonel Rotham sent him after you and Jenna. He's an insurance policy in case you're not with the main group of Christians. The guy's a cold-hearted killer. Quiet. Eyes like a cat. Carries a tomahawk and a crossbow, but he said he lost the arrows."

"Hmm, I might've had something to do with that." Levi chuckled. "So, he's in fact sent by the Federation, huh? Runner, you say?"

"Same name as his dog, who's not nearly as fierce as he'd like her to be, but don't tell him that."

"I've met the Lab as well." Levi sighed. "But her master—he seems persistent, doesn't he? We're a long ways from the Federation now."

"The man's got an ego. I don't know." Brian shrugged. "Everyone has found a different reason to keep on living, driven by their perceived purpose."

"That's kind of deep, Brian." Levi raised his eyebrows. "You've been contemplating your life in Christ, I take it?"

From his pocket Brian drew what looked like a thin Bible and waved it at Levi.

"Hey, I couldn't be a New York street bum my whole life!" He laughed with Levi, then acknowledged Lena by the column. "So, who's this?"

Lena turned partially away, her head down, hiding her eyes. He would know her.

"You two have actually met," Levi said, moving to her. "She's a new sister in the faith. Colonel Rotham shot her in the face and left her for dead. I saw it with my own eyes. But I saw she was still alive, so I found us a way across the Hudson and ran away with her."

"No, I don't think we've met." Brian leaned down, but Lena turned farther away. "A little shy, huh? That's okay. I'm Brian."

He held out his hand. Lena hesitated, her heart pounding. No one better than Brian knew what she'd been—because he'd done the same things. Levi didn't care what she looked like, but Brian was certain to be a different story.

"She doesn't talk much, huh?" Brian asked.

"I said she was shot in the face," Levi said. "Tore her whole jawbone off. She can't talk."

"Wow. Well, we all have scars, right?" Brian's tone mellowed. "Jenna's always reminding me to see our war wounds as war stories to talk about what Christ brought us through, or what He's using to teach us. Some of our scars are little scratches, and some of us lost body parts."

"Brian," Levi said, "this is Lena. God saved her life, and she knows it."

"Lena . . . *Lena?"* Brian's body stiffened. "Wait. *Lena Travers?* Uh . . . I'm not, um . . . Levi?"

"Don't look at me." Levi gestured at her. "She can't speak, but she can still hear and communicate just fine."

Though Lena drew out her notepad and pencil, it took her a few moments to consider what she wanted to say first. Then she realized there was only one thing to say.

"Will you forgive me?" she wrote and passed it to him. Although he didn't know all of the hateful sentiments she'd had for him since he'd left the Federation, her wrath as an Enforcer was known everywhere, and she guessed it was the reason he'd hid underground and gone to the Christians.

"Forgive you?" His voice was weak. He cleared his throat. "Lena, I . . . There's nothing that I have against you. Come here."

He was almost as tall as Levi, so she was familiar with a man's height and long arms around her, but Brian was much less muscled. She cried softly against his chest, bewildered at the newness of everything since she'd been forgiven by God.

After a moment, he held her at arm's length, and one hand reached for her head, as if he intended to touch her cheek. She knew he meant it as a sign of care or sympathy, but she wasn't ready to be touched by anyone but Levi.

"She's still healing." Levi came to her rescue by intercepting his hand with his own.

"I'm sorry, I didn't mean to—"

Lena waved her hand to excuse his apology, and tried one of her smiles, using her eyes, hoping he didn't take offense at her caution at being touched—especially on the face!

"Chen Li, Jenna?" Nathan emerged through the mansion's door, his wife and Jenna trailing behind him. "I want to introduce you to someone."

After Brian had accepted her, Lena moved onto the porch toward her old enemies. Chen Li was looking worn out and a little older, but Jenna's face was the epitome of calmness and beauty.

Holding her head up, Lena allowed Chen Li to look into her veil-covered face.

"Am I supposed to . . . recognize her?" Chen Li asked. "Why aren't you guys saying anything?"

"I think she's the last person we'd ever expect would come to Christ," Nathan said, "but I witnessed God's working myself. She's really a Christian."

"Quit playing!" Jenna pressed. "Someone say something. Levi, are you there? Who is it?"

Lena scowled at Levi, who was obviously enjoying the suspense, grinning as he looked from person to person. She finally took the notepad back from Brian.

"It's me, Lena," she wrote, then drew an arrow up to, "Will you forgive me?"

Chen Li accepted the notepad.

"'It's me, Lena,'" Chen Li read. *"Forgive you?* I don't understand. Please, just take off the mask. I give up."

"She can't take off the covering," Nathan said. "She was shot. Levi kept her alive. It's really Lena. She's been with us for weeks."

Jenna reached out with both hands. Lena distinctly noticed how the blind woman's fingernails were clean, which was rare in those days. She cringed as Jenna's fingers touched her cheekbone, but she held still as Jenna probed lower, across the bridal lace, and then under it. The woman felt gently across her teeth on her upper jaw, then explored to her neck, where her lower jaw no longer existed. But there was no pain anymore.

"Oh, Lena!" The blind woman embraced her abruptly, eagerly. "My father and I prayed for you for years! Lena!"

Crying over the woman's shoulder, Lena held her just as tightly in response. A second pair of arms encircled her, and Lena opened her eyes to see Chen Li joining in. She guessed this was the answer to her written question.

For several minutes, Jenna and Chen Li doted over her, and Lena shyly allowed Chen Li to peek under the veil, but the men seemed to understand their place by staying back.

"Okay, okay," Jenna finally said. "Enough is enough. Where are you?"

Lena was holding hands with Chen Li as Jenna moved past them both, her arm outstretched. Perhaps no one understood right away who Jenna was speaking about, until Levi took a step forward and received Jenna in his calloused hands.

"I'm right here. How are you, sister?"

"You've grown." She felt up his arm to his shoulder. "And your voice is deeper. I've waited a long time for this. There were times after I asked for your help that I wondered if you'd make it all this way."

"I wondered a few times myself. The Lord kept death at bay more than a few times."

"Brian tells me you saved everyone at the bridge."

"Oh, that was all according to some master plan, I'm sure." Levi winked at Lena. "Lena and I were just getting acquainted with one another."

"Sure, now he says he plans things out!" Nathan joked with Brian, which brought a playful slap from Chen Li.

Levi and Jenna embraced, and from where Lena watched, she wondered if his face and emotion had been the same when he'd held her. The two seemed to belong together, so strong and independent, each beautiful in their own way. But Lena remembered Lyla, and guessed that Levi was missing his wife more than anything in the midst of all the emotion.

That night, the men chopped a little firewood, then led the horse inside the front door where they tied her to block the entrance and to protect her from thieves. The back door to the mansion was sealed by twenty years of vine growth. On the empty floor of the den, they laid out their sleeping bags or bedrolls and listened as Levi read from Psalm 107. The fire crackled in the hearth in front of Lena, and Jenna used both hands to hold onto Lena's left hand, as if Jenna were still trying to affirm that the woman beside her was real.

Lena couldn't stop the tears of joy as she watched the fire. It was the strangest, warmest feeling to be so loved, so accepted, regardless of the horrors of her past. Except for Levi, she'd never felt so close to anyone. But here at her side was the woman she'd intended to kill—had tried to kill—for years, and had even taken her father's life in a fit of rage. She couldn't speak to Jenna, and Jenna couldn't see what Lena wrote, but Lena nevertheless realized their hearts were the same. Failed communication by their imperfect bodies didn't discourage a sisterhood founded on much more profound elements.

When they finally bedded down, Nathan and Chen Li snuggled farthest from the fire. Brian made sure Jenna was comfortable, and lay down behind her. Lena and Jenna lay like sisters, side by side. Only Levi was apart from them all. He sat on the floor by the window that overlooked the back yard. Maybe he was thinking of Lyla again. How awkward, Lena thought, that the man everyone seemed to count on was the man most alone that night, even while she was comforted by another child of God.

But it would always be her and Levi, Lena realized. They were bonded by blood and pain. He'd found her bleeding and in pain, and saved her. And then he had accepted the pain of the whipping on her behalf, and bled for days. He would never feel the stripes on his back without remembering her.

Secretly, before drifting off to sleep, she envied Lyla Caspertein, the fierce-looking woman with gray eyes from the GW Bridge who had stood behind Levi.

Chapter Nine

Luigi Putelli used his knife to dig into the rich soil of an abandoned garden. Like the garden, the house in front had been abandoned many years earlier. Virginia seemed to have been hit hard and swiftly by the virus. But people's gardens had continued to grow, and in Virginia, that was about one out of every ten residences.

Laughter from nearby filled the air, and birds in the trees over Luigi's shoulder scolded the invasion of their territory. Luigi listened to the laughter. It was good to hear Levi laugh. He sounded like his father, the great Serval himself. For years, Luigi had loved and served Corban. When he'd been asked, Luigi had gone to watch over Titus as well. But Pan-Day had brought Luigi back to Corban's doorstep. Now that both men were gone, Luigi's last attachments in the world were to Corban and Titus' offspring, Levi and Jenna.

From the garden, Luigi ran past the carport to emerge on the front driveway where the street intersected. He was just in time to catch a glimpse of Levi, Briar, and Nathan escorting Lena, Jenna, and Chen Li. They were heading southwest. Luigi had been running marathons every day, moving between traveling parties, and watching over them from the shade trees and back roads of forgotten communities. Now that the six were all together, he'd been contemplating joining them in person. If it weren't for the danger that Runner and his dog presented, he would've joined them already.

Turning from the street, he entered the vacant house in search of a bag or backpack to use for his garden treasures. Though the house had been abandoned, Luigi didn't believe he was the first to search through the interior. Someone in ages past had tracked mud into the kitchen, and the contents of the hallway closet lay strewn across the floor. Upstairs in one of the bedrooms, the sheets and blankets were missing from the dusty mattress, but he found a pillowcase on the floor that would work for his needs.

Every house had treasures and a past, but Luigi wasn't interested in looting or trading newly discovered items. For decades, he'd sacrificed his own well-being and comfort to ensure the safety of God's people. Since leaving New York, he'd lived off the land by eating plants, mushrooms, and even grass along the way, when necessary. People's forgotten gardens were a sure source of food, and wild roots were an edible source of carbs to keep up his energy. Fruit trees were scarce, but when he found them, he filled his pockets and pressed on. He guarded Jenna especially, and was ready to pounce at the first sign of danger from Runner.

Behind the house, Luigi filled the pillowcase with potatoes that had grown unfettered in the shade of the nearby tree. A bag of potatoes would be a good gift for Levi and Jenna, Luigi decided, once he was able to join their band of merry travelers. With Levi and Nathan at hand, he didn't feel that he was especially necessary any longer, and he could now enjoy the company of the younger Christians. After all, he was weary in body and soul. Now in his seventies, he was truly ready to retire. The weight of loss—first his wife, Heather, and then Corban—was more than he could bear some nights, but he endured to continue caring for God's few faithful.

He tied a knot in the top of the pillowcase and headed off into the woods, hoping to intercept his friends on the next lane before they returned to the interstate. His heart was light as he hiked through the forest, anticipating Levi's hearty laughter and Nathan's gentle strength at his side once again, as they'd been together before Pan-Day.

And to sit over campfires with Jenna, to hear her sing and recite Scripture that Corban had taught her—Luigi envisioned all this as if it were paradise already.

But instead of laughter, he heard crying ahead. Luigi, as he had most of his life, slipped through the shadows of the trees to the east. There, he crouched and observed a toddler in overalls, with blond hair and grubby hands, crying in the middle of a flowery meadow.

The head of a woman rose up and down, and when she paused, Luigi noticed a shovel in her hands. Standing taller, Luigi saw the bundled form of an adult body lying in the meadow grass. She was burying a family member, maybe her husband.

Luigi bowed his head, calling upon God to strengthen America's few survivors in those last days. For people who weren't Christians, the world would become much harsher once the Tribulation years began, as John prophesied in Revelation. But for now, the effects of the Meridia Virus were challenging enough.

Taking a step away, Luigi glanced back at the lonely burial party of the woman and her son. She was in her twenties, Luigi guessed, and the toddler was maybe two or three. If they had any friends, or if she knew anyone else, she would've had others to help her dig the grave. But no man came to her aid or helped her. A woman and her son shouldn't be alone like that, Luigi thought, but then remembered his place beside the Dowlers and Casperteins. What about his vision of paradise in the company of young people who were continuing in the Lord's work after their parents?

He looked down at the sack of potatoes and frowned, but not too sadly. God was speaking to his soul, and as he bowed his will to do the Lord's desire, he couldn't find anything but contentment. His heart shifted, and in just a few seconds of trust, it seemed God's Spirit had drawn him from Jenna, who no longer needed him, to this poor woman and child who clearly needed someone, or anyone.

True, Runner was still out there, but the predator he was would be no match for the witty and wily servant God had made Levi to be. Jenna would be safe with Levi, or even with Brian, who seemed to have taken to the blind girl. No, not a girl any longer, Luigi realized. She was a woman of God, and now she was surrounded by men of God.

Emerging from the tree line, Luigi walked across the meadow. The woman stopped digging and moved in front of her son, who ceased crying and hid behind his mother's legs. She raised the shovel like an ax, and Luigi came to the edge of the shallow grave she'd barely carved out of the earth. He dropped his sack of potatoes and shed his outer layer, a wool sweater he'd scavenged from a home in Pennsylvania weeks earlier.

Down to only his thermal top, he raised his arms to the sunshine, calling in his heart upon God Almighty to strengthen him in this final mission of his life. The Dowlers and Caspertеins were no longer his assignment. Now, with his arms spread and his face turned toward the sky, he dedicated his remaining years to this woman and her child, even though they were strangers. Certainly, her aggressive stance against him revealed the true nature of the state of humanity in that part of Virginia—she didn't feel safe.

Her response toward him also informed him of the type of threats from which he might need to protect her. She was used to violence, because her interactions had been violent. But now she and her boy were his responsibility. It would be his job to bring godly fear to whomever she feared.

He lowered his arms and opened his eyes. She still stood ready to chop him down with the shovel.

"God has directed me to help you." He held out his hand. "Give me the shovel. I'll dig this grave."

She hesitated, then smeared dirt across her cheek as she tucked her hair behind her ear. Slowly, she lowered the shovel and extended the handle to him. He took it in his bony hand, hoping his gaunt features weren't too repulsive. Then, he continued to dig where she'd begun.

Mother and son sat down in the grass and flowers, and Luigi threw the dirt on the other side of the grave. He paused to rest once, and set his potatoes in her lap, and she clutched them and her son as if she would perish without them. Luigi gazed into her tear-streaked face and saw only pain, hurt, and loss.

"You're not alone. I have protected the needy and the innocent for generations. God has made me the best at what I do, and until I die, I am your servant and your son's servant. Fear no more. Weep your tears today, but tomorrow we'll talk about eternal joy. Who do we bury today?"

"My husband."

"Very well." Luigi continued digging. "Today, we bury your husband. Tomorrow, we learn to live again. There will be new hope borne from this loss, and your son will know laughter again. This is my work now."

"There are . . . people." She held the pillowcase to her chest. "Bad people have come here before. They'll kill my son and take me. They've threatened us before. Women my age are in . . . danger all over."

"Danger?" Luigi scoffed. "As long as there is life in my body, you will know no more danger. I serve you now for the God of Corban Dowler and Titus Caspertein. As an operative of the Commission of International Laborers, I extend my hands and my heart to you. Right now, I'm a stranger, but I'll prove to you I'm not just an old man. One thousand have fallen at my left hand, and ten thousand have fallen at my right. Where I go, my Sovereign God Almighty reigns. For decades, He has preserved me. Now, that preservation is extended to you. You are not alone."

Nathan Isaacson stood in the middle of the highway at a crossroads of rural Tennessee.

"You're not hearing me, Levi," Nathan stated, enunciating his words carefully. "Colorado is that way. Erwin is that way. Colorado, west. Erwin, east. Colorado, life. Erwin, death. Are you understanding me?"

"You're overreacting," Levi said. "You heard Jenna and Chen Li. There's a slave market in Erwin. We need to shut it down."

"Well, we're not COIL anymore!" Nathan threw up his hands. "God, help us! Speak some sense into Your stubborn son, Titus! We need to get to Colorado!"

"You just called him Titus!" Jenna laughed.

"That's because he's as stubborn as his father!" Nathan stared down the highway to the west. "I mean, look. It's there, inviting us. We can't rescue the whole world, Levi. Leave Erwin in God's hands. Colorado is calling us home."

"We're not saving the world," Levi said, "just Erwin. It's just down that highway, inviting us to help them."

"It's not on our way."

"Then we go out of our way." Levi shrugged. "It's what we do, Nathan."

"It's not what I do!"

Nathan growled at the sky and shook his head. Sighing, he studied the others who stood and watched him argue with Levi. First, there was Chen Li whose thumbs were stuck in her backpack straps, her face blank, as if she didn't want to take sides, even though Nathan wanted her to take his side.

Next, there was Jenna, her face serene and peaceful as she held the lead rope to the mare burdened with most of their gear. He already knew Jenna would run into a burning barn all on her own if it meant there was a chance to save someone.

Then there was Lena, whose posture and closed fists showed she was barely containing her defensiveness for her protector, Levi.

And finally, there was Brian, who seemed neutral, but Nathan guessed he'd side with Jenna's reasoning to confront Erwin's townspeople, even if they all died doing so.

His eyes settled on Levi once again, who had a calm look on his face as if he already knew exactly what he was going to do, whether he had anyone's support or not. And yet, the very next words out of Levi's mouth convinced Nathan that Levi was actually thinking Christ-like, not selfishly or bullheadedly.

"If you think it's wise," Levi said, "take everyone west, Nate. I've just got to do this in Erwin. It's a couple days' detour for me, but I'll catch up to you guys in a week."

"Aah!" Lena tugged on the side of Levi's pack, expressing her unwillingness to go with Nathan instead of Levi.

"If people are in trouble," Jenna said, "whether it's safe or wise or neither, we need to go there all together. Shaker won't stop what he's doing until we shut down their enterprise."

"They'll start the slave market back up the day after we leave!" Nathan pressed. "We're not the police. We're outside the Federation. There's no authority out here."

"I'd sort of like to tranquilize some human traffickers," Brian said. "I mean, to make a point. It's the principle of the thing, to let people know there are others who stand against slavery, even if we can't force them to stop it."

"It's reckless," Nathan said, but his heart wasn't in his argument any longer. He thought of his own youth. As long as he'd had the resources, he'd done some pretty reckless things for others, but he was an older man now, and Chen Li was in no physical condition to fight the battles they'd once fought together.

"So?" Chen Li said. "Let's be reckless, hon. It's not any more reckless than a bunch of washed-up agents following a blind woman to take over a government. No offense, Jenna."

"None taken." Jenna laughed. "Although I'm not sure that's helping your argument. Operation Esther collapsed toward the end, thanks to unwavering opposition. No offense, Lena."

"Aah-ah," Lena vocalized, gesturing with her hand.

"She says, none taken," Levi interpreted. "But it didn't work out too well for her, either."

Lena slapped his shoulder since he'd apparently spoken too much for her. Nathan couldn't help but see the two as brother and sister already, especially the way Levi was beginning to include Lena in his antics.

"We only have two battle rifles," Nathan said, "and Brian's antique, which could fall apart as easily as misfire."

"And one pistol." Levi drew his sidearm, then tossed it to Chen Li. "See? Four firearms is all we need."

"I'm afraid I'm out of practice." Chen Li studied the gun. "It's been twenty years."

"Ah-ah?" Lena asked.

Nathan glanced at Levi, who raised his eyebrows in question as well, leaving it to Nathan to make the call. He felt his resolve for continuing to Colorado begin to dissolve.

"Go ahead, Chen Li." Nathan sighed. "Give it to Lena. We'll need all the shooters we can get."

"Jenna and I will gladly stay back with the horse someplace safe," Chen Li volunteered.

"Speak for yourself!" Jenna said, laughing. "The horse and I could use a good gunfight. After all, I was to be betrothed to some guy here in Erwin. If anyone's shooting the town up, it should be me!"

"So, we're going?" Brian asked Nathan.

Nathan had been the team leader of COIL's first elite Special Forces team, but with Levi around, he hadn't been too sure how relevant he was in making decisions. Until now. Levi was younger, stronger, and probably sharper, but he was now submitting to his elder, waiting for his answer with the others.

"As long as we have a plan," Nathan said.

"That may not work too well," Jenna warned. "I've heard those Casperteins sort of wing it wherever they go."

"It ain't easy arguing with the truth," Levi admitted, "but I'll try anything once, even a plan."

"Now do you miss all those years when it was just you and me?" Chen Li asked Nathan.

"You have no idea!" He laughed, and held his wife's hand as they led the way east, toward Erwin.

Chloe Azmaveth walked on the right lane of Interstate 80, in about the middle of the group of one hundred refugees. After a couple weeks of partnering with ex-mayor Nick Zoft, she'd come to favor the chubby man's conversation, but at that moment, they were both quiet, nearing the end of the day's march somewhere in the midst of Ohio.

Back to her left, Scooter was telling a story to some of the Christians, using humor to encourage the people's hearts even though their circumstances were unfavorable. Rex had asked for her, Scooter, and Bruno's counsel about walking again during the daytime hours, which would be easier on them all. But food shortages continued, and carrying enough water for everyone was a daily struggle. Shoes were falling apart, tents were tearing, sleeping bags needed washing, and Chloe couldn't remember the last time she'd washed her hair. Every time she ran her fingers through her graying curls, she discovered more debris from sleeping for weeks on the ground.

"What's so funny?" Nick asked.

She realized then that she was grinning.

"Oh, I was just thinking of soaking in a tub. I lived the spoiled life in the Bowery."

"I'd much rather have all this than the luxury I had back in Hackensack."

"All this?" Chloe remembered his life story and the hardships he'd endured as a secret, isolated Christian. "You know, we too often don't remember that Jesus was our example for suffering in this world. Thanks for reminding me to see all that we do have right here."

"Yep!" The man sighed. "I once was lonely in a city that claimed to be unified. Now, I'm with family, even though I may be starving to death."

They laughed until others nearby asked what they were carrying on about. Chloe and Nick explained their view, and joy spread up and down the line of refugees. Or perhaps, Chloe thought, some of the hilarity was that the fat man was joking about starving to death, though the pounds were falling off him on their trek. Whatever the case, Chloe was pleased to have grown close to the man who loved Jesus, and that he had such hope in eternity he could rejoice even in his earthly weakness. God's grace was sufficient.

And the Lord continued to show His care for them in many ways. As Alice led the refugees toward Akron, they came upon a traveler who'd just lost his horse. Rex helped him butcher it, and rather than allow the meat go to waste, the owner gave Rex a quarter of the horse. The following day, Rex stopped to trade with a farmer for as much grain as the refugees could find sacks to fill. The farmer gladly traded some of his horse-drawn wagon full of grain for the haunch of the horse the group had gained the previous day.

Although the meat was good protein for the people, Chloe knew the grain would keep better while they were on the move, and it was necessary for their diet as well. It could be ground down using flat rocks, then baked with a little oil to make flat bread. Chloe had no doubt that Rex, Bruno, or Scooter would find them more meat to eat soon, even if it were dog. None of them had discriminating stomachs any longer, and stray dogs seemed to roam as numerous as the birds in the sky. The dogs were healthy and their meat was lean, so Chloe saw them all as God's provision. Of course, having lived in New York City so long, eating dog was a delicacy since many refugees had been supplementing their food rations with rats.

North of Akron one afternoon, the group had stopped to rest for an hour in the field beside a highway when Alice advised Rex on the radio to stand alert. Rex immediately whistled all shooters to attention. Since learning of the Federation convoy's demise under the Ohio militia, Rex hadn't been deploying a rear guard, so everyone with a weapon was at hand and stood ready for conflict, including Chloe and Nick.

She moved up to Rex's side, appreciating that Rex relied on her counsel and experience at such moments. Following Rex's gaze to the north, Chloe noticed a mass of people moving down a highway toward Akron.

"That doesn't look right." Chloe used the binoculars to study the approaching party, then handed them to Rex. "It looks like they're being herded. I count six gunmen on the sides of them, and two on horseback in the rear. Maybe about forty people unarmed in the middle."

"About that." Rex kept the binoculars against his brow. "Those forty are carrying packs. They look like families. I see a couple of children. If I didn't know any better, I'd say they're prisoners of some sort, being moved somewhere."

He gave the field glasses back to her, then signaled Scooter and Bruno to spread out along the road, placing themselves between the Christian refugees and the approaching party.

Chloe looked back at the hundred God had given them to protect. Most of them were seated on the ground, nibbling on food and visiting in small groups. Milo Rotham, the disgraced colonel, stood near a husband and wife from New York who had more or less adopted the man with no supplies. From their fingers, they shared pieces of meat cooked over the previous evening's fire. If he didn't accept what these simple people offered him, he would die. It was an image Chloe wished Corban could have seen. The humble were caring for the proud. God was the great equalizer.

Rex had relaxed his demands upon Rotham, mostly because the ex-colonel was already so depressed, but also because his identity was now known throughout the whole company. He still wore his Federation uniform, though it was torn and stained. Chloe guessed if the man acted in any way contrary, the people would handle him immediately, since Owen and Obrador's violence against one of their own was still so fresh on their hearts. Although he'd been downcast, Rotham had carried the goat named Ruth every day since joining their number. He hardly ever spoke, and when he did, it was in somber tones.

At that moment, Chloe realized her gaze upon the ex-officer had lingered too long, for he had noticed. He climbed to his feet, skirted the groups of refugees, and came up to them to stand silently beside her. Chloe appreciated that the man, who was about Rex's age, had surveyed the situation for himself.

"So, what's our policy here?" Chloe asked Rex.

He frowned at the approaching gunmen, all with automatic weapons. But Chloe wondered what the gunmen would think of the sight of Rex, who was probably three hundred pounds of muscle and brawn. His beard made him seem older than his early thirties, and the pack on his back added to his mountainous frame. Additionally, he'd been carrying the returned rifle that had belonged to Lyla, so he had one rifle over each shoulder.

"It depends on what they're doing with those people," Rex said. "Our policy is to show grace to all, Levi would say, even if we need to humble some people to get them ready for it. Come with me. Rotham, you stay here. Hold your fire unless you see me shoot first. Understand? Protect the people!"

Rotham appeared bewildered.

"Hold what fire?" he asked, holding up his empty hands.

Rex took his spare battle rifle off his shoulder and set it in Rotham's hands. Rotham was still looking down at the weapon he'd been entrusted with when Chloe stepped out with Rex toward the group of strangers.

As Rex and Chloe advanced, the escorts of the group stopped, and both horsemen from the rear galloped up to the front, then crossed the ditch to challenge Rex and Chloe. Chloe kept her rifle aimed at the ground, following Rex's lead, who she guessed was large enough to wrestle at least one horse to the ground with his bare hands if he needed to. But he didn't react to the charging horses, and the gunmen drew up a few yards in front of them.

"Who are you people?" one horseman demanded. His rifle was a Chinese-made SKS, and he seemed only now to realize that Rex had a number of other riflemen of his own spread out strategically. "You'd better not be headed north. We have a Meridia Virus outbreak on the coast of Lake Erie."

"Meridia?" Rex gave Chloe a reassuring glance, as if he wanted her to know he was reading no immediate danger, and she could stand at ease. "No, sir. We're moving west to Colorado. Deputy Worlawn gave us his approval a few days ago. He even returned one of our rifles that was stolen by a thief."

"I know Worlawn. Good man." The horseman let his own rifle hang on its sling away from his hands. His gaze swept over the refugees, then stopped at Rotham not far behind. "What uniform is that one wearing? I'm not familiar."

"He's a deserter from the Federation." Rex chuckled. "It's strange the way the Good Lord works. He was a colonel who used to hunt us Christians. Now, he's joined us in our march to greener pastures."

"And you trust him enough to give him a weapon?"

"These are all loaded with tranquilizer rounds. We're not trying to permanently hurt anyone." Rex gestured at the group of people behind the man. "You have Meridia Virus victims with you or what?"

"The outbreak required some population relocation. It's our third outbreak in three years. Now we're force-relocating people who refused to find other housing away from the coastline."

"Force relocating." Rex nodded. "Difficult measures for difficult times."

"Tell me about it." The horseman shook his head. "I'd rather be planting crops for my own family than doing this."

"If any want to go to Colorado with us, we're willing to take some off your hands. It's mountain living with hard winters, but plenty of resources."

"Seriously?" The man asked, looking to Chloe for confirmation. "You'd take in strangers?"

"We're all suffering in this fallen world, but some of your people don't look too healthy," Rex said. "They're clear of patchy skin?"

"We've checked them twice a day for the virus."

"Let my people mingle with yours, help them out with what we have. We'll go our separate ways in an hour."

"Hey, my job is to move them from the coast. Where they go from here is their choice."

"Bring them down here into the grass." Rex waved. "We'll share what we have and see who wants to join us for the Rocky Mountains."

Chloe backed away to stand beside Rotham as Rex welcomed the forty Lake Erie citizens into the group of refugees.

"You're seeing Christians at their finest right there," Chloe said to Rotham as together they observed the refugees greeting the downhearted newcomers. "Levi couldn't have handled that any better."

"It's pure insanity." Rotham swung the rifle sling over his shoulder. "Look at your people. You'd think they were meeting lost relatives. Check that out, too!"

Following his gaze to the right, she saw where the Ohio riflemen were congregating with Rex, Scooter, and the others, exchanging food and admiring one another's weapons. Rex laughed loudly at a joke Scooter told, and everyone followed suit.

"You know it's love from God that fills our hearts, right?" Chloe said to Rotham. "I mean, yeah, we're a little crazy, but it's the love of God that inspires us to do things like this."

"I have no words." Rotham looked away. "I didn't know who I was hunting. I don't believe in God, but you people don't need to be eradicated because you do."

"Well, I supposed that's a big step for you to admit," Chloe said. "Come on. Let's join in."

"No, I'm not one of them," he said. "I'm not one of you."

"What's holding you back?" Chloe let him ponder her question a moment, then waved him to follow. "Come on. You just might learn something."

Hesitantly, he walked forward. Chloe patted him on the shoulder, imagining she might've done the same to a son who was taking a bold step forward. At his side, she joined the medley of friends and strangers.

Thirty minutes later, Rex found her and pulled her away from a cook fire that had been lit to feed some of the Erie citizens.

"I've been around to them all," Rex said to her privately. "Can we handle another forty bodies? Because they'd all rather go to the mountains of Colorado than to the unknown of Columbus or Akron where they're being taken."

"But it's still hundreds of miles to Colorado." Chloe frowned. "Did you tell them?"

"Of course, I told them." He turned her by her arm toward the gathering. "Look at them. They haven't known a sense of community like this their whole lives. But forty more?"

"It's at least a couple more fires at night," Chloe said. "Can you hunt for this many?"

"I guess we'll have to find a way." He sighed. "I already made the offer, so I can't un-invite them now."

The armed Ohio men were thrilled that they didn't need to escort the forty all the way south. Instead, they heartily shook hands with Scooter and Rex, with whom they had immediately bonded, and set off to return to Erie where their own families waited.

"Would Levi have invited another forty to travel with us if he were here?" Rex asked Chloe that evening as they marched west.

Chloe knew Rex was just seeking affirmation.

"Rex, you know him better than I, so you tell me. You guys walked across America to rescue Jenna, and he risked his life to save one hundred people when he got to New York."

"It's a lot of people to lead. I know it won't be easy."

"That seems to be the Caspertein way," Chloe said, and they walked side by side toward the setting sun.

Levi Caspertein led his small band of travelers up a forested highway toward Erwin, Tennessee, when he sniffed the air.

"Phew!" he gasped.

"Aah!" Lena waved her hand in front of her face. Her other hand remained on the butt of the pistol in her waistband.

“Something died.” Brian touched his nose and stepped away from behind the mare he’d been following. “That’s not the horse, is it?”

“It’s just fish,” Chen Li said. “There was a wharf in Hong Kong where I grew up. I’d know that smell anywhere.”

They emerged into a clearing where townspeople were coming and going from a three-story house with chipped white paint and two bay windows overlooking a yard of dirt and bushes. Levi handed his rifle to Lena and jogged ahead to meet a man and his wife as they walked down the highway. Between them, they carried a camping cooler with a cracked lid.

“Is the town of Erwin near here?” Levi asked. “My friends and I are just in from the interstate.”

“About two miles this way,” the man said. He had a tattoo of an elephant on his forearm.

“Seems like a long ways for you to carry that cooler. You’ve got fish in there?”

“Yep, it’s Fish Friday.” The man continued with his wife, speaking over his shoulder. “A little walking for fresh fish every week? It’s a fair price.”

“It’s got to be a fish hatchery,” Chen Li said when she caught up. “See where they’re all coming and going to behind that house?”

“The guy said we’re about two miles from town,” Levi said, and nodded to Lena, still trusting her with his rifle. It looked natural in her arms. “Jenna, are you ready?”

“Yes, Master,” Jenna joked. “Finally, I’m part of a Caspertein plot!”

“Quiet, you!” He spoke softly in her ear. “The bait isn’t supposed to be this excited. Come on. There’s a porch ahead, six steps.”

He glanced back at his friends who remained with the horse in the front yard. Jenna held his arm, allowing him to lead her up the stairs where eight men and women sat in rocking chairs and porch swings under the awning.

"Good afternoon," Levi greeted them. Below the porch, people filed past with their containers. The smell of fish was nauseating. "I was told I could make a particularly lucrative trade in Erwin. A couple said we're close to the town. Who should I ask for when I get there?"

A man with a white beard stopped rocking his chair and sat forward. With his glass, he gestured to Jenna.

"The way you've got a hold on that girl, I'd say your trade has something to do with her. Am I right?"

"You presume rightly. She's pretty enough, but she's blind as a possum in a spotlight." Even Levi was surprised to hear his father's Arkansas vernacular from his own mouth. "It ain't easy raising a family with Blind Betty here as useless as a three-legged plow horse. I'm already married. Figured she might make someone a wife, so long as she's not expected to do too much otherwise."

"You came to the right place," White Beard said. "But you need to see Merry in town. This is just the superintendent's residence."

"Superintendent of what?"

"The fish hatchery. Can't you smell it?"

"No offense, but I can't smell anything else." Levi wiggled his nose. "So, this woman's name is Mary?"

"No, he's a Southern gentleman named Merry, like Merry Christmas. He'll see to your trade with your Blind Betty. Tell him I sent you. The name's Reece. He appreciates referrals. He depends on them. You might consider trading that horse there, too. Merry has a taste for horse meat, not just the two-legged merchandise, if you know what I mean."

"I appreciate the advice." Levi nodded at the ladies present. "All of you are part of this Merry fellow's trading circle?"

"We don't spoil ourselves too much." Reece smiled and scratched his belly. "But yes, we've sampled the forbidden wares of Mr. Merry's. He's not a scoundrel, mind you. He never kidnapped anyone. All his trades are fair. The whole town sees to it. I see to it. I'm the superintendent. You don't follow the law, you don't get any fish."

"So, you're all in on it." Levi let go of Jenna long enough to wag his finger at the older man. "You're a clever man, I can tell. You've got your hands in everything. Mr. Merry couldn't have prospered without the say-so of cultured men like yourself. This town is dependent on you, and you keep the merchandise flowing for Merry."

"You have no idea, young man." Reece sipped his beverage. "Without the hatchery, Erwin would've collapsed after Pan-Day. We here are the town's life blood, and Merry, well, he just provides the entertainment—in more ways than one. When you get to town, you'll see the movie theater. Erwin's like paradise—you may not want to leave at all."

The other men on the porch chuckled in such a way that Levi might've tranqed them if he would've had his rifle. He was even embarrassed that Jenna had been there to hear their glee about sin and slavery.

"I'll head into town," he said to the superintendent, "and when I'm finished with Merry, I'll be sure to see to you all here before I leave."

"Take your time." Reece waved. "Plenty to do. Don't forget the Capitol Theater, now. Merry will let you know about everything."

Levi guided Jenna off the porch and back to the horse.

"A lot more stinks about this place than just the fish," Nathan hissed under his breath. "I only heard half of what they said. Levi, you can't let Jenna do this anymore. You used her to get us a contact name. Now she needs to be left somewhere safe."

"*Let me*, Nathan?" Jenna asked sharply. "I appreciate your concern, but I'm not the woman in distress I'm pretending to be, and you're not the man who allows me to do or not do anything!"

"Voices, you guys . . ." Chen Li said through her teeth as Levi led the horse away. "We're not trying to warn them about our real intentions, are we?"

Nathan waited to continue the conversation until they reached the rural highway where they turned left toward the town.

"I'm just saying it's too dangerous for you to proceed, Jenna. Levi knows that."

Levi gave the horse's lead rope to Brian, then stopped on the side of the road to look back at the superintendent's residence. The others continued walking, and Jenna and Nathan continued to argue. Only Lena drew up with Levi and followed his gaze back to the white house. She passed his rifle back to him.

"There's probably only a couple attendants down at the hatchery," Levi said to her. "I didn't see any kids or dogs. At night, this place probably isn't even guarded. They're fat and lazy. Memorize the position of the house and the hatchery below. The river looks like it flows across and down through those woods. What a pity if all the fish were released to the river instead of to the dinner plates of Erwin's complacent and immoral citizens. Tonight, come back here alone. Can you handle the hatchery?"

"Aah."

"We stand for good and not evil, so guard your heart from hating these people, even though it seems the whole town is in on Mr. Merry's business dealings."

"Aah."

Others from town passed them then, and Levi jogged with Lena back up to their friends.

"Levi," Jenna stated forcefully, "kindly tell your friend Mr. Nathan Isaacson that I'm not a child to be told what I will or won't be involved in from here on out. We're catching this Merry and running him out of the flesh trade once and for all."

"I don't know about once and for all," Levi said, "but I do know that you and Chen Li will leave town with the horse before Brian, Nathan, and I pay Merry a visit. The charade is over, Jenna. Our weapons are cocked. If Merry can't be reasoned with, and the town is behind him, we're going to be the ones who are on the run out of this town, not them."

No one spoke for a moment until Brian cleared his throat and addressed Levi.

"You have to teach me to do that," he said.

"Do what?" Levi asked.

"Shut the mouth of a headstrong woman."

"I heard that!" Jenna shouted, then laughed with them all.

Even Lena's eyes showed amusement, Levi noticed, as she enjoyed the conversation with her friends, even though she couldn't take part.

They walked along the quiet highway, townspeople in front and behind them, then descended into "The Valley Beautiful," a sign read, in the midst of the Cherokee National Forest.

Levi had learned to gauge the population of a town merely by how many people were walking around during the day. Erwin must've been about three hundred people, he guessed from the number of stores and businesses that were open on Main and Nolichucky Avenue, one block over. It was hard to miss the Capitol Theater, its bright blue sign recently painted. However, the banner that advertised what shows were playing displayed three adult films from which Levi diverted his eyes.

"Clearly," Chen Li said, "the human flesh trade isn't the only disgusting thing this town turns a blind eye towards. No offense, Jenna."

"What is it?" she asked.

"It's not worth hearing, Jenna," Brian said, then rested his free hand on his rifle. "Levi?"

Two men with sidearms walked past the locals who were carrying fish and running other errands. The citizens had their minds on themselves, but the two gunmen were clearly eyeing the newcomers.

"Spread out, boys," Levi ordered Nathan and Brian. He itched his nose to disguise his words behind his hand. "Chen Li, take the horse and Jenna down to that old building with the flagpole."

Brian wandered left and Nathan drifted right. Only Lena remained with Levi, staying a step behind him.

"Beautiful town you have here," Levi said, the friendliness he'd had with the superintendent gone from his voice as he stopped in front of the two men on the street. "Superintendent Reece said I should talk to Merry about a trade."

"You buying or selling?" one of them asked. He chewed on a twig, and his chipped teeth showed it'd been a bad habit for some time.

"Selling." Levi lowered his head, sizing up the other man, whose right hand rested on a weathered pistol grip, like he knew how to use it. "Maybe buying, if the price is right."

"What's with her?" Twig jutted his chin at Lena. "You make her wear that mask? Pretty eyes, but she can't be the one you're trading if you let her carry that little gun."

Levi glanced at Lena. Her eyes showed amusement, but he had no doubt there was some righteous anger about to pour out as well, like there was in them all.

"Is Merry around?" Levi pressed. "I'm assuming he's got a place of business where we could talk in private."

Out of the corner of his eye, Levi noticed Nathan shift his position up the street. Two more armed townsmen walked closer, their swagger slow, with their eyes on the visitors.

"At the gallery," Twig said, pointing with the stick in his mouth, "around the corner. But he won't be free for about an hour. He's finishing up a deal with another client."

"Appreciate it." Levi nodded. "I'll wait about an hour then, and go see him."

He walked away, feeling within him the fight that was about to occur in the town. In other towns, he'd visited to connect to the locals. But he wasn't in Erwin to connect with anyone. Lena hustled to keep up with him, and they arrived at the horse and flagpole together.

"What'd he say?" Chen Li asked.

Levi waited until Brian and Nathan arrived.

"We've got an hour until Merry's supposedly free," Levi said, "but it could be just a stall tactic to organize. I see eight toughs with guns keeping an eye on us. I can't tell if they're watching us in case we're a threat, or if they're watching us to spot a weakness so they can rob us."

"Aah."

Studying the building nearest the flagpole, Levi saw it was a library, but a plaque out front said it had once been a railroad building. It was built sturdy, like other nearby structures, with thick walls where shooters would be safe from bullets if they were within.

"This isn't going to be easy pickings." Levi checked the cinch on the pack horse and spoke low, where only his five friends could hear. "Nate, what do you think?"

"I counted ten." Nathan's eyes were wide but fearless. "Five pairs. But all handguns. They won't be useful beyond forty feet or so."

"We're definitely attracting attention right here," Brian said. "Maybe we should've hidden our rifles before showing up."

"We can't be the first visitors in town with rifles," Levi said. "If this town moves merchandise, then it's no surprise they've got a security system set up. I wouldn't doubt if there are a few assault rifles behind some of those windows."

"How're we going to do it?" Jenna asked. "I mean, with Merry."

"By getting you out of the line of fire, to start with." Levi pushed the lead rope into Chen Li's hand. "We've scoped the town, so now it's time to set things in our favor. Chen Li, take the horse and Jenna out of town the way we came in. About halfway back to the hatchery, hide on the north side of the highway in the trees. We'll find you on our way out. Don't come back here for anything, no matter what you hear—and you'll definitely hear something."

"You girls have gel-tranqs?" Nathan asked.

"We never leave home without one." Chen Li opened her palm, revealing a rifle cartridge, and Jenna showed she had one in a pocket as well.

"Lena, the sun's setting." Levi nodded at his mute friend. "Be safe."

"Where's she going?" Jenna asked.

"Fishing." Levi shrugged. "It ain't easy keeping this town open for business if its hatchery loses all its fish."

"You're loving this, I can tell." Chen Li kissed her husband, then turned the mare away while addressing Levi. "Just keep my husband safe, or I'll use this gel-tranq on a Caspertein!"

The three men watched the women walk away, Jenna and Chen Li in one direction with the horse, and Lena in another direction, alone. Levi wasn't envious of Brian's obvious feelings for Jenna, evidenced by his gaze following her. It actually relieved him that the two were bonding. He was already thinking of them as a couple, which satisfied him beyond words since he'd have someone dependable to entrust Jenna to when he reached his wife in Colorado.

"Are you two lovebirds ready to talk strategy?" Levi teased.

"You mean a Caspertein actually has a plan?" Nathan jabbed right back, turning his attention to the younger man. "This isn't an easy situation. We could just commence with the sabotage you've already set Lena to, and walk away without a gunfight. I'm sure the town won't manage without that hatchery. We've seen how much they rely on it."

"If you can't beat them out of business," Brian said, "starve 'em out. It could work."

"Erwin's second favorite trade needs to be crippled as well." Levi nodded at the buildings along the street. "We have the advantage of rifles over pistols, at least for now. They have no artillery or heavy guns. If you two pick separate places to hide above the street level, somewhere inside one of these railroad buildings, you should be able to command the street before I come out of that gallery."

"Before you come out?" Nathan eyed the angles. "You want us to bring the thunder while you're inside?"

"Yeah. I'll use it to convince Merry that he's not in charge." Levi gestured at the gallery building. "But getting in there with my rifle is a whole other issue."

They studied the red and white building across the street, then considered a couple buildings down the street for Brian and Nathan to hide in, their distance beyond handgun range.

"You haven't said how you're going to shut down Merry," Nathan said. "We're not sticking around Tennessee, so you have something in mind?"

"Yep. I intend to find Merry and arrest him." Levi tightened the sling on his rifle so he could fire it simply by pivoting his body and pulling the trigger—aiming and firing with one arm. "How do we usually turn hearts toward God?"

"We . . . share the gospel with them?" Nathan frowned. "I'm as confident as anyone in the power of the gospel, Levi, but only if they receive the message."

"Merry will receive the message because he'll be our captive audience. I'm taking him into custody."

"That's absurd." Nathan took a step back. "I'm not having someone like him with us, with the girls! Shaker was going to sell Jenna to this guy!"

"If he's with us," Brian said, "he won't be running things here. I kind of like the idea. I mean, that's how Corban got me to see the truth. He put me with Scooter and Luigi in the tunnels. At first, I was a captive, but then I found freedom in it. Or, through it."

"Exactly." Levi raised his eyebrows. "Like you said, we can't stay here in Tennessee, so we take the man responsible for this evil—with us. It's a citizen's arrest."

Levi watched Nathan struggle with the idea, his face twisting as he seemed to imagine the horrors that someone like Merry had committed.

"We don't have enough gel-tranqs to tranq this whole town, but the whole town is in on it," Brian said.

"Then our statement will simply need to be loud enough to convince the town to get off of it."

"Casperteins." Nathan sighed in resignation and shook his head at Brian. "See what I've been dealing with since New York? He has no reason. Believe it or not, his father was even crazier."

"Jenna talks about him like he never lost a battle," Brian said, "like Titus was protected by God."

"He lost his battle against God," Levi said, "but that just meant he became God's possession. And he never regretted it. Now, shall we proceed while it's still light out? How about five minutes after I go inside, Mr. Issacson?"

"I don't know why you keep pretending like I'm in charge." Nathan chuckled. "But if you need my approval, I humbly concede to your plot. The Lord's always favored the foolish things of this world, so I guess that makes us the three most favored of all."

"Ha, I'm not sure if that's a compliment or an insult." Brian clapped Nathan on the shoulder. "I just hope you two can shoot as well as you can talk."

Nathan led them in a brief prayer for God's will, no matter the outcome. Then the three shook hands. Levi noticed Nathan was smiling, even though his plan had drawn the old operative's criticism. It reminded him of his father's stories about working with Nathan and COIL. Nathan was a military man, so Levi knew he preferred order and structure, but he was no less committed.

"It ain't easy relying on you two," Levi said, "while I put myself in harm's way."

"Don't worry." Nathan backed toward the building he'd chosen to hide in. "If I miss what I'm aiming at and hit you instead, it's just a tranquilizer round. I think you could use the extra sleep!"

Chapter Ten

Levi was seated alone on the slope in front of the library in Erwin, Tennessee, the flagpole at his back. Citizens moved up and down the street, but the armed men were easy to spot since they stood in pairs at nearly every intersection, with four in front of the gallery watching him.

"Lord, Nathan's right," he prayed. "I'm about to get a little foolish. Again. Help me save this town and maybe a few travelers along the way. If possible, no more getting whipped on the back. Lyla's not going to recognize me if I pick up too many more scars."

He climbed to his feet, figuring his companions had had enough time to find their shooting perches at a safe distance.

In front of the gallery, Levi approached Twig, whose partner with the sidearm never seemed to rest his hand anywhere but on his pistol grip.

"How about now?" Levi asked them. "Is this Merry fellow ready for me? It's been about an hour, so it's time to discuss business."

"Where'd the ladies go who were with you?" Twig shifted the stick in his mouth. "How're you going to make a deal without the merchandise? Merry'll want to inspect the brides himself, if he's going to find them some grooms. I might just inspect the wares myself, as I've been known to do."

"Superintendent Reece sent me here, didn't he?" Levi pressed.

"Maybe he did and maybe he didn't." Twig leaned closer. "I don't like your mouth, and I don't like your attitude. You'd better watch it."

"Watch what?" Levi tilted his head and glanced at the man's partner. "What's he telling me to watch? I can barely understand him with all that kindling in his mouth."

The gunslinger flinched, showing surprise at being included in the conversation.

"Um. Your mouth?"

"Is that physically possible—to watch my mouth? Or is it just a sort of idiom?"

"An idi-what?" Twig asked, his eyes darting. "What'd you say?"

"Nothing important." Levi gestured with his left hand. "The door? I don't want to keep Merry or the grooms waiting."

Twig glared at him, but he finally turned and knocked on a reinforced steel door. It was unbolted with a loud clang from the inside and swung outward. Another man, this one with a shoulder holster, stepped through the doorway, his head nearly bumping the top of the door frame. Once outside, he raised his head and looked down his nose at Levi.

"Merry's waiting," the bouncer stated. "I'll take your weapon."

"Of course." Levi moved to slip the sling from over his head. Simultaneously, he slid his left hand into his pocket where he'd earlier deposited three gel-tranq cartridges. "But hold it inside for me, would you? I don't want the fish smell out here to stick to it."

"We'll be waiting for you!" Twig cursed and jabbed his finger at Levi. "When you're done with Merry, then you'll meet with me!"

Levi handed his rifle to the bouncer, who hung the sling over his shoulder, then he turned back to Twig.

"You're too tough for me, Twig." Levi counted the gunmen within sight—ten at the moment. "Look at you, eating wood for dinner. I would never want to waltz with a man who chews on trees in his pastime."

"Wait. What'd you call me?"

"And your teeth." Levi clucked his tongue and squinted while he studied the man's teeth, until Twig snapped his lips closed. "Anyone who can tolerate a mouthful of chipped teeth like you have—I wouldn't tango with that hombre. No way!"

Levi glanced up at the distant buildings, then turned to the doorway where the bouncer moved aside to let him enter.

As expected, it was quieter inside, since Merry apparently kept them all outside, spotting for travelers who might interrupt the town's commerce. Only the bouncer staffed a dimly-lit, narrow room which may have once been a foyer, but now had another door on the opposite end.

The bouncer bolted the outer door, which required both of his hands. Levi drew his left hand and spun on the bouncer, stabbing him with the tranquilizing round in his broad back muscle. As the bouncer's cognition lapsed and he fell, Levi plucked his rifle from the man's shoulder.

Armed once again, Levi checked the sturdy door. Anyone who tried to break through it from outside wouldn't do so quickly or quietly. He guessed he was safe inside to do what he needed to do with Merry.

Noting the time on his watch, he calculated the minutes before Nathan and Brian opened fire on Twig and his friends on the street.

"Well, Lord, no one can ever say we left a town untouched," he mumbled, and strolled to the far door.

Andy Radner stood in the shadows of the forest outside the town of Erwin, Tennessee. The mountains weren't as high as the Rockies, but they still reminded him of home. River Camp was a lifetime ago. In the few long years since he'd run away, he'd become a killer. That's what he was, he told himself with pride, and that fact dictated how he would act.

He stared through the trees in the fading evening light at Shaker's horse. Two forms stood with the horse, but he couldn't immediately identify them until he saw the taller one feel her way to the base of a tree to sit down. *Jenna.* Finally, he had her all to himself. Levi may have outsmarted him to protect her in days past, but no longer. Even if Andy couldn't kill Levi along with Jenna, he could at least enrage Levi with the death of the blind woman.

Moving closer, with Runner also in stealth mode, Andy identified the second person as Chen Li. Easy pickings. Neither of them were even armed. He'd taken these targets as a job, to get into the growing Federation's good graces, but now this was personal.

Suddenly wary, he glanced around the forest. He'd been this close to killing Jenna before, and someone from Levi's circle had always disrupted him. First, it had been Levi himself. Then, there'd been the old, gaunt man. But Andy had tracked Levi and the others into the town, so Levi was nowhere around. And the gaunt man had taken up with a young woman and her kid up in Virginia, maybe relatives of his. Andy hadn't seen the need to push his luck by trying to kill the gaunt man, so he'd left him alone. No one was left to guard Jenna.

Yet still, he hesitated. Shaker had been stripped of his horse and left a hundred miles up the interstate. And Levi had still come to the town of Erwin where Shaker had intended to trade Jenna. Levi hadn't seemed like the vengeful type, so maybe he had business in Erwin that had nothing to do with Jenna at all.

Andy drew his tomahawk and froze, glaring, visualizing his kill. He could hold that stance for hours, and he had before, hunting others across the Mississippi

Valley and into Indiana. It was skills like these, and the lives he'd taken, that had given him the reputation which had caught the Federation's ear. Soon, he would return to Colonel Rotham and prove he'd completed his contract. Then his fame would spread, and he'd pick the jobs with the most prestige, and move around the Federation with authority, respect, and honor.

Just a little darker, he thought, and then they wouldn't see him coming. Chen Li and Jenna would be down. He had no use for a horse, so it would be horse steaks for himself and Runner that night!

Levi opened the inner door to a large display room inside the gallery. He'd wondered what kind of gallery it was, and now he knew. Pottery creations from all kinds of artisans filled the room, hanging on walls, covering the display tables and shelves. Little plaques that described the works of art had been left in place. While the country and much of Erwin itself had been decimated and transformed, the pottery gallery had been preserved.

Beyond the displays, Levi found a blond man at a cluttered desk against the wall.

"You must be Merry," Levi greeted, strolling to his left to fully check that side of the room.

The man was startled as he looked up. His eyes were blue and he took in Levi's rifle hanging over his neck and shoulder, but his wide grin was an instant behind his sense of danger. Yet, Levi had seen the man hesitate, and he knew he had Merry right where he wanted him.

"As Merry as they come!" The man extended his hand. His arms were muscled, his shoulders broad. "I heard we had some visitors in town. Where's the blind woman?"

It was Levi's turn to be unsettled. The superintendent was two miles away at the fish hatchery. Then he noticed a black box on the desk next to files and a chess board.

Before Pan-Day, Levi had grown up in the age of smartphones, but he still recognized a rotary phone for what it was.

"You got it working?" Levi took the liberty to pick up the receiver. "A dial tone, even. I'm impressed."

"Beats a radio. Have a seat, Mr. . . ."

"Caspertein. Levi Caspertein."

"Where's my, uh . . .?" Merry leaned aside to check the gallery. "Wasn't there someone at the door?"

"Oh, he's still by the door." Levi seated himself in an upholstered chair. "He wanted you and me to have our privacy. Don't worry. The outside door is locked up tight."

"I see. Okay, Mr. Caspertein. Can I call you Levi?" He folded his hands behind the desk. "Reece says you have a real prize for us, even if she is blind. I have three potential buyers right now. One might back out with news of her blindness, but the other two will get one look at her and hopefully enter into a little bidding war. My cut is fifteen percent, my standard broker's fee, and we both part ways all the more merry. Get it?"

"Fifteen percent of what?"

"Fish, supplies from anyone in town, whatever you need for your travels—assuming you're moving on. The buyer will put up the collateral, and I'll take care of the rest. It's my pleasure. It's what makes me merry, you get it? I understand she's a real beauty, natural-like, so everyone comes out merry."

"Except the blind woman."

"Well . . ." Merry held out his hands. "She's blind, right? I mean, she'll be happy with a little food and some loving. That's between her and her new husband, of course."

"Actually, I've decided she's not for sale." Levi crossed his legs, watching Merry's grin fade. "She's not even mine to trade. I just used her to get an audience with you. But I assure you, she is beautiful. Nothing in this town, or all the things in town, could equal her value. She's priceless."

Merry's eyes drifted back to the rifle Levi had over his shoulder.

"Uh, so, you wanted an audience with me. Here I am." He flashed a nervous smile. "You have my utmost attention."

"I'm glad to hear that, Merry, because we need to discuss something very, very serious for a moment." Levi paused, then lowered his voice. "Your death."

"My . . . death?" He chuckled and glanced toward the phone. "That's a new one. Discuss my death? You have a way about you, Levi. I can tell when you speak, people listen pretty closely, don't they? And humor. It's in your eyes. I like your style."

"Well, if you like that joke, then you'll especially like this next one. You're under arrest."

Merry leaned back in his chair. All of the entertainment had left his eyes. He licked his lips.

"I'll have you know that, uh, I run this town. You may have noticed the men outside? They let you in, but it's up to me if they let you leave."

"I've gotten in and out of a lot nastier places than your art gallery. *Pottery?* This is really where you buy and sell human beings?"

"It's ironic, yes?" Merry shrugged. "Pottery. Clay vessels. Humans. Get it?"

"Oh, I get it. It's from the Bible. Clever." Levi tried not to envision Jenna in this man's hands. "But do you get it?"

"I'm not breaking any laws. Slavery is legal again in Erwin."

"There's a higher law I'm holding you to today. People have stood before you and you put them into captivity. Now, you walk away with me in captivity. Kind of ironic, isn't it? Get it?"

"What'd I ever do to you?"

"To me? Nothing at all. I'm here to stop you from offending God any further. You're a clay vessel that He made. And now He's allowing me to make you into a vessel of mercy."

"I don't need God's mercy." His confidence rose again. "You don't know who you're messing with, mister. Everyone in this town—"

"No. Repentance will require some sorrow from you, Mr. Merry. In fact, that's your new name—Sorrow, not Merry."

"Well, I have fifty men outside who will tear you apart! They're loyal to me. No matter what you do to me, you'll still have to get through them!"

"That reminds me." Levi checked the time. "It must be almost sundown outside."

"So?"

"I'm placing you under arrest, and the people of Erwin will be reminded that they're not untouchable. That'll be something they carry with them as they move on to another town."

"Nobody's moving."

"You'd be surprised how people begin to scatter once their sins are exposed and their food sources dry up."

Thunder rolled outside as one continuous rumble not far away. Levi watched Merry's eyes widen at the realization. It wasn't thunder. It was gunfire.

"What's happening out there? Why are we just sitting here?"

"My people are communicating with your people." Levi chuckled. "The God of the Bible has given us what's necessary to confront your people's wickedness and to take you into custody."

Merry's face reddened as the gun battle heightened in volume, then drifted to sporadic firing. Finally, all was quiet again outside.

"You aren't going out there?" Merry asked.

"I will when you're ready to join me." Levi took a deep breath, trying to see the man's spiritual needs over his evil deeds. "You've sinned against many people for probably a lot of years. And you've probably justified your wickedness with a variety of excuses, but today your sin is staring you in the face. God is confronting you about the life you need to die to, and the new life you need to be willing to receive. You're lost and perishing, Merry. It's time to lay down your excuses and your selfishness that has made you an enemy of God for so long."

"You're not God!" Merry's confidence was gone, no matter how forceful he tried to make his words sound. "Who're you to judge me?"

"Judge you? No, I'm confronting you about what's wrong, and pointing out to you what's right. I'll leave any final judgements in God's hands. What's right and wrong—I'm helping you to face an urgent need you have."

"I'm doing just fine." His smile was back. "Until you came, my little business here was just fine. Everyone was happy. *Merry*. You think you'll make a difference? I don't keep records of all the people I've given new homes to over the years. Hundreds."

"Sadly, you're right. I won't be able to recover those people. Those people will have to live out their lives where God alone must sort them out. But I can call *you* to repentance. You're old enough to know the words I'm using and what they mean."

"Well, I'm not going with you. You think you can force me? Arrest me? Ridiculous!"

"If you don't come voluntarily, you'll go involuntarily. My horse won't mind carrying you draped over her pack saddle."

"And how's taking me like that any different than what you're accusing me of doing?"

"One of us was perpetuating crimes against humanity, and one of us is about to put an end to those crimes. There's nothing similar about the two. Once we're traveling on the open road, and we endure some hardships together, you'll see that we're meant to be friends, you and me, and eventually, you and God. That's what you'll be open to, okay?"

Levi stood abruptly, making Merry jump in his seat.

"Did you kill my friends on the street?" The man gripped the edge of his desk. "Aren't you concerned about what happened out there?"

"No, I'm not concerned. But I'm glad you recognize the trust I have in God to be able to help you the way you need to be helped."

"I'm not going anywhere with you."

"We're both leaving right now." Levi drew one of the gel-tranqs and held the cartridge up for Merry to see. "I can carry you out after giving you this, or you can walk out like a man. Come on, Sorrow. Let this moment be the first time you take responsibility for what you've done."

"You don't get to tell me to take responsibility!" Instead of shame, his face showed fury. "You can't imagine! I make or break lives! Every stray kid, every lonely woman, every—"

"Come here!" Levi reached for the man.

"No! Stay back!"

Levi couldn't stand to hear the details of the man's victims. After crossing America, he'd already seen the fruit of sensual men's actions. He lunged over the desk, and with a sweeping blow, stabbed the tranquilizer into Merry's ribs. Merry tried to squirm out of the way, but the tip of the gel-tranq had already pierced his skin and burst.

As Merry's face softened into sleep, Levi caught him, then leaned him gently over his left shoulder. Levi thought of burning the room down, since it had been the seat of human slavery. But there was nothing he could find to ignite a flame. Instead, he turned over the desk and left the room in disarray.

He walked out of the pottery gallery and into the foyer, then stepped past the bouncer, who was still sleeping soundly. Balancing Merry on his shoulder, Levi used both hands to unbolt the outside door. When he opened it a crack to look outside, he smiled. Twig was there, laying across other unconscious gunmen, some without their sidearms even drawn.

The street seemed quiet. Levi stepped outside into the dusk of evening, and left the door open behind him. He gazed up at the distant buildings where he knew Brian and Nathan were still perched out of sight.

"That was some fine shooting, boys," he mused, counting the unconscious all the way to the next intersection. Rifles and handguns littered the street.

He walked beyond the sidewalk for a broader view of the carnage when suddenly two gunshots boomed from above and behind him. He felt the punch of the bullets force his body into the street. From years of wariness and keyed-up reflexes, he spun around and fired his battle rifle with one hand at a figure who was leaning off the roof of the gallery. The man was immediately tranquilized. He dropped his pistol, then slid down the roof and thumped to the alley floor.

For another moment, Levi turned here and there, challenging any other shooters Nathan and Brian hadn't put down. But no one else revealed themselves. That's when he felt blood wet the back of his leg. With care, he lay Merry down on the street among his friends. The blood was from Merry.

"Sorry, Levi!" Brian called as he jogged up the street. "That one was hiding behind the apex of the roof."

Levi checked Merry's pulse, but it was clear what he'd find. One of Merry's own men had shot him twice in the back, not realizing he was being carried by one of the strangers in town.

"He's gone. That was Merry." Levi frowned at the dead human trafficker.

"What do you think God thinks?" Brian's face showed concern. "We didn't mean to, but we killed him."

"We didn't kill him, Brian. In trying to save him the only way we knew how, he was killed." Levi rested a hand on the man's head. "That's not on us, Brian. Sometimes our best effort to obey in a bad situation ends badly. Unintended consequences doesn't mean obedience is wrong. We keep being obedient, and trust our sovereign Lord with the consequences."

"It still leaves a bitter taste to what we wanted to do here."

"Yeah, it ain't easy failing with people like this who won't even give you a chance to rescue them from hurting themselves and others."

"Maybe Lena was more successful at the hatchery."

"You're right." Levi slapped Brian on the back. "We'll leave Erwin with something to think about, I hope. Where's Nathan?"

"He'll watch our backs as we leave, then catch up later."

"Then to Colorado we go."

As they passed out of town, citizens peeked at them from darkened doorways and curtained windows. Levi had hoped to make more of a statement to them about God through Merry, but it seemed to be time to go. The town would reflect and change, or it would find someone new to replace Merry and continue in its ways.

They walked for a while in silence, both praying about what had just happened, before they began to speak again.

"What do you think of Jenna?" Brian asked once they were on the highway headed out of town. "I mean, as someone for me."

"You want her to teach you Braille?" Levi asked. "I don't understand."

"Well, no, not Braille. Not exactly."

"You don't want her to teach you Braille?" Levi lowered his voice. "You know, Brian, you really should try to show an interest in Jenna, if you want to be romantically interested in someone."

"What? No! Now you're just—"

"Yeah, I'm just messing with you!" Levi laughed and shoved him on the highway as they approached the horse and the two women. "Of course, I think you two would make a good team for the Lord."

"And by team, you mean . . . ?"

"A couple. A pair. You're thinking marriage?"

"Honestly? I never thought of it before. But . . . *Jenna!* I mean, come on!"

"I know. She's amazing."

"Right? And blind!"

"You know what'd make her happy?" Levi asked.

"What?"

"Ask her to teach you Braille. She taught all the early tunnel dwellers Braille. Chloe told me at the warehouse in New Jersey."

"Braille? Really?" Brian shoved Levi back. "Actually, that's not a bad idea."

"It ain't easy taking sweetheart advice from a clueless Caspertein." Levi chuckled. "You just have to see past all the wit."

"I was going to say *nonsense*."

"Well, you know, I'm well-rounded."

Just before it was too dark to see, Lena finished opening all the gates of the Erwin fish hatchery to the Nolichucky River. She'd only needed to tranquilize one attendant who'd visited the hatchery in the middle of her sabotage efforts. But everyone else in the vicinity seemed to be staying up at the superintendent's estate where a loud party was raging, complete with a live band and singing.

Lena had even taken time to throw traps full of trout eggs into the river, so she figured she'd completed her job for Levi. Between the estate and the hatchery, she stopped on the walkway and looked back at the ruined industry and smiled. She didn't smile for what she'd ruined, but for what she'd accomplished for Levi.

She was a couple years older than he was, but he was mature beyond his years—if she listened beyond his antics. But even then, his constant kidding with Nathan was part of who he was. He joked with people who were dear to him, so he'd begun to do so with her. He meant it to draw her closer, she understood, not push her away. After all, when he cooked anything in camp, he always made sure the pieces were small enough for her to swallow since she couldn't chew them.

Although she knew he was married, she couldn't help but love him. He'd even been allowing her to carry his Bible, like she was that very minute, inside her coat. Since God was so important to him, she guessed that carrying his Bible was as close as she could get to Levi.

The moon was already up, so Lena moved through the trees with ease as she searched for where Jenna and Chen Li were waiting with the horse. She had reflected to herself on how it seemed that God had paired the six of them perfectly. Jenna had Brian, who tried almost too hard to please Jenna, who in turn accepted his attention with patience. Chen Li had Nathan. Those two had been married for more than twenty years, so Lena was witnessing what a mature marriage looked like, something she'd never seen growing up in New York after Pan-Day. Family values had never been a serious interest within the Federation.

And Lena had Levi, though she could never ask him to be anything to her like what the others were to each other. "In Christ" was the term she was learning from the Bible. Being in Christ was a unique fellowship and closeness that rivaled marriage in some ways. She didn't understand it all yet, but she appreciated having connections she'd lacked her whole life, even with her brother Owen.

Suddenly, she stopped. Was that a person? Or two people against a tree? One person moved, and she saw the distinct profile of a dog's head, not a person at all. *The man with the dog!* Levi had said he'd tangled with this hunter not long after crossing the Hudson—the same man who'd prowled into the house when she'd been resting in front of the fire.

Lena smoothly drew her pistol, but when she blinked, she lost the location of the dog. Maybe it had been a stray canine, or a coyote, without anyone else at all. But no, this wasn't a coincidence. Levi had said the hunter with the dog had been after Jenna, and here Jenna was so close.

It was a perfect opportunity, Lena thought, to prove her worth again to Levi, by protecting Jenna, the woman he'd crossed a continent to rescue from danger. Lena would tranquilize this hunter and his dog, and not even make a big deal of it, like it was the least she could do for him, after all he'd done for her. But secretly, she knew it would mean so much to him. And Jenna would see her loyalty as well, and Lena couldn't imagine a more important gesture within their group. They had welcomed her, so she wasn't earning their friendship, but she did want to show that she was willing to take risks for them as well—much more than freeing a town's trout supply.

She took another step, then a bright light glanced through her vision, and she was lying on her back, staring up at twinkling stars above the trees. It seemed a tree had struck her. Or fallen on her. Stunned and immobile, she weakly raised her hands to paw at someone who clawed at her coat. It was unzipped, and this person was searching her. *Levi's Bible!*

"We got him now, Runner!" someone snickered.

Her eyes felt heavy. She felt the dog's breath against her face. No, this was all wrong. Blood seeped into her ear, and her jaw hurt enough to cry, but Lena couldn't even beg for mercy.

"Scream, and I'll finish you!" a harsh voice whispered into her face.

Gasping as he lifted her into his arms, Lena was too weak to fight back, so she surrendered only her body to the enemy. In her soul, she cried out to Levi—to forgive her for failing, and to thank him for showing her the Savior who'd died for her.

She knew she would die now, for without Levi, no one else would know how to care for her. How could she even eat in front of anyone else? Who would defend her? Who would receive a beating for her?

Then she realized the answer to all these questions. It wasn't just Levi. Levi had only done all those things for her because he was following Christ.

Though Levi couldn't be with her now, Jesus had never left her. To that, she held tightly, even as she blacked out from the agony of mistreatment in the cruel hands of the killer.

Levi, Brian, and Nathan reached Jenna and Chen Li with hushed fanfare, though Levi felt certain none of the townspeople were around to witness their reunion.

"That was some noise you guys made!" Jenna praised.

"Lena's not back yet?" Levi looked straight up through the trees to gauge the time by the moon. "I thought she'd be here by now."

"We thought we heard her coming." Chen Li pointed. "Maybe off in that direction? But I guess it was just an animal or something."

Walking away from the group, Levi listened to the night. Nathan set a hand on his shoulder.

"Maybe I shouldn't have sent her off alone," Levi said. "If something happened to her . . ."

"No." Nathan squeezed his shoulder. "Don't go there. It was time she began to find confidence in her own way. Even if something did happen, she's the Lord's child now.

She was willing to carry a gun, and with that comes her own challenges."

"You're right, but she's my responsibility," Levi said, looking back at the others. "Get started on the highway, just in case people from Erwin come after us. Leave me some markings at crossroads so I can follow you. And I'll leave smoke signals for you when I can."

"The hatchery is just a mile away, Levi," Nathan said. "Go find her, and you'll catch up to us in an hour."

"Not if something's happened with that Superintendent Reece guy." Levi jiggled his canteen and tugged on his ammo jacket. "I'll sort it out and meet you on the road."

"Levi, I'd rather we stayed together," Chen Li urged.

"No, if we stay together, we may die together, if Erwin arms itself and comes looking. Look, we're a mile on the wrong side of the superintendent's residence. Right now, you guys need to get back up to the freeway. I'm sure Lena's just being careful, taking her time and all."

"If anyone sees her," Jenna whispered, "I mean without her veil . . ."

"I'll find her." Levi touched Jenna's shoulder, then shook Nathan and Brian's hands. "I'm ready to bulldoze this forest if I need to, to find her."

"Brother, know we'll be praying." Nathan backed away. "We'll go, but not quickly. I don't want to get too far ahead of you like we did with Chen Li and Jenna. Besides, I know how slowly you walk, stopping to drink tea with the locals and whatnot."

"I'll tranq you and tie you to the horse if I have to!" Levi joked, then turned his back on his friends.

"Find her, Levi," Jenna called, her voice breaking. "She's my sister now."

He heard them continue to share their concern as they walked away, and Levi set his mind to the task before him. The forest was dark and the moon was bright, though no longer directly overhead. Kneeling on the ground, he studied the quiet trees, the open ground, and the direction toward the hatchery.

For more than twenty years, he'd been in pursuit of something. He'd tracked criminals in San Diego with his father, and hunted deer in the woods above the city. Whether providing for others, or putting meat in his own pot, his instincts had been honed by experience, often with his own life endangered.

Now alone, he entered that familiar mindset, his senses alert, taking in the forest scents, scene, and sounds. Moving twenty yards north, he paused next to a tree and sniffed, then crouched closer to the ground. Pine needles were flattened. The ground was trampled. And there was fresh dog dung. But a dog hadn't flattened the earth. The feet of a man had stood there—a man with a dog.

Levi didn't allow his emotions to rise. Instead, he moved to the right, now aware of a presence in the woods—someone who wasn't Lena. His eyes shifted from tree to tree, from shadow to shadow. He was out there, the man from whom he'd taken the crossbow arrows. The man he'd underestimated.

Then he saw it—a ribbon of white on the dark forest floor. He aimed his rifle, expecting the item to be some sort of bait. Was it a trap? Running toward the ribbon, he felt for it with his left hand while his right held the rifle steady, aiming where his eyes were focused.

With the ribbon in his hand, he bounded to the nearest tree for cover and checked his surroundings. The man he suspected to be near didn't need a firearm to strike. This was a predator, a man who needed only a tomahawk to make his kills.

Finally, Levi studied the white ribbon in his hand. He sniffed it and smelled the woman he'd been close enough to for weeks to know her scent. It was her bridal lace. And worse—her fresh blood was smeared on it under his hand.

She would want it the second he found her, since she was so self-conscious about her face, so he stuffed it into his vest.

In the darkness, it was hard to see more than shades and shapes of black, gray, and white, but Levi was willing to hunt regardless. Lena was out there, and like Jenna had said, she was a sister in Christ.

For a moment, he paused and recalled God's faithfulness when he'd set off from San Diego on his own, separate from his father who'd just died. First, there'd been the recovery of his cousin Mia from the Brogdons. In the west, he'd saved his wife-to-be Lyla from mountain kidnappers, and Alice from the Brogdons later on. Then, he'd rushed across the States to find and rescue Jenna. It seemed the Lord had tasked him with saving the women in his life, and his body bore the scars of those missions.

Now, it was Lena—a wounded and deformed woman —whom he wanted at his side, even if no one else wanted her. He hoped she knew he wouldn't leave her behind. In fact, he would rather die with her, or for her, than move on without her. More than even running into the arms of his own loving wife just yet, he knew he had one more job to do for God and the safekeeping of His people.

"Hang on, Lena. I'm coming for you."

I pray you've enjoyed *Dawn of Subjection*. Please leave your honest opinion or review wherever you bought this book. It will help me to know if I hit the mark with my writing. Thanks! —*David Telbat*

What's Next?

~ Dawn of Tribulation ~

Enjoy this teaser for Book Four of the *Last Dawn Series*.

Meteors streak through the heavens and ash falls from the sky. The earth shakes and violence hounds God's people. As tribulation draws near, Christians see a new breed of persecution erupt across America.

Levi and Rex Caspertein continue their trek across the States, still heading west to Colorado, but now there is a network of evil that has taken shape in every town. The One Planet Trust (OPT) is a new governing movement that communicates through radios. The Casperteins are hemmed in by natural catastrophe, physical exhaustion, and social antagonism that despises faith in Jesus Christ.

The Last Days of America are upon us. Readers will be hard-pressed in some instances to tell the difference between fact and fiction as they read this final volume of the *Last Dawn Series*. Tribulation is near—perhaps just after the next dawn . . .

Watch for more in the *COIL Series* to come!

About the Author

D.I. (David) Telbat is a Christian author best known for his **clean, Suspenseful Fiction with a Faith Focus**. This includes his bestselling and award-winning *COIL Series*, *Steadfast Series*, *Last Dawn Series*, and other Christian Suspense and End Times novels. He wrote his first book at age 14, and he hasn't stopped since!

David studied writing in school and worked for a time in the newspaper field. Getting into serious trouble with the law as a young man became a turning point in his life. The Lord used that experience to draw David into a personal relationship with Him. Re-focusing his life for Christ, he now seeks to honor God with his life and writing by doing what he loves most—writing and Christian ministry.

Subscribe to receive David Telbat's FREE, bi-weekly **D.I. Telbat Newsletter** with one of his Christian short stories, or an Author Reflection, or his Novel News Update. You'll also receive **exclusive subscriber gifts**, such as his ***Three For Free***—three-novels-in-one eBook! You can join the adventure by visiting his site at books2read.com/DITelbat/ and click on the "**Follow this Author**" button.

www.ingramcontent.com/pod-product-compliance
Lightning Source LLC
Chambersburg PA
CBHW030805210726
48290CB00002B/433

9781737177784